ALL IN

B.E HARMON

Table of Contents

Dedication..1

Acknowledgements...2

Chapter 1..3

Chapter 2..8

Chapter 3..16

Chapter 4..21

Chapter 5..26

Chapter 6..30

Chapter 7..33

Chapter 8..41

Chapter 9..46

Chapter 10..53

Chapter 11..57

Chapter 12..63

Chapter 13..68

Chapter 14..74

Chapter 15..78

Chapter 16..83

Chapter 17..90

Chapter 18..98

Chapter 19..103

Chapter 20..112

Chapter 21..119

Chapter 22..122

Chapter 23..128

Chapter 24..136

Chapter 25..141

Chapter 26..146

Chapter 27..150

Chapter 28..155

Chapter 29..157

Chapter 30..164

Chapter 31..173

Chapter 32..177

Chapter 33..180

Chapter 34..187

Chapter 35..190

Chapter 36..195

Chapter 37..199

Chapter 38..202

Chapter 39..206

Chapter 40..211

Chapter 41..218

Chapter 42..222

Chapter 43..226

Chapter 44..232

Chapter 45..236

Chapter 46..243

About The Author..250

Dedication

To my wife(Taka) and my two son's Shawn and Hashim

Acknowledgements

I would like give praise to special young lady named Shaunasia, for helping me complete this project known as "All In", I will forever be grateful to her and the Pittman family.

CHAPTER 1

As the limousine pulled up, Candy saw a plethora of luxury cars sitting in the church parking lot.

"Whose church is this?" Candy asked inquisitively.

"This was your mother's church," the older woman answered.

"Wasn't she a stripper?" Her tone was flat.

"Your mother wasn't always a stripper, you know. Besides, that was a long time ago." She gave Candy a pat on the knee just as the car came to a stop.

The driver popped the door open, and Candy's aunt climbed out. While helping Candy out of the car, she sensed her niece had something on her mind. "What is it, sweetheart?"

"Nothing!" She uttered, but she was lying. She didn't feel comfortable talking to her Aunt Jackie.

"You sure?"

"Yeah." Candy forced half a smile. "I'm...I'm just ready to see my daddy."

"Let's do this!" Her aunt said sternly as they locked arms and walked up to the church stairs. "Oh yeah, where is Franky? He told me he would be here."

"Probably in jail for stealing somebody's shit! Or up under one of those trees smoking the dope he got from stealing somebody's shit!"

Candy started laughing. It was the first time she had laughed since her father died.

"Why are you so hard on Uncle Franky?"

"Child, please. Your uncle Franky ain't worth a wooden nickel...I know you ain't forget that that boy is a crackhead. Don't get me started! He's my brother, and I love him to death, but he is what he is. Besides, I came to say my last goodbyes to your father! Not talk about your crackhead uncle."

When they first walked in, Candy was overwhelmed with fear. Her knees began to buckle, and her mouth became dry. She flopped to the first available seat.

"What's wrong, sweetheart?" She could see the fear in Candy's eyes. "I'm...I'm scared, Aunt Jackie." Candy had never seen a dead person before. "I gotcha, baby girl." She extended her hand. "I gotcha."

Candy grabbed her hand and was led to the front of the church, just below the preacher, right in front of the casket.

Halfway through the service, Candy noticed that more and more people poured into the already crowded church. "Who are all of these people?" Candy asked with a lost look on her face.

Her aunt took a quick peek around the room, then focused back on the preacher. "Don't know." She gave Candy a soft nudge to stop her from looking around. "Never mind them. Just listen to the preacher."

But Candy couldn't. Too many things were going on around her. There were people constantly moving about viewing the body: some falling out, some trying to claw their way to the casket, others screaming and crying. Plus, it was already hard for her to pay attention to the preacher with all the whispering in her ear.

"Why did my daddy want his funeral to be at my mother's church?" Candy asked, but her aunt didn't respond.

"Aunt Jackie!" Candy nudged her knee.

"What is it, sweetheart?"

"Why did my..."

Her aunt cut her off. "When you go to a funeral, you wait till after the service to talk." She gave Candy a pat on the knee. "We'll talk after the service."

Candy could see the irritation setting on her aunt's face, so she did as she was told. An hour later, the service was over, and Candy found herself standing in front of the church with her aunt, watching the sea of black people dwindle down. They piled into the latest cars and trucks, then flooded the small two-lane roadway leading to the burial site.

Candy couldn't believe her father was gone. What hurt her the most was that she had only known her father for five years. That was one of the reasons why she hated her mother; that and the fact she was strung out on drugs. Her mother, an ex-striper by the name of "Candy Red," had her at the age of fifteen. By the time lil Casandra was three, her mother left her with her grandmother, who at the time was diagnosed with cancer. Two years before she died, she found Casandra's father, a local drug dealer who ran the neighborhood.

Candy remembered the first time she saw her father: it was at her grandmother's house. She came home from school one day and noticed a sky-blue 600 sitting in the driveway. She remembered a very tall, very dark-skinned man with a mouth full of gold squatting beside her grandmother when she walked in. She recalled him promising her that he would take care of her granddaughter Cassandra and for her not to worry because he was going to step up to the plate. He had kept his promise. Although short lived, and despite the fact that she was almost grown, the two became best friends.

As they lowered him into the earth, she blessed him with a single rose. "I promise to stay on my P's and Q's," she mumbled as tears fell from her face. "And I promise to watch my back and trust few just like you taught me. So rest in peace, old man." She blew him a kiss and watched as they filled the hole with dirt.

* * * * *

Sporting a clean shave - a.k.a., the booty face - and deep-dish waves, Todd was posted up at the bus station rocking the latest one-fifties with a matching shirt displaying the same logo. A week before his release, his homeboy, Hope, a long-time childhood friend and partner in crime, sent him a care package. Along with price sneakers, designer jeans and a shirt were a Cuban-link chain and a gold Rolex with a card that read, "You know how we do."

Out of the corner of his eye, Todd spotted a red bone sweating him from afar. Giving her even more of a reason to come holla at him, Todd began to rub his hands together, giving her a view of the Roley. Todd was more into dark skinned women, but he went ahead and spit at the young tender to see where his game was at.

Ten minutes later, he had her number and address. His timing could not have been any better: his mission was complete, and he was ready to bounce. Minutes later, Hope pulled up in a deep burgundy Jaguar, sitting on gold flippers, bumping the latest Scarface. Hope slammed on the brakes Just inches away from hitting Todd and his new lady friend. "Look, but don't touch," he screamed to the on lookers as he jumped out of the Jag, his chain bouncing wildly, "here, so my dawg," Hope yelled as he walked up to Todd.

"Ok! That's what you do, huh?" Todd responded before Hope gave' em a big hug, then some dap.

"Goddamn, homeboy!" Hope backed up to get a better view. "yo ass bigger than a house." He gave one of Todd's arms a light squeeze. "Okay! My dawg ripped up fo them ho's."

"You straight?" Hope asked, pointing to Todd's setup.

"Umm, good," Todd responded.

"You good! Whatever!" He flashed all fourteen. "You know that's clean!"

"It's aiight." Todd knew his homeboy came through, but he didn't wanna blow his head up.

"Who you is, lil' mama?" Hope finally realized how fine Todd's new friend was. More than happy to direct his focus towards her.

"Janet," she answered. Hope found it hard to take his eyes off Lil' Red.

"Well, Janet?" Hope repeated, motioning to Todd's outfit. "Is my dawg clean or what?" Jumping at the opportunity to place her hands on Todd's body, she stroked his stomach with her small manicured. "I like his little outfit," she said seductively.

"Damn, lil' mama! What, you bout dat?"

"About what?" she questioned, her eyebrow rising up.

Hope stared at the lil' tender for a moment. "Don't worry about it," Hope said and laughed. "Umma spare you dis time cuz my dawg fresh out." Hope looked at Todd, back at the young girl, then back to Todd, "Let's bounce."

"You trying to ride? Todd asked the young tender.

"You gonna take me home, right?" she asked.

"I got'cha," Todd assured her.

"Where's your stuff, family?" Hope asked.

"My property over there." Todd pointed to a small plastic bag by the phone booth.

"Your what!" Hope mumbled as he walked away.

When he returned, Todd and the lil tender were curled up in the back seat. "Where she stays at, dawg?"

"She from the Mount," Todd answered.

Hope blew big smoke cruising down seventy-five while his homeboy had his way with the young tender in the back seat. "I Hope you put something on the seat?"

"I got dis," Todd assured him.

Halfway through his second blunt, Hope recalled the number of times Lil' Red was flipped around in the back seat. My dawg smashing lil' mama, Hope thought, his lungs full of smoke. But Lil Mama ah animal - referring to how Lil' Red was right with Todd step-for-step, even though she was steady being folded up and tossed around.

"You off glass," Hope blurted out while blowing out a dark grayish green smoke.

"Tighten up, homeboy! We almost there."

"How long before we get there?" Todd asked.

"Twenty, thirty minutes at the most," Hope answered back.

Twenty minutes later, they were in Altamont. Getting dressed, Janet gave Hope the directions to her apartment. Ten minutes later, they were parked in front of her front door.

"You gone call me, right?" she asked Todd.

"Gimme a few days." He rubbed her chin. "I gotta handle some business, but I'll hit cha' up."

"Cool!" She got out and went into the house.

Todd jumped in the front seat.

"Dat lil' hoe like dat," Hope spat lustfully, watching Lil' Red strut into the house.

"I know dat head is off the chain," Todd spat.

Hope started laughing, and then he tossed Todd a cell phone.

"This me?" Todd asked.

"Oh, yeah." He handed him a small card.

"What's dis?"

"The number to the phone."

"I'm glad you gave it to me after she got out of the car!"

"Stop playing," Hope said jokingly. "Man, you know how we do this.

Check this out, right. After we get your clothes, we gotta go get your ride out the shop. Damn, my bad dawg." He reached into his top pocket and tossed Todd a key. "This to the house?"

"Yeah! Yo house," Hope spat.

"So where I'm at?" Todd asked skeptically.

"Oh, you straight." He fired up another blunt. "You out there wit' dem white folks."

"Cool!"

Hope turned over the engine and changed ed's, a mixtape by J.P.E. (Jam Pony Express).

Always ready to show out, Hope flashed a four thousand plus gold and diamond smile at three young women hopping out of a Honda.

"You kill me when you call yourself grilling dem hoes," Todd mumbled.

"Man, what are you talking about? You been gone fo bout eight of dem." He passed Todd the blunt. "Trust me, dawg, these hoes love it when a nukka come through like dis."

After Todd hit the blunt, everything Hope said went in one ear and out the other. That was the first blunt he smoked in three years. Truth of the matter is that he wasn't a big weed smoker when he was on the bricks, that was Hope's thing, not his.

"Damn, dawg! You gonna pass dat." Hope had to repeat himself twice before giving Todd a slight nudge.

"What's that?" Todd asked with a slumped face and bloodshot eyes.

"Man, pass...da blunt," Hope chuckled lightly. He could tell his man was high as hell.

"Dawg...what the hell is this?" Todd had never been that high before in his life.

"Dat's that drow"

He looked at Todd. "Man, dis dah bomb!" He started laughing at Todd, pointing his finger at him.

"Mann, yo ass is out there, dawg. You look like a olly molly right now."

"Man, I don't want...no...more...of...that." Todd could feel his heart pounding in his chest.

"Dawg, ah nukka glad you home. A nukka miss you fo real."

"I feel ya!" He gave Hope some dap. "Being locked up is for the birds, man. Dem folks treat ya like crap."

Hope could see the pain setting on his homeboy's face. "Don't even sweat dat, cuz. You home, nah."

"Fo'sho," Todd replied as he leaned back in the plush leather.

"What's up?" Hope asked.

Todd was just staring at him. "Let me hit dat again."

Hope passed his homey the blunt. "That's you, homeboy."

Todd nodded his head in concordance.

"Nock ya self out." Hope chuckled.

Todd hit the drow once again. And once again, he was back on cloud 99 as J.P.E. blasted through all six twelves.

CHAPTER 2

It's been almost a year since she lost her father. For Candy, some days were better than others. She began to feel lonely. She needed to do something with her life. She needed a change. She decided to go back to school. She knew her father would have liked that. Slowly but surely, her life started moving along after that. Besides, she didn't have anything else to do. It was time for her to move on. She knew that. And what better way to find her way in life than to go to college? She even thought about joining a sorority on the drive to the university to register for her classes.

Candy's ol' boy was a real go-getter, and because of that, he was able to leave his baby girl over one hundred thousand dollars in cash. Her aunt gave it to her a few days after the funeral, along with the keys to her father's sky blue Benz.

Florida was no ATL. Candy was glad that she was ready for a change, and Central Florida was just that. A change. When she arrived at the college, it took her a while to find the administration building, but she wasn't too mad: the campus was far more gorgeous than the brochure had led her to believe and much bigger.

Blessed with her mother's hand-carved, Coke-a-Cola bottle shape, she was considered a true dime piece. Normally, her hair fell past her shoulders, but Candy decided to go short for a while. When she hopped out of the sky blue 600, rocking the same color pants suit, the question of whether she could wear a short hairstyle was quickly answered. Catcalls came from a group of guys posted in front of the administration building almost immediately.

"Damn Red! All dat you?" the tallest of the bunch yelled.

She spoke without looking either one in the eye as she walked toward the building. "How y'all doing?"

"Let me holla at'cha, Red," another blurted out but was politely ignored.

When she came out, they were gone. She was glad. She hated it when guys approached her like that. Her father used to call them "Cold Busters," but what he meant was cats like that didn't have any game.

"Daddy, you dead ass right," Candy said aloud with a light chuckle as she popped open the door.

"I'm sorry. Were you speaking to me?" an older woman asked, startling Candy.

"Oh, I...I...I was just...."

"Talking to yourself?" she asked with a warm smile.

"Something like dat...I mean, that," Candy replied.

The lady could tell Candy was embarrassed. "Well, baby, so long as you don't answer back, you'll be okay." The lady walked towards the building, stopped, then turned around. "By the way, you are wearing that pants suit."

"Thank you." Candy looked at her reflection in the car door. She ain't tell nothing but the truth, Candy thought before flopping in the driver's seat and pulling off.

The only thing she hated about Florida was all her friends were back in ATL. No friends in Florida meant a lot of lonely nights and cold showers. Today was no different.

* * * * *

Born Howard Sneed, Hope was just two months old when his father was killed during a bank robbery. At twelve, his mother moved him to Florida to live with his grandmother. That move turned out to be a bad move for Hope's mother than for him.

The year was '87' and the crack era was in full swing. That summer, he met a friend for life: his name was Todd, an up-and-coming foot soldier known for boosting expensive cars and having a mean 'wholla' game, among other things.

By the age of fifteen, Todd had been to the juvenile at least three times; that, and the fact he was always sporting the latest name brand gear, made him somewhat of a celebrity among the local hot girls. One of those trips to juvie, he went because he took charge of Hope. That particular charge landed Todd a two month stay. After that, the two became best friends, which turned out to be a good thing for Todd.

A few years later, Hope shot two dudes who were acting like they wanted to jump Todd after the club one night. Although Todd was in the wrong, Hope wasn't going out like that. It was always like that between those two.

Hope thought about all the things he and his homey went through as teenagers as his Jag swayed in and out of traffic. Todd's ride wasn't going to be ready until Monday. But it wasn't a big deal: they were homeboys.

Hope's cell phone vibrated between his legs. He set it on that mode, knowing he wouldn't hear it because of the music. When he picked it up, the screen read "T." He quickly pushed and talked. On the other end, Todd started drilling him about his whereabouts. Before he could speak, he had an incoming call. He told Todd he'd be there in twenty minutes and clicked over to the other line.

Waiting impatiently on the other end was Hope's used-to-be business partner, Rosco, an overweight Puerto Rican whose hands were in everything illegal. From drugs to counterfeit, stolen cars, racketeering, you name it.

Hope never trusted Rosco. He only dealt with him when no one else was available. The two had done a lot of business together. That was until a few months ago when Rosco paid Hope $20,000 in funny money. The situation was resolved without violence, but Todd felt it would be best to cut all ties. So, when Rosco called, his guard automatically went up.

"Que holla?"

"What's up, Fatboy?" Hope knew Rosco hated being called a Fatboy.

"You haven't called me in a while...what, you don't do business wit me, no mo?"

"What'cha want, Rosco?"

"Damn, my nukka! Is that any way to talk to the one who put yo ass in the game?" There was a few seconds of silence. "Where you at?"

"I'm on the road,"

Rosco could tell he wasn't up for conversation. "On da road, huh! Same ol' Hope." For as long as Rosco knew Hope, he knew he never gave his location over the phone. "Well, since you already on the road, how bout you swing by the spot before we close up?"

Before Rosco could get out another word, Hope hung up. Hope turned the music back up, fired up a fresh one, and headed to Todd's.

* * * * *

"So, is he coming?" Lewis asked with a sense of urgency. He'd been trying to make something happen for the last two months now and was starting to get aggravated.

"He 'll be here," Rosco promised. "He bout his business. Trust me!"

"So when is he coming?" Lewis demanded.

"Relax, Gringo! I said he'll be here."

"Do not call me a green-go." He shoved a finger into Rosco's chest.

"And do not tell me to relax, you lil' prick. The only reason this here little operation is even afloat is because I allow it. Don't you forget that, Fatboy."

Rosco began to chuckle. "You might need to take anger management or something... maybe you should turn your life over to crime...being a cop is stressing you out, homeboy."

Lewis hated Rosco. He hated his kind. He hated the fact that Rosco thought the two of them were equal, or even partners, for that matter. So, instead of feeding Rosco's sick sense of amusement, he got straight to business. He slid Rosco a piece of paper. "Have him pick up the car at this address."

"When?" Rosco asked.

"3:00 o'clock in the afternoon."

"You sure you know how to fit sixty keys into a car?" Rosco asked, "Cause you know I can have my boys do it for you."

Lewis shot Rosco a dog-eyed look. "Yeah! I'm sure I'll manage."

"Okay, if you say so," Rosco responded.

He looked at Rosco with a foul stare. "I can't afford any screw ups on this, so make sure your little tar baby follows the instructions."

"No, screw up," Rosco repeated. "Monday, 3:00 o'clock in the afternoon." Rosco's first mind told him to kill the white man and take his sixty kilos, but then he thought about all the heat that would bring to the shop. For some reason, he didn't trust the detective. He felt they were too much alike, and that was good enough of a reason for him. Rosco was used to getting over on whomever he did business with, not the other way around. And to make sure this venture wouldn't be less lucrative than the others, Rosco had yet another trick up his sleeve.

* * * * *

Todd was coming up on his second week of freedom, and any true hustler knew that a lot could happen in a two week period. A lot of money could be made in a two week period. But being a vet, Todd was not about to jump out there. He knew if he played his cards right, things would fall into place. A lot had changed in eight years, and to a certain extent, he was green to how the next generation ran things.

He'd swung through the hood a few times with Hope to grab a few outfits from the local boosters, but they didn't hang out. Hope was always ready to go as soon as they bought the clothes. He never did like hanging in the hood. It was Todd who liked being in the trenches. Even when they were young, Todd always believed the hood was going to be his mill-ticket.

When the door opened, Todd's thought process was interrupted as Hope barged in.

"What's up, family?" Hope asked, being trailed by a thick grayish blue fog. "You ready?" he asked between pulls on the blunt.

"Yeah. Let me just grab my shirt." Todd walked to the back room.

"I thought you were already ready!"

"I am," he replied, returning with his shirt.

"Tighten up, prettyboy!" Hope was the only one who could call Todd that.

"You can miss me wit all dat prettyboy junk!"

Hope started laughing. "Tighten up, we gotta go see Rosco."

"Rosco? Who the hell is Rosco?"

"Rosco! Oh, fat ass Rosco, stay out there on Conway?"

"Man, I don't know no damn Rosco," Todd said off handedly.

"My bad." Hope saw the confusion on Todd's face. "I forgot that's what we call him now. You remember Fat's, right?"

"Okay! Yeah! Yeah! I know who Rosco is now. We used to boost cars for him back in the day. What's up with him?" Todd asked.

Hope broke everything down to Todd about Rosco, how he came up, how he's a snake, how they used to do business, and how he had tried him with the fake money.

"So it's been, what, a little over six months since you did something with him?" Todd inquired.

"Yeah," Hope nodded. "About six months."

Hope gave him a curious glare. "You know what he wants?"

"I think so. I believe he wants me to fill an order."

Hope wished his money was on point; that way, he could have told Rosco's fat ass to kick rocks. But times were hard, and money was low. Hope always spent more money than he made; that was the main reason why he put the dope

11

sack down and went back to boosting cars. He enjoyed the luxury of the modern-day-barter trade he mastered while Todd was locked up to meet all his wants and needs. Hope would boost cars for people who were in position to make their desires or necessities a reality. But just like his short lived, instant gratification lifestyle, his overlooked tomorrow had finally come... So, for now, he had to see what Rosco was talking about.

"If he ain't talking right off I-O-P, we bouncing," Todd stated firmly to Hope right before they jumped out the Jag and walked towards the office.

"What's up, Fatboy?" Hope blurted, walking through the office door.

Rosco motioned to two folding metal chairs in front of his desk.

"Have a seat. Thirsty?" He lifted up a soda.

"We straight?" Todd replied evenly as they sat.

"Todd! My main man." He gestured to Hope, "Now, see that. He didn't even call and tell me you were home." Rosco flashed a stained smile,

"I could have had you a welcome home party."

"Maybe next time," Todd spat.

"Yeah! Maybe next time." Rosco's eyes shifted back to Hope. "You trying to make forty g's."

"Depends on what I got to do!" Hope replied.

Rosco slid a small piece of paper to Hope. "Easiest money you'll ever make in your life, homeboy."

Hope scanned the list. "Forty grand for dis?" The only car that troubled him was the Lamborghini. He never stole a Lam before.

"We do business, yes?" Rosco asked.

"Say I do do dis here. When you want the cars?"

Rosco handed Hope another slip. "Each car has an address. They have to be picked up and brought to me before Monday...except the 600. That will be delivered on Monday at 3:00 o'clock in the afternoon."

"Why dat?" Todd chimed in.

Rosco shoots Todd a unit, "Things have changed, homeboy. When money talks, bullshit, pay attention."

"Don't get it twisted," Todd shot back a unit, "ain't nuttin change but the players."

"Let me ask you dis here, can you come up on a Lam?" Rosco gave Hope a crooked smile. "I mean, I know you never bammed a Lam before."

"Forty grand!! On delivery, right?" Todd asked to be sure.

"Forty g's on delivery," Rosco repeated.

Hope looks over to Todd. "What ya think?"

"If you can get the Lam....run it."

That's all Hope had to hear. His main man was officially back on the grind. All three worked out all the ifs, ands, and whats. The only problem was that Hope lied about getting the Lam. Truth of the matter is he had never seen a Lamborghini in person, more less seen the inside of one. But he was determined to get those forty grand. And with his partner in crime back on the bricks, that was just what he intended to do.

Hope tapped Todd on the knee. "Let's ride, dawg." He turned around at the door and pointed at Rosco, "Oh yeah, don't try me like you did last time!"

Rosco flashed a smile. "Ease up, homeboy. What happened last time was a misunderstanding. Ain't nobody try you like dat."

Hope shot Rosco a unit. "I am just letting you know, I ain't gone be wit all dat, Eddie."

Rosco did all he could to keep from laughing. He always thought Hope was soft. "You got dat killah." It was Todd Rosco felt he had to worry about.

When they got back to the car, Hope saw the funny look on Todd's face.

"I thought you said you don't fuck with da dude?" Todd blurted, hopping in the Jag.

"I don't! But I do dem forty he stressing." He handed Todd a cigar.

"I don't like it!" Todd said, glancing over at Hope. "Why you? He know y'all on bad terms. And what I don't like the most is this time and place he wants for you to pick up the cars. It sounds like ah..."

"First of all," Hope said, cutting him off, "we need dem forty. Second of all, I am the best of the best." Hope bragged, trying to reassure his homeboy. "Besides, you gonna help me bam dem cars, anyway." He gave Todd some dap, "What could go wrong with the two of us on the spot?"

"Man, I haven't stolen a car in almost ten years!" Todd confessed.

"You trippin'," Hope turned over the engine and pulled off.

"Umm, just saying!"

"Saying what?" Hope asked. "Dawg, you showed me the car game...So you telling me you forgot how to sell dope?"

"That don't even sound right!" Todd shot back. "How you forget to sell dope?"

"Exactly!" Hope exclaimed. "Man, is you gonna bust dat down?" he shouted, pointing to the cigar.

When they came to a stoplight, Hope tossed Todd a sandwich bag containing a light green color weed with red hairs.

"Twist dat up," he ordered, "and don't waste none in the car."

"Man, I know how to roll! It wasn't like a nukka wasn't burning in the joint."

Hope snorted back a laugh. "You wasn't burning dat in no joint! Betcha dat."

"All of it da same," Todd mumbled as he cracked the door, dumping the tobacco onto the road.

"I taught, yo ass," he snarled, looking over to Hope. "Remember?"

Hope just started laughing. He missed being with his homeboy, and as he watched Todd masterfully twist up the blunt, he sensed things were going to be gravy for the two of them.

Todd fired up the blunt and took a deep pull. As soon as the smoke entered his lungs, he erupted into a death like cough. His eyes turned bloodshot red, and mucous pushed through one of his nostrils.

Hope burst out laughing. "Yeah, nukka, dat's dat dro. Play wit it if you want too." In a more serious tone, he asked Todd if he was willing to help. "You down?"

"Yeah, I'm down!" Todd assured him.

"I know you is," Hope said jokingly. "Trying to act like you ain't bout dem forty."

"Look, man! I don't play games all the time," Todd tried to hold a straight face, but he couldn't. As soon as Hope started laughing, he did, too.

* * * * *

After the fourth ring, Lewis finally answered the phone. "Detective Lewis speaking."

"I would like to report my car stolen, it's a black..."

"What do you want, Rosco?" Lewis snapped angrily, cutting him off.

Rosco's chuckles echoed in his ear.

"Relax, detective."

"Don't tell me to relax." He hated when Rosco talked to him as if they were friends. "I, just..."

"What do you want, Rosco?" he asked in the same angry tone.

"To tell you everything is on point. But, there was a little problem. Not a big one. Don't worry, I took care of it."

Lewis hated problems. "What problem?"

"I had to pay him upfront. Something about his car needing to be fixed; baby momma behind on rent; his homeboy..."

"What the hell are you talking about? Who said anything about paying anybody anything!"

Rosco could hear Lewis's blood pressure shoot up.

"You told me he was one of your workers." There was a few seconds of silence before Lewis spoke again. "How much did you pay?"

"Forty thousand," Rosco replied flatly.

"Forty thousand! Are you crazy?"

"If I didn't give him the money, he would have walked. If he walked, you don't get your stupid promotion, and I don't get broke off. Ya, feel me? Besides, you only got to give me back twenty five."

Lewis chose his words carefully before he spoke again. For some reasons, he felt as if that Fat Hispanic knew how bad he needed this bust to go down. He couldn't trust him. At some point and time, he knew Rosco would try and cross him. Lewis's lips set in a thin, grim line. He didn't have a choice. "Okay," Lewis agreed.

"Okay? So we straight?" Rosco asked.

"Yeah, we good," he assured him. "So he'll be there Monday, right?"

Rosco conceded. "Monday, as planned."

Lewis's tone was menacing when he spoke again. "Rosco, he'd better be there, or your ass will be the one who boosts my career."

Rosco grinned and rubbed his hands together. "I ain't got no problem wit dat. Just make sure you bring the twenty five with'cha."

Lewis didn't even acknowledge his demand. "I'll be over there tonight with the car, so be ready."

Rosco wasn't letting him off that easy. "So you gonna bring dat?"

Lewis blew out a noisy breath. "What, the money?"

"Yeah."

"Yeah, whatever. I'll bring that," Lewis was lying, he would never let some fat, overweight Puerto Rican pull the wool over his eyes. He made a mental note to kill his fat ass as soon as he got his promotion.

Rosco replaced the phone on the receiver, then leaned back in his chair.

"So what he say?" the young boy asked excitedly.

Rosco looked at the young boy with greedy eyes. "What you think...He gone get dat money up!"

"You like dat, papo," the young Cuban boasted as he walk out the office. "You like dat."

Rosco decided he would have the detective killed as soon as he got the money and find another way to grab the sixty kilos of cocaine.

CHAPTER 3

"How you wanna do dis?" Todd's asked as he sat behind the steering wheel of a mobed out LeSabre.

"Soon as he pops the door, I gotta have'em." Hope pulled a nine from his waist. For the next twenty minutes, Hope and Todd shared a blunt and some small idle talk while waiting for their victim to come out of the restaurant.

"There he go!" Todd's words were soft and slow. "Go, go, go!" Todd yelled as the middle age white man lifted up the door to the Lamborghini.

Before he could react to the screeching tires, the decor of a metallic green Buick swung open. Out came an average built black male wearing a ski mask. The only thing he saw was a mouth full of gold and a 9mm Glock.

"Let me get dat," Hope demanded before slapping the older man with the pistol.

"Please don't kill me," he begged, as the top of his head began to bleed.

"I ain't playing wit you, white boy." He slapped him with the gun once more. "Gimme da dam keys."

"Here, here! Take the damn keys." He looked at Hope with pleading eyes, his face covered in blood. "Just don't hit me with that damn gun anymore, please!"

Hope snatched the keys from his hand and ordered him to lie on the floor. "Back yo butt up and lay over there." He waved the pistol to the back end of a car parked next to them.

In fear of his life, the white man did as he was told. Before he could lay completely flat, he heard the tire's high pitch screeching noise as they gripped the asphalt, and just as fast as it happened, it was over. The only evidence that could prove the masked thug's green Buick or his Lamborghini was ever there were the skid marks printed on the parking lot.

Damn, this bitch fast," Hope yelled out loud as he almost ran into a minivan coming out of the shopping plaza. Hope had been waiting for a ride like this his whole life; he couldn't believe how fast he took off. He'd never been behind the wheel of anything so powerful. As he bobbed and weaved through traffic at speeds close to ninety miles per hour, he made a mental note that as soon as his bread was straight, he was going to cop one.

When Hope arrived at the stash spot, Todd was already there, waiting with his arms crossed. He knew that meant his homeboy was hot mad.

"Damn nukka!" Todd lashed out. "I been here over twenty minutes now."

"You wouldn't believe how...."

"Man, we ain't got time fo all dat, Eddie. You know we gotta go get the Lac, and you know we ain't got that much time. He pointed to the open garage. Park that, and let's bounce!"

After Hope hid the Lam, he made sure to run a rake over the dirt to cover the tire tracks before he jumped into the burgundy Acura.

"You gotta tighten up, homeboy," Todd mumbled as he pulled off. They had less than an hour to bam the Cadillac. The only problem was that they were at least thirty to forty minutes away. Hope mentioned a club he wanted to take Todd to called "La'Roose." Todd agreed, but first, they had business to handle.

* * * * *

When Lewis arrived at the shop, Rosco's men were more than ready to load all sixty kilos of cocaine into the 600 Benz.

"You ready?" Rosco snatched open the door before Lewis even killed the engine. "Because my men are ready to go to work," he stated and flashed his stained smile, then backed up so Lewis could exit the car.

"Why doesn't that surprise me!" Lewis said sarcastically. "They...you, only had two weeks to prepare them," He pushed the door shut and walked to Rosco's office.

Rosco asked about the twenty five grand, but his words were drowned out by the constant banging as Lewis shoved his way through the small group of bandits right on his heels. Rosco stumbled into the office, his heart pounding and his mouth dry.

"Why you walk so damn fast?" Rosco asked as all three hundred plus pounds crashed onto the couch.

Lewis signaled for silence, picked up the phone and dialed out. He waited a couple of seconds, then spoke a few words. Shortly after, he completed his phone call and focused back on Rosco.

"Who was that?"

"That was neither here nor there." He tossed Rosco the keys to the Benz. "Do yourself a favor, try not to worry about things that do not concern you... you'll live longer." Lewis pulled a piece of paper out his pocket, "by the way, make sure those idiots don't get happy handed." Lewis picked the phone up and flashed a fake smile. "We wouldn't want anyone to get the sticky fingers, now would we?"

"It's your world," Rosco responded.

"My world?" Lewis thought to himself. "You're a funny guy, Rosco." Lewis looked at his watch, "I got a few more calls to make...give me a few seconds, and I will be down there."

Ten minutes later, Lewis was back downstairs. With the eyes of a hawk, Lewis watched as Rosco's men packed the Benz with what he considered the purest coke Florida had seen in a long time.

"You got that from the evidence room?" Rosco asked, glancing over the carefully packaged cargo.

"About the money...."

"Yeah, I don't see it!" Rosco uttered.

"That will be tomorrow."

17

"Cool!" Rosco looked over to the young Cuban. "What are you looking at? Load that up and do as you were told. And anybody wit dem sticky finger will be delt wit," he met eyes with all his workers. "Trust that!"

* * * * *

Cadillacs were always easy for Hope to steal. He'd been stealing them since he was fourteen, so when they arrived at the address on the list, it was like taking candy from a baby. The job took less than two minutes.

Afterwards, they went to Todd's crib to get clean for the club. Being that this would be Todd's first night out, he wasn't really feeling the whole club scene. But, when they pulled up, snatching all the attention as they leaned back in the deep burgundy sitting on gold flippers, blasting "All eyes on me," Todd switched to flipmode real quick.

Hope was the master of flossing, so when he saw a young, bowlegged red catch eyes with his homeboy, he slowed down and cruised by.

"I told you it be thick out here!"

"Thick ain't da word!" Todd responded.

Hope tossed Todd a blunt. "Twist one up, they don't let'cha roll nuttin' up in the club." Hope thought about it, then pulled half a blunt from his top pocket. "You ain't gotta twist nuttin' but one, I forgot I put one together earlier."

Thirty minutes later, they were on the third floor, posted in a V.I.P. Booth. Boosting cars had its advantages, and Hope was good at finding them. Once a year, he would give the owner of the club a new ride free of charge. In exchange, he was allowed to bring two friends, free admission, drinks and a personal table in V.I.P.

The night was young, and Todd was starting to feel loose. He was glad he decided to come as two honies cuddled up under him.

"Boo, you trying to get some head?" the moca fudge honey with gray contacts asked.

"Some head?" Todd repeated.

"My bad," she mumbled politely. "I just figured since yo boy was..."

When Todd looked over to Hope, he couldn't believe his eyes. The two honies Hope had were all over him like animals. One sucking his dick. The other licking his chest.

"Right there," Hope instructed the lil' red with the vicious head game as he ran his fingers through her Halle Berry haircut.

Before Todd knew what was going on, the mocha fudge honey was trying to swallow him whole.

"Fuck me wit dis," the other brown skin freak begged. Seductively. As she pulled out a dildo. Todd took the dildo and placed it on the lips of her pussy.

"No, boo," she lowered it down, "not there, here."

"You want me to fuck you in the ass!" Todd asked, a bit confused.

"Do it!" Hope yelled as his two animals switched positions.

Todd put their ass to the test. Everything he ever read about anything freaky while he was locked up, he tried on them. And for the next hour and a half, both of them had their way with their new lady friends. After the club, they gave the young freaks cab fare and went to the local eatery to grab a bite to eat.

* * * * *

Rosco walked back into his office. Lewis was still on his phone, still in his chair. His feet propped up.

"Your feet belong on the floor," Rosco uttered, but his complaint fell on deaf ears.

Lewis gave a nod of the head and held up a finger, signaling Rosco to be quiet. Lewis continued his conversation for the next ten minutes, then placed the phone back on the receiver. He was about to tell Rosco to let him finish his call, but he saw something in his eyes and decided that that wouldn't be a good idea.

"So, what time you plan on bringing the money?"

"I'll call you when I'm ready." Lewis was lying, all he wanted was to buy some time.

"You'll call me when you ready?" Rosco repeated the irritation in his voice present.

"You'll have your money home...boy."

Rosco hated it when people played on his intelligence. He was trying to hide his frustration. He knew right then that the detective was going to cross him: If he didn't get the money now, he was never going to get it. Now, he didn't feel so bad about the ten kilos he instructed his workers to switch out. Then he thought about it? Maybe all the dope was fake.

"I'm cool," Rosco tried to force a smile.

"When I call you, you'll have to come and get the money," he said as though reading Rosco's eyes. "We'll meet somewhere."

"I'm cool," Rosco repeated.

This is too easy, he thought. Rosco was too slick for his own good. He knew Rosco was trying to get him for twenty five grand, and he was going to cross him. Lewis had everything planned. All ends were covered. With an awkward smile on his face, Lewis began to visualize the press conference:

"Detective Lewis, how were you able to come up on such a bust as this?"

"I am a detective, ma'am. That's what I do. That's my job."

"Detective! Detective! Would you say a bust of this enormity has put a slump in our city's drug trade?"

"I won't say that, but I will say that I have committed my life to leave this beautiful city of ours from all that brings harm."

"Detective! Detective! De-tek-tive," Rsoco's heavy accent crept into the slanky detective's muse. He quickly brushed off his fantasy and got back to business.

"Are they done with the car?"

"Almost," Rosco answered.

Rosco's men placed the last couple of kilos in the trunk of the Benz. Both men watched with a precarious smile. For Lewis, he wasn't sure if he should kill Rosco before the bust or after. For Rosco, it was less complicated. He knew how he was going to kill Lewis and when it was more of a choice of what.

"We all done!" the young Cuban shouted to Rosco.

"Well, that will be you, detective." Rosco patted Lewis on the back.

"Great." Lewis looked at his watch, "I'll make it on time."

"So I'll see you Monday, right?"

"Yeah, Monday," Lewis snarled.

"Cool! and don't forget the money."

Lewis made one more phone call, then left in one of Rosco's Cadillacs. After he was long gone, Rosco called Hope to come and pick up the car key. After Hope left, Rosco sat back in his office... daydreaming about all the dope he was about to come upon. I should never be broke, he thought. Not me, I am too good.

CHAPTER 4

Hope and Todd were right on schedule. The list Rosco had given them was almost complete. One Benz left, and they were forty grand strong.

"Once we get the money, we need to invest it."

"Invest it into what?" Hope asked.

"The market. A small business. Don't matter. We just need to be smart about our money."

"What, like a grocery store?" Hope started laughing. "You trying to sell milk and eggs..."

"A grocery store? Where the hell you get dat from?"

"You said a market!"

"I'm talking about the stock market! Not a damn grocery store. I said when I got out dat we were going back to school. "He looked over to Hope, who was rolling one up.

"School?" Hope repeated. "Man, I ain't going to no damn school house," he fired up. "For what?"

"What you mean...for what? Dawg, a nucca ain't trying to be out here like dat, and I'm damn sure ain't trying to go back to prison."

"Ain't nobody said nuttin' bout going back," Hope said.

"You ain't got to. You stay out here long enough, and you will."

"Dawg, I'm wit'cha." He passed the blunt to Todd. "Ya feel me. But let's get dis money first... then we decide what to do wit it." He gave Todd some dap.

"I'm cool wit dat," Todd responded.

"Cool! Now let's go get this raggedy ass car of yours."

"Raggedy. Whatever." Todd started laughing. "When you see the Ackk, I'm gonna make you put the Jag up."

When they arrived at the shop, Todd was expecting to see his 92' Acura, but instead, he would be surprised with a new wipp. A brand new black on black Escalade sitting on twenty two's sound system that brought nothing but pain; ll' t.v. Screens and the softest leather known to man. It was the ultimate truck.

"Everything tight?" Hope asked the nerdy looking black boy.

"Yes, sir." He flashed an honest smile. "If you would follow me, I'll take you to your ride."

"What all they do up in here?" Todd asked as they walked through the side door that led to the paint room.

"They put down up in this spot," Hope boasted.

"We try our best," the nerd looking boy followed up. "Yes, we do. We do everything: paint, music, bodywork, engine detail, sound systems, rims, toys..."

"Toys?" Todd started laughing.

"Toys," he repeated," You know, games, tv... Dawg, daa do eeeverything," Hope uttered.

When they reached the paint room, Todd didn't see his Acura. At first, he thought that they may have been bringing it around, but Hope didn't ask for it. "Where da Ackk?" Todd asked, concerned.

"What Ackk?"

"What'cha mean, what Ackk? The one my people brought in bout a week ago." He looked to Hope to verify. But he just stood there.

"I'm sorry, sir, but the only rides we received a week ago were their Lexus and this here Escalade."

"I thought you said you brought the car to dis..."

"He didn't tell you?" the assistant asked, cutting Todd off.

"Tell me what?"

"Hope you crazy." He pulled a key out of his pocket and tossed it to Todd, "This is your truck, family. Hope brought it to us personally."

Todd took a good look at the Escalade, then back at Hope.

"When did you...How did you...Dis here clean?" He muttered as he opened the door and jumped in, setting off the alarm.

"Dawg, you gonna turn that off?"

"Oh, my bad." He hit a button on the key chain, "Dawg, I seen one like dis on Trick's new video."

"Where you think I got the idea for the spinning rims?" Hope asked. "So you straight?"

"Hell yeah, I'm straight."

"Good, then let's ride. We gotta get you some more clothes."

"Let's hit tha mall! I wonder if they got some new one fifties?"

"Hold up," Hope uttered as he answered his cell phone, "Hello? Yeah, what's happenin?" His eyes shifted towards Todd. "Gimme bout twenty minutes. Yeah, yeah. Cool, aight."

"Who was dat?" Todd asked.

"Dude, name Pollcat from in town. He been owing me for the longest, and now he got my money," Hope explained.

"Want me to ride wit'cha?"

Nah, you go ahead. I'm cool, Pollcat, my dawg. He just fell off, dats all.... Trust me, he good peoples."

"Aight! I'll hit'cha up when I bounce from tha mall." He gave Hope some dap, then closed the door. "Yeah, dis here me," he thought as he crunk up the system. 400 degrees was blasting out of the slew of twelves packed in the back of the truck. The whole paint room shook.

* * * * *

Todd decided to go to the newest mall out west: THE CENTRAL FLORIDA FASHION PLAZA. It was the first of its kind. Not only was it the biggest in the state of Florida, but also on the east coast. The parking lot alone looked to be five to six football fields, or at least that's what Todd thought as he drove around for fifteen minutes looking for a parking space.

Todd never saw anything like it. It was huge. He visited four stores, and all of them seemed to have this high life aura to them. Some he recognized, most he didn't. Todd felt like a new man as he went in and out of stores, putting together some of the cleanest combinations only a chosen few had the skills to do. Heading to the last store to cop a pair of blue and white one fifties (Air Max Nikes), Todd saw the badest bitch he'd seen in years rocking a fly business suite, matching tent designer glasses, and low haircut. She was bowlegged with a pecan brown complexion. A true dime piece, and Todd had to have her.

Her favorite color was blue, but the dark brown blouse brought out the softness of her skin. One by one, she held each blouse up to her chest as she pranced in the full length mirror, trying to decide which to buy. "Girl, you look good in both of them," she boasts to the curvaceous figure staring back at her. "I should buy both of them," she muttered softly.

"Maybe you should."

His voice startled her, causing a near smack to the face as she spun around wildly, dropping one of the shirts. When they came face to face, she was Impressed, but the only thing she was Interested In was slowing down her heartbeat.

"Excuse me," she uttered, placing one hand over her chest.

Todd was speechless for a few seconds. He couldn't believe his eyes. From afar, the curious eye Candy had appeared to be elegant and easy-on-the eyes, but up close, she became a gift from God. She was gorgeous. The last time he saw a woman this fine, she was on a Nelly video.

"Da brown one," he managed to muster out. "Dat's you all day." He reached down and picked up the blouse. "Here you go."

"I'm glad you picked dat up!" Candy voiced with a mixture of uneasiness and flirtatiousness.

"My pleasure," Todd uttered. He was more than happy to assist her, plus it gave him a chance to check her out thoroughly: Her lips, her eyes, her hips, her thighs. His nose was wide open.

"You shouldn't go around scaring people like that!" Candy's words came out casually as her eyes traced the outline of Todd's muscular frame.

"Like what?" he asked boyishly. "You asked me which one you should buy, so I told you!"

"Boy, I did not ask you anything." She started blushing. "I didn't even see you stalking me!"

"Stalking you! How am I stalking you when you were flirting with me in the mirror?"

"Flirting! Child, please, I was not flirting with you," she was lying. She knew he was watching her. She was hoping he would come over and holla.

"So what's your name?" he asked, disregarding her statement.

"What's yours?" Candy asked sharply.

"So, you gonna make dis hard fo me, huh?" He chuckled. "But I'm cool wit dat. "He extended out his hand. "Dat's cool, umm, Todd."

"Well, Mr. Todd," she said, placing her small, manicured hands into his. "It was nice meeting you."

I wonder if the rest of her is as soft as her hands? Todd thought, reluctant to let her hand go.

"Can I have back my hand?"

"Damn, my bad." He acted like he forgot.

"No problem." She flashed a perfect smile.

"You know what? I changed my mind."

"About what?" she inquired.

"You look better in blue," Todd insisted.

"Blue?" she repeated, "you think I look good in blue?" She raised the blouse up to her chest. "I do look good in blue, but then again..." she placed the other up to the chest. "The brown one brings out my eyes."

"Blue's my favorite color."

"Child, please!" she gave a light chuckle. "Boy, I know you ain't drop dat on me."

"I'm dead serious." He flashed a playful smile.

"If you say so." She looked at her watch. "Well, I was in a rush."

"Hold up!" Todd reached out for Candy's hand. "How you gone act? You know a nucca trying to holla at'cha."

"Is that right?" Candy teased playfully.

"Don't do dat. You know I'm trying to get at'cha."

"I can't tell, all you had to do was ask me straight up if I was interested in you or not."

"Are you?"

Candy reached into her purse and pulled out a phone. "Maybe, maybe not!" She flashed a smile. "Give me your number. If I am, I'll call you sometime this week."

After she logged the number into her phone, Todd decided to hang around and help her put together a few more outfits. Two hours later, he was walking Candy to her car. After Todd saw what she was driving, he was impressed, to say the least. "Dis yo nucca car?" he asked.

"No!" She snapped. "Boy, if I had a man. I wouldn't have taken your number."

"Where you work?" he asked as she climbed into the 600.

"I don't...I choose to go to school instead."

"Let me find out you got dem thangs for the low-low."

She burst out laughing. "Didn't you just hear me say I go to school?"

"School, my ass," he shot back over, looking the sky blue Benz on dubs. "You stunting harder than the nucca's out here," he said jokingly.

"You are so silly."

"What's your name?"

"Candy!"

"Well, Candy, I'm not gonna hold you up any longer...make sure you hit me up." Todd closed her door and watched as Candy pulled off, blasting Maxwell's latest CD. I gotta have lil momma, he thought as he jumped into the Escalade and headed back home.

CHAPTER 5

When Todd arrived at the house, he noticed ten messages on his answering machine. Maybe Hope gave a few broads the number, Todd thought as he rewound the tape. To his surprise, they were all from Hope, He'd caught a fresh one on the house --so he said-- and was being held without a bond. He claimed he'd called Todd at least twenty times. No answer.

"I know my.." Todd snatched the cell out of his pocket. "I'll be damned," he shouted. The battery on his phone was dead. He couldn't believe he forgot to charge the battery from the night before. Todd hated not being there when his dawg called. He decided to stay home and wait for Hope to call. Finally, a little after one o'clock in the morning, Hope called back to the house. This time he was there. Waiting. He picked up on the first ring.

"Goddamn, my nucca!" Hope's voice blasted from the phone. "I been trying to get at you all day, where you been?"

"What happened?" Todd asked, concerned.

"Dawg, as soon as I got in the house, Pollcat tells me to hold on. He walked to the back room to get the money, right? Now check dis out, some jit came flying through the door. I wasn't in the house for three minutes. Come to find out, his clown ass was on a highspeed wit dem folks. He calls his elf, busting at the po-po's. Before I could get my bread and dip, da police were all in the house. They found dope, money, trees, and basers in that bitch blowing. They find guns, bowls...dis nucca got a federal warrant."

"Who?"

"Pollcat bum-ass." Todd could feel his dawg's pain. "Man, I know I ain't gone get my money now!! Dat nucca going to daa fed's, and I ain't got no damn bond!"

"You holla'd at the lawyer?" Todd asked

"He was at court, so I left a message... dawg, I ain't worried about no bond. Most likely, I'll get one when I see the judge. The only bad part about it is that won't be until Monday or Tuesday, ya feel me!"

"Hell yeah! Todd said in a confidential tone, "dat got to be dun by Monday.." As an afterthought, Todd added, "Don't worry, I got it."

"I left the list on the table at the house."

"You or me?" Todd asked.

"You," Hope shot back.

"Cool, I'll holla when you touch down. One."

"One!"

* * * * *

Todd was up early. His partner in crime was temporarily M.I.A., four of the five cars were hidden in various locations, and they all had to be delivered at the same time. He was only short one Benz, but, being that he would have to do it all by himself, he found out real quick that he had a far place to go and a short time to get there.

Todd parked the undercover, jumped out and walked through the parking lot. His first mind told him to just walk away, but he ignored it. He thought it was just nervousness. He convinced himself it was only butterflies due to his ten year hiatus. Besides, they needed the money more than ever. He could hear the lawyer all in Hope's ear: "Mr Sneed, I can beat the charge for about eight grand. You see, your record is very bad, and the judge you are going in front of is a real hard ass about these types of cases. Without a doubt, Hope was in desperate need of that money, and nothing or no one was going to deny Todd from getting it for him.

Not even Detective Lewis, who just so happened to be sitting in a van a few feet away or the ten plus undercovers scattered about.

The first thing Todd noticed was that the Benz he had to cop was sitting off by itself. At first, he thought the owner might have parked it away from the other cars to avoid any bumps or scratches, but then he took a good look around and saw a slew of expensive cars; some more extravagant than others, but none the less, they were all lavish in one way or another.

"No one moves until I say so," Lewis spoke softly but firmly into the small hand device. "No fuck ups...remember, the suspect is more likely to be armed and dangerous. Most drug dealers are, so I want everyone to be cautious when we approach the car." Ten minutes later, Todd was spotted.

Although he hadn't stolen a car in ten years, he was still on his square. He stayed out of jail and in harm's way for the most part because of that, and this was no different. He knew better than to just jump right in the car, his first mind told him to walk around first. Scope thing out. If everything looked straight, bam the Benz and get the hell out of there. He looked at his watch, it was a quarter after eleven. Perfect time. He figured it would take at least twenty minutes to scan the whole parking lot, which would give him close to an hour and a half to grab the four other cars on the list.

"Sir, is that our target?" a voice chirped through Lewis's earpiece.

"Affirmative!!"

"Are you sure, sir? He appears to be lost, sir," he responded as Todd strolled freely in and out of the cars.

"He's not lost, you idiot; he's cautious." Lewis wasn't too thrilled to be going up against a pro, but he welcomed the challenge all the same. Although he structured his little escapade around an easy snatch and grab, this could be just what he needed to spice things up and make it more real. More dramatic.

"Change of plans, ladies and gentlemen," Lewis spat into the mic. "Looks like we got ourselves a bona fide criminal. So listen up, I want everyone on his ass like bees on honey the second he puts one foot in that Benz."

After two trips around the lot, Todd felt safe enough to bam the Benz. He looked back at his watch, a quarter till twelve. The parking lot was bigger than he thought. Before he opened the door, he took a few seconds to look around, something he did back in the day. It made him feel safer. He called it his second opinion before he was off to the races.

This can't be happening --Todd thought as the parking lot came alive with cops. He had scanned the whole parking lot and came up with nothing, but as soon as he got a foot in the car, cops were coming from everywhere. Some plain clothes, some uniforms. All were coming in fast, drawing firearms.

"Kiss my ass!!" His words came out unconsciously as Todd fumbled with the key before jamming it in the ignition.

"Get out of the car!!"

Todd looked up. Two plain clothes stood in front of the Benz. Guns pointed.

"Gun!! Gun!! He has a gun. He got a gun," the plain clothes officer crouched down in his shooting position and fired off six rounds.

Todd couldn't believe what was happening. Where did they come from? Why were they there? Why were they trying to kill him? Before he realized it, two more rounds ripped through the Benz. Todd stayed low, trying to avoid getting hit. Then it happened, his mind went blank, and his instincts kicked in.

Quickly, he turned over the engine, snatched it in reverse, and mashed the gas. When he looked up, he mashed the brakes. His rear end was mere inches away from a brick wall, but that was the least of his worries as a slew of bullets tore through the windshield; one managed to graze his shoulder.

He snatched it down to drive and mashed the gas. The car lunged forward towards the cops, swaying from left to right, trying to avoid any more hits. This was his first time being shot at by the police, and if he had anything to do with it, it would be his last. That was his exact thought as he came crashing through the sea of armed men, knocking many to the pavement before the Benz bounced off the variety of parked cars and slammed into a squad car.

Without hesitation, he threw it in reverse, pulled back, and took off again. One of the officers got off one last shot before Todd shot out of the parking lot. He accelerated up to one hundred miles per hour. With one hand nursing a flesh wound, panic began to settle when Todd realized his troubles had just begun. He'd been shot --at least, he thought he was; The Benz was a total bust, and he was in need of a hiding place.

Just like that, things went from bad to worse. Hope was in jail with no bond; he was one car short of forty grand, and now, he was a fugitive on the run. A million things ran through Todd's mind as he tried to figure things out: what if he would have done this, or If that would have happened, and he should've done this, and he should've seen that. His cell phone went off. He tried to ignore it. Scared to answer it. But, after the fourth or fifth ring, he answered. There was a few seconds of silence before a voice popped up.

"May I speak to Todd?"

"Who, dis!! Angie?" Todd asked with a hint of nervousness.

"Angie?" Her voice became flat. "Maybe I called you at a bad time, this is Candy, not Angie."

"Candy, where you at?"

"Why?" she asked cautiously. She sensed an alarm in his voice

"Man, where you at? The house where you live at?"

"Yeah, I'm at the house," she acknowledged. "Is something wrong?" She could tell something had him shook up.

"You stay near the school?"

"What school?"

"The college?" Todd asked with urgency

"Yeah, about twenty minutes away...are you in some kind of..."

"What street you live on?"

Candy knew what he was really asking of her. He was in trouble, and he wanted her help. If she was to help, what would she be getting into? She'd just met him. For all she knew, he could be a serial killer.

"Candy!! I'm fucked up...I need, I need yo help."

Maybe it was how he said it or what he said, she wasn't sure, but despite her better judgment, she gave him the directions to her home. After she placed the phone down, she put her hands over her mouth and sat back on the couch. I can't believe I just did that, she thought.

CHAPTER 6

After his so called well planned drug bust blew up in his face, Detective Lewis spent the next two and a half hours cleaning up a self inflicting misfortune. Afterwards, he tied up the last loose ends and headed to Rosco's place. The entire ride over, Lewis replayed the chain of events in his mind. Over and over again, he tried to figure out where the hell he got that key from. And how did he know they were out there?

"Rosco!! You, fat bastard," Lewis yelled. He could hear his words echo throughout the car as he drove his fist into the steering wheel. "I'm gonna kill you. Rosco caused him the opportunity of a lifetime, not to mention sixty kilos of cocaine. Who else could have given that lil tarbaby a key to the car? For all he knew, the two of them could have teamed up to rob him for the drugs. He knew he couldn't trust a nigger and a spic. There was going to be hell to pay; he would make sure of that. Killing Rosco was something he already deemed necessary. He just thought it would be under different circumstances.

Killing him now was purely personal for taking away his shot to the top. Rosco saw everything on the news, so he was expecting Lewis to pop up. So when Lewis arrived at the garage, Rosco's men were positioned and waiting on him to bring an unpleasant visit. Rosco saw a look of death on Lewis's face when he walked into the office.

"You do good out there?" Rosco asked sarcastically.

"Something like that," Lewis responded with daggered eyes.

"You brought the money?"

Lewis was so enraged with Rosco. Who the hell did that fat bastard think he is sitting there like everything's fine and dandy... and just how long was he going to play this out? Lewis knew he gave that black boy those keys. They planned that together, and that was why Lewis had to kill him.

"Detective, detective!" Rosco noticed a dazed look on his face.

"What?" Lewis growled.

"The money?"

"The money? Yeah, yeah, yeah, the money," He waved Rosco out of the office. "It's in the car." He tried to smile but couldn't.

"I'm ready when you ready," Rosco responded.

As the two walked downstairs, Lewis finally realized they were the only ones in the shop. How perfect, Lewis thought. Instead of driving Rosco to his death, he would let him walk into it.

"Where is everybody?" Lewis asked.

"They all quit...said something bout giving their lives to god," he gave a light chuckle.

"Very funny…Fatboy."

Rosco began to laugh, and that made Lewis even madder. He wanted to pull his gun out and shot him right there, but he couldn't. He wouldn't allow himself to be cheated out of watching Rosco's eyes turn from sugar to shit when he pulls his gun on him while he's counting his money, only to realize he's about to die.

"You wouldn't believe what I went through to get your money," Lewis mumbled as he picked up his step, Rosco right on his heels. When they climbed in the car, Rosco barely had the strength to close the door. Walking fast always did that to him.

"Very funny," Rosco muffled in between breaths.

"What's that?" Lewis asked.

"What's what? Man, you know what I'm talking bout."

"Hell, you walking so fast fo?"

"Here!" Lewis tossed him a bag from the backseat, then placed his back to the door, giving himself a better angle.

"All of it's here?" Rosco asked as he flipped through the small bills.

"That little bastard had a key…go figure," Lewis voiced bitterly.

"How dat happen?" Rosco asked, trying to look surprised.

"If I had to guess, I would say that either he was tipped off or someone gave it to him."

"These days, these guys are like dat," Rosco responded, "deh steal cars like you wouldn't believe."

"Was it all there?" Lewis asked.

"Yeah!"

"You sure?" Lewis asked. "Because I don't need you calling me later on talking about I was short."

"You afraid you put too much money in the bag, detective?"

"Something like that…you mind counting it again?" He flashed half a smile.

"No trust?" Rosco asked boyishly before recounting.

This was the moment he was waiting for. Rosco was just too predictable. Lewis knew that Rosco was so obsessed with greed that he wouldn't notice the gun in his face until he heard It go off. By then, It would be too late.

"Do you believe all great minds think alike," Rosco asked as he thumbed through the last stack of twenty's.

"I'm not sure I understand," Lewis responded.

"You mind if I smoke," Rosco asked but was already lighting up a cigar before Lewis could respond.

"Was it all there?" Lewis asked as he eased for his pistol. It was time.

"The money isn't my problem. My problem is that you came all this way to kill me."

At that moment, both men's eyes met, and an alarm went off in Lewis's mind. Before he could react to his suspicions, a young Latino catapulted from the back, spraying his eyes with a hazardous mist.

"You fat bastard!" Lewis screamed as he fumbled with his pistol in the corner of the door. The teenage boy was well prepared. After spraying Lewis, he snatched away his pistol.

"Good job, Papo," Rosco cheered before pulling out a gun. "You know what your problem is, Detective?" Rosco asked in a satiric manner.

"Damn you!" Lewis cried as he squirmed around.

"You were too much of a cop for me." Rosco began laughing.

"I'm a cop, for Christ sake, you can't kill me!" Lewis began begging.

"For… Christ sake," Rosco repeated as he rubbed his plump fingers over his chin. "No, no, no, my friend, I am not going to kill you for the sake of Christ," he said, then laughed while screwing on the silencer. "You're going to die for the sake of me." He placed the gun to Lewis's head. "If you didn't mind, tell Christ I said I am very, very sorry missing church dis year."

Those were the last words Lewis heard before three bullets tore into his skull. After he disposed of the body, all Rosco had to do was wait for Hope to bring the cars so he could get his dope. All fifty.

CHAPTER 7

Todd's sleep was overpowered by the sound of soft jazz and the smell of French fries and hamburgers floating through the air. As his eyes opened slowly, he could feel a stiffness in his back, while the deep bruise in his shoulder gave an irritable throbbing pain.

"You need to lay your butt right back down." Candy walked in carrying a plate of food.

"How long have I been asleep?"

"Since yesterday!" She placed the plate down. "You lucky it was only a flesh wound." She watched as Todd rubbed his shoulder, taking notice of how professional the wrapping was. "The way your car looks, I might be talking to a ghost."

"What's dat, burgers and fries?"

"Yeah, I made you lunch. You hungry?"

"You mean to tell me you let me sleep for a whole day?

"Me?" She began to laugh. "Boy, please, if god wanted your butt to wake up yesterday, you would have." Candy left the room and returned with a wash cloth and towel. "Here!" She tossed them to Todd. "The shower is down the hall on the right, and don't leave no ring around my tub either."

Todd mumbled something under his breath, climbed out of bed and headed to the bathroom. For the next hour, Todd soaked in the oversized tub. When he reemerged, he felt fully energetic and hungry, which was quickly satisfied by the burger and fries Candy left next to the boxers and t-shirt. "Good lookin' out," Todd thought as he dived into the plate of food, devouring everything in minutes. When Candy walked back into the room, he was washing the last bit down with cherry Kool Aid.

"Boy, you just eating that food? It got to be cold."

Todd shook his head yes. "That big ass tub had a nucca slumped over...it was cold, but a nucca fucked that shit up!"

"Poor thang," Candy chuckled. "By the way, what are you going to do with the car?"

"Oh, dat's a done deal, it'll be outta here by tonight," Todd assured her.

"Why were the police shooting at you?"

"What makes you say dat?" Todd eyed Candy closely.

"I just figured if it was anybody else, you would have gone back to get some straightening."

Todd just smiled. Fine and thuggish, he thought to himself. I gotta have her.

"Don't do dat," he said jokingly, heading to the garage.

"Do what?" Candy asked, right on his heel, "Do, what?" she repeated, but Todd was somewhere else.

All Todd could do was thank God. He couldn't believe what he was looking at. How could he have survived the hail of bullets that tore through the Benz like Swiss cheese? How could anyone have survived?

"They tried to do my ass," he expressed angrily as he snatched open the car door.

"What's dat?"

"What?"

"That!" Candy pointed to the off white pover pouring onto the floor. "Man! That white stuff?" Candy asked.

"That's that money, that's what that lo," Todd announced as he continued his search.

"Is that cocaine?" she asked fearfully.

"What kind of tools you got?..Candy!"

"What kind of what?" she snapped out of her thought.

"Tools...a screwdriver, hammer, wrench. What'cha got?"

"I have a toolbox."

"Let me get it," Todd ordered.

Candy left and returned with a power drill in hand.

"Those other ones will take too long," she handed him the drill.

Inside the driver's door were five kilos of cocaine. In the passenger door was the same amount. With a disturbing gaze, Todd turned to Candy.

"I don't think that was the cops busting at me."

"Why not?" she asked, but he didn't respond.

Todd went right back to searching for more kilos. His gut told him there was more dope, and the more he ransacked, the more he found. He was right. In each door, he found five; fifteen in the backseat, twenty-five more in the trunk. What bothered Todd was the ones in the trunk: they weren't hidden. It was as if someone just put them there just to be seen. He wasn't sure what to make of it all. Everything was out of place. He needed to think. Hope was in jail, someone posing as the police tried to kill him, and now he had sixty kilos of cocaine stacked up in front of him in a garage at some broad's house he just met yesterday. He didn't even know her full name. And then there was Rosco. As his mind raced to piece things together, he realized those bullets were meant for Hope. Not him.

"Rosco!!" he uttered out loud.

"Rosco? Who's Rosco?"

"He the one who set this whole thing up? Dat nucca almost got me knocked Off. He gave my dawg this bogus list for us to bam a few rides when all along," he rubbed his shoulder, "he wanted Hope to pick up his yahh. That's why he offered forty grand."

"Forty grand for what? And who ls Hope? And what the hell does bam mean?" Candy asked, feeling things spinning out of control.

"Hope is my dawg," Todd explained. "And to bam means to do yo thang...and the forty grand was for the list of cars."

Candy sat there for a minute, hand on hips. "Yo, ass a car thief?" Her tone confirmed her disapproval. "Dis nucca a damn car thief!"

"Man, I ain't no car thief." He couldn't believe how she tried him. "I'm a go getter, ya feel me, I get money," he voiced in a matched tone.

Candy tried not to laugh, but she thought he was being very comical.

"Man, you trippin! You up here laughing, my dawg cased up, people trying to kill a nucca." He gestured at the stack of kilos. "I bet Rosco had us rob those people for this dope."

"So what now?"

"I gotta see how this plays out first."

"Then what?"

"Don't know yet. But I do know this, it ain't going down the way Rosco thinks it is. That's on everything I love."

Candy was about to comment, but Todd's phone went off.

It was Rosco, he wanted to know if Todd had seen Hope, and if he did, where was he?

When Franky took his seat, he knew his life was about to change. He wasn't sure how, but he was certain a change would come as long as he stayed drug free. As he gazed out the window, lost in thought, he prepared for the future. Strapped with less than a hundred dollars, a gold chain his ex-wife gave him when they were sixteen, and half a sandwich, he was on his way to Florida. His niece had moved there after his brother's funeral. He was hoping Florida would bring something new to his life. He'd spoken to his niece a few times during his recovery. They'd talked about him cleaning up and her starting fresh. Things were slow to pick up, but they did. He found himself more impressed with her determination than her accomplishments. Maybe...just maybe, if he was lucky, he thought, he'd be able to come up like his niece.

"You mind if I sit next to the window?"

"Nah, go ahead." Franky bounced to his feet, giving way to the seat. Standing before him was one of the rawest broads he'd seen since he was sixteen. Blessed with wide hips, a small waist, and a deep mocha fudge complexion, often mistaken as a video vixen.

"Thank you." She flopped down, obviously tired, "I hate the isle seat."

"So where you headed?" Franky asked the second she sat down.

"Florida."

"Florida?" He sensed a bit of excitement in her voice. "What part? If you don't mind me asking......"

"Are you flirting wit me?"

"Am I flirting with you?" He tried to lie, but his ear to ear smile told the truth.

Instead of a cordial handshake, lil' mama gave him some dap. "I'm Dee Dee."

"So that's what you do?" Franky joked with her about her hood like greeting.

"Boy, please." She flashed a girlish smile. "I do not know where your hands have been."

"Fo real, fo real, these hands just might be what makes all your dreams come true."

"Is that right?" she asked comically. "And just how do your hands plan on making my dreams come true?"

"Funny you would ask." He rubbed his palms together. "First of all, they get money. Secondly, they know the true essence of the woman's anatomy, and last but not least, they don't hit women, that is."

Born a breadwinner, Franky was one of the last true hustlers of his time, but, like all great hustlers, he, too, had a flaw: he smoked dope. Even at the age of eleven, he showed signs of a go-getter when he organized a lawn service gig by bringing together a few kids from the neighborhood. All he had to do was keep their tanks full as they went out to cut his clientele's yard, then collect at the end of the day. But that was a lifetime ago, and Franky wasn't eleven anymore. He was a forty two year old recovering drug addict trying to make his last comeback. He'd been off drugs for over two years now and was feeling that drive to get money again. Factoring in that with his natural ability to make money, Franky was destined to come into some major bread. Not even he knew he would come into it faster than he thought.

The ride to Florida was longer than expected. At one point, he wished he would have caught the trains; at least that way, he could have rode in a cabin. But, the more he talked to Dee-Dee, the more he felt good about his bus ride. It gave him an opportunity to brush up on his skills. Although he was a bit rusty, he was still on point. Before Dee-Dee got off the bus, he knew her whole history: from her first boyfriend to her last mud pie.

Hours later, the bus was pulled into the station. He made it. Down for whatever, Franky was ready to mark his claim. He hopped in a cab and was on his way.

* * * * *

A little after ten o'clock, Jamie Lightbourn's mind went into overdrive. Standing over the body of a dead cop, a million thoughts ran through her mind as she rushed for answers to solve yet another homicide. The body was found around nine o'clock the day before, which meant she only had seventeen hours to do what she did best. Catch a murderer.

Jamie watched as the medical examiner read from his chart. "Ok, Doc, give me what you got."

"Cause of death three bullets into the brain." He walked over and pulled the sheet down to the waist, exposing the upper body. "Here, here, and here."

"You run a toxicology test?" Jamie asked casually while overlooking the entry of the wounds.

"Yeah!" He thumbed through the stack of papers. "Give me a sec. Okay, yeah. Here we go. We found traces of hydrochloride, MDMA, and THC."

"What's MDMA?"

"Ecstasy!! Go figure, I thought ecstasy was popular with the kids. Oh yeah," he flipped back through the file, "although he was found about nine, he was dead before 5:00 p.m."

"Anything else?"

"Yeah, I found pepper spray on his hands."

"His hands?" she repeated.

"Yeah, but look at this," he placed the open file on the table, "his clothes were soaked in rubbing alcohol and the spray was washed out his eyes..."

"Figures," her voice was flat.

"What do you mean?" he asked curiously.

With her eyes fixed on the ceiling, she spoke as if she were searching for an answer. "It's just, whoever killed him made damn sure it would be hard to find any evidence. If any."

Jamie knew the examiner wouldn't be able to help her. Whoever killed Detective Lewis was well aware of the procedures followed after the discovery of a dead body. It was quite obvious after she read the field report that her trip to the coroner's office would be more of a formality. After she received a copy of the corpus delicti, she headed back to the station to compare notes. But first, she swung by the house to shower up and grab a bite to eat.

* * * * *

Franky was more than impressed when the cab pulled up to his niece's house. Besides being in a nice neighborhood, the house was laid out. She said she was handling her business, Franky thought as he paid the fair. "She gotta have a baller?"

"A ball?" the driver asked cluelessly.

Franky hopped out of the cab, grabbed his bags, and began to walk, then came to a halt. When he looked back, he saw the driver wrestling with his last comment. "Don't woory bout it," Franky said with pride, "it's a black thing."

After four knocks and three doorbell rings, Franky decided that his niece wasn't home. Maybe she went out to the store, or maybe, and he hoped that wouldn't be the case, but maybe she went to the bus station to pick him up.

After a few seconds rationalizing his next move, he took it upon himself to check the door. He was right. The door was unlocked. She had to just run to the store, why else would her door be unlocked? "Just because you stay in a white neighborhood doesn't mean you can leave your house wide open," Franky mumbled as he made his way into the house.

The second he stepped in, the smell of the new carpet rushed up his nose. And from where he was standing, everything in the house looked new. But that wasn't what had him star struck. What had him mesmerized was the fish tank. Never in his life had he seen a fish tank cover two walls before.

"This girl got sharks In her fish tank," He dropped his bags and walked through the living room to have a better look.

"Well, I'll be damn." Pranky wiped the glass with one miraculous swipe, "This girl got all kind of shit in dis bitch: octopus, eel, shark," he looked around the house, "I see she budda-budda, kinto-kunta right now," referring to the Afrocentric decorating.

Franky couldn't believe his niece's house. Four bedrooms, two baths, garage, pool. She was doing her thang. This must be the wrong house? Franky thought as he pulled out his pocket the address he'd written down earlier. It was the right house. Franky knew she was doing okay, but not like this. Curious as to which room would be his, he decided to take a tour of the house.

Each room was beautifully furnished. They all had their own Individual characteristics. His first choice was the snow white room, but then he got to thinking. Too girly. He settled for the one with the hammock and futon. Franky was very proud of his niece. Her first time away from the family, and she was holding her own. At that moment, Franky decided to make his lil' niece lunch. That was the least he could do for her after she told him he could stay as long as he needed. Rent free.

"I knew this was too good to be true," Franky mumbled as he rummaged through all the cabinets and the fridge in search of something to cook. All he could come up with was a six pack of yogurt, half a chicken sandwich, a pint of spumoni, and a few bottles of water. Man...she tripping, he thought as he leaned back on the island.

She has a woman's dream kitchen with no food, he thought, his arms above his head. "This heifer doesn't even have any peanut butter and jelly. What black person on this planet doesn't have peanut butter and jelly."

At first, he thought he was hearing things. Maybe one of the neighbor's children was outside playing. He focused his attention on the far end of the kitchen. The sounds he was hearing were coming from the other side of a door that led to the garage. The closer he came to the door, the louder the whispers became. The door was too thick for him to make out just how many were in the house, but he could tell it was more than one. Just to play it safe, he thought it would be a good idea to pull out his pistol before he opened the door. Franky wasn't about to take any chances. With one hand on the door knob, the other wrapped firmly around his chrome .22. Franky counted to three and then drove his broad shoulder into the solid oak just as he turned the door handle.

"No one moves!" Franky yelled, brandishing his pistol.

"He gotta gun," Candy screamed, then dove to the floor.

Todd decided he'd rather take his chances going out with a fight. He rushed Franky, taking him to the ground. As the two wrestled wildly, Candy recognized her uncle.

She began pulling on Todd. "Get off him!"

"What the hell are you doing? He trying to rob us," Todd yelled.

"Get up, crazy." She pulled as hard as she could to snatch Todd off her uncle, breaking a nail in the process.

"Boy, what the hell is wrong wit you?" Franky struggled to get up, "You must be one of dem butterheads rushing me, and I got a gun." He raised up the small handgun and flinched at Todd with the.22, "I aught'ta, slap yo ass..."

"Franky, chill out!" Candy ordered. "It's not what you think."

"Yeah, Franky, chill out," Todd repeated.

"Boy," he took a step towards Todd before Candy stopped him: "That mouth of yours gonna get yo ass in a lot of trouble."

"Dawg, you need to stop pointing that gun at me!"

"Yeah, Franky, put that thang up!" Candy ordered.

"OK. But first, tell me what you two were out here doing, and secondly, where do you know him from? He yo boyfriend or something?"

Franky wasn't green by a long shot. He was good at reading people's body language, and Candy's body told him something was going on.

"So nothing is going on?" He asked suspiciously.

At first, Candy was going to lie, but lying wasn't one of her strong points; in fact, it was one of the things she despised the most.

"Okay, okay. If I tell you, will you put that gun up?"

"I don't believe this, yo ass can't hold water," Todd grunted in disapproval.

"He might help us if you give him a chance."

"One of y'all need to spit it out." Franky shifted his eyes back and forth between the two. "What's up!!"

Candy walked her uncle to the other side of the car.

He couldn't believe what he saw. "Is that what I think it is?"

"It's exactly what you think it is," she assured him.

"Let me guess, you.." he pointed to Todd, "robbed the dude who was putting you down, and she helped you. Now, you're backing out of whatever you promised her." He walked closer to get a better look. "So this how you paid for dis house?"

"Boy, please! He did not rob anybody for no dope? She looked at Todd, "You didn't, did you."

"Hell nah! Crazy girl," Todd snarled. "You know damn well what happened. Besides, I wanna know how yo uncle here can help us."

"So, can you help him, Uncle Franky?"

"That depends," his eyes shifted back and forth from Todd to the pile of kilos.

"What'cha mean? Depends on what?" Todd asked.

"You still in the streets? Candy asked.

"Yeah, I'm still plugged in," he lied. He was never plugged in, - but dat's not important right now. "You two say he didn't rob anybody for the dope, and from the way, you two are acting, ain't no one give it to you...so where it come from?"

"Long story".

"Dat's okay, I got time. As a matter of fact, Candy, why don't you go get us something to eat."

"I'd rather she stay." Todd shot Franky a unit. "I trust her more than you."

"I respect dat, but at the same time, she ain't got no business getting any deeper."

Franky loved his niece to death, but he knew she spoke very freely, and what he was looking at was the opportunity of a lifetime. The last thing he needed was for his niece to blurt out he used to be a smoker. Lucky for him, she felt the same way. She decided to go grocery shopping. That way, she could give the two of them time to talk.

For the next hour, Todd filled Franky in on what happened a few days ago and how he came up on the sixty kilos of cocaine. Still weary of Franky, he felt it would be better if he held back a few details until he got to know Franky a little better.

CHAPTER 8

"Let's look alive, people," Jamie walked into the small conference room. "We have a cop killer to catch. So what'cha got?" She fixed her eyes on the young man with curly hair.

"For starters, we recovered his pistol. Apparently, some eight year old found it this mourning at some park."

"What else?" Jamie asked,

"We can't find his backup, not yet anyway, but we do have a few leads."

"Shoot!!"

"We were able to come up with three types of hair, two blood samples and a card with the name "DIENTE" on the back. Also, inside his black book, we found a number to a payphone. He could see Jamie wasn't getting it. "The number is to a payphone across the street from the car garage listed on the card found in his coat. We also have tire tracks from either a '98 Camry or a '92 Acura Legend. Both cars come with that standard tire."

"The lab results came back for the hair?" Jamie questioned.

"Yeah." Curry flipped through a few papers. "One was his, and the others belonged to someone of a Spanish or white trace. Jamie, whoever killed Lewis, knew exactly what they were doing. They went out of their way to cover their tracks. The tire track is a long shot, considering we could not find a single footprint within twenty yards of the body."

"Where was he coming from before he got killed?" Jamie asked.

"He was supervising a controlled buy." He flipped to a filed report, "This says he had a buyer for sixty kilos of cocaine. The buy went bad, shots were fired, and the suspect got away." He closed the folder and threw it onto the table.

Jamie picked up the folder and thumbed through it. "That's interesting. He leaves a drug bust gone bad, a deal for sixty kilos of cocaine and two hours later, someone kills him. We have no witnesses, no motive. But, we do have hair and blood samples, a card with the name Diente on the back and a number to a payphone across the street from a car garage." She looked at her team of five. "I say we have a shot at solving this case. "You with me or what?"

They all shook their heads in agreeance.

"Then let's do this." She looked over to Pete. "Hey, let's say we take a trip to that car garage and see what we can come up with."

"Whatever you say, boss!" Pete said sarcastically.

"Maybe you should meet me at the car." She tossed him the car keys.

"I'll be there in about ten."

"Whatever you say, boss!"

As Pete walked out of the office, Jamie couldn't believe the way he was acting. She'd noticed a change in his behavior two weeks ago. At first, she thought it might be because she found a new sex partner, but that couldn't be it; he was married, for god sake. Maybe he was going through a mid-life crisis? Maybe he wasn't. Pete wasn't only the first man Jamie had sex with within two years, he was the first of his age and the first co-worker. Ever. A mistake she regretted, but one she knew she had to put right as soon as possible.

When Jamie came up to the car, Pete was smoking a cigarette. Jamie hated all tobacco products, especially cigarettes. She went out of her way to stay clear of anybody who smoked. Even after they'd smoked, the stench trapped in their clothes made her stomach queasy.

"I thought you quit?" she asked as she opened the car door, reluctant to get in.

"So did I." He took another pull, then flicked it out the window.

After a few minutes passed, Jamie stuck her head in the car to see if it was aired out. Not as much as she'd like, but due to circumstances, it would have to do.

"Next time you feel the urge to dirty your lungs, don't do it in my car."

"Yes, boss lady!"

At first, she was about to say something, but she ended up biting her tongue instead of lashing out. She turned over the engine and whisked off. The whole time they were in the car, neither one said a word to the other. If Jamie knew what it was that brought about all the tension, she wouldn't have minded the way Pete was acting or the fact he wasn't speaking to her. Then again, it did bother her. It bothered her a lot.

"Are you mad at me because I stop having sex with you?"

"No! No!" He was lying, and he knew she knew it.

"Pete, I think you're a nice guy and all, but like I told you before we got involved, we were only good for one year. After that, we would have to move on."

"Sorry to burst your bubble, Ms Prima Donna, but the sex wasn't all that."

Jamie felt bad that his feelings were hurt, and she could tell he was getting way too attached, but for some reason, she felt that that wasn't what was bothering him. But what was it?

"Jamie, do you love me?"

"Do I love you?" The words echoed in her head. "Do, do I love you?" She couldn't believe he just asked her that. How could he be in love with me after only seven months? But he's married. "In what way?" she asked with an unsettled tone.

"Is it my age?" Pete asked regretfully.

"No, it's not your age, Pete," Jamie voiced without confidence.

"Then what is it, Jamie?"

"What is what?"

"Is it my wife...because if it is, she's..."

The look on Jamie's face told it all. She wasn't in love with him in any way, shape or form. They were so sure. She had to be the one. She had to.

"I'm sorry, Jamie, I just thought...."

"Pete, I will always be here for you, but just as a friend." She was about to pat 'em on the knee but didn't. She didn't want to send mixed signals. "You okay with that?"

"Yeah, I'm okay with that. Jamie?"

"Yeah?" Jamie appeared more shocked than relieved.

"I think you passed the car garage." They both looked back.

"I believe I did." She stopped the car and backed up. When they pulled into the garage, the first thing Jamie noticed was the payphone across the street and a big insurance company sign.

"Hey, Pete, what was the name on the card?"

"It didn't have one. Just an address. Why?"

"So, how did you know it was a car garage?

"We called in on it. Turns out the building used to be owned by Triple C Insurance a long time ago, but now it's what you see before you. How about we get out, ask a few questions, and then get the hell out from over here? There's nothing but niggers and spics over here." "As long as you're in my presence or under my command, you will never, ever refer to them as that. Do I make myself clear?"

"Yeah, sure, whatever!"

"Pete, I'm very serious about this." Her voice became very stern.

"Okay, geesh!" He hopped out of the car and headed toward the office.

She hadn't noticed earlier, but the second Jamie exited the car, she felt the weight of a dozen eyes pulling down on her. Unfortunately, they were well hidden, but she still could feel their presence. Why would Lewis come to this Rankydanky garage? Jamie thought as she caught up with Pete right before they walked into the bay of the pit. Once they were in, Jamie was shocked by all the expensive cars being worked on.

"What's wrong with your car?"

Jamie and Pete turned around to find a young boy covered in oil.

"Do you work here, kid?" Pete asked.

"No, I'm just covered in oil to help keep my skin looking nice."

Jamie let out a little laugh. "Very funny!"

Pete pulled out a photo of Detective Lewis. "You ever seen this man come here to get his car fixed?"

"You ah cop?"

"Yes, we are cops." Jamie offered her hand. "I am Detective Lightbourne, and this is Detective Wise.

Before the young boy could respond, an older man walked up and spoke a few words in Spanish, and just like that, the young boy ran upstairs to the office.

"How can I help?" His voice was flat and hostile.

"You the owner?" Pete asked.

"Something like dat. Who wanna know?

"Hi!! I am Detective Lightbourne, and this is Wise." She offered her hand once again, and once again, it was denied.

"Obviously, you're not here to get your car fixed, and as you can see, I'm very busy. So, if you don't mind, would you get to the point of why you're here."

"Pete?" Pete handed him the photo.

"We're looking for our friend. We believe he was here right before he…"

"Disappeared," Pete cut into her sentence.

"Sorry." He handed Pete back the photo. "I can't say for certain if he was here yesterday or not. A lot of people come through here in a day. Besides, your friend looks white. He would be easy to notice around here," he waved around his arm. "You know, the only people around here are blacks and Spanish. If a white person came around here," he paused and gave them an evil eye," they dee police. Dah police ain't welcome round here. We don't trust'em. We don't need'em."

"Thank you for your time, Mr.…"

"Bobby, Bobby Johnson," he replied with half a smile as he offered his hand.

"Well, thank you again, Mr. Johnson." Jamie shook his hand. "If you hear anything or remember…"

"I don't think I will, but if I do, you'll be the first one I call."

His lustful eyes played over Jamie's curves.

When Jamie and Pete left, the older man was waved up to the office. When he walked in, he could see the look of concern on his partner's face.

"Cops?"

"Yeah, they're looking for Lewis."

"For Lewis, huh? What did they ask the kid?"

"Nothing really, but they did show him a picture."

"Of Lewis?"

"Yeah."

"Think they'll be coming back?"

"I would think so. The dude she was wit seems like an asshole, but she…"

"She thinks she's got all the sense, that's what she is," the heavyset man explained.

"Hey, Rosco, what's up with the lil' black kid? He still hiding out with the dope?"

"I don't know if he hiding or locked up!!"

"Locked up? Where you get that from?"

"The kid say he heard that Hope was in jail. He got busted trying to serve a dude named Pollcat."

"So what happen to the yao?"

"That's what I'm trying to find out." Rosco picked up the phone and dialed out. "Maybe his homeboy can tell us where my shit at, ya feel me."

"But if they tight like dat, he ain't gone tell you anythang."

After a few rings, someone picked up on the other line. Rosco threw up a finger, commanding silence.

"I figured you be calling me real soon, Fatboy!! So what can I do for you?"

"Where's Hope?"

"He ain't here… but I guess you already knew dat, Fatboy! So what'cha want!"

"He never brought in his car to be fixed on Monday."

"Oh, yeah, about that car, he got into an accident." Todd let out a slight laugh. "Totaled that bad boy. We had to sell it to the pound, I mean junkyard, ya feel me. But we were able to save a few items. A couple of car seats, steering wheel…"

"Don't play wit me, you lil' street punk. You think dis a game?" Rosco griped the telephone so heard his knuckles turned white." I tell you what, wherever you at, you better stay there cuz when…"

"Cuz what!" Todd's voice blasted so loud through the phone Rosoc's friend could hear him. "You ain't gone do a muthafuckin thang Fatboy, cuz fo'real fo'real, I don't see ya!" His voice suddenly calmed down. "But check dis out, Fatboy, if you tryin' to get'em fo daa low, you need to get at me before it's too late." Todd hung up the phone before Rosco could get out a word.

Rosco couldn't believe the nerve of Todd. Who the hell did he think he was talking to? He carrying it like he was…like he was some sort of gangsta. Rosco couldn't wait to get his hands on Todd, especially after the way he talked to him on the phone, but Rosco wasn't a dummy, he knew Todd wasn't a pushover and that if he killed him, he wouldn't be able to get the rest of his dope. He leaned back in his chair, thinking of a way to kill two birds with one stone. He came up with a master plan. Rosco wondered why he hadn't thought of it earlier as he ransacked his desk.

"What'cha' looking for?" he asked as Rosco frantically went from drawer to drawer.

"Frank's number." He looked up. "You seen it?"

"Frank, who? The lawyer dude?"

"Yeah, I had it here a few days ago," Rosco answered.

"Check the rolldesk!"

"Why didn't I think of that?" Rosco thumbed through the list of names. He found the number.

"What now?" he asked Rosco?"

"You'll see," Rosco picked up the phone and dialed out. "Frank Sticks, please."

When Frank got on the phone, Rosco got straight to business with no small talk. He gave Frank Hope's full name and instructed him to call him back with how much it would cost to get him out of jail.

"Nucca, you trippin." He gave Rosco a dawg-eye stare. "They just hit you for fifty kilos, and you talking bout paying for dis cat a lawyer."

"Trust me on dis one…When everything falls into place, oh' bad ass Todd is going to hand me every brick, and not a gram short."

Twenty minutes later, Frank called back. He had the information he needed to do what Rosco asked of him. Now Rosco was one step closer to getting back his dope.

CHAPTER 9

"So what do you think?"

"About what?" Pete asked plainly.

"About the man we just spoke to... think he has something to do with Lewis's death?"

"Depends!!"

She looked over to Pete, but his focus was more on the road than on her, "depends, depends on what?"

"Depend on how you look at it? Personally, I feel all them thugs are guilty of some type of crime," he paused for a second, "professionally, he didn't say anything incriminating, at least not to me."

"I wonder what he said to that kid in Spanish?

"Probably kill whitey."

She gave him a soft tap to the shoulder, "Not all Spanish people hate whites."

"Believe me, when it breaks out, and you're not on the right side of the fence, you'll see just how much Spanish and blacks don't hate you."

"What kind of KKK crap is that!!!... us against them, them against us."

"I just see the world for what it is, that's all," Pete stated matter-factly.

"And I don't?" Jamie asked angrily.

"I just think you've been sheltered from harm's way."

"Whatever!"

"Maybe we should Juat drop this and focus back on the case," Pete suggested.

"Good idea!"

Jamie thought that Pete was a good person at heart, but for some apparent reason, he hated all non-whites. That alone made her question his ability to serve and protect unconditionally. Maybe he grew up with racist parents, or maybe he had a bad experience with Blacks and Latinos as a child. But what bothered Jamie the most was that the two of them shared a very intimate relationship for quite some time, and when it all boiled down, she barely knew Pete at all. Lately, Pete had been acting strange, and Jamie was starting to feel as if her breaking things off wasn't the reason why Pete was acting out. She made a mental note to do some research into the matter once they solved the case, but for now, it was back to the station.

* * * * *

THREE MONTHS LATER - things were starting to look real good for Todd, money was starting to roll in, his skills on the stove were coming up to par, and he and Candy were officially a couple. The only thing that bothered Todd was Hope. Hope was still in jail without a bond. Hope's lawyer tried explaining to Todd how the system worked and why his friend was still in jail, but Todd wasn't trying to hear it. He knew the system oh too well, and he knew how lawyers worked: out for the beat. Now that he was able to afford a top notch lawyer, Todd was seriously thinking about hiring one. And why not? The one they had had more excuses every time Todd spoke with him, and for the ten grand he was paid, Hope should've been out. "Fuck that," Todd thought. Just as he reached out for the phone, it rang. It was Hope's lawyer.

"Hello?"

"What happen? I thought you were supposed to call me back last week?"

"What they talking bout with my dawg?" Todd asked

"didn't I tell you I gotcha," his tone was felt with a strong presence

"So what'cha saying, he straight!!"

"I'm saying that Howard should be home within the next hour or two…"

"So you gott'em to drop the charges?" Todd's voice showed some relief.

"Not yet," he began to laugh, "But that's my next move. For now, he'll be coming home on bond…"

"I thought you said they wouldn't give'em no bond?"

"At first, no!! But I ended up pulling a few strings, calling in a few favors." He paused for a few seconds, "a lot of favors. The important thing is that he has a bond."

"How much is the bond?" Todd asked.

"Twenty thousand, but I already took care of it, I'll add it to the bill, and you can pay me when he gets out."

"You paid the whole twenty?"

"No, no, I only had to pay ten percent, but listen, I have another client waiting in my office. Tell Howard to call me in a few days so we can go over a strategy."

"You got dat!!" Todd said, then pushed the off button on the cell phone.

When Franky replaced the phone back on the receiver, he leaned back in his chair and eyed the scruffy looking old man. Two things Franky couldn't understand; one was why was this old man so interested in Howard Sneed? And two, why did he pay him ten grand to put Sneed's case on the back burner and then turn around and give him another ten grand to get him a bond?

"So, how long before he goes to trial?" Rosco asked.

"In about a year, a year and a half," Franky words came slow as he eyed Rosco carefully.

"Good," he licked his thumb, then swiped his brows, "So can you beat it?"

"He might plea out!!"

"He 'll go to trial, trust me, Hope just like dem other nucca's." Rosco paused for a second, "think he's tough."

"Well, Mr. Rosco, I did what you asked…so if our dealings are squared away, you can give me my five grand, and we can call this a day."

"Bout them five," Rosco flashed a cricket smile, "I'll shoot dat to ya when you get'em to the office."

"You're not going to kill'em, right?" fear was present in his voice.

"No, no, no," Rosco assured him. "He owes me too much money, besides, all I want to do is scare'em up a little, you know, rattle his cage."

"Rattle his chain?" Franky asked, "Nothing else, right?"

"Franky, you've known me for what… four years?" Rosco walked over to him and gave him a playful tap on the jaw, "now, have I ever lied to you?"

"Hell yeah," Franky thought. But never did he lie about killing anyone. Franky couldn't believe Rosco was capable of killing anything other than a fly. Like Rosco said, they've known each other for four years.

"Okay," Franky said submissively.

"Okay," Rosco repeated, "so we cool, and you'll have him here tomorrow?

"I guess so."

"That's not good enough, Franky," Rosco gave'em a kill stare, "you need to have'em here. Tomorrow. Three o'clock sharp. No if's, and's or but's about it. Three o'clock, Franky. Three. O'clock."

* * * * *

On the way to the house, Todd explained how Rosco tried to cross them with the dummy car scheme, but he wanted to wait to tell him about the dope. He wanted Hope to see with his own eyes just how much things had changed.

"So, who is Candy?" Hope asked lustfully, "She bout it?"

"Nah, she ain't bout it," Todd started laughing, "we hooked up right when you went to jail, she looked out when I went through it wit dem folks I was telling you bout."

"Where she from, the 'o'?"

"Nah, she from Georgia."

"Georgia, what part?

"ATL, I think." Todd reached into the ashtray and pulled out a freshly rolled blunt.

"Stop playing." Hope grabbed the blunt and fired it up in one swoop.

"You know damn well you don't smoke. So lil' momma a peach, huh?"

"Something like dat" Todd was lying, Candy was one of the rawest broads in Central Florida. Hope would soon see that for himself. Not to mention all the dope Todd came upon.

"Where you get dat from?" Todd asked curiously.

"Get what from?" Hope questioned.

"What is that? Some sort of smoke ritual?"

"Dawg, a lot of people smoke weed, but they don't know how to smoke weed, right?" He pulled on the blunt in a professional manner, blowing the smoke out of his nose and giving the fire breathing effect. "I know how to smoke, and whoever rolled dis knows how to smoke." He lifted the blunt to eye level, admiring the craftsmanship.

"My baby rolled dat!!" Todd said proudly.

"The lil' peach know how to roll?"

"Lil'momma like dat." Todd expressed proudly, "One thang fa'sho, she keeps it in the raw." right in the middle of their conversation, Todd's phone rang

"Hello, yeah, bey, what's up? I'm pulling up now." He looked over to Hope, "Yeah, he wit me. Go ahead and open up the garage." Seconds later, they were pulling into the two door garage.

"I hope she can cook," Hope blurted out as he hopped out of the Lex.

"Can she!!" Todd stressed, right on his heels.

When Hope seen the house, his first thought was, "damn," dis crib is tight, but when he walked through the door, the expression on his face showed it all.

"Dawg, you got dis bitch laid out, clean" Hope dashed out the kitchen, through the living room, and headed to the overly sized fish tank. He was so caught up on the fish he didn't notice Todd had slipped into the back room. When they returned, Hope was still stuck on the tank.

I see you've met the babies, Candy's words came out soft and warm.

"Babies, dees ain't no..." When Hope turned around, he couldn't believe how fine Candy was. "So you the Georgia peach my dawg crazy about."

"They still calling us that?" Candy responded as she watched Hope eye her up and down with a lustful look.

Trying not to stare, Hope averted his attention back to the tank. "So these your babies, huh?"

"They sure are," she began, pointing out each fish. "That's Trigger, Blue, Moo, oh that's Queeny, and that's Majior, Flame, Goat, Butterfly, Wrasse and Hog. And that little cutey over there is Babyboy. That's Nemo!!"

"Flame, Goat, Butter...Fly, Trigger?" Hope shot Candy off the wall and looked, "Who in the hell names a fish 'Trigger'?"

"The name of the fish is Clown Trigger fish, Crazy man," Candy rolled her eyes playfully.

"Peaches?"

"Who's that?" Candy asked curiously, thinking it might be one of Todd's old flames.

"Dat's you, Georgia peach...man, I know yo fine ass gotta sister, cousin, friend brother girlfriend sister, man put a nucca down."

Candy burst out laughing. She'd heard all about Hope and how he looked after Todd when they were young, but now she had someone to talk to about Todd. Someone who really know him. To her, Hope was very outspoken and straightforward. She felt she could use that to understand Todd just that much better.

"Todd said you were off the chain," she gave Todd a quick wink.

"I'll see what I can come up with, but in the meantime, have you guys eaten yet?"

"See, that's what I'm saying," Hope blurted. "Fine, and can cook. Boy, you done came up!!"

"Trust me!! He knows." Candy walked over and gave Todd a kiss. "Now get out of my kitchen, 'cause I don't need you two hovering around my food while I am trying to cook."

Todd gave Candy one more kiss and then took Hope to the back room. When Todd told Hope he wanted to show him something hundred, thoughts ran across his mind. What was so secretive he couldn't tell'em until now? And if it was that big of a deal, why tell'em over some broad house?

"Why is you smiling like dat?"

"Like what?" Todd asked

"Like that," Hope responded.

"You'll see," Todd reached for the doorknob but didn't turn it. "Check this out first. You my nucca right, and we go back, way back-" Todd's expression let Hope know he was serious. "Dawg, no matter what happens, I gotcha back."

Before Hope could respond, Todd opened the door and walked in. At first, Hope was thrown off. Todd gave him this old heart to heart about them having each other's back right before they walked into the room, talking about showing him something, but now that he was in the room, all he saw was a bed halfway put together, two dressers, a few boxes, and a closet full of clothes and shoes.

"So what'cha think?" Todd asked.

"Good looking, but you know I got a gang of clothes at the crib," Hope expressed with a slight frown.

"Clothes? man bump deem clothes." Hope was so excited about the dope that he didn't realize the boxes were closed. "Dat's why you talkin' bout some damn clothes, the damn boxes closed!!" Todd walked over to one of the boxes and ripped it open. "This what I'm talkin' bout."

Hope came within a few steps to get a better look. "What dat suppose to be?"

Todd pulled out one of the packs and opened it up with a box cutter he had tucked in his pocket. The smell raced up Hope's nose instantly.

"Dis yo mill ticket."

Hope's face balled up in defense, "Damn dawg, dat shit loud as hell!!"

"Who you telling? That's why mine wrapped tight and put up."

"Oh, so dat's me? Dawg, is that a whole one."

"Better be," Todd responded. He opened another box, "but dawg, I said a mill ticket. You can't make a mill with one of these...but you can wit twenty."

Hope just stood there, this was the most dope he'd ever seen in his life. Who in the hell did Todd rob for twenty bricks? And how did he pull it off by himself? As Todd continued to express his joy, Hope unconsciously blocked him out. Whoever Todd robbed wasn't going out like that, and even if he knocked the dude off, his people can't take a loss like that. Twenty bricks is enough to have whole families dome-checked, and Hope knew that. So, while Todd was counting his millions, Hope was devising a war strategy.

"Dawg, who you touched for twenty bricks?" Hope asked over concerningly.

"Touched! Nucca, I ain't robbed nobody for no dope!!"

"So, what if just fell out the sky?"

"Man, you know damn well if I hit somebody for twenty bricks, I would have told you off rip!! Besides, we sitting on sixty of dem thangs?" Todd pointed to the three boxes on the floor. "them twenty your, mines put up, you feel me."

Todd ran everything down to Hope. How Rosco planted sixty bricks into one of the cars, how he found a connection through Candy's uncle, who also taught him how to cook up the dope and helped open up three traps. One in North Florida, one in Georgia, and one in Tennessee. He told'em about the threats Rosco made, why he gave his cars away and let his apartment go while he was locked up. Hope listened with a keen ear as Todd explained who they would hustle, what time of the day they would hustle, and how they would distribute the dope to each trap. The way Todd spoke, one would think he had planned for this moment his whole life. Everything was mapped out to the "T." From through aways to jump outs and honeycombs. He was on point. It was because of Candy that Todd decided to run things as if he were a C.E.O. of a major corporation. Although he didn't let Hope know where most of the ideas came from, he did let'em know she was on the team. After Todd was finished, Hope seen what Todd seen. A fast and easy way to make a couple of millions.

"Bey," Candy's voice came through the wall intercom, "just wanted to let you know that dinner will be ready in half an hour."

Todd walked over and pushed the button on the intercom, "Okay, bey."

"What time is it?" Hope asked curiously.

"Probably five thirty, why?"

"She on county time, let me find out peaches done been the country."

After Candy delivered one of her many three course meals, they all sat around the pool for a nightcap. The more of the house Hope seen, the more he was impressed. The backyard in itself was a scene straight out of a movie. Very exotic. Very original. Designed by an old Chinese gardener recommended by one of Candy's professors, the yard was laced with mini waterfalls, fishponds and a family sized hot tub.

"So you and Todd go back to when ya'll were kids?" Candy asked,

"Fo show," Hope leaned over and gave Todd some dap, "We like family."

"So what as he like, I mean, when ya'll were little?"

"Green as hell."

"Green!!" Todd repeated.

"Keep it real, dawg, you was square as hell," Hope looked over to Candy, "Umm, just playing, dis nucca here was one of the realest cats I know. He showed me the game when I was only twelve. Back then, we were only into bamming cars."

"What else was he like?" she asked eagerly, "What was some of his girlfriends like?"

"Wasn't none of 'em finer than you, but fo'real, we didn't do the boyfriend-girl-friend thang." He reached over and gave Todd some dap, "Deem hoes was sweating ninety going north. And me and I-Man stayed shitty clean."

"T-Man, how long you been calling him that?"

"Oh, you don't know bout the I-Man," Hope tapped Todd on the shoulder. "She don't know bout the T-Man?"

As Candy listened to Todd and Hope reminisce over childhood memories and old war stories, it was evident that Hope being home was a good thing. Todd's whole demeanor seemed to change the moment Hope came home. He didn't seem stressed, and he was smiling more. Candy was really enjoying her night, noticing the wine was getting low, so she went to grab another bottle from out of the house. When she returned, Hope and Todd were deep into the streets rather than bother them. She turned around and left for the store to pick up another bottle.

CHAPTER 10

When Jamie pulled up to Pete's house, she politely blew her horn three times. One right after the other, a pause, than one more. Although his wife was unaware that they had had an affair, she felt it was for the best that the two of them did not become the best of friends. For all she knew, the two of them were only together to fight crime, and Jamie wanted it to stay that way.

"I could stay home today if you like," Pete placed his wife's fragile hand into his.

"Why does she never come in the house?" her voice was barely audible.

"I told you why," he wiped her forehead with his handkerchief, "she feels awkward being around you, she just, just...."

"Just being a woman, right?" she tried squeezing his hand.

"I could stay," he reminded her. "Jamie and I don't really have any leads. Besides, the case is three months old," he looked at his wife with pleading eyes.

"I..."

Jamie blew the horn three more times, then yelled out for Pete to hurry up. "She's bossy. I like that. You're going to need a woman to keep you grounded."

Eva was the best thing that ever happened to Pete. She was caring. Honest, and most of all, very open. By far, she was the most beautiful woman he'd ever been with or seen, for that matter. They started their courtship when he was only thirteen. She was fifteen. That was thirty years ago. Eva was everything to Pete. His first love, best friend, mother of his child. She taught him the true meaning of life. Pete hated seeing his wife like that, they'd been through so much together; just two years ago, she lost their second child, and for the past seven years, they have been struggling to keep their house. Pete was determined to keep his wife alive for as long as he could. When they found out she had cancer, the doctor told her that it was too late to start treatment, that the cancer had spread too far, too fast. He told her that she had no more than four years to live. That was seven years ago. That was all the hope Pete needed when he decided to take out a second mortgage on the house to pay for a special treatment he heard about from a friend through a friend. Eva never knew where the money was coming from, and he wanted it to stay that way. But now, things seemed worse than ever. It was evident that Eva was going to die. Soon. And to make matters worse, Pete was flat broke. Their life savings were exhausted, and the bank was in the process of foreclosing on their house, but what hurt the most was the fact that he didn't have any money to give his wife a proper burial when it was her time to go. After a few more minutes, Eva convinced Pete that she would be fine until he returned and that if she needed anything, she would call his cell phone. Against his better judgment, Pete kissed his wife goodbye, hurried downstairs and jumped in the car with Jamie.

"Jay just called!" Jamie said excitedly.

This was their first break in the case. The deputy coroner called and told Jay that a small dot was found on Detective Lewis's upper neck. He explained that the chemical found was called prime a coat. A chemical used when painting cars. Finally, Jamie thought. Finally, she had something solid to go off on, she was starting to think that she wasn't going to catch whoever killed Lewis. She'd seen it too many times. Cop gets killed, Clues fade away, and the file is tossed to the side with the other cold cases.

"You okay, Pete?" Jamie asked she noticed he wasn't answering any of her questions.

"You could have at least come in, you know."

"Excuse me?"

"She knows!" Pete looked at Jamie with watery eyes.

"Knows what?" Jamie asked what she already knew.

"That we're having an affair. I told her I had too...."

"Well, did you tell her it was over!! Did you tell her I called it off?"

This was the first time Jamie felt ashamed about the meaningless affairs she would have from time to time. This was the first time one of her fling's wives found out about her. At least, to her knowledge, they never knew. At that moment, she decided she was going to change her life. No more fling. No more one night stands, married men or women. Especially women, they were too emotional for her. For now own, she was strickly dickly, and whomever she chose to lay down with would have to be her man. Pete's wife made her feel like a whore, and she hated that feeling.

"So what did she say?" Jamie asked slowly.

He looked over to Jamie, "Not much, just that she forgives me, and she loves me very much."

Jamie wasn't sure how to respond to that. She'd never been in a situation like this. It was bad enough that Pete was a constant reminder of what she'd done, but now it seemed as if he wanted her to be his confidant. Jamie felt it would be best to change the subject to the case at hand. This was the first real break, and Jamie knew she had to move fast before the lead got cold. As Jamie hopped on the highway, she ran a few ideas to Pete about how they should attack their first breakthrough.

"Did Lewis have a personal car?"

"Not sure," Pete responded. "I've always seen him driving the unmarked."

"That's odd, Jay said the corner said the chemical on his neck was from a paint shop or a place where they paint cars."

"Did they paint cars at the garage we went to a few months ago?" Pete replied.

"Not sure?"

Jamie grabbed her phone and hit speed dial, seconds later, Jay was on the other line. Jamie instructed him to call the garage and see how much it would cost for him to get his car painted. Three minutes later, her phone rang. It was Jay.

"Jay? Yeah, what he say? You sure?" Jamie looked over to Pete and waved her hand under her chin. "Okay, yeah, yeah, that's fine with me," she checked her watch. "Give me about an hour, I wanna check on something," Jamie hung up and then jumped off the next exit.

* * * * *

For the first time, Florida felt like home for Candy. Although it could never replace ATL, it had what ATL didn't, Todd. Candy was in love with Todd. She knew it the first time she slept with him. She knew not to tell'em just yet, being that they've only been together a few months, she understood guys got scared when women told them their true feelings. Most street dudes want that ride or die bitch, and she was cool with that. She figured she'd play her position. Keep it real, show support, and let him be the man. In due time, he will tell her he loves her. After that, it's a wrap. But for now, she thought she needed to put Hope down with one of her classmates. That way, they can all hang out, and Todd won't be out tricking with Hope, slick ass.

Just as Candy was pulling off from the ATM machine, she thought she seen a car that was behind her a few blocks earlier, Todd made it his business to teach her how to look out for people following her just in case somebody he was serving or beefing with tried to get to him threw her. At first, she started to call him and tell'em she was being followed, but when the car turned in the opposite direction, she figured she was safe and that she might have had too many drinks or maybe that blunt she smoked earlier had her trippin'. Being on the safe side, she rushed into the store, grabbed the wine, and rushed right back out. She was moving so fast she didn't see the old man until she nearly knocked him down coming out the store.

"Are you okay?" Candy yelled as she latched on to his arm, keeping'em on his feet, dropping her wine in the process.

"I am so sorry!" Candy stressed.

"Quite, alright," he fixed his shirt.

"Is there anything I can do?"

"Maybe," he reached in his pocket, "I was on my way in to get change for this here ten, you wouldn't happen to have a change, would you?"

"Let me see?"

When Candy reached down into her purse, she felt a blunt object hit her across the head, knocking her unconscious.

"What about the truck?"

"Leave it, all we need is her," he picked her up and tossed her over his shoulder.

"Where's her phone? Boss said to make sure we get her phone."

As the young boy fetched the car, the older man searched for the phone. By the time the young boy pulled up with the truck, he found the phone in her purse.

The young boy popped the trunk and stood watch as Candy was dumped in the back of the trunk.

"So when can we have her?" the young boy asked with lustful eyes.

"As soon as Rosco gets what he wants," he responded, "and not before then," giving the boy a threatening stare, "comprende!!"

"Si!" the young boy agreed disappointedly as he made a quick left headed for Rosco's.

CHAPTER 11

Frank couldn't wait to get back to Florida, he'd been in Tennessee for almost two weeks now. He hated that he had to sit up there for those extra few days. Being that he was holding over a hundred grand, he felt a little uncomfortable being so far from the crib. He would have been home, but DeeDee's lil brother decided to change his game room, and because of that, money came closer than usual. Frank was cool with that. Matter of fact, he was impressed by how the young buck was running his house. He was very precautious and well planned. Franky was just ready to go home. He and Dee-Dee had been on the road for almost a month, and he was just eager to lay it down.

"Here," Dee Dee walked into her old bedroom and tossed a bookbag on the bed next to Franky. Junior said it's all there, and if you wanted to, to count it." Franky opened the bag and poured the money out.

"Help me count this!" he ordered as Dee Dee flopped down next to him.

"How much is this?" she asked while taking a rubberband from around one of the stacks.

"Should be seventy-five," he responded.

"My baby be, getting, that, bread," Dee Dee mumbled in a nursery rhyme like manner.

"Man, count dah money, crazy," Frank said Jokingly.

Two days after Franky met Dee Dee on the bus, he knocked her off. After that, he ripped her a few more times before finding out she had a little brother who was hustling in a little town in Tennessee, which was perfect considering his niece's boyfriend had just come up on sixty bricks. This was his chance to become a major baller, and he had every intention of making it happen. Moving to Florida was the best thing that could have happened to him. The money was counted out, and just as he expected it was, a few grand short. Franky wasn't trippen, Junior was good people, and he knew it would be thrown in the kitty next month. For now, he was just ready to hit the road.

"Let's ride!" Franky shouted as he passed by the bathroom.

"I'm coming!" Dee Dee responded, checking her nose before she came out. After she said goodbye to her mom, they jumped in the car. Florida, here we come.

* * * * * *

When Todd woke up, the taste of cognac was still on his tongue. He was in the same clothes from the day before, and instead of being by the pool, he was in the living room. Hennessey is a unique liquor; when drunk without a chaser, you were guaranteed not to have a hangover the next day; the only thing is that that next day, you would still feel the Hennesey. Todd was reminded of that the moment he bounced to his feet too quickly.

"What dah hell wrong with you?" Hope eyes were barely open when Todd fell back on his heels onto the couch.

"I told cha bout that yak!" he stretched out his legs, "Dawg, I'm hungry, see if Peaches ah cook something."

Where is Candy? Todd thought, looking at his watch. It was almost eleven, and she didn't come and make them get out of her favorite part of the house. "Candy!!" Todd called out a few times, no answer.

"Maybe she is at the school house," Hope suggested.

"School?" Todd repeated with uncertainty as he rushed to remember her schedule, "Today's Tuesday! She doesn't have a mourning class on Tuesday."

Todd jumped up and dashed to the back room, Hope right on his heels. When they got back there, they searched for Candy. Nothing. The room looked to be untouched, and the bed appeared to have not been slept in. Hope seen a slight panic on Todd's face as he pulled out his phone and hit speed dial.

"Who you calling?"

"Candy! Who else!"

"Hello?"

"God, damn!"

"What's up?"

"What's up! You trippin' that's what's up, me and Hope round here thinking..."

"Gotcha! Candy started laughing, this is a recording! Leave a message."

Hope was confused when Todd hung up and stuffed the phone back in his pocket.

"What happen? The phone cut off."

"Naw! That was her answering machine," he slammed his fist into his hand. "She thinks that junk is cute or something."

"So where she at?"

"I don't know, her punk ass..."

"Try it again, Hope suggests."

Without thinking, Todd pulled out the phone and hit speed dial. Again, her answering machine picked up, and this time, Todd left a message. Where could she be? Why didn't she come home last night? Just where did she go last night, and why isn't she answering her damn phone. All these thoughts, plus more, ran through Todd's head.

"She might be at some nucca house!" Hope blurted out.

Todd shook his head in disagreement, "She more 'G' than dat, if she was out trickin', she would have answered her phone by now. Something has happened to that girl!!!"

"You think she got into an accident or something?'

"Damn!" Todd slammed his fist into his hand. "I don't believe dis..."

"That might be her?" Hope blurted out as Todd's phone rang.

"Hello! Hello!"

"Que holla mie hombrea," the heavy Latin voice echoed through the phone.

"Where she at, Fatboy?" Todd asked poignantly.

"Quien esta?" Rosco let out a slight giggle.

"Oh, you think dis a game, you think a nucca..."

Hope snatched the phone from Todd. "What you trying to do, Fatboy?" Hope asked calmly, "Even swap, no swindle?"

"Something like dat," Rosco responded.

"Okay, cool, so when and where?" Hope asked.

"That's what I like about you, Hope," Rosco let out a light chuckle, "You be bout your business."

"When and where, Rosco?

"I haven't told you what I want first."

"What you mean?"

Hope knew Rosco all too well. Anytime he had a chance to get over, he took it. Hope knew Rosco wasn't going to come off Candy just like that, and if he did, it was going to cost them more than sixty bricks.

"I want four hundred grand by tomorrow and another four hundred by Friday. Once I get my money, you can get ya lil nappy head."

"Eight hundred! You dun lost yo damn mind, you can keep dat hoe," Hope hung up the phone then handed it back to Todd.

"Is you crazy? They gonna....."

The phone rang again and again. Hope took the phone from Todd. "Hello? Dawg, quit calling us, I told you could have dat hoe for eight." Hope hung up again but kept the phone.

"Gimme dah phone!" Todd demanded.

"He not gonna kill her," he motioned for Todd to stand still, "Trust me."

Rosco bout his money, and he know if he hurt her, he can't get paid. I know his fat ass, if he thinks he can work you, he will. Now, dis is how we going to do dis when he calls back, I'll let'em know that he can get his sixty, plus ten and nothing else. After that, we'll set up a time and place to go get her. He extended out a closed fist, "Cool?"

"Cool!" Todd repeated as he slammed a closed fist on top of Hope's. Seconds later, the phone rang. It was Rosco.

"Talk!" Hope ordered.

"Maybe eight was too much, maybe I'll take four."

"Goodbye, Rosco!" Hope took the phone away from his ear, he could hear Rosco pleading for him not to hang up. "You were saying."

"Now that I think about it," he paused for a few seconds. "You right, she not worth that either," he paused again. "So what did you have in mind?"

Hope explained to Rosco how he explained it to Todd, sixty plus ten. Rosco agreed after a few more tries of negotiating. They were to meet at the garage later that night, around three o'clock.

* * * * * * *

Dee Dee was an animal. She was barely in her twenties and already a pro.fes.sion.al head hunter. And to make things worse, not bad meaning bad, but bad meaning good. She was willing to try anything. Frank decided to give the road a break, and the two of them decided to stay the night at one of the apartments in Tallahassee before going home.

As Frank lay flat on his back with his knees inches away from his chest and Dee Dee's tongue sliding in and out the crack of his ass as she stroked firmly up and down, he couldn't believe she was so vicious. Just when he was about to bust, she stopped.

"Turn over, baby," she asked softly before running her manicured hands down his stomach.

He did as he was told. Now she was licking him from the back, pulling on his dick very slow, very soft. She learned Frank very well. She knew what he liked and how he liked it. She was good at pleasing her people. But she wasn't finished with Frank just yet. You see, Dee Dee was blessed with an unusual tongue length, and because she was so blessed, she didn't mind blessing others. Ice cold, she moved her stiff tongue deep into the crack of Frank's ass and began pulling on his dick at a heartbeat's pace. This time, she did it until he busted off, and without hesitation, she flipped him over and stuck it in her mouth; of him being over sensitive, he busted off again. She caught that one and kept sucking until he fell asleep. The next morning, he got up, recounted his money, and headed home.

* * * * *

"Do you have'er?" Rosco asked instinctively.

"She's in the back, just like you asked," the old man assured him.

Rosco thought it would be safer to have Candy sent to an old friend rather than have her at his spot, at least until he could reach an agreement with Todd.

The first thing he noticed was her legs. They were extremely toned and lustfully thick. This was Rosco's first look at Candy, and what a sight it was. She was completely naked, bent over a desk chained down, her high yellow skin glistening with sweat.

"I see Todd went and got'em a video chick' he walked over and slapped Candy on the ass, "Not bad! Not bad at all."

"I didn't think you were coming?" He mumbled between breaths as he pulled up his pants.

"So, let me guess? You were so bored you had to find some means of entertainment!" Rosco asked sarcastically."

"You want a drink?" he asked on his way to the mini bar.

"Whatcha got?" Rosco replied, then took a seat.

"So when do you need her back?" He walked over and handed Rosco a cup.

"Tonight!" Rosco replied.

"You bringing her back?"

"I'm afraid not," he looked over to Candy. "I plan on killing her and her little boyfriend."

"Is that right? You plan on killing lil Mama," He started groping himself. "You mind if I come"

"For what?"

"Man! Lil Mama was a great fuck. I wanna get it at least one more time before it gets cold."

"I see you haven't lost yo sense of humor," Rosco chuckled. "What the hell? An extra gun won't hurt to have a round."

"That thang sweet, Rosco. I'm telling yah. You should try it out," he motioned for Rosco to go and have his way with Candy.

"PLEASE! NO! NO! NO! SOMEBODY HELP!"

Candy screamed and yelled at the top of her lungs as tears flowed down her eyes. But her pleas for help was reduced to only mumbles and whining, her abductors had a sock stuffed in her mouth with duck tape holding it in place. Rosco thought about it for a minute but was reluctant to pass up a chance to go up in something as fine as Candy.

"Umma kill yo ass anyway, so I midas well fuck yah," Rosco blurted out before kneeling down, "You might even enjoy dis."

With her sacred spot within inches of his lips, he carefully opened her up and began licking and sucking both holes. Candy tried her best to resist, but the more she jerked and pulled, the tighter the chains became and the more excited he got.

"Dat's it, girl! Throw it, throw it!"

To Rosco, this was just another whore who couldn't wait to have him, but for Candy, this was a nightmare. For the love of God, why were these men doing her like this? Candy couldn't understand why or how her world got turned upside down so quickly. Rosco finally stood up. She was nice and wet, just like he liked it, well she should be. He'd been down there damn near twenty minutes, and now he was ready to go up in her.

"I saved the best for last," Rosco mumbled as his pants fell past his knees.

As Rosco slammed in and out of Candy at a rabbit's pace, he felt he was at his moment of glory while Candy felt she was at her moment of truth.

Although she was already num from the other three violators, his presence was felt. He told her he was going to kill her, so she took what time she had left to ask God to forgive her of all her sins and to look after Todd while she's gone. She even asked God to forgive her for the time she stole twenty dollars from her grandmother when she was eleven. Overly excited, Rosco busted within a few strokes.

He tried to get another hard-on but couldn't. Upset, he pulled up his pants and ordered her to be cleaned up for the night's transaction.

"Make sure you wash the blood out her hair," Rosco reminded him, "don't want for anyone to act out prematurely before I get me!!"

"See yah in an hour, strawberry" Rosco kissed her in the center of her back and taped her on the ass."

For now, her nightmare was on hold, but she'd said her peace and was ready to die.

CHAPTER 12

The first thing Frank did when he hit the city was called Todd. The last two months have been like a dream come true for Frank. He finally felt as though he had a purpose in life. Yes, it was Candy's vision and Todd's dope, but it was Frank who did all the leg work. He was the one burning up the highway for weeks at a time, and it was he who showed Todd how to put that clack together. Despite all that, he understood his position and accepted the fact that Todd called the shots, which were in accordance with his niece's vision. After Frank got off the phone with Todd, he hurried up and dropped Dee Dee home, then rushed to Todd's house. He could tell something was wrong with Todd's voice. Once he got there, Todd introduced him to Hope, and they both explained the turn of events, as far back as when Rosco first gave them the list of cars to steal up to the last phone call they had with him. They gave him a few minutes to let it all soak in, then they gave him their plan.

"So what time do we go get'er?" Frank asked.

"Around three!" Todd responded.

"So where is she? Did you get to talk to her?"

"We're not sure. Rosco said he'll call and give us a location."

"When he suppose to..."

With a carefully steady voice, Hope made stern eye contact with Todd and Frank. "Listen up, you two. When we go to get'er, don't be wit dat John Wayne, T.J. Hooker dumbshit. Wait for my signal, then move as we planned." "Remember," he pointed at Todd, then Frank, "our goal is to bring home your baby and your niece. No matter what!!"

After Hope gave his little speech, he checked to make sure they had the right firepower. Rosco had no intentions of letting either one of them live after tonight, Hope knew that. He also knew of Rosco's history with women. He didn't tell Todd, but he did pray that Rosco didn't get off too bad on Candy. The call came in a little after two o'clock. Rosco gave them the location and then reminded them of the ramifications if they were to cross him. It was on and popping.

Pussy was a great bargaining tool. Since the beginning of time, it's been used to take down some of the best-known men. This was no different. Rosco called back the lawyer and told him that he changed his mind and that he wouldn't be needing his help after all. Not trusting him to keep his mouth closed, Rosco sent a few of his men to quiet the lawyer permanently. Now, everything was going according to plan.

Rosco chose an old Public warehouse on the west side of town to conduct business. That was a bad sign of the rip. The west side was considered off limits to anyone who wasn't from there, especially street dudes. Po Po's had the meanest parameter out west. Easy rope off action. Because of that and the time of night, they were going over there, Hope chose the black on black six with a light tent. Frank was the oldest, so he drove. Hope played shotgun while Todd cuffed the backseat. Todd was quite the whole ride. Hope only spoke to let Frank know when and where to turn and which way to go. No one said it, but they all thought it; PLEASE LET CANDY BE OKAY. The second they reached the parking lot, Hope hoped in the driver seat, Todd climbed up front, and Frank crept around the back of the building, looking for a way to sneak in. Rosco never seen Frank, which was a good thing considering he was the one who had to get the drop in him.

"Where she at?" Todd seethed.

"Where's my dope?" Rosco countered as he stood on the top balcony.

"We got yo dope, Fatboy," Hope lifted up a duffle bag, "all we want is Candy."

"Candy?" Rosco repeated as he ran two fingers down the side of his mouth. I couldn't have described her any better myself. He thought, "She's here, don't worry."

Rosco signaled for one of the workers to retrieve the duffle bag. When he reached out to Hope, Todd pulled out his pistol. "We doing this at the same time, Fatboy," Todd demanded.

"I'm cool wit dat."

Rosco cut the air with his finger, and shortly after, Candy was pushed out on a pallet, hog-tied and gagged. Meanwhile, Frank was slipping in and out the shadows, taking out Rosco's men one by one. Some throat he cut, others, he whispered into their ear from a distance. Strapped with two 9 mm, each with a silencer, extra clips, and an "AK" tied to his back, Frank was quickly evening out the playing field. Frank was the first one to see Candy. It made him sick to his stomach to see his niece tied up like that. He could hear Rosco and Todd talking, but he couldn't see them.

His first mind told him to wet up the group of men posted around Candy, but he didn't follow through; he gave Hope his word he would wait for his signal, and he did. Just as Hope suggested, Candy was swapped out with the dope. Everything was as planned, or at least Rosco thought it was. He gave his men specific instructions to gun down all three of them once the dope was secured. The warehouse was the perfect stage for a bloodbath. The men were positioned up high, which allowed them to not only have a clear shot but also to stay out of harm's way from friendly fire.

"Hurry up and untie," Hope mumbled as he watched the young boy rush to a side door.

Candy was trying to warn Todd, but she couldn't. Her mouth was gagged. Todd seen the fear on her face but was more concerned with freeing her arms and legs than her mouth.

"Man, hurry up!!" Hope shouted.

Something wasn't right, and Hope wasn't the only one thinking that. The plan was for them to start shooting the second the boy reached the side door, but when he got there, nothing happened. "Kill'em!!" Rosco screamed as he backed away from the rail.

Unable to reach all of Rosco's men, three started to unload as ordered. Bullets began to come from everywhere. "Frank!!" Todd yelled out as he and Hope fired up into the shadows.

Unlike Hope, Todd shot only one pistol at a time; he held Candy up under the other arm, trying to shield her from strays.

"Get'er out of here!" Hope screamed.

Holding on for dear life, both arms wrapped around Todd's waist, Candy felt the other pistol and, without thinking, snatched it from his pants line and began shooting. She knew Hope and Todd couldn't do it alone. They risked their lives to come save her, and she would be damn if she went out like that. Once Hope seen how Candy handled a pistol, he knew this wasn't her first time picking up a gun. Her third shot came with success as one of Rosco's men fell over the rail down to the floor. She was very calm and very accurate. If it wasn't for Frank, things might have turned out a lot differently, he was the determining factor. As a result of that, six of Rosco's men paid with their lives. It wasn't until the gunplay stopped that Frank came out.

"It's time to go!" Frank insisted.

"Yeah! Let's ride, baby girl," Todd said to Candy, who was wrapped ever so tight on him.

"I thought they were going to kill me!" Candy cried, squeezing Todd tighter.

"I wasn't going to let dat happen!" Todd assured her.

"Man, let's bounce," Frank repeated, "I know somebody heard their shots, so I know dem folks coming."

"Hell, yeah," Hope co-signed as he directed them to the side door. "We can go out that one," he suggested.

Todd led while Candy held on tight to Hope and Frank right on their heels. The six was parked on the other side of the parking lot behind a big dumpster. Frank parked it there just in case someone passed by. It wouldn't be in plain view. Todd recommended that they walk to the car one by one, being it was almost four o'clock in the morning. He didn't want to look suspicious. They all agreed, and each one waited until the other reached the car before the other came out. Frank went first since he was driving, then Hope and Candy. The nightmare was almost over. Candy was starting to feel safer by the minute, and when she saw Todd coming across the parking lot, she experienced a type of relief words couldn't explain. Within the last twenty-four hours, she'd been kidnapped, raped repeatedly and, on top of all that, almost killed during a heroic rescue. Why God chose her to go through such an ordeal, she'll never know. She was just glad he felt she'd been through enough and was gracious to send Todd and them to come get her. Candy yelled for Todd to hurry up. She could hear sirens closing in. Todd was very much aware of the sirens and sped up his pace. He'd gotten close enough for Candy to see his facial expression. He was smiling from ear to ear when, out of the blue, a shot was fired, then another one and another one. He tried to open the door but fell a step or two short. Frank jumped out and released a flurry of bullets in all directions while Candy and Hope pulled Todd into the backseat. Once he was inside, Frank hopped back under the wheel and mashed down on the gas peddle.

"Who dah hell was dat?" Hope screamed.

"He's bleeding everywhere!" Candy cried out as Todd laid limp in her lap.

"Where you hit at?" Frank asked, but Todd didn't respond. "Candy, see where he's hit."

Candy was in the backseat going crazy. Todd was losing a lot of blood, and his words were starting to slur. His beige button-up was drenched in blood, making it hard for Candy to tear it.

"PLEASE GOD! DON'T LET'EM DIE!" Candy pled.

Finally able to rip off the shirt without moving him, she saw firsthand what a real bullet womb looks like. Todd tried to speak, but Candy quickly quieted him. She told him to save his strength, and that help was on the way.

"Can you see where he been shot?" Frank asked again.

"He, he, he got two in his back," she stuck her finger in a hole in his pants, "and I think it's one in his leg." She pushed a little deeper until she felt blood, "Yeah, yeah, that one."

"Hang in there, homeboy," Hope yelled, then turned around to have a look.

Hope wanted to cry when he seen Todd covered in blood. They were like brothers, so when he seen Todd slumped over Candy's lap with two holes in his back, to him, he looked dead.

"Nucca, don't you die on me!" he ordered.

Candy felt helpless. She didn't know what to do or what to say, so she did the first thing that came to mind. Sing. Rocking back and forth, rubbing on his head. She hummed a tune to the song they made love to for the first time.

"Remember this song?" she mumbled in between tunes.

"Candy!" she looked up, and their eyes locked in "he's gonna be aigh't" Hope gave her a thumbs up, and even though the words weren't audible, she heard every word.

"Which way to the hospital?" Frank asked with a little panic.

He was watching Candy through the rearview; her face was covered with agony, and it was clear Todd meant more to her than he thought. At that moment, Frank zoned out. Todd could have let Candy die. He could have kept what happened to her between Hope and himself, but instead, he risked his life to save hers. Frank made up his mind not to let Todd die, not to bring more grief to his niece and not to lose a friend.

He pushed down on the gas peddle even more, exceeding over eighty miles per hour. He knew if Todd didn't get medical attention soon, he could bleed to death, not to mention anything internal that could be wrong.

"Just hold tight, baby," Candy whispered, "Just hold tight."

Frank never felt this nervous before in his life. Here he was, speeding down some interstate that seemed as if it would never end, with some guy he had just met bleeding to death in the backseat. As he passed through the third traffic light, he glanced in the rearview at his niece, who, in his opinion, was going crazy. He had to do something. It was she who gave him a second chance to be somebody. He owed her for that. When Hope told them that the hospital was less than ten minutes away, Frank speeded up. That was all he had to hear. Nothing mattered from that point on. The fact his niece was in his ear screaming and yelling for him to slow down didn't matter. The color of the lights didn't matter. Nothing mattered. Frank wasn't about to stop or yield to anybody or anything. He was on a mission, and his mission was to save a life. Hope wiped the tears from his face and then turned to look at Todd and Candy. He didn't want Candy to see him cry for more reasons than the obvious. Things had seemed discouraging at first. Candy was kidnapped, and only God knows what Rosco had done to her. Todd was shot three times while rescuing her, and now he was in the backseat of a car, bleeding to death. Everything was just crazy for a minute, but now Candy was back, and the hospital was just around the corner. Things were more hopeful. That was until the six hundred was sideswiped, causing it to flip three times before hitting a tree. Things just went from worse to worse.

CHAPTER 13

Pete hated his life. He hated his job. He hated the fact his wife was dying. He hated the bank for not allowing him to take out another loan on the house. He even hated God, although he wouldn't admit it out loud, taking Eva through so much torment. Normally, Jamie would pick up and drop off Pete, but occasionally or every other Thursday, he drove himself to work. Thursday was the day he and Eva became an item, so he chose those days to come home early to be with his wife.

The first thing Pete saw when he walked into the house was the stack of mail. At first sight, it appeared to be at least two weeks worth. Eva would've never let it build up like this, Pete thought as he scooped up the letters, walked into the living room and flopped down in the Lazy Boy. Sifting through the small pile of envelopes, he came across a letter from the bank with the word "URGENT" stamped in bold red letters. In one motion, he dropped the other letters into his lap and opened it. The bank was notifying him that his application for an extension was denied and that the bank was making preparations to take over the house within the next forty five days. It also informed him that unless a full payment of twelve thousand, three hundred, sixty two dollars and ten cents was paid before the forty five day deadline was up, all his personal accounts would be forfeited. Their cars would be repossessed, and their names would be turned into the credit union; at that moment, all Pete wanted was his wife. Disappointingly, he stuffed the letter in his pocket and headed upstairs.

"I guess my best wasn't good enough," Pete sighed, staring at Eva from the doorway.

This wasn't how her last days were supposed to be like. They both knew her condition would worsen with each day but for Pete, seeing it was much more harder than actually knowing she was dying. Seeing Eva like this hurt Pete's heart. Literally frustrated, he walked over and buried his face into her stomach. "Till death do us part," he mumbled, placing her fragile hand in his.

Fifteen years ago, Pete was a star running back in college who was a sure-in for the pros, and Eva was this sexy, vibrant, exotic looking twenty three year old model who, at the time, was on the cover of every major magazine there. She was the first non-white model to feature on the cover of "Palace." They referred to her as the new face of fashion, but Eva's looks weren't always a plus for her. As a child, she struggled to find her place in society. Her mother was Chinese-Jamaican, and her father was Haitian-Dominican. All the girls hated her because all the boys wanted to jump her bones, so she stayed fighting. That was until she met Pete. He always loved the way she looked. He made no secret of that. If it wasn't for him, she would not have gotten into the modeling business. But that was so long ago, and so much has changed since then.

A stream of tears began to run down Pete's face as he began thinking about how his life would be without his Eva, so much so that the sheets Eva was up under started to dampen.

"What's wrong, baby?" Eva ran her fingers through his hair.

He didn't even notice she'd removed her hand from his. Amazingly, that's all it took. A simple touch and the tears stopped.

"Nothing wrong," he responded, face still buried in her stomach.

"Let's talk." She moved her hand to his chin, lifting up his face.

"You're my wife! You're my wife, and your dying! And I can't help you!"

"Go on." She sat up.

"I don't know how to live without you!"

"You're so silly, you know that." She let out a light giggle.

"I'm serious!" he retorted, but her giggles increased, causing him to get up and walk to the window.

"Come here." She extended her hand.

"This isn't funny," he responded but was unable to stay by the window. He walked back over and sat down.

"I'm sorry." She tapped his nose. "But you're crying," she said and cupped her hands around his face, "and you know how adorable you look when you're crying."

"I'm scared," he uttered.

"We promised!" Eva pulled him close to her. "Besides, God will give you another wife."

"That's the problem," he rejoined, lying down next to her, "I don't want another wife. I don't..." she pressed her lips hard against his. "I'm scared," he repeated.

"So am I," she pressed her lips on his again, but this time she slid in her tongue. "Make love to me, Pete," she entreated while unbuttoning his pants.

They hadn't made love for over three months. Pete just wasn't there mentally, but now his emotions were at an all time high. He was full of anger but also depressed and somewhat doleful. Eva, on the other hand, was always up for it. She never pushed the issue because she knew what he was going through. But tonight was her night to reconnect with her husband. Gracefully, she laid him on his back and then straddled around his hips.

Instantly, he was feeling the warmth from between her legs as she wore nothing but a tank top. That warmth was all Pete needed to stiffen up.

Eva felt the bulge coming through Pete's boxers. She repositioned herself to where his face was between her legs. Pete was on point as he slid his tongue in and out of her. In return, she pulled his boxers down to his knees and then placed him in her mouth. The more they sucked on each other, the closer they became as one.

The common couple. Most couples expressed their love through gifts or romantic getaways. Not these two. They had more of a physical relationship. For them, sex was a tool they used to deal with anything emotional. A ritual they performed as often as the sun rose and set. The two of them understood each other to the "T." Whenever Eva was on top, Pete would allow her to be the aggressor, and vice-versa, so when Eva began rubbing herself up and down Pete's face, he became fully aware that she was seeking special attention for her other spot. Her small hole. Pete wasted no time accommodating her wishes. With the tip of his tongue, he traced the outlining as slowly as possible. That was her favorite part of making love, and Pete knew that. But without warning, Pete brought something new to the table. He spread her ass far as she could go, then eased his tongue as far as it could go. Once he was in, he rolled it in a wave like motion. That was only the phase one. Phase two was what sent Eva over the top. As he freed his hands, her cheeks clamped down on his jaws, which in return stiffened up his tongue that much more. With one hand, he ran the tip of his fingers up and down her stomach and with the other, he brought out her little man in the middle, placed him between two fingers, then pulled and rubbed her clit until Eva moistened beyond her control. This was Pete's show now, and he took full control. With each stroke of his tongue, in unison with his hands, she began to have multiple orgasms.

Eva stopped sucking on Pete the second she reached her first climax. Not that she wanted to. Besides, he was still in her mouth. Everything locked up on her. Her body was functioning without her control. She couldn't even stop her eyes from rolling to the back of her head. Pete was amazing, he was giving it to Eva just the way she wanted it. He didn't miss a beat. His focus was impelled from all his emotional hardship and stress, but for Eva, it was an intimate bliss as she released puddle after puddle onto Pete's chest...

"Please, baby..." Eva was finally able to get out a word. "I can't take anymore," she pleaded, but Pete just sped up, interesting things even more. Eva was losing it. Her orgasms were coming faster. Each one was more profound than the other. Then, without warning, he flipped her onto her back and shoved himself in her as deep as he could. At that point, her whole body went numb while Pete started pumping as fast and as hard as he could. He was able to keep up that pace for the next twenty minutes before releasing what felt to be a thousand babies into Eva.

As the warmth of his eggs sat just below her tummy, she wrapped her legs around his back and pulled him in for a passionate kiss. One that lasted for at least three minutes. That night was a Long night coming for the both of them and a special one at the chat. It was the first time in a long time they put their feelings back into their lovemaking.

Before they fell asleep, they promised never to let that happen again.

* * * * *

"So what do we have?" Jamie asked the tall, redhead man holding a mid-size camera.

"Not sure yet," he answered while photographing the body of a young Spanish boy.

"So why you have me called out here?"

"The kid had a gun on him when we found him." He moved her to shoot a different angle.

"What does that have to do with me?"

"The serial number wasn't scratched off," he said, hovering over the body to take a close-up, "so I called it in." He looked up at Jamie. "You wanna guess who it belongs to?"

"Who?" she asked, but in the back of her mind, Lewis was her first choice.

"You ever heard of a Robert Lewis? Or should I say, Detective Lewis?" He stood up and signaled for a blonde-haired woman to bring him the gun. "After I process it, you can get it." He focused his attention on the warehouse. "I'm not sure, but I think they said it's eight more bodies in there."

"I'm surprised the flies aren't around," Jamie responded.

"You know how reporters are! They just come out of nowhere," he uttered...

"So when is the best time to come get it?"

"You can pick it up from ballistics tomorrow." He waved over another set of hands. "I'll sign it over to you." He turned and gave the man specific instructions, then turned back to Jamie. "As you can see, I'm kind of busy, so..."

"Well, let me get out your way," Jamie responded.

She pulled out her cell phone and called Pete. No answer. She tried again and again. No answer. She looked at her watch to see it was a little past three in the morning. She redialed on her cell, but this time it wasn't Pete she was calling. She was calling the rest of the team to meet up later that morning. This was the break she needed to solve the case, and she would be damned if she let this one get away. Whoever killed Lewis, days were numbered.

*****

"Is he going to die?" Candy asked Franky tearfully.

"Nah, he ain't gone die," he responded as he looked out while Hope hot wired them a getaway car.

"I hate leaving him like that," she said half aloud.

"You can't do him any good locked up, and that's just where you're going if we don't get out of here. Hell, that's where all our ass going if we don't get up outta here."

Hope was moving with Godspeed. He popped the lock and started the car in record time. Once in, he gave the signal for the two of them to jump in. Candy was in the backseat, remorsefully silent. While Hope and Frank were upfront devising a plan to get all four of them out the mess they were in. "You can't do him any good locked up." Those words replayed over and over in Candy's head the whole trip home, and they weren't going anywhere. They ended up following her to sleep, and her dreams turned into nightmares...

When she woke up that afternoon, the house was empty. Frank and Hope were long gone. She tried calling them, but neither one answered their phone.

* * * * *

Jamie was feeling that sense of urgency she would always get right before she solved a big case. Two weeks ago, the case was officially cold, Meaning it was no longer on the to-do list. From the beginning, there were no eye witnesses, and as time went on, all leads turned up cold. That was two weeks ago. That was before a fortunate chain of events occurred. First, the backup gun was recovered, and just two hours ago, she was informed that a man was shot with that same backup gun and was being held at the Memorial Hospital. As the team of four listened to Jamie debrief them on her new findings, it was apparent how excited she was. But she wasn't by herself. Whenever a fellow cop was killed, whether they were corrupt or not, it hit home hard. The killer had to be caught, if not just to send out a message. No stone was left unturned.

Jamie was in a zone. Everything was mapped out. It had to be. Jamie was very clear that this might be their last shot. She told them to reinterview the little boy who found the gun in the park. She wanted for them to run a hair test with the slain Spanish boy found earlier that morning and to find out who Lewis was going to sell the kilos to, something she should have done the first time around.

"What about the car garage?" the curly head man asked.

"Check it," she responded, "but don't let'em know you're a cop." She looked around. "Where's Pete?"

"He called and said he'll be running late," a voice blurted out from across the room.

"How long ago was..."

"Was what?" Pete asked, coming through the door.

At first, Jamie was going to give him a piece of her mind for showing up late, then decided not to spoil the moment. Besides, the team needed to leave on a positive note.

"Good, you're here," she uttered. "Okay, people, let's get this show on the road." She looked over to the curly head man. "Call me the minute you know something. I'll be at the hospital if anybody needs me." She tapped Pete, then walked out of the office.

"The hospital!" Pete repeated right on her heels." What's at the hospital?"

"I'll explain in the car," she yelled, her pace picking up dramatically.

Just as Jamie and Pete were pulling out of the parking lot, a short, chubby woman came flying out of nowhere, waving a small piece of paper and shouting Jamie's name at the top of her lungs. Jamie immediately stopped and waited for her to catch up. It was obvious she wasn't in the best of shape as she struggled to breathe and talk at the same time. In her best effort, she explained the message from the lab confirming that the hair sample found on Det. Lewis didn't match that of the hair from the body found earlier that morning. She handed her the note, then wobbled back to the precinct.

"So if he's not the killer, how did he end up with the gun?" Pete asked half aloud.

"Who says he's not the killer!"

"The lab confirmed that his......"

"All the lab did was let us know his hair didn't match the sample found on Lewis, but..." But we'll just have to wait and see how this plays out with our gunshot victim." She looked over at Pete, "I believe he has the answer to all our questions."

The first thing Jamie noticed was that there wasn't anyone guarding the suspect's door. With one potential suspect already dead, she thought it would be best to have around the clock watchmen. She politely flashed her badge to the desk clerk and demanded to see whoever was in charge.

Ten minutes later, she was approached by the hospital administrator.

"How can I help you?" she asked as Pete and Jamie rose to their feet.

"Hi, I'm Detective Lightbourn," she pointed to Pete. "Detective Wise. We're here about the gunshot victim from last night."

"You mean this morning?"

"Yes, I mean this morning," Jamie repeated. "Is it a good time for us to question him or should..."

"Now is good." She pointed to room 112. "He might be a bit sluggish, though. He came out of surgery about an hour ago."

"Surgery!" Pete asked curiously.

"Yeah, doctors had to remove a few bullets, but he's fine now." She looked down at her pager, which was flashing crazy. "I'm sorry, but I'm needed back upstairs. If you need anything else..."

"I think we can manage from here." Jamie thanked her, watched her walk off, and then tapped Pete on the shoulder. "She's on women. And she's not your type."

Pete gave her an off the wall look as he trailed behind her to the room.

CHAPTER 14

When Todd awoke, Candy was right by his bedside. Still woozy from the anesthesia, it took him a few minutes to regain full consciousness. When he fully came around, the first thing he noticed was that he was wearing a cast on his whole arm. Because he was shot in the back, he was forced to lie on his stomach, so when he first opened his eyes, he couldn't see Candy. But the second he tried to move, she knew he was up.

"Hey, you!" Candy came from around the bed and positioned her chair so they would be face to face.

"Heeey, hey, baaa..."

"You need some water?" she asked, concerned after hearing the dryness in his voice.

He shook his head, and she went and retrieved a cup of water with a straw in it. A few sips later, he was able to speak much clearer. After they began to talk, Candy realized Todd had no recollection of the accident, so she filled him in. She told him about the car coming out of nowhere and how she thought she'd lost him. She explained how he got to the hospital and why she had to leave him in the middle of that field. She was just about to tell him about Frank and Hope when suddenly two strangers walked into the room. Although they were casually dressed, the moment they entered the room, Todd got a funny feeling in his stomach.

"Todd Patrick?" the woman asked very politely as she walked over to the bed.

"Are you his doctor?" Candy asked, thinking she was too pretty to be anything else.

"No, ma'am." She offered a warm smile, then extended her hand. "I am with the sheriff's department, and you are?"

"Tasha Stokes!" Todd chimed in, "And yes, I'm Todd Patrick. How can I help you?"

"Well, I'm Officer Lightbourn, and that's my partner, Officer Wise. We've come to ask you a few questions." She fixed her eyes on Candy. "But if this isn't a good time, I could have you come down to the station next week and we..."

"It's all good. Right now, straight." Todd fixed his eyes on Officer Wise. "Whatcha wanna know?"

"Whatever you can remember about the night of the accident would be fine." She pulled a small pad from her back pocket.

"All I remember is that this car came from nowhere and knocked my ass silly."

"And where were you coming from?"

"I was going to the club!" he answered.

"The club?" she repeated while writing on the pad. "And what club would that be?"

"I'm not sure the name of it. Some eighteen and up spot I heard be jumping."

"Were you drinking?"

"I had a friend die from drunk driving, so I don't do it."

"Were you with him, ma'am?" She looked over to Candy, then back to Todd.

"Why would you ask that?" Candy responded.

"You have a scratch on your chin," Officer Lightbourn explained.

"Oh, that." Candy ran a finger over the scar. "One of my cats scratched me the day before."

"I didn't mean to make you feel uncomfortable," Officer Lightbourne mumbled as she wrote down on the pad again. "Asking questions comes with the territory."

"Anything else, Officer Lightbourn?" Todd faked a yawn. "These pain pills are starting to take their toll."

"No." She wrote on the pad again. "That'll be it. Thank you for your time, and I hope everything turns out okay for you. Miss Stokes, it was nice meeting you." Just as she was about to walk out, she turned around. "By the way, what happened to your back?"

"I got jacked two weeks ago for my chain and sneaks," Todd explained.

"Did you report it?" Officer Lightbourne asked inquisitively.

"For what?" Todd retorted. "That wasn't gonna get my stuff back."

"The wheel may start off slow, Mr. Patrick, but in the long run, it does catch up with its man. You two have a good day."

As Jamie and Pete walked down the hallway, she sensed Pete wanted to say something. She was right. The moment they got into the elevator, he gave her a piece of his mind.

"What the hell was all that about?" Pete asked confoundedly.

"Would you relax, for Christ's sake? I made a judgment call."

"Asininity was the first thing to come to mind," Pete replied.

"Why question my methods, now?" Jamie asked.

"Well, for one, you've never gone in left field on me like today." His eyes were screaming out disappointment as he eyed her coldly. "We've been on this for what...two, three months at the least, and what do you do when we get our first real break?" He slammed his fist into his hand. "Absolutely nothing!!"

Jamie was about to reply, but the elevator door opened, and a group climbed aboard. At that point, she felt it would be best to hold her tongue until they reached the car.

* * * * *

"And they didn't say anything before they bounced?" Todd asked.

"Like I told you before, when we got to the house, I didn't speak to them. I was so mad that they talked me into dropping you off like that, I just went and took a shower and went straight to bed. When I woke up, they were gone."

"And you say you hit them on the cell, but ain't nobody answer?"

"I hope they didn't get arrested!" Candy mumbled.

"They would've hit you up if that was the case," Todd said.

"Todd, I'm scared." Candy started crying. "I don't know what to…"

"Listen to me, baby girl," he said, reaching for her hand, "I promise you this will be over real soon. I just have to figure out how this lady cop is going to play this."

"I don't understand?" Candy professed. "You mean the lady officer who just left?"

"That hoe up to something. She know something."

"Is that why you lied about my name?"

"Check this out," he paused a moment to gather his thoughts, "when you leave from up here, don't come back unless I call you."

"Boy, I ain't trying to…"

"Just listen for a minute." He squeezed her hand tighter. "I was shot!"

"I was there, remember," Candy replied sharply.

"Anytime someone comes to the hospital for a gunshot, they have to call the police."

"Okay, so what? They call the police and…"

"The only cops came to holla at me was that lady and her partner… talking bout some car accident."

"So I can't come see you because they didn't ask you about the shooting?" Candy began crying harder.

"Listen!! You're going to stop crying and stop asking questions." Todd wiped the tears from her face.

"I need you to do just as I tell you. No more. No less. Do you understand me?"

Reluctant to answer, she took a moment before nodding in agreeance.

"I'm listening," Candy answered.

"First, I want for you to tell Hope and Frank to close up shop, then tell them I said to flip the phones. All the phones, Even yours."

"Then what?" she asked.

"Then, I want for y'all to put up all the whips," he paused a second, "except for you. You keep the truck. Do you remember what I taught you about people following you?"

"If I would've done like you showed me the first time, we wouldn't be in…"

"Shit happens," Todd explained. "We can't change that, but you do…"

"Yeah, I remember."

"Good. I have a feeling you're about to be followed for a few days."

"By that lady cop and her friend, or that fat bastard who…" Candy almost told Todd Rosco raped her, but she caught herself. "Who kidnapped me?"

"Just look out for either one," he instructed. "Oh yeah, don't tell them about the two cops coming here to see me until I say so." From the look on her face, he could see she was confused about not telling them that, but as long as she did what he told her, things would be alright.

"You said not to come out here unless you call me first, but how can you call me if all the numbers will be changed?"

"We'll make contact through my lawyer, Frank. As a matter of fact, once all the numbers are changed, call him. No, have Hope call him and..."

"I can call him!" Candy stated.

"Okay. You can call him!"

Hope understood Candy needed to feel she was part of what was going on. Besides, he would rather have her making a few phone calls than doing anything else. "Set up a meeting. Tell him it's urgent. When you go down to his office, tell him everything that happened the night we went and got you. Make sure you pay the retainer fee first, that way, it's attorney-client confidentiality. And don't tell him about Hope and Frank. Leave them out. Let him know he needs to come to see me ASAP."

Candy stayed until visiting hours were over. After she left, she did just as she was told. And just as Todd predicted, she was being tailed; At least she thought she was. And just to be on the safe side, she took a scenic route.

Meanwhile, Todd's brain went into overdrive as he devised a plan to dodge the law and clean up his money. He couldn't help but think of his old celly from the state who was indicted by the feds. He remembered him explaining how the feds came at him. Todd knew he had to come up with something fast, or he could end up like his old celly: serving twenty to life in the federal prison.

CHAPTER 15

After the nurse finished bathing Todd, he got a surprise visit from his lawyer. "How you holding up?" he asked with much concern while taking a seat. "I'm aight!" Todd responded, Franky could see the pain in his face. He wasn't aight! "So what the hell happen? And where's Hope? He has a court date coming up."

"Knowing Hope, he bout out there tricking."

"Is this about the sixty grand you owe Rosco?" Frank got straight to the point.

"Rosco! Sixty G's," Todd repeated, "you seen Rosco?"

"Yeah, he told me a little over a week ago you owed him that?" But he told me he wasn't gonna hurt you... I guess he lied."

Todd was thrown. Why would Rosco tell his lawyer about the dope?

And why didn't his lawyer tell 'em about Rosco yesterday when they spoke? And what the hell he meant by 'he wasn't suppose to hurt 'em.' At that moment, Todd chose his words carefully.

"I thought you were coming tomorrow."

"Me too, but I have to fly out to Seattle tonight. Friend of mine got'er self in a real bind."

"So you did dat?"

"Yeah. As far as I can see, you're clean."

"What about the others?"

"Everybody's clean. Unless."

"Unless what?"

"Unless you have a close indictment. If that be the case, then it wouldn't show up, and my friend down at the federal building wouldn't know unless he was on the case."

"So what the hell is a 'closed indictment?'"

"In simplest terms, the indictment won't open until you catch a charge cognate to those in the indictment. Being the only thing you're guilty of is being shot a few times, it remains closed."

"But what I wanna know is why you think the Fed's are after you?"

"I just do!!"

"If they are, you better hope it's not a crack case, and you better hope they don't hit you with the C.C.E."

"What the hell is CCE?" Todd asked with a puzzled look, "and what difference does it make if it's soft or hard?" Frank just shook his head. He couldn't believe how many young blacks came into his office who were knee-deep in the dope game but really had no idea what they were into. Over the last ten years. Frank has represented dozens of young black men who were just like Todd. Blinded by fast money, beautiful women, and street credibility, they took more time committing the crime than they did studying the consequences and the few who did started only after a lengthy prison sentence.

"A CCE is what they call a CONTINUAL CRIMINAL ENTERPRISE." He gave Todd a harsh look. "Whoever they consider the leader gets life. And as far as soft or hard goes, hard is 18 to 1. So, for every gram of hard equals 18 grams of soft.

"When they started dat?"

"Dah started dat in 87'." Franky tried his own Impersonation OF ebonies. "Its called the "Crack Law..." Oh yeah, that and the career criminal alone can start you at fifteen."

Todd was trippin. He'd never heard of a damn "crack law," and he had been selling dope since 89'. The more Todd llstened to his lawyer talk, the more he felt like a scrub. All these years, he thought he was on his square. You couldn't tell'em he wasn't two steps ahead of the game. But in reality, he wasn't. He was no different than the thousands of dope dealers the Fed's got caught up in the system. The way Todd took it was that the only way to beat the Fed's was not to get caught up in their system. The only way to do that is to find out how it works and how they move. Todd planned on finding that out real soon.

"Do deh got like a..."

"Guideline or procedural book," Franky cut into his sentence. He could see the look of knowledge on Todd's face.

"Yeah." He got up, walked over to his briefcase and pulled out a thick greyish blue book. "I thought you might've been interested in this." He placed it on the table. "Take your time and read carefully." Before Franky left, Todd informed him that Candy would be calling him from time to time to relay messages to him.

"That's cool," Franky responded. "Just let'er know that I'll be out'a town for two to three days. I told you about my friend out in Seattle. And if you see or hear from Howard, tell him he has a court date on the 8th of next month."

After Franky Left, Todd tried to take a nap but couldn't. For some reason, the book Franky Left was calling him like he was a dope flend. After a few more minutes of mental wrestling, he grabbed the book. On the front, read "The Federal Guideline Book." Just seeing the bold white letters awoken his awareness as he began to thumb through the table of contents.

* * * * *

It was official, Dee Dee had herself a bonafide baller. She knew he had bread, but in order for him to bring her to some private island In Jamaica, she knew he had to be sitting on a bank. Jamaica was a childhood dream for Dee Dee, but nothing like this. The reality of her trip was far more magical than her banal fantasy. Never been on a plane before, Frank let her sit by the window. The view of the Atlantic was absolutely breathtaking. The look on her face told it all... She was as close to heaven as any living person could be. From the airport, they were driven to the shoreline by some kid who was barely tall enough to see over the steering wheel. Once they got there, a girl looking just as young and short as the driver charted them over to the villas on a mid size sailboat.

When they arrived at the eighteen acre mountain top estate, there was a full staff awaiting them, including a personal chef and butler. Even Frank was impressed by the eight thousand square foot, three bed, two bath villa laced with a satellite tv and home theater.

For Hope, the trip was simply a means to an end, and unlike Frank, who brought only one woman, being on some lovely duby time, he brought two amazons with him. One black. One Spanish. Both are under twenty-five. Although it was strictly business for Hope, he didn't see any harm getting off glass with two 'bout its.'

"I'm glad you decided to come," Hope uttered. "I know Dee Dee happy. She been on cloud nine since she got on the plane."

"Yeah, dis suppose to be some type of childhood dream for her, or something like dat. Frank had a boyish grin on his face as he watched his black queen splash around with Hope's freak-aleks down by the beach.

"I think Candy is the reason Todd wanna close shop," Hope expressed in a flat tone.

"How you figure dat?"

"Think about it!" He looked Frank straight in the eyes. "Broads always asking their people to get out the game. Don't get me wrong, I love Candy girl, too, and I feel where she coming from...you know, with all that has happened to'er and all... but at the same time, ah nucca ain't trying to be broke round dis bitch."

"So what'cha saying, youngblood? We back in business?"

"Dat depends on if you're willing to get dis money the way I see fit!"

"Lay it on me, youngblood," Frank said cheerfully.

"First, we gotta carry it like it ain't nuttin'. That mean we gotta keep Todd and Candy out our game room. But if Candy's the one trippin' and not Todd, why not just keep her out of our business." Frank asked.

"I know you ain't forget dat, dat's Todd connect we getting the dope from. You remember, my folks got out dah game."

Hope pulled out a blunt and fired it up. This was the first time Frank smelled any type of drug since he left rehab. Candy made sure of that. She wouldn't allow any smoking in her house. She knew her uncle was once an addict, so she stayed on him about staying clean.

Although his choice of drug wasn't marijuana, she felt one could lead to the other in a heartbeat.

"I thought about dat too?" Hope expressed. "But whatever he knows, she knows. You know they swear deh in love. I just think it's best we keep him out the loop, too."

"What about the plug in?" Frank asked with skepticism.

"Dat's not a problem!" Hope assured him.

"I can't tell," Frank uttered. "You act like you gotta connect?"

"I do!!"

"You got one." Frank studied Hope's body language. "Den, who is it?"

"What you need to be worrying about is if your people can handle thirty to fifty a week."

"Instead of once a week? Why not once a month?" Frank asked. "That way, we'll be more under the radar. Besides, I ain't trying to hit the highway like that...ya feel me."

Hope didn't respond right off the bat. He took a few toots from the blunt while staring up at the sky. After one more pull, he fixed his glass-glazed eyes back on Frank. "You might be right, you know dat?" He offered Frank the blunt, but he refused.

"So we gonna do it once a month?"

"Yeah, we can do it like dat. I ain't got no problem wit dat."

"Cool. So how are we gonna break dis money down now dat Todd's out the picture?"

He offered Frank the blunt again and again, but Frank refused. "My nucca can never be out the picture! Don't get dat twisted! As far as the money goes, the only thing dat'll change is Todd will only get half of what he was getting. The other half will go to you." He locked eyes with the old man. "You straight wit dat?"

"Yeah, I think I can swing dat," Frank expressed with a hint of joy.

Phase one of Hope's plan was complete. Frank was down with his plan. Now, faze two. Faze two was going to take a little more finesse because Hope needed to convince Todd's people that Todd was out of the game for a while and that he would be taking over until his return. Two things stood in his way: one was that Todd's people were very reserved individuals, and although Todd never said it, he knew the real reason why he only met them once; the other problem was them reaching out to Todd for whatever reason... "Hope you feel better," or "no rush," or "your friend is good people." Whatever the case may be, he didn't want them to reach out by no means necessary.

Hope felt himself thinking too hard, and when he got to thinking too hard, he knew he tended to overthink the situation, so whenever that started to happen, he'd just push everything to the side, roll up a fat one and kick back. "We'll talk later," Hope announced, waving over his two sex toys.

"Um wit'cha when ya right!" Frank acknowledged as he lustfully gazed at Dee Dee strutting her way towards him. Unlike Hope, his whole intention was to have a romantic getaway with his Egyptian Gods. Although she could tell from the way he started having sex with her, he wanted this trip to be the time he told her how he truly felt about her. He was in love. And who wouldn't be? She was twenty three, no babies, and was fine as hell with a mean sex game, ride-or-die type chick who was all about him. Oh yeah, she got a mean sex game, and every time she was around him, she made him feel like a real king. There was nothing he wouldn't do for or about her.

"Hey, you." Dee Dee wrapped her arms around his neck, pulling his mouth to hers. Dee Dee was very open about her attraction towards Frank. She knew it made him feel good when young dudes saw him with something so fine on his arm. After a short but passionate kiss, she pulled back, acting like she had to catch her breath. "Your lips are just too soft," little boy."

He loved it when she called him that. "So I guess you enjoying ya self?"

"Am, I," She flashed a big smile.

"Other two girls straight?"

"Don't know?" She looked over to the two of them wrapped around Hope, "but I know dem hoes gay as hell!!"

"Gay?" Frank repeated between giggles. "Dah don't look gay to me!"

"Trust me, dem hoes gay."

"So dinner for five is out the question for tonight?"

Dee Dee placed her hand on Frank's dick. "Do you really want to be bothered wit dem tonight?" She began stroking softly. "Or do you want Mama to put dis pussy on ya?"

Frank raised an eyebrow as if to think about it. "Let me think about it?"

"Child, please!" she retorted with a big smile. "Boy, you know you want dis pooh nanny!"

"Yeah." He started laughing, "I'm faking like hell."

"You ain't gotta tell me." She lowered her eyes to the bulge in his pants.

Frank yelled to Hope that he and Dee Dee were going to skip the dinner and stay in for the night.

CHAPTER 16

When Jamie arrived at the station, the whole team was there, each with the information she was requiring. She had a glow about her that was brazen optimism. Armed with her notes from the night before, she took her seat among the foursome.

"Give me what you got?" she asked sternly, her eyes scanning each individual.

"Well, I took that trip back to the garage you asked about," Curly uttered.

"What'cha come up with?"

He leaned up in his chair, "they are definitely doing dirt at that garage. My guess is that they're into chopping cars...but I think they're into something more heavy, like dope!"

Jamie pushed a button, and her assistant came within seconds, "could you make four copies of everything in this folder ASAP." The assistant took the folder only to return within minutes with the copies. Jamie took'em, thanked her, then passed them out. Once she closed the door behind her, Jamie got straight to business. Jamie buzzed her assistance once more. When she came back, she handed her a piece of paper with a name and address on it. She instructed her to have a uniform, go to the address, pick up the young girl and bring her down for questioning. She told her about the boyfriend, then suggested that if he was there too, bring him and his cellphone.

"You think Lewis was dirty?" one of the detectives asked.

"Let's not get carried away here," Jamie suggested, "Our job is to find his killer, not..."

"That might be true, but you may see things a little differently when you see what I found."

He slid Jamie a small note pad, "looks like the I.A. is just as or was, curious about Lewis as we are.

Jamie thumbed through the small pad devotedly. "This says he's been under investigation or was under investigation for almost a year before he was murdered?" she blurted out, her eyes still glued to the paper.

"Actually, he was under investigation two years before that. For whatever reason, they closed it, then opened it back," he explained to Jamie.

"So why was Internal Affairs watching Lewis?" she asked while flipping through the pages, looking for the answer to her own question.

"On or off the record?"

"That's a new one," someone blurted out, inciting a slew of fictitious commits.

"All right, guys. I said alright!" Jamie rose her voice to a commanding level. "Like I said before, our focus is to catch Lewis's killer." She looked the whole room in the eyes. "Their lil" Investigation is simply a means to an end for us. No more. No less. "Now, what did you mean by on or off the record?"

"On the record, they say he was taken bribes from street gangs."

"For what?" Jamie asked.

"You know, regular stuff. Tip off, looking the other way, arresting the competition. But off the record, my sources say they were really after him for distributing large amounts of drugs." He gave Jamie a worshipful grin. "I'm talking kilos on top of kilos."

"Kilos of what?" Jamie asked instinctively.

"Cocaine!" he uttered. "also, my people."

"You mean your snitches," someone blurted.

"No! I mean my people," he focused his eyes back on Jamie. "When called that, they are less inclined to perform, so I call'em...my people."

"What did your people come up with?" Jamie asked eagerly.

"According to them, our man Lewis popped on he scene three years ago, snatching up all the big dope boys. Now, while he was stacking his resume with high profile arrests, he was marking his territory at the same time. The younger generation loved him because he made it possible for any and everyone to sell drugs. So long as you got it from him, whereas before, the older, more established dudes didn't allow such things to go on."

"Where are we talking about?" Jamie inquired. "The trail. Paramore. Mercy Drive. Eatonville."

"You're thinking about the blacks from up north," he gave Jamie a belittled look, "the blacks down here aren't as organized. Besides, the blacks down here thrive on being the man. Not working for him. I think Lewis knew that. I believe that's why he chose to deal with the Spanish out east." Before Jamie could get out her next question, her assistant came in to let her know that the young lady she requested for questioning was being brought down to the station. Jamie was also informed that the boyfriend escaped on foot, but the cellphone was recovered. After Jamie thanked her, she instructed her to have the girl put in one of the interrogation rooms and not a holding cell and to notify her the second she was in the building. Jamie leaned back, crossed her arms and rested her chin on top of her thumb.

"What do you mean, didn't allow?"

"Simple!" he suggested. "They control who sells and how much, which means they control the streets."

"Let me guess," she finished the sentence, "they control all profits, am I right?" Things were starting to come together fast. Now that she found a possible motive, her clues were starting to look more and more vivid.

"Yes! and our friend Lewis capitalized on the youngster's ambitions for his personal gains."

"So what do you think?" she looked over to Pete.

Pete rose to the edge of his chair, both elbows flat on the table. "I think he was killed by that kid in the hospital, and I think the dead Spanish boy shot'em out of revenge. That's what I think."

"But why would he wanna kill Lewis?"

"Because he was giving the drugs to the Spanish people! That's why." Pete suggested.

"I don't think he was shot over Lewis's death, uuum, that's, that's not what it looked like at the warehouse." She tweedled her finger for a few seconds, gathering her thoughts. "The more I think about it, the more I am convinced..." Jamie's tone dropped to a whisper. She jumped from her seat to the file cabinet, snatched out Lewis's last case, and then wildly turned one page after another.

"What is it? What?" Pete asked tensely.

"She found something." One detective cheered in honor of her brilliance. When Jamie reached the page, she stopped. Read a few lines, and just like that, the excitement in her eyes was gone.

"So much for my hunch," she mumbled in defeat. Jamie figured the shootout was about sixty kilos of cocaine, but when she checked, it showed the drugs were recovered on August 16, 1999, the same day of the deal. Now that her motive wasn't consistent with her clues, Jamie needed a new angle. Something that could put two and two together. She was tired of just collecting data that would draw her to false conclusions, she needed that niche, and she needed it fast. So when her assistant buzzed her, letting her know the alleged perpetrator was in T.R. #6, she put her game face on and then went to business. She gave her team a brief prep-talk to stay focused and then whisked away on that high note. Jamie was good at putting positive spins on bad situations; she was also good at putting on bad ones if she thought it was necessary. When she walked into the room, she knew it was one of those times. "This should be fun," Jamie thought as she took a seat across from the young lady.

"You sound much younger than you look," Jamie acknowledged playfully, placing a tape recorder directly in front of her.

"I didn't do anything!" She pleaded, but her words fell on deaf ears as Jamie started reading through a file. "I...said I didn't do anything! Jamie ignored her again, focusing more on the file than her, but after a few more minutes of silence, she looked up.

"I don't think you're aware of just how much trouble you're in young lady." Jamie gave her the look of death. Her favorite interrogation tactic. "I have reason to believe that you've partaken in the theft of a cellphone."

"Ah, cellphone?" she repeated. Jamie could see the relief forming on her face.

"Dis bout a damn cellphone? Man, you trippin', cuz I ain't stole no damn cellphone. "I don't even own no cellphone." She rolled her eyes and shrubbed her shoulders.

"So, how do you explain the conversation I recorded of the two of us on the stolen cellphone we had last night?" She looked down to the small recorder and removed the young girl from her comfort zone.

"You need to understand that that phone belonged to a cop...a cop who was killed a few months ago by whoever took his phone. So either it's gonna be you or your boyfriend who takes the rap." Jamie tossed the file onto the table and then waited for the words to sink in. By that time, Pete was coming through the door. Just as he was told, he came to get her in ten minutes. Jamie excused herself, and they both walked out.

"So, who is she?"

"Hopefully, someone who can give us that niche," Jamie responded.

"What do you think she knows?"

"For one, her boyfriend had one of Lewis's cellphones." "What'cha mean, one of?"

"Come to find out, Lewis had two phones. One no one knew about until now. Last night, I found the number and called.

"Let 'me guess," Pete uttered. "She answered and thought you were the other woman?"

"Something like that, but anyways." She waved her hands to dismiss the whole concept. Lewis had to have both phones on him the day he was murdered...

"And you think her boyfriend killed him and then kept the phone?" "Maybe, maybe not," she retorted. "MY main concern is to find out how and when he or she got it." "She say anything yet?"

"Not yet!"

"What if she...can't remember or holds her ground? Then what?" "That's not gonna happen," she assured him.

"All I'm saying is that we've had a few doors slammed in our faces trying to solve this murder!"

With her arms crossed and her bottom lip tucked under her teeth.

Jamie stood there staring at the ceiling. "Give me twenty minutes was the last thing she said before she went back into the room. Ten minutes later, she came out with two names, an address, and a hang-out spot. One of the names was her boyfriend, and the other was his friend. The one who sold him the phone for fifty dollars. The address was to the boyfriend, but both could be found at the hang-out spot. Jamie told her assistant to hold the girl for two more hours than to let her go. She figured two hours should be a sufficient amount of time to catch up with either of the two.

Dee-Dee knew that the only way she was able to have herself a true baller was because he didn't know about her track record. Her best friend told her to hide her history until she got pregnant. That way, she'd be locked in no matter what. Not only was her friend six years older than her, she had babies from two street ballers who broke bread every month. She had to know what she was talking about. Dee-Dee told her they would be in Jamaica for two weeks, so she gave Dee-

Dee ten ex-pills and told her to get him to take them with her. She guaranteed her she'd be pregnant before they left Jamaica. "Trust me she said, that's how I got Nod punk ass." And with that in mind, Dee-Dee was ready to put her plan together. Everything had to be special. The music had to compliment the mood, and the conversation had to be meaningful and romantic; this was her night to bring him all the way in. She made a mental note to have all champagne, no hard liquor or beers. Her homegirl told her that champagne would have him nice and tipsy but not drunk. Ex-pills and champagne will have'em just right. She was told he'll remember everything cuz he ain't drunk, she explained, and he will be in tuned with his soft side because of the pills. Everything her homegirl taught her ran through her mind as the two of them walked to the villa, hand in hand. When they got in, she went straight to the bathroom and started his bath water. The bathroom was enormous. Bigger than anything she'd ever seen in her life. Equipped with his and her sinks and toilet, walk-in shower, jacuzzi size tub that looks to hold at least six and a surround sound with a forty inch television, and a full stock of exotic toiletries. After picking what she thought were the most romantic smelling bubbles, she made sure to dim the lights and spark a few candles before calling him in. With an old cut from Donnie Hathaway whispering through the speakers and the combined smell of French vanilla and wild strawberries sipping into the air, she'd created a scene straight out the movies.

"You like? Dee-Dee asked, wearing nothing but a towel.

Frank took a second to check out the whole setup, "you like dat, Boo!" he responded.

"I am like dat," she repeated as she offered her hand, flashing her girly-girl smile.

"What made you do all this?" He took her hand, then followed her lead towards the shower.

"I just wanted to do something special for my man, that's all," she started undressing him. "Since we hooked up, you've been nothing but good to me, and I...I, I just wanna let you know how grateful I am towards you." She placed her lips on his, then his cheek, then his neck. "Frank, I will do anything for you. Anything!"

"I believe you, baby girl, I believe you." Frank couldn't help it, but every time he came around her, he would get a hard on. The smell of her skin alone drove him crazy.

"Baby, take a shower wit me," she suggested, pulling him within inches of her face.

I thought you'd never ask!" He walked up the stairs, pulling her with him. Inside the shower, it was like entering a whole new world for Dee-Dee. Not sure if what she was feeling was of her own or from the two pills tucked under her tongue, but she was starting to feel very sexy. Without warning, she pulled Frank in, then pushed her tongue along with one of the pills deep into his mouth. The initial bitterness of the pill raised a red flag, but her passionate twirl of the tongue quickly conquered all his doubts. Besides, what did he have to worry about? If anything, she was chewing on one of those sweet and sour hard candies that girls love so much. "Fuck the world," Frank thought as she washed him from head to toe with the luffa sponge, occasionally rubbing the tip of his dick against her lips while cleaning him thoroughly.

After her slow and sensual wash up, Dee-Dee put'em in the oversized tub. It was there where she worked her magic. First, she straddled herself across his lap, then began to rub down his neck and shoulders. While doing so, she felt him stiffen up, not quite to full erection, but just enough to slide up in her. For them, sex was never without protection, so when she saw he wasn't resisting going bare, she was more than happy to bless him with some flesh on flesh. Making sure the next kiss was more passionate than the last, she added the hand game for insurance. With both hands cuffed around his face, Dee-Dee twirled her tongue in and out of his mouth with full lustful kisses. Each twirl inspired him to stiffen more and more, which led to her next move. Dee-Dee rose up just enough to position herself right above Frank's dick as she switched up from twirling her tongue to sucking on his. Frank was lost in total bliss. His sense of touch was so sensitive he could literally feel every hair on his body stand up while Dee-Dee sucked and pulled on his tongue like she was giving him head. After a few moments of that, she straddled back on his lap, pushing him inside her, causing him to release his first load. The warmth of that first load drove Dee-Dee crazy. She herself was very sensitive to the slightest touch. She couldn't believe a pill so small could make her body feel so alive.

But, what really amazed her was the effect it had on Frank. It was like he was this piece of wood that wouldn't bend, that, and the fact he was holding her as if it was life or death. But what really got to her was when she could feel a pulse throbbing between her thighs while sucking on his neck, seconds later, he released another load. That was two within ten minutes. She was on a roll. Frank found himself in a zone. Although he knew he was forty three, he couldn't help but feel sixteen again. As far as he could remember, that was the age he was at when he could get as stiff as he was now.

"I want you to beat it from the back, baby," Dee-Dee moaned out loud. "Whatever you want, baby!" Frank sprang to his feet with Dee-Dee still wrapped around his waist. From the tub, they made their way to the bedroom. She reached down, pulled him out of her, then fell to her feet.

"Don't move," she commanded, lowering down further to her knees, placing him in her mouth, creating long, slow strokes. When Frank looked down, his eyes met hers. She knew he loved for her to give him head while looking at him at the same time.

"Like dis daddy?" she asked, putting as much in her mouth as possible.

"Do what you do," he responded. His facial expressions conform to each stroke. Dee-Dee teased him with a few more strokes before rising up to her feet. The look on his face told her she had full control as she led him to the edge of the bed.

"I still want you to beat it," she giggled, bending on all fours.

When Frank went in, he could feel her muscles pulling on him. "You got skills like dat?" Frank just stood motionless as she performed one of her many tricks. Fascinated by her physical ability, Frank pulled out to have a look. He wanted to see how it looked in motion. Not only did he get to see it jump, he saw a clear liquid sipping out of her vagina. Dee-Dee was having an orgasm. Known to most women as a phenomenon due to the fact no more than forty percent of them get to experience such a sexual pleasure. That was enough for Frank, he pushed himself back into Dee-Dee and then went jumping up and down in her like a madman. The more she moaned and streamed, the faster he pushed his hips, causing her to have multiple orgasms. They kept up that pace for ten minutes before changing positions. After a few more tricks and a gang of positions straight out the karma sutra, Dee-Dee managed to slip o'boy another pill. After hours of beating off in Dee-Dee, Frank didn't have a single sperm count left in his body. His last release was all the confirmation Dee-Dee needed to start wrapping things up. It was about time. Those back-to-back orgasms took a real toll on him. Besides, her stuff was so soar it was starting to hurt. But she knew she had to end things on a high note. And that's just what she did. She laid him on his back and sat on his face, then bent down and placed him in her mouth. Both were tired but managed to suck on each other throughout the rest of the night. That afternoon, they woke up in that exact position. Ready for round two.

CHAPTER 17

While Hope and Frank remained in Jamaica, Candy was trying to get her life back on track, and being in school helped the transition a great deal, it gave her the mental stability she needed to stay focused, while Todd gave her the emotional support she used to rebuild her foundation. She understood things weren't going to change overnight, so when Todd promised to leave the streets, she promised herself to take that promise one day at a time. After one of her night classes, Candy was invited to dinner by a few of her classmates. Normally, she would have declined and then rushed home to Todd. But Todd wasn't expected to come home for another week or two, so on this go around, she quickly accepted. At first, they all agreed to go out for pizza, but by the end of the night, they were all spread out on Candy's living room floor, gulping down hot wings and breadsticks. Candy even went as far as renting a couple of chick flicks for them to watch, which was rare for her to do. What initially started as a few classmates going out for pizza ended in a sleepover. For Candy, that was the first time she'd done anything like that since she was a young girl, and although she wasn't that close with them, she seemed to be really enjoying herself, considering they were all white.

"So, Cassandra, Lien tells us you're from Atlanta?"

"Born and raised," she said proudly.

"Do I look fat?" one of the girls mumbled with a distorted face as she walked into the living room.

"Well...your ass is a little big for that nightgown."

"Pissed off, Lien," Rachel shouted, "you know how she 18 about her weight."

"Which is why I can't understand why... she's always asking about it."

"Honey, you look just fine. Cat shot Lien a devil's eye, never mind Lien, she's just jealous, that's all."

"Jealous my ass! I am just a realist, and most people spend their whole lives avoiding the truth. I don't."

"Casandra, what do you think? Do I look fat to you?" Sam asked.

"You off the chain! Dat's what you is."

"I am off what?"

"Off the chain, silly," Step blurted out. "Please tell me you're not that lame?" Her head shook in the discussion.

"I am not lame! Okay, I just never grew up speaking...Sam looked over to Candy, ebonics. That's all. So sue me for not knowing if my chain is off." Candy was the first to burst out laughing, but it wasn't long before they all joined in.

"Ladies, I have an idea. So if you would, come with me." Candy led the crew into the kitchen and then started pulling out things to make a dacary. "Let's get drunk!" she suggested, overlooking the group's expressions.

"I'm in!" Lien chuckled.

"Me too," the rest of the girls cheered in unison.

While making the drinks, Candy took the opportunity to tell the girls a little bit about herself. Nothing major, just a few details about her upbringing, minus her mom's heydays and of course, she couldn't leave out the love of her life, Todd. The girls followed suit, but unlike Candy, they told it all. At least, she thought they did until they got that liquor in them. It wasn't until they knocked down a few that Candy realized just how much of a character her new friends were.

"This is my Todd," Candy boosted, handing Rachel a stack of pictures.

"Ahhhh... aren't you two just the cutest," she held the stack to her chest, rocking side to side.

"Don't you just love being in love?"

"So where is Todd now?" Step asked.

"He's in the hospital... he had to get an operation on his back."

"Nothing serious, I hope?"

"Nahh, doctors said he'll be home in a few days."

"Cat, don't drink too much, Step insisted, you know what too much liquor does to you!"

"She does it on purpose," Lien uttered, "I think she likes it."

"That's not true!" Cat shot back.

"Okay, I'm lost here, Candy admitted, what?"

"Bad girl, bad...girl," Sam grabbed Cat's hand and gave it two playful taps.

"What does alcohol do to you?"

"It gets her all wet in the paints," Lien blurted aloud.

"Well, that's all the excitement she'd gonna have because she sure isn't given any up!" Sam was always trying to peer pressure Cat into losing her virginity, and Step was always there to defend her.

"She 'll have plenty of time for sex," Step explained in a motherly tone, "right now she needs to focus more on school and less on boys... Ms. Samatha."

Like a child being admonished for being bad, all the girls lowered their gaze and then began fumbling with their hands. All, except for Candy and Stephaine. Candy was trying to figure out what was going on. While Step sat there, mouth twisted, shaking her head.

"You guys are sooo... silly," she said playfully, steering her eyes towards Candy, who looked dumbfounded. "They call themselves... I don't know what they..."

"Yes, Mother superior," "You're always right, Mother dearest," they all cheered in harmony. Normally, something as corny as their lll sing-along would be less than funny to Candy. But, because of her high powered dacaries, she was laughing so hard she excused herself to the bathroom. Rushing not to pee on herself. When she returned, the gang requested more dacaries. Happy to oblige, she whipped up the drinks and then came back to an ongoing heart to heart. Led by who else? Stephanie.

"But seriously!" Stephanie patted her hands in the air to draw their attention, "I know that college is supposed to be the best times of your life, she eyed her younger colleagues carefully, but it also is supposed to be the time you start building your foundation for the future."

"My future is already set," Lien shot back. Her overbearing pride kept a thorn in her side that she had to learn to overlook.

"The only reason you feel that way is because your parents are millionaires," Samatha explained.

"That is so untrue!"

"So if your parents weren't rich, you..."

"Money doesn't make me or my family...what makes us is our morals and our character. I know you might think I'm some sort of a brat."

"If my parents were rich, I'd be a brat too," the cat blurted out.

"Just hear me out. I was raised to pride myself on being the best. Being perfect. No matter If you're rich or not. It's not like I had to come to college and get a degree to earn a lot of money. I came so I could be a better person."

"Well, I came to meet Mr. Right, Rachel exclaimed, he's gonna be tall, dark, smart, and handsome. Oh, yeah, he is going to be really good in bed."

"That's what you said about Alex, and Steve, and Joe, and Tori."

"I just hope you're using protection finding Mr. Right," Stephanie's tongue lashing was mild but firm.

For the next hour or so, Candy listened as the girls talked about their dreams and fears and how they would always stay close. They talked about past loves, current lovers and the advantages of being a women In the new millennium. Although her expectations of white women remained solid, her ideology, on the other hand, quickly changed. Yeah, they were a bit weird, maybe even corny. But they loved each other very much. Candy always wanted to see firsthand what real friends look like. She saw just that with Lien, Rachel, Cat, Sam, and Step.

Stephanie was the first to leave. Her babysitter called and said she had a family emergency and needed her to come right home. Soon after that, the rest of the gang followed suit. The house was back to its norm, and so was Candy. Her thoughts were back on Todd, and as usual, she had one pillow tucked between her thighs, and another pressed to her chest while she fought to go to sleep. The fact she was still tipsy, plus the mental vision of Todd hitting it from the back, didn't help matters any better. She was in for a long night.

* * * * *

Slumped in the chair with her feet propped up and arms crossed, her eyes seemed to be the only thing alive as she decomposed the mall Security tape on the day Lewis's drug bust went astray. Three things bothered Jamie after watching the tape. One was the date on the security camera did not match the dates on the police affidavits. Two, the alleged perp was no other than Todd Patrick. The gunshot victim had been under her nose the whole time, and last, she couldn't understand why his name was nowhere on any report. He was a convicted felon who'd been to prison, so his identity was no secret. Yet still, he was out the picture. Why? That and a number of questions ran through Jamie's mind. But the more she dug, the more she realized all her answers were within arms reach, sheltered between the pages of Lewis's closed cases. She was able to identify Hope in the surveillance tape of Candy's house with an old mugshot Lewis had. There was also a picture of a young, well-built Hispanic male. Unfortunately, there was no name to go with the face. After learning of Todd and Hope's adolescent tag team car theft escapade, she was able to connect most of the dots, all except for the well-built Hispanic. He was her missing link. For now, she was willing to stick with what she had and work from there, knowing two heads were better than one, she called Pete.

"Hello?" Pete always answered his phone on the first ring.

"You were right!"

"Right about what?"

"You remember the drug bust that flopped?"

"What about it?"

"Todd Patrick...rang a bell?"

"The gunshot victim, what about 'em?"

"He was the buyer for the kilos the day Lewis was last seen alive!"

"Go on," Pete could hear in her voice she was on to something.

"Well, one of the men we got on surveillance leaving Casandra James's house name is Howard Sneed. Sneed and Patrick go back to when they were kids. Lewis was the arresting officer when they got busted for stealing cars. Fifteen years ago, by the way, Sneed was on bond for possession charges."

"But Lewis doesn't do car thefts," Pete explained.

"Exactly! She shot hack, but that's not it. Mr. Patrick wasn't on any report, although Lewis knew him."

"If none of this is on paper, Pete asked curiously, where is it coming from?"

"Lewis told me," Jamie answered.

"If Lewis told you all that... ask 'em for the lottery numbers for this Friday. Oh yeah, while you're at it, ask 'em what Elvis and J.F.K. are up to."

Jamie could hear Pete's ignoring chuckle growing louder. She hated to be made fun of. "He didn't come back from the dead and tell me, I went back over his old cases and found it."

"It's about time we got something solid," Pete exclaimed, "so what else do we have?"

"Where are you?"

"At the moment, I'm cross town, why?"

"I need everybody back at the station. Pronto!!"

"I'll be there in twenty minutes," Pete responded.

"Good!" James said, "I'll call the rest of the crew so I can catch everyone up." Twenty minutes later, everyone except Curly was there. He explained to Jamie that he caught a flat and would have to catch a cab to the station. Time was of the essence, so Jamie briefed the gang and brought them up to speed. Curly was informed over the loudspeaker instead of sitting in at the meeting. All Jamie was concerned with was that all her people were on the same page, no matter where they were.

* * * * *

THREE WEEKS LATER

"Congratulations!" She walked over and gave Candy a hug, "Looks like you're gonna be a mommy."

"Pregnant?" Candy blurted out of her distorted face, "This can't be happening!"

"Don't be so hard on yourself, she patted her on the knee, a lot of women have babies out of wedlock. Not that I agree with it, but..."

"But you don't understand!" Candy dropped her face into her hands, "I don't know if Todd is the father."

"Who's Todd?"

"That's my boyfriend."

"I see. So you've been unfaithful... Things happen, but the most important thing right now is the..."

"I don't want it if it's not Todd's baby. I can't have it if it's not his. I just can't."

"Having someone else baby is not the end of the world."

"You don't understand!"

"You keep saying that. Understand what? What is it I don't understand?" As the Images of the men raping her flashed in and out of her memory, her eyes began to swell with tears, "I was...I, I, was raped," she whispered.

"Do you know who raped you?" She bent down on one knee, pacing Candy's hand into hers.

"Only by face," she muttered, "not name. But my...my."

"Your what?"

"Nothing!"

"So you haven't reported this yet?" she raised her chin up 50 so they could be eye to eye, "you know you're gonna have to report this to the police?"

"Are you sure that I am pregnant?"

"That's the only thing I am sure of right now."

"What is that supposed to mean?" Candy snatched her hands away and then bounced to her feet, almost knocking the doctor down, "you think I am making this up? Like I'm lying or something."

She took a step towards Candy, but Candy took one back, "I am sorry if I upset you, but that wasn't what I meant by that. I am curious as to why you didn't report the rape and why you're so reluctant not to. Do you feel it was your fault because..."

"No! No! I don't feel like it was my fault! No, I am not gonna swear off men, and no, I am not mentally scared. Yes, I do feel violated, and yes, I do hate who did it to me."

"When did this happen?"

"A month ago," Candy answered.

"Would you like to take an Aids test? You know, just to be safe."

"A.I.D.S.!" Candy repeated with alarm. She'd never thought that those bastards could have given her Aids or any sexually transmitted disease, for that matter. The mere thought of her contracting any disease brought about too many what If's, causing Candy to once again lose her composure as she broke back down into tears.

"It would be in your best interest to have one taken now, just...I just think it would be best."

"Aids!" Candy repeated under her breath.

"How many partners have you had in the last six months?"

"A.I.D.S.!" Candy repeated again, but this time in a slower drawl.

"Ms. James. Ms. James! She gave Candy a slight nudge, I asked you did you know how many partners you've had in the last six months?"

"Just Todd."

"Are you sure?"

"Yes! I am sure!" Candy snapped, "I don't get down like dat. Trust me."

"What about Todd? You think he's been sleeping around?"

"Todd's a one women man. We've talked, he doesn't believe in cheating."

"You don't think you were the victim of a hate crime, do you?"

"Why would you ask me that?"

"You know how crazy white people are these days," she responded.

"My attackers weren't white. They were Spanish."

"A Spanish person did that to you?" Her tone was astounded as she shook her head in disbelief, "I tell you, the world is getting crazy by the minute." She placed her hand on Candy's shoulder. Are you sure you don't wanna report this? Because if you do, I'll go with you."

"I'm sure."

"Ooookay, but if you ever change your mind, give me a call. For now, I'll accept your answer. She gave Candy one of those "you gonna tell" looks. For now! But right now, I am going to have someone come in and take some more blood. We'll run a few more tests, then take it from there."

"You think I might have Aids?"

"I think anyone who engages in sex without protection might have that same possibility. I'll be back with your results in about half an hour."

From the time the doctor left to the time she came back was the longest half hour Candy had to endure in her whole life. She sat in that room with only her thoughts and fears to accompany her. Growing up, she would always see commercials about A.I.D.S. or hear in school that such and such had it, but that was such and such a problem for her. The people on television were probably actors who really didn't have it? And if they did, she didn't know them personally, so it didn't count. That was then. This is now. Her tears begin to fall as fast as her heart. Her stomach started to tighten from an overpowering fright that caused her palms to sweat and her head to ache. The wait was literally making her sick, and just when she couldn't bear the unexpected any longer, the doctor walked in. The doctor's body language wasn't telling Candy anything. Her eyes followed her every move. From the time she came through the door to the time she took a seat. Her fingers ran up and down and side to side, the blue chart snuggled in her hand. She looked up only once to make eye contact with Candy while flipping through the file. Candy was going crony Inside. The moment was growing too intense for her, she felt like she was about to explode, but she was too scared to ask.

"Don't you wanna know what the results are?" She asked Candy impassively.

"Isn't there supposed to be a preacher or something with you when you give people had news?"

"Honey, you watch too much TV," she let out a slight giggle, "anyways, you came back negative." Once Candy heard the word negative, the doctor could see her facial expression clearing up.

"Thank you, thank you, thank you, thank…"

"Not so fast, young lady! She walked over to Candy, we will still need a follow up test in about three to six weeks."

"But, I thought you said I was clean?"

"I never said you were clean, all I said was that the test came back negative."

"I don't understand? If the test is negative, I should be….."

"I am not saying you have Aids or the virus for that matter, and I am not trying to scare you," she placed her hands around Candy's cheeks, "but this particular disease has the ability to lay dormant in one's system. As your doctor, it's my job to inform you of that."

"So what do I do now?"

"The only thing I would recommend is for you to concentrate on your baby. Let me worry about the other stuff. You'll just be back here to see me in three weeks."

"I don't know what to do about the baby!" Candy confessed.

"Talk it over with your male friend. I am sure you two will come up with something."

Before Candy left the doctor's office, Todd called and told her he was being released from the hospital within the next hour and for her to come and pick'em up. Normally, she would have been more than thrilled to have heard such good news. But that was before she found out she might be carrying another man's baby, and on top of that, she could have a life threatening disease. Now, all she could do was find a way to buy time before she broke the news to Todd. She figured she'd play it by ear when she could ease the news on him about her being raped. "I hope this nukka doesn't trip when I tell him the whole deal," Candy thought right before she entered the hospital.

CHAPTER 18

Jamaica ended up being a huge success. Hope was able to convince Frank that his way of doing things would be in their best interest, not to mention most profitable, with Todd out of the picture. Even though Todd would still receive his share, Hope just used the pitch line to feed Frank's fantasy of being a big willy. But Hope wasn't the only success story, Dee-Dee proved to be just as persuasive. Her objective was to get pregnant, when they left Jamaica that morning, she was a twenty to one favorite. Twenty was the number of times Frank couldn't pull out. When they returned to the states, Frank and Dee-Dee went shopping for a house. While Hope shot straight to the crib to check on Todd. He called from the plane to see how he was doing. Candy was on her way to pick him up from the hospital. Hope was pleased to hear his Ace-coon-boon was coming home, but at the same time, he wished he could've stayed at least another week or two. He needed that time to set up the meeting with Todd's connection and to lay down a few ground rules for the street generals to pass along to the foot soldiers. He knew it was imperative that all news, good or bad, came directly to him and that all problems, big or small, be handled under his discretion. Now that Todd was home earlier than expected, Hope would have to be more creative than ever.

"Wuz up, Fireball?" Hope blurted out as he walked into the living room. "You got jokes, huh?" Todd replied with a smile equal to his.

"You straight?"

"I still got a lil pain in my back... but I'm aight. Doc told me to chill out for bout a month or two, you know, for everything to heal up straight."

"Where Candygirl?"

"Oh, she had a class early dis morning", he looked at his watch, "She should be home in a few hours, she told me you wanted us to close shop... What was up wit dat?"

"Did you?"

"Yeah! I closed shop", Hope gave Todd a harsh look, "but at the same time, my nukka, you could have holla at me yourself, ya feel me!"

"Did you switch cans and change phones?"

"Man, we did all dat," frustration started to sit on Hope's face, "Dawg, you act like... like we being followed by the feds?"

"We are," Todd shot back.

"What'cha mean, we are?" Hope's tone indicated fear- "Dawg, deem people came out to the hospital?"

"Who, the Feds?"

"Who else we talkin' about, Einstein?" – Hope asked harshly.

"I'm not sure... well, I think they sent someone to see me."

"So they did come out there!"

"No! Not themselves, but..."

"Man, hold up! You trippen! You've thrown me with this yes then no shit. Either they did, or they didn't."

"What's the first thing the hospital does when someone comes in shot?" Todd asked.

"Man, get to the point!" Hope's lack of patience was starting to show.

"They call the police!" Todd could see the confusion on Hope's face, "but they didn't do that with me, if they did, the police didn't come and holla at me about it."

"That's why you and me close shop? Because the police didn't come and ask you who wet yo ass up," Hope was unable to hide his anger.

"You don't think something's wrong with dat?" Todd asked concerningly.

"Maybe they hollard at the doctors."

"There was two cops who came in plain clothes, faking like they were regular poo-poos," asking about the accident.

For the next few minutes, neither one said a word. Anytime the two came close to having an argument, they would automatically go into silence. It was their way of avoiding saying something out of the way towards each other. After Hope twisted one up, the silence was broken.

"You trying to go?" He offered Todd the blunt and a lighter.

Todd sparked it up and took a long pull, only to let out a small cloud. "We gotta be smart about dis." He took two more pulls then passed it back, we made it to the top, and I ain't trying to go back to the bottom, ya feel me."

"I hear ya, but what I'm hearing sounds more like candy than you, homeboy."

"Candy! Dawg, don't try me like dat. What I look like letting some squad tell me how and when to move, umm G – bout mines", Todd reassured his longtime partner in crime. "Umm, just saying... you know how chicks get when things get a little crazy."

"Candy ain't like dat!" Todd shot back, "She down for me like you is."

"Ain't nobody down for you like me, Homeboy, don't get dat twisted!"

"You know what I'm saying... she got my back, but I'm the one who runs dis."

"We run dis," Hope responded with cold eyes.

"Yeah, us, we run dis... man, you know what I was talken bout. You trippen!!"

"Now what? You still talked bout closing shop?"

"Maybe for about a few months... you know, to see how everything plays out."

"Exactly what is a few months?"

"Bout five..."

"Five!" Hope screamed.

"Nah, bout three, bout three or two months, yeah, but two months dat's too long," Hope mumbled with his lungs full of smoke, "In a couple of months, you'll have another cat locking down our traps. Dawg, the streets are watching, and cat's out there starving! They trying to eat like we eating! They got mouths to feed, too! If we wait that long, they might breaking bread with another circle." He gave Todd a dense stare, "Or did you think we were the only ones with dope?"

"One thing I've learned, and that's dope… good dope, not that bowkickha, sales itself. Are you thinking about losing customers? I'm thinking about losing my freedom, we can't make a damn thing locked up, homeboy."

"The market," Todd responded.

"A grocery store! You wanna nukka to fo from bricks to apples and oranges…"

Todd started laughing, "You trippen, I ain't talken bout no damn grocery store, I'm talken bout the stock market!" Frank said he could hook me up with some brokers dat's like dat."

"Frank!" Hope repeated, "Frank don't know nutten bout no damn stock market. Besides, I ain't givin' my money to no whiteboy to jack me off."

"It ain't like dat, dem people professionals, they went to school for dat stuff. Besides, we gotta find a way to clean dah money we already got."

"Wallstreet for white people," Hope shot back, "They ain't trying to let no blacks up in they spot."

"All dem people care bout is if you have enough money to cover your losses, they don't give a damn about your color, creed, or gender because they make money regardless."

"You talking like you already got dis mapped out?"

That was Todd's cue to start convincing, "Check dis out. I added everything up," he grabbed the blunt from Hope, at least what was left, "We got a lil over nine hundred grand put up, plus two-fifty to re-up wit. Now, that's not including the seven bricks we got in Georgia and Hamilton. That's another hundred and something, so altogether, we over a mill."

"Why Frank ain't getting paid from the market? Why he ain't no millionaire if he got dat hook up."

"Oh, he got bread. Trust me!"

"He sitting on a mill?" Hope asked sarcastically

"Try six. Not one," Todd acknowledged

"Damn, whiteboy caked up like dat?" His change of tone sent Todd a positive signal, "yeah, and for a small fee, he's willing to help us stack some major paper."

"He charging us to use our money! I told you that Wall Street is for white people!" Hope blasted, "Knock it off! You know damn well, ain't nobody gonna help you just make hundreds of thousands of dollas on the house… dah man, only asking for twenty percent of our take. So what do we need to jump in?" Hope asked as his snow rose up, exposing his doubts. "Fo-Fifty," Todd answered, "well actually, two an a quarter, but he said we'll have to clean up the money first. Then start flippin' it."

"Homeboy, either you in or out."

Hope knew what Todd was really asking of him and that his answer would determine a great deal as far as their relationship was concerned. If he said yes, the two of them would embark on a new chapter in their lives. If he said no, he knew that the two of them would have no choice but to part ways, for they were no longer on the same side of the fence anymore. Hope thought diligently about his response before he gave Todd an answer. Then, after weighing out his options, he said "yes".

"Dat's what I'm talken bout!" Todd exclaimed.

"To hell wit these streets", Hope shot back, giving Todd some dap and then a hug. He only agreed to the stock market scheme so he and Todd could remain close. But what Todd didn't know, and neither did Hope, was that trouble was right around the corner.

"So when we suppose to do this?" Hope asked

"I told Frank to give me a few days to run things over wit'cha first."

"Okay, now what?"

"First, we take'em the money to get cleaned up... Then we go holla at his peoples."

"You talken bout the broker?"

"Yeah, the dude he gonna hoke us up wit. After dat, it's a wrap. Although Todd didn't have to twist Hope's arm to convince him to invest in the stock market – which he would have had no problem doing – He found it to be a little too easy, but at the same time, He was so happy he'd agreed that his suspicions vanished the second they started counting up the money to take to Frank.

* * * * *

After declaring "business management" & "corporate marketing" as her major, Candy's schoolwork took on a life of its own. Every day except for Sunday – Which she often called her "day of sleep" – was comprised of three demanding and often tiresome, arduous work assignments. Everything had to be analyzed, researched, and memorized. With all she'd been through, her assignments were allowing her to feel normal again, and she needed that more than anything. But at the same time, she was neglecting everything else, including her strip life. She decided to do something about that. Instead of researching for the next three hours, she drove home to taste–down Todd's manhood. "I guess I can bless my baby with a quicky," Candy mumbled to herself as her juices started to flow throughout her body. Forty minutes later, she was walking through the front door. At that point, all she could think of was eating Todd up, who just so happened to be coming out of the shower.

"You must've read my mind?" Candy asked while taking off her clothes. The sight of her banana red skin gave Todd an instant hard-on.

"Damn, bay!! Your ass dun got thick."

"You, like?" Candy asked teasingly as she poked out her hip, one hand snuggled deep in the curves.

"Fo,sho!" Todd blurted out his approval as fast as he could.

"Well, in that case, you have two hours to do whatever you want to do to me," Candy announced. For the next two hours, Todd did just that. Any and everything he even did, tried, or thought of was put to the test and being the team player she was, Candy pulled a few tricks out of her hat too. Candy wanted to stay and continue her mash-n-tuck but decided to pull the plug right at the two-hour mark. "We needed that," Candy thought after she washed up and got dressed. While passing the bedroom, she noticed Todd was laying on his stomach. "Poor thing," she mumbled, walking out the door. The only time he laid on his stomach after sec was when he was trying to undo an erection, and Candy knew that. That thought stayed with her the whole trip to the library. That was until a parade of bullets ripped through her beloved Benz.

CHAPTER 19

Here you go, she handed Jamie a red file with the word internal affairs stamped across. "What is this?" she asked while staring blankly at the bright red folder.

"You asked me for it," her assistant replied.

"No! I asked you to find out who the Spanish guy in the picture was.

"And I did!" She flashed Jamie a smile, "just read it... I think you'll find it very interesting."

"But this says internal affairs?"

"I know," the assistant mumbled right back right before she walked out of the office. Jamie stared at the file a few seconds longer before opening it up. Caveated to a few page report were two photos, one was identical to the one Jamie had of the well-built Spanish guy, and the other appeared to be a more recent photo of the same person, or at least Jamie thought so. Maybe they were brothers? Or close relatives, like first cousins. After she read the file, she noticed that the only two names mentioned were Lewis and Jose Rumerez. Neither one looked like Detective Lewis, which could only mean one thing? Both pictures were of Rumerez. He looked ten years older and two hundred pounds heavier. According to the report, Lewis and Rumerez were being investigated by internal affairs for extortion, murder, and stealing confiscated drugs from the evidence room. The report indicated that the case went cold after one of the C.I.s ended up missing. That was three years ago before the informant disappeared. There was never any solid proof to connect Rumerez to Lewis or to show that Lewis was involved directly in any depraved activity. Shortly after Lewis's death, it was placed with the other cold cases, and just like that, Rumerez was no longer an issue. At least not as far as internal affairs were concerned, but for Jamie, he was the last piece of the puzzle she was looking for. Now, all she had to do was put'em together.

* * * * * *

While Frank was getting on heavy coke, Dee-Dee was in the back, taking a nap. Not wanting to get high by himself, he offered her a folded twenty-dollar bill full of the dark beige powder, but she declined; she said she quit. When she tried to explain why, she was quickly waved off. "More for me," he mumbled as he scooped a small pile with his pinky finger, shoveling it up his nose. That was two days ago and a half ounce later, something he hadn't done in a longtime. He'd been for two days straight getting high, so when Dee-Dee came home from Traci's to find him wearing the same clothes, sitting in the same spot from two days ago clutching a sandwich bag half empty of cocaine, she knew it was time to take matters into her own hands.

"Frank!! I know yo ass ain't been up for two days getting on raw?"

Frank placed one finger to his lips, "why you so loud?" He whispered, looking around as if someone was hiding. "Girl, you trippen!"

"No! you the one trippen," she started opening up the curtains, "you acting like you Tony Montana, gimmie dat!" She walked over and snatched the sandwich bag out his hand. "Boy, you done lost yo mind! You can't snoot all that stuff like that, you could've burst your head, crazy."

"You heard dat?" Frank asked with an alert, ignoring her warnings.

"Heard what?"

"You ain't hear it."

"Don't start that bull…"

"Chill out, chill out," Frank motioned for Dee-Dee to back up and be quiet.

"Dis boy done lost his damn mind," Dee-Dee mumbled as Frank tip- toed past her to sneak up on whoever was in the kitchen. Halfway there, he reached for his pistol, and after a few taps on the hip, he looked back to Dee-Dee. "Throw me my (Fi)," he whispered. Dee-Dee looked down to the table, on it was an all-black glock forty.

"Boy! Ain't nobody in dat damn kitchen," she yelled while disarming the handgun.

"You bout to get us killed in here!" he rushed over and grabbed the gun instinctively. He ran to the kitchen, gun first, pulling the trigger the moment he turned the corner, but it was too late. The clip she'd tucked in her purse, and she wasn't coming off of it. The look on her face told it all. "I'll be at Traci's house – call me when you calm your ass down," Dee-Dee announced right before the door slammed. He was so peeped-up that he pointed his gun in the direction of the loud bang and stood there for the next twenty minutes, waiting for someone to come from around the corner. That was one of the reasons why he stopped sweating coke and started smoking crake; smoke made him less paranoid, not to mention it was a lot cheaper.

* * * * * *

"Kevin, thanks again for the info, you're a lifesaver, I owe you one." Jamie placed the phone back on the receiver and then thought about her last reply. "I owe you one!" she thought aloud, laughing to herself as to how Kevin might have taken that. She knew he had a crush on her, and because of that, she would exploit the possibility of them hooking up to get tip-offs and information from less guilty and more inclined to do it again. "This is it," she thought as the fax machine began chirping. After reading two of the three-page report, Peet popped into the doorway.

"You ready?"

Jamie raised a finger, requesting a few minutes to read the final page, "Almost ready," she suggested.

"You found anything else?"

Jamie tossed the last page onto her desk and then stuffed Rumerez's picture into her purse, "wouldn't you like to know?" she gloated as she walked past him.

"You play too much," he mumbled, snatching up the papers from her desk. He was only able to read a few lines before she came back.

"I thought you were ready to go?" she flashed a half smile, "Come on," she waved'em on, "I'll explain it all in the car." Trying to squeeze in a couple more lines before tossing the papers back onto the desk, he managed to spot the name Jose Rumerez.

"So who is Rumerez?"

"Rumerez was the missing informant, internal affairs had on his case."

"Ok, so how does he tie into James Patrick, Howerd Sneed, Candiace James and Lewis?"

"Do you remember the young man who had Lewis's cellphone?"

"Yeah, how did that come out?"

"Well, according to him, he got the phone from his cousin Flex. Now get this, when he shows me a picture of this Flex character, it turns out to be the kid killed at the warehouse!" Turns out that Flex was bragging about knocking off some dirty cop for his boss..."

"Lewis!" Peet blurted out.

"Now, we know that Patrick and Sneed are running buddies and that Lewis, Patrick, and Sneed crossed paths here and there..."

"Yeah, we also know that Patrick was supposed to buy these from Lewis that day. Things went crazy," Peet acknowledged.

"And being that Sneed and Patrick run together, it's highly likely Sneed was apart in some way," Jamie added.

"So where do Rumerez fit into all this?" Peet asked.

"I'll show you," Jamie pulled the picture out of her purse, "look familiar?"

"Son of a bitch!" Peet announced at first sight, "I knew something wasn't right about him, he snatched up the radio..."

"What are you doing," Jamie exclaimed.

"I'm calling in for back up to meet us at the garage," He responded – "We are going to the garage, right?" He questioned with an estranged look.

"Not so fast! Jamie replied, opposed to Peet's impulsive reaction.

"What do you mean?" He looked at Jamie, "we need to grab him before he gets ghost."

"Who says he will?" Jamie shot back, "Maybe, just maybe, he might think he's uncatchable!"

"So you just want us to go over there and say what? You're coming with us."

"You think it would work?"

"I'm serious," Peet replied... Jamie needed for the time of them to be on the same page, so when she looked over to them to see if he was paying her any attention, it upset her to find him playing with his pages.

"Have you listened to a word I've said?"

"Dammit! Gimmie your phone", Peet insisted, patting himself down. "I think I left mine on your desk?"

"What is it?" she asked sharply, sensing something wrong.

"It's Eva," he uttered, dialing as fast as possible.

"Who?"

"My wife! Eva's, my wife, Jamie." He looked at her as if she should have known that.

"Is she…"

"Dammit! She's not picking up. I need to go to my house."

"Now? But we're almost…" The look on Peet's face told Jamie all she had to know. Twenty minutes later, they were pulling up to Peet's house."

From the outside looking in, Hope appeared to possess the qualities of a true leader. His demeanor showed self-restraint, confidence, and poise, but on the inside, he was a nervous wreck. Over a hundred thoughts raced through his mind while being patted down by some young dude with fag eyes and big lips. After being thoroughly searched, he was whisked to a windowless room occupied by two small sofas and a chess set. Ten minutes later, a man looking fifties-ish walked into the room.

"So what is it I can do for you?" He walked over to Hope with his hand extended. His accent was non-American, but his pronunciation was perfect. The two shook hands and then sat down, one in front of the other with the chess board in between.

"I came to talk to you about my brother."

"Something wrong with Todd?"

"No, just the opposite," Hope uttered, "He's doing real good for himself. That's what I'm here to talk about. My brother is calling quits."

"Is that right?"

"Yeah, he umm, he bout to get married and all. You know, the family life?"

"Married?" He flashed Hope an all-white smile, "to who?" "The girl from Georgia?"

"I ain't know you knew Candygirl," Hope uttered.

"Something like that," he responded, "So Todd sent you here?"

"Not exactly," Hope responded, watching the old man turn the black side of the board to himself. "Would you mind finishing up this game with me?" the old man asked, "seems like I can never finish up this damn game."

"Yeah, I'll play."

"Good. It's your move."

Hope moved up to the edge of the couch and then made his move. "I hope I wasn't out of line calling you out of the blue like that," Hope asked.

"Nice move!" the old man mumbled to himself, his eyes never leaving the board – "looks like I've found myself a chess played." After a few minutes, the old man made his first move. "Your move!" He suggested.

"No disrespect, but I ain't come way out here to play no chess. I came to talk business."

"Ok, you wanna talk business?" – he leaned back into the sofa, legs crossed, arms folded – "Let's talk business."

"Like I was saying, Todd is calling quits, so I'm here to take his spot."

"Go on," the old man suggested.

"Now, what I need from you is simple, I need you to keep me with the same quality of coke, my brother been getting from you in the past. Oh yeah, you're gonna have to come down at least two grand a square."

"I see, and what else do you request, Mr. Hope."

"Umm sure you think dat I'm trippen, but the way I see" – He made strong eye contact with the old man – "My brother isn't as street as he should be, but he's good people's, so it kind of worked itself out."

"Works itself out? And what you mean by that?"

"Look, my lil brother grabbing fifty of deem thangs from you at fifteen a brick, you talkin' seven fifty each drop."

"And your point?"

"Look, I came to you out of respect that you and my lil'bra used to break bread, but at the same time, this here a business, ya feel me? And if you want for us to get dis money together, you gotta come down."

"Come down to what?"

"At least six fifty."

"Six fifty!..."

"I know," – Hope cut'em off, "That's a hundred grand short, but it ain't like you can't afford it. Besides, why would you let a hundred grand cause you to go outside your circle? Risk hooking up wit the wrong person.

"And because of that, you feel as though you have an angle to hustle me out of a hundred G's."

"Ain't nobody trying to hustle you... I'm trying to eat like you earing, ya feel me?"

"And just how am I eating, the old man asked curiously."

"You eating damn good pushing fifty at fifteen a piece."

"Anything else?"

"Naw, dat's it" – Hope leaned back, stretching his arms the length of the sofa, crossing his legs simultaneously. This was the most confidence he'd ever felt in his life. He was playing with the big boys now, putin' down just like he practiced in the car. This was too easy. Before you know it, He would be coping them thangs at ten a piece. Once "I get'em down that low, it's a wrap," he thought to himself.

"Good! Now that you've said all you had to say, you'll be able to listen much better. First thang first – He leaned to the edge of the seat – "you won't be grabbing fifty nothing for no six-five. That's not going to happen! Secondly, never threaten me,"

"But I..."

The old man raised a finger, cutting Hope off – "To me, a threat is a threat, whether it be physical or not."

"I feel where you coming from", Hope uttered, "but at the same time, look at it my way. This ain't no threat, all I'm saying is that you been eating good off me and my peoples for a minute now. We making money, true enough… but we ain't eating, ya feel me!" With his eyes fixed on the ceiling and his mouth twisted, the old man waited a few minutes before responding – "If you can handle seven flat." – He made eye to eye contact – "We have a deal."

"Can I get back to you on that seven?" Hope asked flatly.

"No! He shot back, "Right now would be best for both of us."

Although he felt he was being pressured, Hope agreed – "OK, I'll do seven for now."

"Glad to hear that… so when would you like to start?"

"Gimmie bout a week to get my money right."

"No problem."

"So, do I call you, or do you call me?"

"I'll call you," the old man suggested. After the old man explained to Hope how to carry himself accordingly, the two had lunch, and then Hope left. On his way back to the house, Hope noticed he was being followed. Reluctant to shake his tail, he felt it might be one of Nijé people making sure he was straight. He was right. But what he didn't know was that Nijé had him followed from and to the house, among other things.

* * * * * *

When Jamie and Peet arrived at the house, Eva was long gone. A letter was left behind informing Peet of his wife's whereabouts. Twenty minutes later, they were at "ORME". Jamie tried asking Peet if he wanted for her to stick around, but he jumped out the car with god speed. She decided to stay, guessing he wasn't in his right mind, considering he catapulted out of the front seat before the car could come to a complete stop. Unable to find a parking space, Jamie ended her ten-minute ring- around-the rosey by parking in a no parking zone. "What's the use of being a cop if you can't park where you want to!" she thought as she rushed into the lobby.

"So, how is she?"

"Don't know yet… The nurse said a doctor was coming to see…"

"It's probably nothing," she cuffed her hand around Peet's jaw, "You know a woman would come to the hospital for a hangnail."

"Yeah, you're probably right." – Peet tried to smile, but the truth of the matter was that things were more serious than he led on to believe. His wife was dying, and Jamie didn't have a clue. "I think that's the doctor," Jamie announced, pointing to a usually tall Asian man wearing the traditional white coat.

"Mr. Wise?" the doctor extended his hand, "How are you? I'm doctor, people."

"How is she doc?" his voice a bit broken up.

"I'm afraid it doesn't look that good, she…" "Is she dead?" he asked calmly.

"No!! She's not dead" – He glanced over to Jamie, then back to Peet – "But she is in a coma."

"Ah, coma?" Jamie sputtered with a dumfounded look, "What happened?"

"When can I see my wife?"

"You can see her now, but she won't be able to respond."

"I just wanna see her. It doesn't matter if she can talk or not." "Take all the time you need," Jamie suggested as the doctor walked Peet to Eva's room. Jamie felt it would be best if she stayed in the waiting room. That decision proved to be bene-ficial in more than one way as two EMAs burst through the door, each one holding the arm of Candice James.

"I'm fine!" Candy repeated for the um-tenth time, "The airbag just…"

"We just wanna make sure, ma'am!" one of the EMA's acknowledged as they whisked her past Jamie. "What is it with this girl and hospitals?" Jamie mumbled, instinctively bouncing to her feet, right on their heels. "Excuse me!" she shouted, hoping her voice could catch up with their fast pace. But, by the time she turned the corner, they were gone. Just when she thought she'd lost them, Hope and Todd scrolled right by her. Because she was bent over the water fountain, they never noticed her. "Just the man I was looking for," Jamie thought as she trailed the two of them.

"May I ask why you are following those two gentlemen?" He grabbed Jamie's shoulder – bringing her to a halt.

"Keep your hands to…" when she turned around, there was a uniformed offi-cer in front of her, she looked him up and down a few times, then pulled out her badge – "I'm a cop!"

"I'm sorry, you just looked…"

"Don't worry about it. Are they with?"

"No, but their lady friend is."

"Ms. James, you mean?"

"Yeah, that's her name," he pulled out his cuffs, "is she wanted?"

"What is she doing in the hospital?"

"She crashed her car into a light pole after being shot at by some kids with paint guns."

"Did you catch'em?"

"We caught two of them, the other one is still loose." "Is she hurt bad?"

"Not really, just a few cuts and bruises" – the young officer eyed Jamie closely – "How did you know who she was?"

"Do you mind if I came with you to question her?"

"Well, actually, I just came to get her to sign the affidavit, but you're welcome to tag along. When they walked in, all three were there, including a very attractive Asian doctor.

"She's cute," Jamie thought as the two of them met eyes.

"Ms. James, could you sign this statement for me," he handed Candy the affidavit.

"I'm sorry," she grabbed the paper, signed it, then handed it back.

"You following me?" Todd demanded, staring at Jamie with cold eyes.

"I was about to ask you the same thing," Jamie uttered.

"I'll be right back with your results, Ms. James," she gave Jamie a look over before walking out.

"Are you arresting anybody?" Hope questioned.

"Not at this moment," Jamie proposed.

"Then I'm out'a here!" Hope gave Todd some dap, then walked towards the door.

"I know why Lewis tried to set you up!!" Jamie expressed confidently.

"You just rapping white girl!" Hope uttered, slamming the door behind him.

"Your friend is in real danger" – She fixed her eyes on candy – "and I'm afraid the two of you are caught in the middle of it."

"Tell us something we don't know," Todd voiced comically.

"So you do know about the sixty kilos of cocaine?"

"Right plan, wrong man, white girl," He pulled Candy close to him, "All I was agreeing to was that young black males are in grave danger of being extinct... 'we' don't know anything bout no sixty nothing."

"What about you?" Jamie asked Candy with sympathetic eyes.

"I just told you we don't know anything," Todd snapped.

With her eyes fixed on Candy, she spoke to Todd. "Rumerez isn't going to give up until he gets the drugs back." She focused her eyes back on Todd. "He's already tried to kill you once... Who's to say he won't try to kill her if he can't get to you or your friend Howard?"

"So, let me guess? This is the part where I help you help me, right!" Jamie suggested.

"Baby, I..."

"I got dis baby girl," Todd quickly cut her off – "I'm sorry we can't help you on your case, detective, like I said, 'we' don't know anything. So if you don't mind, we'd like some time alone.

"Ok, Ms. James," – The doctor announced, coming through the door, "everything seems to be normal, and by the way, the baby appears to be just fine."

"Baby! What baby?" Todd screamed.

"Baby, I'm so sorry. I was going to tell you, but..."

"Pregnant? You pregnant, and you weren't..."

"Can we have some privacy!!" Candy demanded.

"Okay, Okay," – The doctor mumbled on her way out the door.

"Congratulations, Ms. James, and to you, Todd. Now that a baby is involved, I hope you'll take me up on my offer...if you do..."

"Goodbye!! Detective! Todd snapped.

"If you do, Ms. James, call the station and ask for Detective Lightbourne," she patted her stomach before it was too late. Jamie looked at her watch and then left Candy and Todd alone to talk. When she arrived back at the lobby, Peet was already there. "I know who killed Lewis," Jamie blurted.

"Who? Peet bounced to his feet.

"Rumerez" that's who Jamie filled Peet in on her little talk with Todd and Candy about how she felt Candy could expose Hope and Todd. Her plan was to sit and wait for Rumerez to come out of hiding. She knew it wouldn't be too long before his palms got to itching, and he came after Hope and Todd.

"You said Rumerez was the killer, but without a witness or some sort of physical evidence putting him at the crime scene, we..."

"But we do have evidence," Jamie uttered, cutting off his sentence.

"We do?"

"Yeah, remember the third blood sample? I'll bet my life he left it there."

"I hope so, Jamie, I hope so."

CHAPTER 20

Four months, ten days, and sixteen hours. That's how long it took for Jamie to find out who killed Lewis and why they did it. Normally, for her, it wouldn't take that long to put all the pieces together. A true hound dog in race form, never resting until she got her man or woman for that matter. So, for the record, this victory wasn't one she'd be dancing in the blue suede shoes about.

"So watcha got there?" Jamie questioned, strolling into her office, Peet was on the other side of the desk. Resting on the edge of the seat, elbows planted firmly on the table. In front of him was a single sheet of paper, some sort of phone list.

"Earth to Peet! Earth to Peet!" Jamie repeated, snapping and waving her hand inches from his face.

"I heard you the first time," He glanced up then back down, all while performing some sort of ritual by tapping a pencil in an unorthodox rhythm. The lines on his face told Jamie that whatever it was, it wasn't good.

"Do I need to sit down?"

"Here!" He handed her the paper.

"What is it?" she grazed her eyes over the list of numbers, then back to him.

"Those are the numbers Lewis called either the day he died or the day before."

"But we've been over this list a thousand times." she handed it back.

"This case!" She began talking with her hands, "We've overlooked so much, trying to...trying to come up with...anything."

"Maybe you're right." He leaned back in the chair, locking his fingers behind his head.

"Is Curly still in the field?" She pulled out her C-phone and then pushed the speed dial. Seconds later, a ringtone came blaring through her door.

"I'm guessing this isn't a social call?" the young redhead with freckles handed Jamie a folder.

"What's that?" Peet asked.

"Just some information I need to fill in the blanks on my reports." She looked at her watch, "it's time to go!" She pulled out her sidearm, checked it over, then replaced it back in the holster. "I told the others to meet us at the garage."

"About time!" Peet's voice spent.

"I thought you'd be happy about that," Jamie responded. All three power walked down to their cars. Jamie and Peet rode together while Candy drove the unmarked.

It wouldn't be long now before this case would be over and done.

"What about Sneed and Patrick?" Peet questioned.

"What about them?"

* * * * * *

"You're going to arrest them, right?"

"They aren't my problem." She waved her eyes in his direction.

"Not your problem?" He gave her an indeterminate gaze, "Where the hell did that come from?"

"Who killed Lewis?"

"Who killed… what's your point?"

"My point is, we" – She gestured to herself than him – "do homicide cases not…"

"So what, just let'em have the drugs, pollute they whole goddamn city?"

"You know that's not what I meant." She peeped through her rearview… "Did you see Curly pass by us?"

"He's still behind…" he took a look back, but Curly was nowhere in sight. That's odd, he was just two cars behind us.

"Here," – She tossed Peet the phone, "Call and see if he's having car trouble."

"What's the number?"

"Hit speed dial, too."

Peet did as told, but what happened next left knots in his stomach. Nothing about this case made any sense, and just when things started to incertitude would creep back into play like a thief in the night. How did Curly play into this web of smoke and mirrors? Why did Lewis call him the day before he died? Why didn't Curly bring such valuable information to the table? What was he hiding?

"If you don't push send, it won't dial," Jamie suggested, looking over to Peet. Peet didn't respond. He couldn't. He was in shock. "She's going to be fine, Peet." She eased the phone out of his hand and called Curly. Two rings later, he was on the other end.

"I took a shortcut. How far are you from the garage?"

"Ten, fifteen tops," Jamie looked over at Peet, who was lost in a daze.

"I thought it would be best if we came at different times, hope you're not…"

"No! No, that's probably the best way. No one moves until I say so."

"Oky, doky," Curly responded before hanging up.

"He took a short cut, should be there by now.", Jamie explained to Peet.

"What division was Curly in before he joined us?"

"Quite a few, why you ask?"

"Just curious," He responded.

"Curious," Jamie repeated. She knew he was lying. He never just asked questions, there was always a catch twenty-two to his acquisitiveness. "So where is this coming from?"

"I know what you're thinking," He waved her off, "It's not even like that."

"Like what?"

"It just dawned on me that I've been working with him for about six months now, and I don't really know anything about'em. That's all."

"If there was anything else, you'll tell me, right?"

"Of course I would!!" Peet was lying, but he had good reason to. He understood Jamie better than anyone. The thoughts in his head were all circumstantial, and because of that, he didn't want Jamie going out there on a whim. He had to do some backtracking first, check a few traps, call in a few favors, and see what came up, then bring Jamie up to speed. Besides, if he was right on his hunch, taking down Rumerez first would be in their best interest. Peet had a few questions he needed answered, and Rumerez was the only one who could answer them.

Jamie looked Peet over a few times before responding. She thought she might've been able to pick up on something, but she didn't. "Let's see," her eyebrow arched up as her memory began to reclaim past knowledge, "he's been with forensics, coroner, internal affairs task..."

"Drugs?"

"Yeah, something else... can't remember though."

"Wife and kids?"

"Not that I know of, no." Jamie glanced through the rearview for the ninth time, she didn't feel like she was being followed, it was just some habits never die. "Why do I get the feeling I'm being..."

"You're not!"

"You don't know what I was going to say?"

"I'm not interrogating you if that's what you're thinking."

"Feels like it," Jamie mumbled to herself.

"Are you sure he's there?"

"He said he took a shortcut..."

"Not Curly. Rumerez?"

"Oh yeah, he's there," she made a silly face towards herself, "thought we were still on Curly?" "Is he armed?"

"Most likely," Jamie uttered before putting the car in park. From where she was parked, their view was limited by a tall wooden fence, only allowing them to see who came out or who was going in. That was the bad part. The good part was that whoever was behind the wooden fortress wouldn't see them until they made their presence known. Jamie was banking on that to be her rabbit out of the hat trick. After a few minutes of watching the abnormal ins and outs of the garage, Jamie pulled the crew together four blocks away to go over the plan. This was it. The day she looked forward to. The day she was able to arrest the killer of Detective Lewis.

"I want him alive!" She waved her finger down a line of plain clothes officers, "But if it comes down to you or him... you know what to do."

"Okay, boys and girls, pare up. It's showtime!" Peet's tone vocalized both fear and excitement as they loaded back into their unmarks and headed to the garage. Normally, Peet and Jamie would always be together on any raid, but on this day, she felt it would be best if Peet rode with Curly. This was his first raid. Although he was on task, he never made an arrest in the field. No matter how many times

Jamie went to arrest a murder suspect, she would always get butterflies. For her, it was a vital tool she used to stay alert. Unlike her first takedown, during her first thirty-six months on the force – better known as the rookie years – when she was all gun-ho, causing her partner to be killed after she took a bullet for her, back then, she had those same butterflies, she just misinterpreted them for an adrenaline rush rather than a cautious light. But that was then, and this is now, and right Jamie had a time of eight – two to each can – positioned at their designated spot. She placed every one according to their capability, she didn't want anyone doing more than what they could do. She went out of her way to eliminate all gaw-ho's and to make sure no one died under her command.

"Listen up, everybody!" Jamie demanded in her soft but stern voice, "As soon as the older couple come out, we're going in. Peet?"

"Yeah, I know. Be careful. Be smart, Be..."

"Just checking," She let out a light giggle.

For the next twenty minutes, Jamie and her crew waited for the older couple in the white Cadillac to exit the building and get out of harm. Those twenty minutes felt like twenty years. The butterflies in Jamie's stomach started to turn into knots, her palms began to swell, and her mouth became dry. It wasn't until those last moments – the quiet before the storm – the point of no return that everything seemed surreal, time was at a complete standstill, and the only sound within reach was their own heartbeat as they watched the Cadillac pull out. Make a right and drive toward the safety mark. It was on and popping. The game plan was airtight. Team five covered the back ally, leading one of the doors to the garage, they used the car as a traffic barrier while both men manned the door. Team two covered the front entrance, duplicating team fives strategic tactics, while teams six, seven, eight, and three bee-lined into the garage, Jamie at the helm. As the sound of roaring engines and blaring lights crammed into the already cluttered chop shop, Jamie noticed something strange. The place was empty, not a villain in sight, and not even the watchdogs were in earshot. Peets can was the last to pull up, but he was the first to jump out. He'd notice just as quickly as his counterpart did.

"Gone!!" Pet blurted out furiously, "That bastard got away." he waved his hands franticly. "They're all gone..." He pointed his finger at Jamie, "This is bullshit," he fixed his eyes on Curly. Then it happened. Curly's eyes inadvertently shifted to the left, a few seconds later, multiple rounds were being fired. Jamie took two in the upper back. The force of the shots pushed her headfirst back into the passenger seat. Peet screamed for his partner, but she didn't respond. He tried to get near her, but the slew of bullets kept him pinned down. Besides the sounds of metal rippling through metal. Peet's agonizing cries for her to hold on would be the last words Jamie heard.

* * * * *

Neither one of them said a word during the ride home. Candy's reason for not speaking was simple, Todd didn't speak. Her plan was to play by eating, let him open up first, then feed off his vibe. When they were alone at the hospital, he never acknowledged her being pregnant, he was more or less concerned about her accident – at least, that's how Jamie took it. For Todd, it was a little different. His silence came out of confusion. Todd wasn't sure how he should be feeling after hearing his girl was pregnant, doubt was painfully setting in one hand, and joy was rapidly rushing through his veins on the other. He was on an emotional roller-coaster pulling him in so many directions he became physically exhausted. Her silence told him that she knew about the baby before the accident, but why she wouldn't tell him the day she found out raised red flags everywhere. That was the doubt whispering in his ear. The joyous part told him to play it cool, take her home, boil some tea, talk things over and figure out their next. He followed his heart and listened to his joyous past.

"Be right back," Todd kissed Candy, then walked into the kitchen. Minutes later, he returned with two cups of orange flower, Candy's favorite tea. "Thanks!" she reached for the oversized mug, legs crossed Indian stance while sitting solo in the loveseat.

"Figured... you know, you need to start eating and drinking healthy, baby and all," he responded before squatting in front of her, his back resting on her knees.

"I'm going on two months," Candy whispered between the sips of her tea.

"Are you sick?"

"Sick, how?"

"I thought when women get pregnant, they get all sick and stuff?"

"It's called morning sickness, and no, I'm not expecting any of that."

"But I thought you said...well, I heard the doctor say you..."

"Not all women go through that," Her words came out like a schoolteacher.

"So you're two months pregnant?"

"According to the doctor," Candy implied, her index finger making circles on Todd's nape.

"Are you planning on keeping it?" When he realized what he said, he quickly turned around. To his surprise, Candy had an indeterminate gaze in her eyes. "I didn't mean it like that!" He wrapped his arms around her, placing her head into his chest.

"Baby, I'm scared," Candy mumbled.

Todd leaned Candy back in the chair – "Don't you go worrying yourself over nothing. We are in this together." He wiped the tears off her face and then gave her a kiss.

"Do you love me, Todd?" She placed the cup of her hand under his chin.

"Of course I do!"

"No, I mean really love me... In love with me, I should say."

"Same difference!" He took both cups back to the kitchen.

"No, sweetheart, it's not," She retorted. Todd returned with two fresh cups, handed her one and then sat back between her legs.

"You complete me if that's what you're asking," Todd responded.

Candy wrapped her arms around his neck, resting her cheek on top of his head – "I'm keeping the baby I told you I didn't mean it like that."

"What about you? You want the baby?"

"You said you was keeping it, right?"

"That's not what I asked you! Yes or no!"

"I'll be right back," Todd bounced to his feet, gave Candy a kiss, then fast walked to the back, leaving Candy alone with only her thoughts to comfort her. Twenty minutes later, he returned to find Candy balled up in the chair, her knees pulled up to her chest, face buried in her lap, arms wrapped around her legs.

"Come on, baby," He extended his hand.

When Candy looked up, Todd was wearing house slippers and a towel wrapped around his waist.

"Where we going?" She asked, already knowing the answer.

"Just come on," He grabbed her hand and led her to the bathroom. The bathroom was one place Candy could find serenity, she designed it that way, and Todd knew that. Because of the impassioned nature, the two of them share in the bathroom, all Todd had to do was light a few candles and spread a few petals to create the exact mood he was looking for. Words could only describe how he felt to a bare minimum, so he decided to only use a few. Sex. Sex between two people who shared the same passion equalled fireworks, but between the shit taken, orgasms, and pipe dreams, sex in itself wasn't what he was looking for. He wanted their souls to hop on the ninth cloud and ride to places such as Zion, Laputa, Goshen, the land of Beulah and back. He wanted utopia.

"This was what you were doing?" Candy voiced in a girlish tone, her hands muffled around her mouth, "I can't believe you did this...but why?"

"I'm glad you asked," he flashed a boyish grin and then started undressing her. After she was completely naked, he placed her in the tub of warm water and rose petals. He added a bottle of baby oil to give the water a silky feeling and to enhance the fragrance. So far, so good. The back of Candy's thighs rested on top of Todd's. Her wide hips did not leave much room for his knees, forcing them to bow out. He positioned them to it within arm's reach, he put just enough water to cover their hips, leaving the top half exposed.

"Before we begin." He gave Candy a stern look... "This isn't about sex."

"We've never been that way, any way," she responded.

"Not saying it like that... just need for you to come in with that mindset, that's all."

"Come into what?"

"Here," Todd extended out his arms, palms flat, upright, "Remember..."

"I know, I know," she placed her palms on top of his, "this isn't about sex. What're we doing?"

"Utopia," he voiced without words but just the motion of his mouth, "I'll go first, then you'll go. Okay?"

"Okay, but how are we going to do Utopia?"

"First, you have to find a place where your heart and mind can become one. Once you've found that place, block out all your bad vibes. After you've accomplished that, you'll be able to purify my skin with your hands and your mouth, not your tongue, will be used to intertwine our souls. Then, and only then, will we consummate."

"I thought you said no sex."

"Trust me, it's not what you think... close your eyes, take four deep breaths, then open them, okay." Candy did as she was told, she closed her eyes, took four deep breaths, and then opened her eyes. Using his hands as cups, Todd poured the warm water down Candy's back, around her neck and off her shoulders. Next, he took his thumbs, pressed them against her forehead, and wildly massaged in small circular motions. He performed the same technique on her temples and right under her jawbone. He did that for the next ten minutes, afterwards, he used another then minutes to handwipe her down, starting from her face, down to her toes. Once that was completed, he commenced kissing. According to Todd, the mouth was the focal point for convergence, through it alone, would their souls be able to intertwine. With his lips slightly opened, Todd pressed them firmly against the lower half of her neck, creating a suctioned like feel when he pulled away. From there, he went on to her shoulders, back up to her face, then her chest and stomach, arms and hands, thighs, then ending with her feet. What Candy was feeling at that moment was unimaginable, it was as if her insides were almost at a standstill, but her outer parts were vibing with godspeed. For her, this level of intimacy made her feel more of a woman than she'd ever felt, and as a person she felt completely whole. Candy's touches were identical to Todd's touches. She performed the same ritual to a tee. Lil'mama was on point, and thanks to Todd working his mojo. Things seemed that much easier for her to find that place in her mind. He enabled her to block out everything negative and concentrate more on intertwining their souls as she kissed away, focusing her plump lips more on his face, neck, and ears. After she finished mimicking his every move, Todd pulled Candy's hips up to his, sliding in her at the same time, never unlocking his arms from around her lower back. The consummation was complete with that move. The fifth element made its 360, and Todd and Candy were able to find their utopia. There was no turning back after that. It was official; they were soulmates for life.

CHAPTER 21

Time was running out, and things were getting worse by the minute. Jamie, while laid, slumped over the driver seat. Feet hanging out, showing no signs of life, Peet remained pint at the rear of the car, wisely avoiding anyone taking shots at him. He tried getting close to Jamie but was pushed back by a handful of hot. He tried calling her, but like the last time, she didn't answer. Just two years ago, they were in a similar situation, the bad guys had the ups on them, and time was of the essence. Jamie pulled them out of that with one of her "T.J. hooker out'a body experience," but Jamie wasn't able to do that this time. Peet knew that this one was his shoulder.

"I need for everybody to listen up," Peet said with one stern tone, reload and hit me back.

"Sir, what about you?"

"Hopefully, the diversion will give me enough time to make it up the stairs." Peet waited a few seconds, gathered up his courage, then gave the signal. All teams did just as they were ordered, giving Peet his chance to make a break for the stairs, but before he could take it, curly was already in full stride, climbing the flight of stairs heroically, forcing Peet to back down and give him cover. The counterattack was executed at the right time, giving them that edge they needed. Now the tables were turned, they began picking off Rosco's men one by one.

"Going somewhere?" Curly's voice reached Rosco's ears at the same time his bullet entered the chest of his righthand man.

"Hell naw...yo ass supposed to be..." Images of Rosco shooting Curly rushed to the front of his memory bank.

"Dead?" Curly replied with a hostile sneer, "I told Lewis to kill you a long time ago, but he wouldn't listen" – He aimed the gun at Rosco's head – "and now, now, I have to chase two street punks and a bitch about my dope, when I should be somewhere in bora-bora getting my dick sucked." He pulled the trigga twice more, hitting Rosco once in the head and the other in the chest. He walked over to Rosco, pulled a gun from out of his desk and placed it in his hand, Rosco's finger to discharge the small handgun. Now that Rosco was dead, there was no one left to implicate Curly to Lewis or the kilos of cocaine stolen from the evidence room. Curly anticipated that Lewis wouldn't take heed to his warnings and eventually die at the hands of Rosco for not doing so. He saw that because he set the stage and let nature take its course, but what he didn't expect was for Rosco to be robbed for the dope by two wannabe thugs. Before Rosco made such a hodge-podge of things, all Curly had to do was wait a few days after Jamie couldn't find any clues, go and kill Rosco and get the dope – which he didn't – get all fingers to point his way, kill him then get the dope. The only problem with that was that the longer the case stayed open, the more of a chance he could be exposed. That fact alone forced him to kill Rosco ASAP and go after Hope and Todd later on. When Curly came out of the office, he saw Peet helping Jamie take off her vest.

"Next time you decide to play hooky while we're in a gunfight, could you at least take down one bad guy," Peet let out a slight laugh.

"What the hell did I get shot with?" Jamie asked.

Peet held the vest up to his face – "Looks like 45 slugs."

"Feels like I got hit with a sledgehammer."

"I would imagine so," Peet coped a squat next to Jamie.

"Shouldn't you be helping me get up?"

"Paramedics on their way," He tapped her on the knee, "so until then, relax."

"Was any of our people hurt?"

"Nothing major, but I think one of the new guys ended up with a flesh wound."

"What about Rumerez? Did we…"

"Rosco's dead," Curly informed the two of them.

"Did you kill'em?" Peet's request was more of a challenge than a question, and Curly sensed it.

"I tried to take him alive," He fixed his eyes on Jamie, "but the bastard had a gun and said he wasn't going to prison."

"What made you run up the stairs when you knew I was…"

"I was closer to the steps," Curly cut into Peet's question, "I figured I had a better chance of not getting shot rushing up the stairs, that's all!"

"Or maybe you wanted to get to Rumerez before anyone else?"

"Meaning what?" Curly asked.

"Meaning you wanna tell me how they knew we were coming!" Peet bounced to his feet, jumping straight into Curly's face, his fist balled so tight his knuckles turned white.

"You think I set this up!!"

"Maybe!"

"Peet, what the hell are you doing?" Jamie staggered to her feet, putting herself between the two.

"What the hell is your problem?"

"You're my problem," Peet reached over Jamie and shoved Curly, "you've been…"

"Been what?" Curly asked, shouting him back.

"Stop it, you two." – Jamie fixed her eyes on Peet, "where is this coming from?"

"Forget about it," Peet snapped, "the paramedics are here anyways, I'm going to check up on the rest of the team," He gave Curly the coldest stare over, "See how they doing."

"What is his problem?"

"Cut'em some slack, it's not every day your partner is almost killed, ya know."

"Maybe you're right," He glanced over to Peet, who was shooting daggers at him with his eyes.

"Trust me, U know my partner."

"I believe you do," Curly responded, but he wasn't buying it. He knew Peet was holding back on something, but what? Whatever it was, he had to find out fast. Then he had to kill him before he told anybody. After the medics checked over Jamie and her crew, they spent the next hour or so cleaning up things.

"Excuse me!" Jamie raised up a finger, then walked away from the small crowd to answer her c-phone – Detective Lightbourn.

"You told me to call if I had any information for you."

"Who am I speaking to?" the voice sounded familiar, but Jamie wasn't sure.

"Where are you?"

"Is this..."

"You want my help or not?"

"Gimmie, what'cha got?" Jamie replied.

"Not over the phone... but if you can find a place where no one can see us, I'll..."

"What about your place?" Jamie implied.

"I don't think that would be such a good idea."

"How about the university?"

"That'll work...Know your way around campus?"

"Not really, I've only been out there a few times," Jamie explained.

"Meet me at the science building behind the cafeteria."

"On my way," – Jamie hung up, waved Peet over and explained what was going on. He offered to ride with her, but she insisted on going alone. Thirty minutes later, she was pulling into the student parking lot.

CHAPTER 22

After all the "job well done" pats on the backs and numerous articles in all the local newspapers and magazines about them solving the case of the slain dirty cop. Peet decided to tail curly for a few days. His gut told him that Curly was responsible for both Lewis and Rumerez's deaths and that he was still up to his eyeballs in some type of dirt. The first two days turned out to be nothing of use. He followed Curly around to a few spots, nothing out of the ordinary, not as far as Curly was concerned. Then, on the fifth day, things were starting to look more productive. That turned out to be a bust. He followed Curly for nearly six hours only to observe him getting a blow job from an overweight Spanish woman in a Winn-Dixie outfit. Thinking this day was going to play out like the others, Peet almost called it quits. Almost, but he was determined to find something... anything, and just like that, his stubbornness paid off. I'm not sure what he'd come up on, but his gut was telling him it was worth hanging around for. Judging by the manicured lawns, foreign cars, and oversized homes, it was obvious that this wasn't a place to come sight see. Because the community was so spaced out, Peet had to fall back further than he expected so that he wouldn't be noticed when Curly pulled over. "What're you up to?" Peet thought out loud. His eyes pay attention to Curly's every move. "Was he parked in front of one of his drug buddies' house? Was he about to meet someone he was supplying? Or was he seeing if anyone was following him?" All those thoughts crossed Peet's mind, but in the end, his stubbornness overpowered all doubts. So he stayed and waited for his next move. Twenty minutes later, for his confirmation, he noticed a young black woman right out of a Spike Lee movie come to the door to meet with the cable guy. To no surprise, Curly's focus was on the same ghetto diva.

"I'm coming," DeeDee yelled from the bathroom, rushing her feet to the front door as the doorbell continued to ring – "I said I am coming," she repeated, but the bell kept ringing. "I said...I was coming," She snatched open the door. "Oh, hell naw – yellah boy?"

"Man, I thought yo ass was some white girl on the phone?" He uttered.

"White girl?" she waved'em in, "You know you tried me then. Boy, I thought you were working for frito-lay?"

"I am, I just do this cable thing Mondays and Thursdays. I'm trying to get this money, ya feel me."

"I feel ya," she responded, then walked him to the living room, "the socket over there."

After showing Yellah where to hook up the cable, Dee-Dee went back to the bathroom to check on her test. "This can't be right," she mumbled, balancing the small white stick on the corner of the sinktop. Maybe she did something wrong?

Being this was her first time taking a pregnancy test, she could have misread the instructions. She re-read it, then read it again. Everything the box said to do, she did. Yes, and still, she wasn't pregnant. What was it? What went wrong? Was it his age? Or maybe those damn ex-pills messed Franky up so he couldn't get her pregnant. Dee-Dee thought of all that, but when it all boiled down, she realized her homegirl just didn't know what the hell she was talking about. Discouraged and frustrated, she moped back into the living room.

"Gimmie a sec!" he mumbled, sensing her presence in the room, "I'm almost finished."

"How do you know I was in here?" she asked before flopping in the lazy boy.

"Cuz umm like dat!" He rose off one knee and stuck something in his back pocket.

"Is that right?"

With a slight arch in his back, Yellah stuck out one foot with his arms spread out up to his chest, "All a nukka mussing is a few chunks, some gear and a nice whip…I ain't ugly", he gave himself a quick look over, "man if I had any f that a bitch ah be giving me head every night!"

"Child, please… you would want your dick sucked every night"- They both start laughing.

"I'm just keeping it real."

"You just like your brother!"

"Talk yo ass off, I don't know ah nukka out the hood who think otherwise." Yellah looked around, "Where ya bathroom? I gotta piss", He grabbed his crotch and twisted his knee.

"Down the hall to ya right – yo ass better not piss on my seat either, Mr.Thug-life." When Yellah went into the bathroom, he was surprised to see a pregnancy stick hanging halfway off the sink counter – He took a peek, it was negative. He took his piss and returned back to the living room.

"So where's pops?" He asked slyly.

"Who?"

"Yo pops," he started laughing, "Word around the hood is that you dot ah old ass cat."

"Frank ain't dat old," Her words were more of a challenge than a statement, "Trust me, my baby fuck game is up to par."

"Whatever," he replied.

"Whatever, my ass! My baby knows how to lay pipe better than yo green ass!"

"Get out ya feelings." He pulled out a sack of green, "Since you ain't pregnant, you wanna blow one?"

"Pregnant?" she asked cautiously.

"Knock it off, you know a nukka seen the lil test – what's up we straight?" He flashed the clear sack of green.

"Yeah, we straight...I need to clear my head anyways", she confessed. Dee-Dee went and grabbed a couple of blunts from the kitchen, came back and began her smoke session with her childhood friend Yellah.

* * * * *

The only thing Frank could remember before the collision was the feeling the cocaine gave him the second it rushed through his bloodstream. He couldn't recall jumping lanes and running into a minivan, caring for a man, wife, and newborn. He had no recollection of the metal rod piercing his shoulder on the face that he'd been cut out of his car by the fire department and rushed along with the family of three to the hospital. To make matters worse, when he finally became conscious, he found himself handcuffed to a bed. When he pulled his arm a few times, the rattling noise from metal on metal woke up a distinguished man sitting in the corner wearing designer glasses and a silver badge around his neck.

"I would take those off if you ask nicely," he suggested to Frank.

"Who the hell is you?" Frank demanded.

"Where are my manners?" he offered his hand, "I'm agent Skies."

"Agent who?" Frank shook his hand but quickly pulled it away when he heard the word "agent".

"Agent Skies!" He repeated, "But I don't want to harm you." – He pulled his chair to the side of the bed. "Yes. You're in somewhat of a bind."

"A bind?"

He looked at Frank with a half smirk – "Like I was saying, you're in a bit of a bind, but luckily, you can get out of it with only a few bumps and bruises."

"What type of bind am I in? And just how am I supposed to get out of it?"

"Very simple," he leaned in closer, "just tell me everything you know about Nigí Rousseau."

"Nigí Roo-see-me what, me what?"

"Rou-say-u", Agent Skies responded, "Nigí Rousseau."

"Never heard of 'em!"

"Maybe if you'd look, you might have..."

"If I could help you, I would, Agent...Skies, but I'm afraid I don't know."

"Anything or anybody for that matter."

"So far, I've lost two agents and close to three hundred grand in equipment and manpower." He rearranged the pictures, "So, if I didn't think you, no, if I didn't know you knew something," he handed Frank the pictures, "I wouldn't be here wasting my time."

"I told you I..."

"Once you look at them, you might see things a little more clearly." Reluctant to view the photos, Frank thumbed through them anyway. In his hands, he held a surveillance picture of him and Hope at the Magic Mall – he thumbed through some more, another picture. This one was of him and Dee-Dee. The rest of the pictures were people he'd never seen before.

"Am I under arrest?"

"Of course you are," he lifted the badge from his chest.

"So what the hell was all about taking off these damn cuffs?"

"You didn't ask nicely," Skies shot back, "or are you?"

"Maybe! Maybe not!"

"That's not gonna cut it," Skies informed him, "As of right now, you're being charged with possession with intent to distribute cocaine— possession of a firearm by a convicted felon manufacturing…"

"Manufacturing?"

"The glass bowls we found had residue in them." – Skies snapped his finger a few times, "I forgot about that crack! Remember when I told you you were in a bit of a bind? I lied. That crack we found, that crack plus your past history, just put your ass in a slingshot." - Skies was starting to see the fear in Frank's eyes-

"I told you I don't know no damn Nigî", Frank snapped.

"And I believe you, but that doesn't change the fact that you crashed out with twenty kilos of cocaine hidden in your SUV. What were you doing with this?" He tossed a glass tube into his lap, "You back smoking that stuff? I thought you quit. Don't look so surprised, like I told you, if I didn't think you could help me, I wouldn't be here."

Frank looked down at the glass pipe, feeling ashamed about relapsing – "So what if I didn't?"

"This isn't the time to be on that soldier… whatever you call it, you're looking at forty years." "Forty," he repeated, hoping it would sink into his head. "You're forty-two now, you wanna spend the next forty years in a federal prison?" -Frank didn't respond- "I didn't think so!" Tears of anger began to roll down Frank's face. He was caught between a rock and a hard place. From the moment Skies introduced himself, Frank knew what the lick was, he just played it by ear to see just what the white boy knew, which was everything. Frank didn't know the name of Hope's plug-in, just that he was Haitian, but he knew Skies knew that. Judging by the picture, they'd been watching them for at least three months, maybe longer. But why not grab Hope and Nigî? Why him? Why was he so important? And how did he get to the hospital so fast? Now, Frank had to figure out how to get the mud off his shows before he walked on the rug.

"So what you talking bout?"

Skies handed him his cell phone – "Call Hope, tell him you were in a car accident…not unless that's some sort of code? Do you use phone codes?"

"We don't have codes," Frank uttered.

"Okay, call him and let'em know you'll be home in a few days. Tell him everything is straight on your end and that he has nothing to worry about."

"That's it? That's all I gotta do?"

"For now," Skies mumbled

"What dat mean… for now."

"It means just that! For now, that's all I need for you to do – don't worry, I will only be a phone call away." A million reasons why he shouldn't be making the phone call ran through his mind as his finger pushed away at the seven-digit number. After only two rings, Hope's voice came blaring through the phone. Skies adjusted the volume so that he could hear what both men had to say. Frank hated it had to come to this, but what other choice did he have? He had to tell himself that the game was hard, but it's fair and that you only get to play with the cards you were dealt.

Hope: Talk to me?

Frank: Just calling to let'cha know dat I got into a lil fender bender, but dat um okay.

Hope: You at da crib? Or you still at ol'girl house?

Frank: Um, still at ol'girl house…well actually, um, at the hospital, mess my shoulder up!

Hope: You had the kids in the car, wit'cha?

Frank: Yeah, but they all had on seatbelts, so they straight.

Hope: You want me to come and get'em

Frank: Nah, they cool, I called my Uncle George to come and get'em.

Hope: Your Uncle George?

Frank: On my mama's side, the one used to stay off of Washington and Jackson

Hope: Oh, ok, ok, now I know who you talking bout! So, how long before you make it to the crib?

Frank: Doc said I can bounce tomorrow.

Hope: Den, I'll just holla at'cha tomorrow. One! Frank: One!

"That was colorful," Skies commented on their illusory jargon.

"Now what?" Frank asked coldly, disregarding his comical attempt to get a buddy buddy with him.

"Nothing! Just let the doctors do their doctoring, and I'll call you when you get back to Florida."

"Call me how? I thought my cellphone was broken up in the crash?"

"You thought wrong." – Skies pulled the C-phone out of his pocket and tossed it to him, "you were the only one hurt. Thank God! You just get better, and I'll call you in a few days."

After Skies left the hospital, Frank was desperate to call Hope back and explain to him what had just taken place. He wanted to tell him that the feds were deep in their game room and that they were trying to use him (Frank) to build a case on Nigí. But then he thought about it. How was Hope going to react after hearing something like that? If given the opportunity, would he throw him (Frank) to the wolves in order to save his own ass? Maybe he was already working with Skies from the jump. That would explain the picture, and it would most definitely explain how he got to the hospital as soon as the crash happened – Frank didn't want to feed into any of his ambivalence, he understood from that point on out, every move had to be calculated, and like the old saying goes: "Bet carefully because dead broke is a muthacuker."

CHAPTER 23

Two years ago, Todd would have never entertained the thought of hanging out with old white men involved in the stock market or putting his own money into it, for that matter. Back then, he thought – and most back people, young and old – that that was a white man's thing, like thug life was a black man's thing. Growing up in the hood, you were taught that if a black person bared a hand in such things as the stock market, they were either high class or bougie. Something looked down on in the hood, but that was then, and this is now. Todd was eager to learn as much as possible, so he decided to sit in on the first day of trading. He'd pictured flying first class to New York, visiting that exchange building he had seen every time he would go to his lawyer's office. He even envisioned himself rubbing shoulders with some of these big-time stockbrokers, but instead, he found himself downtown in some high-price lawyer's office on the twentieth floor, staring at three oversized monitors, each displaying colorful charts that changed by the minute. At first, things were boring, then things started to change. Todd began to feel that rush he would get when he was chasing cars as a youth. He wasn't sure why he was feeling as such, but the thrill of anticipation got his blood flowing.

"Ok, no... that's fine... talk to you tomorrow", the old man hung up the phone, then leaned back into his chair. "Congratulations," he announced to Todd.

"Congratulations?" Todd repeated in a disgusted tone – "What type of time you on!"

"'Type of time?', what does that mean?"

"It mean I just lost ten grand, and you act like dat ain't nothing... dat's what dat mean!"

"Mr. Patrick"

"Todd!"

"Ok, Todd." He walked over to the wet bar – "drink?" he lifted up a small glass, he got no response but took the liberty of fixing two drinks, then took a seat next to Todd. "What bothers you the most – the amount you lost on the loss itself?" He handed Todd a drink – Todd thought about the question, then took a sip – "Both!" He responded.

"I don't understand?"

"Understand, what?" Todd uttered.

"You're acting as if you never took losses when you were in the streets?"

Flashbacks of when Todd had to throw nine ounces away came to mind – "You know what, you right."

"You will make money, young man, I promise you that" – He gulped down the 17 year old congniac – "And I'll all but guarantee you'll take a few losses here and there," the old man got up and fixed another drink.

"So you're saying I'll make more than I lose..."

And as the old saying goes: Therein lies the challenge! For the next two hours, they said and picked each other's brains while downing a few more drinks. They talked about everything from marriage living in the hood, to corporate America. Although Todd wasn't as inclined to world events as the old man, he was surprised by his vast knowledge of the infrastructure of the American government. A government he recognized as the biggest mafia family in the world, the corlions to the hundredth power.

"Are you serious...ah mafia family!" The old man burst into a deep, bellow laugh.

"Knock it off!" Todd retorted, matching the old man's ear to ear grin.

"Mafia family?" He repeated, his laughter a little louder – "So what! I'm a part of the mob, too?"

"Hell yeah!" Todd snapped, doctors, lawyers, judges, policies, CEOs of big companies. All y'all clicked up. Y'all just can't bang wit dem boys.

"You have quite an imagination, young man."

"You can call it that, but where I'm from, we call it being on ya square."

"Would you like to get high with me?"

"Naw, old head, I don't fuck wit no dope."

"I thought all young blacks shared marijuana?"

Todd started laughing – "You trippen old man! First of all, all black people don't smoke weed, and secondly, we don't call our tree dope... you said dope, and I'm thinking... getting on raw or smoking hard."

"Raw what? I thought hard meant being badass."

"Nevermind. Yeah, I'll blow one wit'cha. Yo, rich ass aught to have day fly." The old man left the office and returned with a sandwich bag full of a hydroponically grown weed. Its dark purplish color and orange hair told Todd that the old man had good taste in the greenery department and expensive taste at that.

"Don't drag on that too hard," he warned Todd, "this batch came out more potent than expected."

"Dis batch? You grow your own green?"

"Of course.", he replied, but the redness of Todd's eyes and the heavy coughing let the old man know his warning came too late.

"What dah hell you put in dis weed!" Todd screamed, the panic in his voice overshadowed him, beating his fist against his chest.

"I tried to tell you to take it easy," the old man reminded him.

"Thanks for warning," Todd replied facetiously.

"Have you thought about what type of legacy you want to leave to your loved ones? Say, a hundred years from now." Todd pondered over the question, then shrugged his shoulders – "Never thought about a hundred years from now!"

"So why would anybody take such…risks… so many chances, day in and day out, if it wasn't for the benefit of generations to come?" The old man's question was more of an admonition than an inquiry.

"Not all young blacks turn our backs on our kids," Todd snapped, "some of us are hardworking!"

"What about their children?" He asked in a subtle manner.

"My children gonna raise their children the way they see fit," Todd responded.

"Typical," – the old man began giggling. "You wanna know why the rich stay rich and the poor… you know the rest, yeah let me hear yo version?"

"It's simple. Rich people look at their money as mean tools in the game of life to build a strong future, while poor, the poor is just the opposite."

"Meaning?"

"Meaning, the poor don't look towards the future so long as they have money today."

"Overlooking their tomorrows!" Todd answered.

"Exactly!" the old man shot back, "the market goes deeper than just making money, young man. The market will allow you to open up doors and structure foundations for you and your family long after you're dead and gone."

"The hundred years you talken bout?"

"That's the legacy I was talking about!" the old man advised Todd. After a few more joints, the old man talked to Todd about business cycles, candle stick charts, market structure, and how interest rates affect the stock market. Todd might have left the office ten grand short, but before he left, he had a better understanding of life, making him that much more determined to leave the street alone.

* * * * * *

Curly's patience was all but run out. He'd been sitting in his car for the last hour or so, and the cable guy was still in the house with the young black girl; on top of that, he was growing tired of Peet's "good cop – bad cop heroics," and the fact that he was snugged in an unmarked – just a few yards away – behind him irritated him even more. Forced with a deli man, he weighed his options: Not sure how long the cable man was going to be, it just might be best for him to leave and come back. But if he were to just leave after waiting so long, he might raise doubt that he knows Peet's been following him. On the other hand, he could follow through with the plan and risk Peet overreacting and bolting into the house. He decided to risk raising red flags he turned over the engine and drove off, and just as expected, Peet wasn't too far behind; incognito, of course, or at least he thought so. "I'm sick of this crap!" Curly thought aloud, his eyes fixed on Peet, trailing six cars behind. Only took his eyes long enough to dial out on his e-phone. After two rings, someone picked up.

"Wuz up homey? Long time no hear, I thought."

"How far are you from Webb and Trailhome Road?"

"Bout, bout twenty. Why? What's cracken?"

"Fo show, big homey! – please believe me", he shouted with excitement.

"Dress her up! She has a date... don't be late, little homey." "I gotcha, big homey. One!"

"One!"

Curly b-lined to Webb and Trailhome Road. He parked in a shopping mall plaza and went to a Chinese eatery. Once inside, he hit Peet on the c-phone and invited him to lunch. Peet wanted to decline, but the tone of Curly's voice hinted that this was more than lunch and that he was aware of Peet's spy games. Peet accepted ten minutes later, they were sitting at the table, face to face.

"So, what have you learned so far?" Curly inquired.

"That you're a disgrace to the badge" – he paused to let the waitress pour their tea, smiled, then waited for her to walk off – "like I was saying..."

"No, need." – Curly took a sip of his tea – "I get it!" he gestured at himself then Peet – bad cop. Good cop. "Is this what this is?" he gave Curly a death stare, "some sort of... game! Because of you – asshole."

"An officer lost his life," he leaned closer, "Jamie almost died, you bastard!"

"Does she know you've been following me around like some rave lunatic?"

"Did you kill Lewis? Is that why you killed Rumerez, so he wouldn't rat you out?"

Lewis was a means to an end – he took another sip of his tea, and Rumerex was an idiot.

"So you admit to killing the both of them?"

"Of course not!" Curly voice spent as he took a second to oversee the crowd – "All I'm saying is that he was bound to get what was coming... after all, he was a bad cop."

"So are you!" Peet suggested.

"Ever got a lil too physical with a suspect or bent a few corners to make an arrest, Peet?"

"What does that have to do with you killing cops and stealing drugs from evidence," the look on Curly's face confirmed Peet's thesis – "Surprised! Like you said earlier, a bad cop is bound to get what he got coming."

"How's their wife?" He snapped his fingers a few times to recall her name, "Eva! Right?"

Without warning, Peet leaned over the table and grabbed Curly's wrist – "You're threatening my wife, you bastard?"

"Relax, crazy man!" Curly massaged Peets prints from around his wrist – "It's just the opposite. I believe I can help you, stupid ass."

"Excuse me!"

"You're not the only one who's been doing his homework... I hear you got money problems?"

"You heard wrong." Peet snapped.

"How you gonna foot the bill this time? If you don't mind me asking?"

"You know that I've been following you around, trying to find something, anything to arrest your sorry ass" – Peet leaned back and placed his hands on his stomach, "And what do you do? Invite me to lunch to... what bribe me?"

"The hospital is asking for forty. I'll give you a hundred, leaving you with sixty to play with."

"A hundred grand. You wanna give me a hundred to what?" look at the other way.

"And you think I should've offered more."

"I think you've lost your damn mind. What in the hell would make you think I would do something so stupid?"

"Not what. Who, as in, penny nickles." "Am I supposed to know what that mean?"

"I know thirty thousand reasons why you might know, Penny nickles was the name of the sixteen year old girl you caught giving oral sex to the mayor... turns out she was carrying his baby and that they'd been seeing each other – for two years," He flashes Peet a crooked smile, from my understanding, you looked the other way. Peet chose his words before speaking – "That was ten years ago," Peet explained, "He wasn't even mayor at the time."

"You right!" Curly suggested, "But that's not my point!"

"What's your point?"

"Opportunity and circumstances." "Being?"

"Under the circumstances, you needed the money, when the opportunity presented itself, you took it!"

"This is no different," Curly's words danced off his tongue like a ballerina.

"Opportunity and circumstances," Peey repeated, sounds more like bribery.

"Think about Eva." – The second he said her name, he could see the blood rush to Peet's eyes, "Just hear me out." – He motioned for Peet to remain seated, "Eva needs this money more than both of us... love is as love does. If you're afraid of getting caught, don't be. I have a way to clean the money. Free of charge." Everything he was saying was true. Exa needed that money. A hundred grand would be a real safety net; besides, it wasn't like he had never taken a bribe to ensure her well-being before, so this was no different. Peet agreed to Curly's proposal. The whole time Curly was explaining what he needed to be done, all Peet could think about was Eva. He reminded himself of her and what he was doing to the point. Every word coming out of Curly's mouth was saying – "This is for Eva... This is for Eva." Once both men came to an understanding, they had lunch. An hour later, they were in the parking lot. Before Peet climbed into his car, Curly asked him how he would like to receive his money. Out of nowhere, a person wearing all black rode up on a motorcycle and pumped six forty-four calibers' bullets into Peets head and chest. He died on the spot.

* * * * * *

When Jamie walked in, Eva was sitting up in the bed, her lunch straddled across her lap. Their eyes meet, and reality struck. Jamie became aware that the message she received from Peet was really from his wife. "I wasn't sure you would come?" she waved her over to sit by me, but Jamie was unable to move her feet.

"There's something you need to know," Eva insisted, "I know about you and Peet."

"He told you!" her words came out too fast.

"Come here, sweetheart," she extended her hands and then waved Jamie over again. This time, she accepted and took a seat next to Eva – "He didn't have to tell me anything, you see, I chose you for my Peet chose me!" Jamie repeated, "What does that mean? You chose me?"

"I see that I've upset you... maybe you're right? I probably shouldn't have..."

"I'm not upset!"

"I thought since I am..."

"What did you mean when you said you chose me?"

"He asked me not to tell you, but..."

"Who asked you? Peet asked you not..."

"You're mad" – Eva smothered her hands over her face, wakening her words barely audible – "I should've listened to Peet. Now I've ruined everything."

"Eva, listen to me" – Jamie pulled down one of her hands, exposing her eye – "I am not upset. I'm not mad."

"I just wanna know where all this is coming from."

Eva cuffed one of Jamie's hands, looked her square in the eyes and told her she was dying. Although her words were as soft as her eyes, the moment Jamie heard her say, it brought her a pathos she'd never felt before. She and Peet had been partners for almost eight years, and up to that day, she'd never sat down and had a meaningful conversation with his wife. She never said more than five words to her since the two of them teamed up, and none during their so-called affair. Guilt sat on Jamie's face like dried concrete. Her loss of words kept clamps on her lips while her brain scrambled for the appropriate response. "Does... Peet know you're dying."

"Last time I talked to him, he did," Eva let out a silent giggle. "Don't look so serious," she patted her hand, "my doctor told me it was okay to laugh." But Jamie did just the opposite. She began to weep. From weeping, she went to sobbing, and from sobbing, she turned on the waterworks.

"All this for me?" Eva asked in a waggish tone, referring to Jamie's tear-stained face.

"I'm sorry... I just lost it, that's all."

"I would consider it a natural reaction, considering the circumstances."

"So all this time you've known about the..."

"Two of you sleeping together? Yes! I knew."

"Eva, I don't love Peet.", Jamie acknowledged.

"But you can learn too! Besides, the two of you already share a bond."

"We're just partners.", Jamie suggested.

"That's my point", Eva replied, "the two of place each other's lives into the hands of one another, day-in and day-out, and although he's not the most attractive man in the world, he has a good heart and he's a great lover."

Jamie pulled her hand away and walked over to the window – "Just so we're on the same page! You want me to be Peet's wife after you've passed away? Was that the plan?"

"Yes! But only..."

"Did the two of you ever think that, maybe, Jamie doesn't want to be anybody's wife?"

"Not his legal wife... just by spirit."

"I am sorry, but I can't do this..."

"You can't, or you won't?" Eva's soft eyes harden up a little, "I am going to die. That much certain, and if I know my Peet, he's going to come to you for comfort. When he does, will you turn him away?" Just as Jamie was about to answer, her phone rang, she threw up a finger and then answered it.

"Lightbourne"

"Your partner just been shot!"

It only took Jamie a minute to recognize the voice – "Are you sure?"

"Yeah, I'm sure. I'm off Webb and Trailhome Road. He was shot by some guy and a motorcycle... Jamie, he was hit a few times."

"What guy?" Jamie asked, her eyes focused on Eva, who was resting with her eyes closed.

"Don't know, but the guy that was with your partner shot the guy on motorcycle."

"How long ago?" She asked, trying her hardest to hide her fear from Eva.

"Looks like your partner made the wrong enemy."

"How long ago?" She repeated.

"Just happened... not even..."

"Hold on! I gotta incoming call – When Jamie switched lines, it was one of her teammates calling to tell her what her E.I. just informed her. She wrapped up both conversations, then got back to Eva. Out of all people, she had to be the one to tell a dying lady – A lady whose husband she cheated with – that her partner for life was just taken away. As Jamie looked ever Eva, she thought about what she'd told her about her and Peet's plan. She thought about all the husbands she'd slept with and in some strange way, how Eva represented all their wives. Was she the ploy in their twisted schemes, like she was in Eva's and Peet's? Or was she just some homewrecker looking for attention? "I am trippin'," Jamie spoke aloud, shaking off her daydream. "Eva!" She placed her hand over hers, "Wake up, honey... I need to tell you something." She tried holding back her tears but was unsuccessful – "Eva," she repeated, this time giving her hand a slight nug. But Eva didn't respond. She tried it again and again, but Eva didn't respond. Just as the words were coming out of Jamie's mouth, the machines hooked up to Eva began to buzz high-pitched noise. Moments later, a whole staff crew busted into the room. Things began to move too fast. As one doctor pushed over Eva's chest, another injected a fluid type substance into her I.V. "Clear!" the young lady yelled at the top of her lungs before shoving Jamie out of the way and placing two metal plates on Eva's chest. Jamie watched as the team of doctors fought to revive Eva despite their efforts. She died.

CHAPTER 24

The young man who shot Peet was being rushed to the "Winter Park Hospital," and so was Jamie. Peet was pronounced dead at the scene, so Jamie didn't feel any need to go and see her partner's dead body. After watching his wife die, she knew she wasn't strong enough to hold a mental picture of the two of them. Besides, she could read the report later on down the line. For now, it was all about Peet's killer and how he would be punished for killing one of the finest cops Florida had, "Thank god Curly was there to stop the young assassin from getting away and possibly hurting someone else." Jamie thought as she sprung out of the car and into the hospital inside, she was surprised to see the whole crew was in the waiting lounge, No one went to the murder sight – instead, they were all waiting for the doctors to produce a miracle so the wheel of justice could crush the life out of him.

"How bad is he?" Jamie inquired.

"Don't know yet!" Curly explained – "He's still with the doctors."

"Who's gonna explain to his wife?" A voice blurted from the small crowd of badges.

"Eva died half an hour ago!" – Jamie wished she didn't have to say that, but she knew they deserved to know. "Who is this kid anyway?" She looked at all their faces for some sort of clue – "Do I know him? Is he an old case?"

"There go the doctor!" One of the members pointed towards a tall man with thick lips and cornrows.

"I am afraid your friend didn't make it, but before he..."

"I'm sorry" – Jamie cut in – "but are you a doctor?"

"He let out a light laugh – you talking about my braids." He pointed to his head, "I'm allowed to be myself around here." He shrugged his shoulders- patients seem to love it.

"I didn't mean it like that."

"No problem. But like I was saying, he kept saying something about 'he paid him.'"

"Who paid him?" Curly intervene.

"Some kind of nickname!" The doctor implied, but to tell the truth, "I wasn't paying that much attention to what he was saying. I was just trying to save'em."
"You win some, you lose some." Jamie acknowledged her, and the crew dispersed back to their cars. Not knowing what to do with herself, Jamie just went home. There, she balled up like a baby and cried all night. It wasn't until then that she realized how much Peet meant to her.

* * * * * *

After Frank crossed the Georgia-Florida line, the realization of what he was about to do started to sink in. Agent Skies was very clear about what he wanted from him or, better yet, who he wanted him to set up, and although their first encounter was succinct – Frank felt that Skies was still holding a rabbit in the hat. Now, all he had to do was figure out a way to save all he'd hustled for, keep Skies from crossing him, get Todd and Hope out of the picture and turn over the Haitian. The only problem he was facing was getting under Nije and getting him to drop his guard. The only thing that bother Frank was when Agent Skies gave him back the twenty kilos, then allowed him to have one of his workers come and pick them up, but at the same time pressuring him to set up one of the biggest dope boys in Florida. Skies even went out of his way to have his car fixed. Even though he appreciated it, he didn't trust such an amiable gesture coming from a federal agent, Especially when that agent was forcing him to go against the grain. Frank bee-line straight to the house. Normally, he would stop by the mall to buy Dee-Dee an outfit or pair of shoes. He used that old trick to see if he was being followed but in this case. He didn't need such a ruse. He knew exactly where the feds were, instead of pulling into the garage, Frank sat halfway into the driveway, admiring his home. Never in a million years would he have thought that he would own something as magnificent as what he was looking at. "Now, how in the hell am I supposed to let this whiteboy take all this from me." Frank thought aloud as he struggled to climb out of the car and into the house. Dee- Dee always greeted Frank in the garage with a hug and a kiss, but he didn't pull in. She took it as some sort of game. Eager to play, she dashed out the front door. When she saw his shoulder all bandaged up, her smile quickly faded. A closer look flaunted deep bruises under his eyes and multiple gashes throughout his face and neck.

"Baby happened!" Dee-Dee cried out, instinctively assisting him into the living room.

"Some white chick ran a red light and hit me from the side," he complained as she eased him onto the sofa.

"Your care must be a…"

"My car is fine! But the rental car was totaled."

"Baby, you could've died!"

"I know," the doctor said. I was real lucky – he gestured to his swollen shoulder – "said if the poll would have moved over a little further, it would have hit my heart."

"I don't know what I would do if I lost you," she confessed – "But don't you worry cuz I am gonna nurse you back to full strength."

"You're just too good to me," Frank admitted.

"Doing my job." – She leaned in to kiss him.

"Wifey, huh?", He questioned, "Fuck a wedding… fuck putting it on paper, we just married."

"Child, please!" she started laughing. "I don't need anything but my man. No pa-per. No wedding. Just my man, and yes," – she rolled her eyes, "you 're my husband!"

"I feel ya," Frank acknowledged while laughing.

"You hungry?"

"Not like that, but a sandwich and some tea, ah, would be nice."

"You wish is my command," Dee-Dee revealed before bouncing to the kitchen. While Dee-Dee was making Frank lunch, he jumped on the phone to call Hope. They talked about everything except Agent Skies. Frank decided to keep everybody on a need-to-know basis, and for now, all Hope needed to know was that their spot up North was doing its thang. He understood that Jope had to know as little as possible in order for him to get up under the Haitian, that way, Hope's actions would be pure hearted when he introduced him to the Haitian face to face. Frank set up a time for Hope to come and pick up the money, but Hope suggested doing it the next day and told him to enjoy his first day back with his wife. When Frank replaced the phone, he started to laugh aloud, "I guess we're married." He chuckled.

"What you laughing about?" Dee-Dee asked as she came in with his food, "where you want for me to sit at?"

"Over there would be fine," He pointed to an end table,

"What was so funny?" She kneeled between his legs.

"I was just laughing at Hope... He called you my wife, you know?"

"Well, now, he can call us a family!"

"Everybody knows you, my people."

"No, silly!" she took his hand and placed it on her stomach – "A real family. Like, mom, a baby, and daddy."

"Are you sure?"

"About me being pregnant? Of course, I am!"

"You've been to a doctor? You're absolutely positive!"

"Yes, I am positive! Why are you looking at me like that?"

With a disappointed look, Frank leaned back – "Dee-Dee, I can't have children. I never could." Dumbstruck, Dee-Dee just sat there as tears began to swell in her eyes.

"You figured a baby would lock me in? Let me guess, one of your older homegirls told you to try me with that." He let out a light giggle. "Are you even pregnant?"

"I wanted to be." her words were barely audible, "I wanted to have your baby so bad..."

"So why lie? Why now? Haven't I been real with you?"

"I thought you just like fucking a young Frank, and as soon as I get old to you, you would find another find another girl to take my place." Her tears began running down her face.

"You might as well hold them tears for another time," Frank suggested, "Matter factly."

"Are you gonna leave me?"

"I should! Crazy ass, but you're young, and I knew that before we got together, so no! I'm not going to leave you, but we're going to have a serious talk about what I expect from you here on out." Dee-Dee remained quiet while Frank laid down the law. She knew he was angry, but to her surprise, his words were understanding and gentle. The perfect gentleman, but at the same time, Chasten. Frank was nobody's fool. To get rid of Dee-Dee at this point in his life would be detrimental to his big scheme. Although she tried him, he knew she would do anything for him, and now she had all the motive in the world to prove it. He would make certain of that. For the next three days, Frank began his clandestine campaign to hand Nije over to the Feds, but Jope was reluctant to bring the two face to face. "You know I can't do no shit like dat!" Hope snapped to Frank's absurd request as the two of them headed to Todd's spot. "You need to tighten up, young buck! What if something happens to you? I wouldn't have a connection to keep our little gig afloat – know I can't holla at Todd." He emphasized, "Dude ain't like dat! He ain't trying to be on front street."

"He sorry like that?"

"He cautious like dat... I'll be too if I was bricked up like dat."

"We are bricked up!" Frank implied.

"We called up, not bricked up,"

"Caked up! Bricked up! All I'm saying is that we're major nukkas in this game, and should be treated as such, you lil Haitian need to come in all the way." – He gave Hope a questionable eye – "Keep it real! He knows all about us, and we don't know all about him. Dis ain't 75', cats don't move like dat in 06', besides, He don't know all our business!"

"You just started doing business with them, I've been dealing with them since they came over here with that blow-up back in the early eighties... They think they smarter than us."

"What dat supposed to mean?" Hope let out a slight chuckle, "Where all dis coming from?"

"I'm just trying to pull your coat to who you dealing with," Frank pointed out just as they pulled into the driveway. Hope agreed to think about it, but the look on his face said otherwise. Unfazed, Frank was meanly trying to plant a seed. He knew hope was going to give some sort of resistance, but after he agreed to think about it, he took it as a victory and a step closer to the Haitian. He left things as they were, and both went into the house.

* * * * * *

August 15, 2006 – Jamie only took four days' leave of absence after the funeral, deciding to return on that Tuesday instead of Friday. Without any expectations, she slowly began her morning watching the news and sipping on an extra strong cup of coffee. After hearing how both Hezbollah and Israeli leaders declared victory, and some fifteen-year-old Ohio girl was sentenced for bank robbery or Kate

Hudson was getting a divorce. The only thing that seemed to bring a smile to her face was when the news reporter would announce "Boy George" was ordered to pick up trash in New York. That and the outfit he is on. "I wouldn't be caught dead wearing that!" Jamie declared. "That's very considerate of him.", Jamie thought aloud as the story of an NBA basketball star was raising money to build a hospital in his homeland of Africa. "We need more people like that in this world," she mumbled while getting dressed. After only a few bites of her breakfast, Jamie headed out the door only to be pulled back in by the ring of the phone.

"Hello?"

"Is this Detective Lightbourn."

"This is she, but who is this?" "Doctor Urus."

"I'm sorry, but did I miss some appointment or something."

"I'm not your doctor, but..."

"So, how did you get my number?"

"Some Spanish lady at the police department, I thought this was a cellphone."

"Maria", Jamie mumbled.

"Excuse me!"

"Never mind, so what can I do for you?"

"It's about that kid that died last week, the one who shot that cop."

"What about him?"

"I remember who said paid him to kill that cop!"

"What's the name?"

"Sanguinary!"

"What is that the name of? A place, person, thing?"

"Dunknow! Just called to tell you what I remembered."

"Are you sure that's what he said?"

"I'm not willing to bet my life on it if that's what you're asking."

"Well, do you know what it means?"

"Never heard of the word."

"Thanks for calling doctor."

"You're welcome."

Jamie wrote down the name and then stared at it for a few seconds. Images of the double funeral flashed through her head. The funeral was paid for by the department after Peet's financial status showed he was unable. "Sanguinary" the name gave Jamie a chill through her body, she stuffed the paper into her pocket and walked out the door.

CHAPTER 25

Agent Sky came to Florida with the sole purpose of killing two birds with one stone. A man on a mission, he was determined to put an end to his three years of bureaucratized shenanigans and deceptive role playing. His pawns were strategically placed by way of patience and perseverance, because of that, Agent Sky was in a place he'd been looking forward to for some time. Putting Nije behind bars for a long, long time. Frank was merely a means to an end. But, because Sky hated all drug dealers of any kind, he was a bonus added to the list of thugs he was more than happy to rid society of. His first order of business was to check into a room, lay low, and oversee his pawns as if he were god himself. Not letting Frank or Nije know he was in Florida was vital for the jump off. But Sky wasn't the only one moving under the radar. While the agent was mobbing incognito, Curly was also putting a few pawns in place. Lewis always spoke of this Haitian he used to do favors for during his rookie years by the name of Nije. He spoke so highly of me, Haitian, you would think he was a politician rather than one of Florida's major cocaine distributors. According to Lewis, he was the heartbeat of Central Florida, so Culry figured if he wanted to get all his dope back, he would have to go through the Haitian named Nije, and if everything went as planned, he would get his drugs back plus more.

Curly wasn't sure what to make of this Nije character. Based on his house, he was far bigger than what Lewis explained. While being escorted to the backyard, Curly couldn't help but notice how young the house servants looked or the fact that none of them made eye contact with him as he walked by.

"Monsieur Dupont est á vous dans seconde," the young girl announced in French as she pointed to a heavily cushioned lawn chair.

Not knowing what she said, Curly just nodded his head and sat down – "Thank you!"

"Aimeriez-vous á boisson san alcool?"

"No, thank you!" Curly said, waving his hand in a "No" motion. The young lady accepted his answer and walked back to the house. Ten minutes later, Nije came. "Lieutenant! How can I help?" Nije extended his hand.

"I came to offer you my services." Curly stood up – shook his hand, then sat back down. Curly had never seen Nije before and, like most people, had already put a face to the name. For Curly, he was expecting a short, dark-skinned man with high cheekbones. Instead, he was face to face with a very tall white man who appeared to be in his late fifties and was physically fit.

"And what might that service be, Lieutenant?"

"I was thinking maybe we could pick up where you and Lewis let off."

"Lewis... Now, that's a name I haven't heard in a long time." He looked Curly in the center of his eyes without changing his facial expression – "How is my old friend?"

"Dead!"

"Dead?" Nije let out a light laugh, "did you kill'em?"

"No! But I did kill who killed him."

"Now, who would want to kill the detective?" he asked with a factious smile.

"Some two-bit street thug named Rosco."

"Rosco?" Nije began laughing.

"Let me guess? That's a name you haven't heard in a long time."

"I'm sorry... I don't mean to... but the thing is that the only service you've done for me is telling me two people I once knew are now dead."

"What if I told you I had friends in customs who could guarantee you eighteen months of worry-free shipping and handling!"

"I already have such friends."

"What is your definition of friends? Mr. Nije."

"Excuse me!"

"Let me explain. For one, you're being taxed. Two, they're inconsistent and sloppy. Lastly, they are spread too thin if you ask me. With me, like Lewis, you would be our only focus."

"Is that right?"

"More than you'll ever know."

"How much?"

"No money. Only your friendship."

"My friendship... How is being my friend going to bless you?"

"Your friendship is going to bankroll my run for governor."

"I'm listening."

"For eighteen months, I will assist you free of charge. All I need from you is to hand me a few big licks... off the record, of course, then..."

"Off the record?" Nije repeated.

"Yes, these two hand me downs won't make it to the spotlight, sort of speak."

"So you want me to back door a few people?"

"Only the small ones, and I promise..."

"Let me guess, I do business with them, then you come later and rough them off of the goods? The money I get from them will be washed through one of your businesses at thirty cents on a dollar. You will, in return, finance my start-up company as one of your subsidiaries. From there, I pull you into a world you've longed to be a part of."

"What makes you so sure I want to be a part of politics?"

"Let's just say an educated guess?"

"When do we start?" Nije asked.

"We start with Todd and Hope?"

"With pleasure."

Things couldn't have come at a better time. After Nije had hope followed, he realized his operation was at risk of being exposed. Now, instead of killing the two of them, he could simply hand them over to the very same people who wanted them in the first place and at the same time, make a few hundred grand out of it.

Thanksgiving was less than two weeks away, and the only thing Agent Skies could think of was his ex-wife's roast duck as he sat a few houses down from Candy's place. This was his third stake-out, and just like the first and second ones, everything was going according to plan. From his observation, Hope and Todd didn't expect anything, which was a good thing. But he also noticed that Todd was spending more time at some broken firm than he was with Hope and Frank, which wasn't such a good thing. Todd was the key to the whole case. For Ski, he was the only person who could place Nije in a room full of kilos of cocaine. He thought he had his chance with an informant named Rosco, but all Rosco had for him before he died was some dirty cop who did a few favors for Nije back in the day. Just Skies luck, the dirty cop died, and his silent partner was never identified. The only good thing that came out of all that was the final report Detective Light-bourn turned in. Skies pulled a few strings to read it. While closing out her case, Lightbourn unknowingly helped keep Agent Skies alive. In his opinion, it was an opportunity to meet Faith. Commonly known as a second chance. A chance he planned on taking full advantage of. Feeling the need to spice things up a little, he decided to reach out to an old friend.

"Hello?"

"Where are you?"

"Hello! Who is this?"

"The tooth fairy... where are you?"

"I'm at the crib, why, what's up?"

"I thought I told you not to call me when I'm with my girl."

"Relax Casanova... I just called to inform you that I'm not in town and that you need to pick your things up."

"Can I call you later?"

"When you do... have something for me."

"Cool. I'll hit'cha up tomorrow then." Frank tossed the C-phone on the table and then leaned back into the couch. He tried his handset to avoid any eye contact.

"Man, you know how dem ho's act after you put dat dick on dem." – Hope blurted out.

"I'm glad I'm down with just one girl." – Todd boasted – "Fucking with too many broads gets old!"

"What the fuckever! Hitting one droad is what gets old." – Frank started laughing – "But fo'real, what about the loss we just took?"

"What about it?" Todd asked.

"I'm trying to get that back."

"The clubhouse clean... besides, we legit now, fuck dat dope."

"Fuck dat dope? Youngblood, that was twenty bricks we loss! Twenty!"

"And?"

"Twenty times 60 equal what? I'll tell'ya what it equals... one point two mill, but that's dirty money." – Todd shot back – "Besides, we a mill clean. Legit. Just like I promised." – Todd went to the back room, then came back with a shoe box – "Here!" He tossed Hope and Frank two thick envelopes.

"What is it?" – Hope inquired.

"Your freedom!" – Todd responded, "Go ahead and open it." Inside of the envelopes were several legal documents. Ownership papers to shelve corporations, deeds to property in the states of Florida and Georgia and a check from Matt Trade Brokerage Firm for two-hundred fifty thousand dollars.

"How you pulled this off?" Hope asked.

"Through the whiteboy."

"Whiteboy pulled this off?"

"What whiteboy?" Frank asked.

"My people" – He fixed his eyes on Hope – "The same one my boy didn't trust."

"I trust his ass now!"

"This two-fifty is cool, but what about that one, point two?" – Frank asked.

"Do you understand what you have in your hand?" Todd asked.

"All I'm saying is..."

"Let it go homeboy," – Hope intervened – "like my dog said, we legit now."

"But..."

"Just let it go!" – Hope insisted.

"Dog, that's a hundred and fifty short." – Frank explained.

"The risk isn't worth the reward." – Todd explained.

"Hold up" – Frank answered his c-phone – "Hello?"

"You have a guest coming through the bathroom with a pistol!"

"Ah, what?" – Frank dropped the phone and ran to the bathroom with his gun.

Although Hope was right on his heels, Todd not too far behind, Frank was able to get off four shots before the two of them reached the doorway. By the time they entered the room, the intruder was slumped over in the tub.

"Who the hell is this?" – Todd asked, fear creeping into his voice as the intruder bled profusely.

"A dead ass whiteboy in yo' tub" – Hope exclaimed.

"This ain't the time!" Todd shot back – "Dis ain't the time."

"Fuck!" Frank blurted out, but in a low tone – "Out of all the bullshit dis had to happen."

"You think he came to Rob us?" Hope asked.

"Man, I don't care what his intentions were... I got a dead whiteboy in my tub."

"Where Candy?"

Todd looked at his watch – "Shit! She's on her way home from school. She gonne trip!"

"Hell yeah, she gonne trip nekka, you got dis dead whiteboy in her tub... don't she love this tub or something?"

"Didn't I tell you this ain't the time..." Just as Todd was about to straighten Hope, there were three loud knocks on the door. "Police!" "Open up!"

CHAPTER 26

Saturday mornings were always the same for Jamie; With a routine that was at least six years old, she would wake up at 5:00 am, eat a small breakfast, run three miles, showers, and then read the paper with her favorite tea. All was going according to plan until she grabbed the wrong paper. He didn't once until she saw the picture of her standing next to Peet and Curly on the front steps of the police headquarters. That picture of Peet brought back a slew of memories she didn't love him, but he was such a big part of her life, and although she barely knew Eva, looking at Peet's picture made her feel some sort of connection to her as well. "You really never know a person." Jamie thought out loud as Eva's dying confession played back through her head. While it was the most loving thing she'd ever known for a person to do, it was by far the strangest thing she had ever been a part of, and for Jamie, that was saying a lot. Seeing Curly in a short sleeve was also a surprise. Up until then, she'd never seen him in anything but long sleeve. But what really caught her eye was his tattoo. Even though she wasn't attracted to Curly physically, she had a thing for men with tattoos or women for that matter. Not able to identify it, she went and got a magnifying glass. What she saw when she placed the glass on the paper literally took her breath. On the inside of Curly's forearm read "Sanguinary". Immediately, she ran to the phone and called her sergeant.

* * * * * *

"So, what did he say?" the older man with sunk-in eyes asked.

"Just what you said he would say.", Curly replied with a wide smile, "but how did you know the political thing would do the trick?"

"It's called a thumbscrew!" the tallest of the four announced as he walked through the door.

"Jacki!" the old man shouted before giving his friend a hug, "It's been too long."

"I agree," Jacki acknowledged.

"Have a seat... have a seat", the old man pointed next to Curly, "and where are my manners? Curly, this is Jacki, and that young man right there is the 'old Tomcat.'

"I don't know why he always does that." – He leaned over and extended his hand to Curly – "You just call me Tom."

"So, when do we start?" Jacki asked the old man.

"You would have to ask him that." – He directed the question toward Curly – "I put'em in charge of this here mission."

* * * * * *

As all three men fixed their eyes on Curly, he began to feel the immortality of infinite power. There he was amongst three very powerful, influential men who were waiting on his command before they could make any mor of their own. Any and everything would be done according to his liken. He was the king of kings.

"Day after tomorrow". Curly informed the others.

"Good... that's very good", the old man's approval was present, "So Tomcat, how are we gonna do the boats?"

"First, I'm going to need a list of all the ships he plans on bringing in for the year. I'll need time and dates of arrival." Tom was chief director of the U.S. Coast Guard, which meant he was in charge of the day to day operations.

"Anything else?" Curly asked.

"That should do it," He answered.

"And what about you, Jacki? What do you need?"

"All I need to know is when the deal is going down so we can back door'em. Trust me, my people will be on point and ready for whatever." Jacki was head of the DEA and second in command of the FBI.

"Noo blood!" the old man said, "Last thing we need is a..."

"Not to worry, old friend," Jacki assured, "in case you forgot – this isn't our first sing and dance. Besides, it's like taking candy from a baby or has it been that long?"

"So, who's going to move the goods once we collect it?"

"That's a very good question, Tomcat." – the old man fixed his eyes on Curly, awaiting an answer.

"Jacki... the first one you backdoor... can you hold'em until I get there?"

"I wasn't aware I would be babysitting."

"You're not. I just need the first one put up so I can talk to him."

"What if it's a She?"

"It won't be." – Curly pulled out a file and tossed it on the table.

"Who are they?" – Jacki asked as he thumbed through some surveillance photos.

"You're looking at your first backdoor," Curly announced.

"So why hold'em... what's the catch?" Tom's curiosity was growing bigger.

"That's who is going to move the dope for us."

"Brilliant, my boy... brilliant, we bust them, then force them to move our dope for free or spend the rest of their lives in Leavenworth.

"Not quite," Curly uttered, "I plan on giving it to him on the street value."

"Him! You said that as if the two of you have made some agreement of some sort. Do you know these people?"

"Let's just say that I've had my eye on them for quite some time now."

"So why backdoor'em... Why not just set up a meeting with him on them or whoever." – Tom asked with a lost look.

"Because we're not friends, and he's the type who's going to need a push..."

"Well, start pushing!" the old man announced, "in case you've forgotten, we're on a tight rope here, and time is of the essence."

"Yes, sir, I'm on it."

And just like that, all four men shook hands and left the table. All headed back to their normal lives as if the meeting never took place. Phase one was now complete. Meanwhile, back at the police headquarters, what seemed to be a clear-cut case for Jamie was just the opposite of her captain.

* * * * * *

"Why would Curly kill Peet?" he captain asked matterfactly.

"I just told you!"

"Maybe you need to explain it again... but this time with more explaining?"

"Peet told me he had a bad feeling about Curly... something about him wasn't right!"

"And?"

"And Curly knew Peet was about to expose him."

"Go on," the captain suggested.

"That's it!" Jamie responded, but the look on the captain's face told her what she knew the second she blurted out, "That's it," that she didn't have anything coming – "I know what you're about to say," she implied, "but you're just gonna have to trust me on this one."- she tried reading his face, but nothing was there – "For Christ sakes, captain, that son of a bitch killed Peet!"

"Calm down, detective. I wasn't to help you, I really do. But the truth of the matter is that you aren't helping me help you."

"What the hell does that mean!"

"It means... I need something, anything, to push forward. In case you've forgotten, the man you are accusing of murder is a fellow bluecoat!"

"With all due respect, so was Peet!" Jamie announced sardonically.

"When did you find out?" the captain asked, trying to break the few moments of silence.

"Today. When the doctor called, he told me what Peet's shooter said before he died."

"He said Curly killed Peet?"

"No! He fingered who paid him to kill Peet."

"So, he said Curly paid him? Is it on tape?"

"Not exactly..."

"What exactly did he say?"

"Sanguinary," Jamie uttered, and that son of a bitch has that tattooed on his forearm with two..."

"Snakes intertwined through a purple heart," – the captain intervened as he rolled up his shirt, exposing the same exact tattoo... "If that's all you've got, I'm afraid you just hit a brick wall. There's got to be at least three, four thousand ex-military men and women with this tattoo." he gestured at his arm.

"But only one of you killed him!"

"I'm going to act like I didn't hear that."

"I'm sorry, captain... I'm just."

"I know, that's why I'm going to give you seventy-two hours to either bring me something of sustenance or his ass handed to me on a silver platter." he looked at his watch, "You got until Friday."

Whatever Peet knew was worth his life, which meant that Curly was either knee deep in something really big or way over his head in something too big. Whatever the case, Jamie was going to find out or die trying. After she left the captain's office, she went down to evidence and collected all she could, along with her personal file of Peet's murder and the case they were all working on. "I'm going to get yo'ass Curly." She thought aloud as she climbed into her car headed home to study all that she'd gathered. That morning, she called Kevin to see if she could squeeze one more favor from him. He was more than happy to help.

CHAPTER 27

"Police, open up," a loud voice ordered. Followed by three bangs on the door. "Them crackers at the door!"

"This some bullshit!" Todd screamed.

"We fucked!" Hope cried out.

"Man, chill out."- Todd announced – "The two of you clean this mess up. I'll go handle them crackers."

"What you gonna do?" Hope asked panically.

"Just clean this shit up."- He looked down at the dead whiteboy – "I'll be right back." Todd ran to the living room, turned up the T.V. full blast, then answered the door. To his surprise, it was only one cop, and he was in plain clothes.

"Police? You don't look like no dame police."

"Well, I am." – Skies flashed his badge, then barged in – "Now what the hell is going on in here? I heard gunshots."

"What you heard was the surround sound system." – Todd pointed to his 72" TV.

"Surround sound, my ass."- Skies pulled out his pistol – "I know what gunshots sound like."

"What the hell..." Todd took a few steps back – "Man, if you don't have a warrant, you can get yo ass out my house, whiteboy!"

"Do I need one." – He asked while looking around before he bolted towards the bathroom, Todd right on his heels, yelling and screaming to get out, but it was too late when Skies burst through the door, he caught Hope and Frank trying their hardest to push the dead body through the bathrooms tiny window.

"Don't. Fuck'n. Move" – Skies ordered, his pistol pointed at Hope's head – "Unless one of you wants to end up like your friend there, I suggest you listen up very carefully. You two drop the stiff and follow me to the living room."

As ordered, the two of them, along with Todd, followed Skies into the living room. After turning down the television, Skies got straight to the business. He got on his c-phone, called the crew, and told them to B-line to Todds house. He instructed them not to bring the locals but to bring the coroner as quiet as kept. While placing the phone on the table, he fixed his eyes on Todd.

"So why did you kill'em?"

"You trippen... I ain't kill nobody."

"What about you?" He gestured to Hope.

"Miss me, whiteboy... right plan, wrong man."

"So I guess I can muss you too!" – He pointed to Frank, but he didn't respond. For the next hour, Skies tried everything from scare tactics to life sentences threats. Nothing. Just as Todd opened his mouth, a young man sporting a crew cut walked in through the door, followed by four others.

"What's on the menu?" he asked Skies nonchalantly.

Sky pointed to the back of the house, then took the man with a crew cut into the garage.

"How are we doing this?"

"Off the books for right now," – Skies informed – "but eventually. I'm bringing this to the light!"

"What's the hold up?"

"Nije!"

"I thought we were through chasing that Haitian. You almost lost your job because of that Haitian... we, I, almost lost my job because of your obsession with him, and I'm..."

"Hear me out before you go all ape-shit on me. Please!"

"Talk!"

"The last time was different... this time I have his ass..."

"You fucking kidding me – you always say that dumbshit."

"I'm serious this time" – Sky replied.

"You're always serious, Sky, and who the hell are those people in the living room?"

"That's what I'm trying to explain to you. The older one is my mold, he's my ace in the hold."

"Ace in the hold, huh?"

"Ace in the hold." – Sky repeated while flashing the biggest smile he could muster up.

"Last time, Sky, last time. After this, you're on your own."

"So, you're in?" – Sky extended a closed fist.

"I'm in." – He bumped his fist with Sky. For the next twenty minutes, Sky brought his five-man crew up to speed; with colorful detail, he drew the perfect picture of how they were going to catch and out away the biggest drug lore Florida has ever seen and in the process, bolster their law enforcement career to new highs.

"Which one of you fucks is taking the wrap for the dead whiteboy?"

"Don't everybody speak at once." – Sky suggested.

"Man, what kind of cops are you?" – Hope asked.

"This some creep ass shit!" – Todd said – "all of a sudden, some bad body whiteboy break in the house, and two seconds later whiteboy hatcha come busting through the door!"

"So, you killed him for breaking into your house?" – one of the men asked.

"Man, I ain't kill nobody!" – Todd shot back.

"So, if you didn't... who did?" – He gestured to Frank – "You did it!"

"Hell naw!"

"What about you?" – he pointed to Hope.

"I want my lawyer." – Hope demanded, "And I mean right now!"

"Oh, lawyer boy wants representation," – Sky acknowledged.

"If he doesn't start talking, the only thing he gonna get is a life sentence!"

"I know my rights." – Hope yelled – "I know my rights!"

"Sir, the house is clean, and the body is being put into the truck." – the young man eyed down Hope, Todd, and Frank while waiting on his next order. "Sir, sir, what do we do with these three?"

"Lock their ass up for murder!"

"This some bullshit!" Todd yelled.

"I'll be dam'd," – Frank mumbled – "Ah nigga going to jail for murder!"

After they were read their rights and placed into handcuffs, Sky walked them one by one into different vehicles. "This isn't about you." – He whispered to Hope – "Let Todd know he has the power to make all this go away. He helps me I help you!"

"Cracker, fuck you! I ain't telling my dawg a muthafucken thang!"

"Yeah, yeah, yeah, tough guy." – Sky replied – "Man, get your ass in the car, you little shit eater." – Sky shoved Hope into the backseat of the car, causing him to bump his head.

"Laugh now whiteboy... but I promise you'll cry later." – Hope screamed as he kicked violently on the car door.

"Would someone shut him up!" Sky demanded as he walked over to the other car and made that prick stop kicking my goddamn door! "Okay, T-man..."

"My name is Todd!"

"Okay, Todd... How about we have a little heart to heart?"

"Kick rocks whiteboy, cuz what's in my heart you really don't want to hear!"

"You should think before you speak, asshole." – Sky replied just before he slammed the door –"Maybe your friend will be smarter?" Sky mumbled just as he pulled open the car door.

"What kind of junki-stunt was that?"

"Play times over, Franky."

"Man, talk to me down at the station... you trippen!"

"We had a deal."

"What, you deaf or something? I can't talk to you like this, Not like this. Where's Nije." – Sky reached in and punched Franky in his stomach, knocking the wind out of him – "You think you can play me? Do I look like..."

"Punk as cop!" Todd yelled and screamed while kicking the door – He'd seen Sky bend over and punch Frank and was furious that the cop would resort to violent tactics just because neither of them would rat out the other.

"I'll get that Haitian for you." – Franky said in between moans – "I just..."

"Hold that thought." – Sky intervened, then walked over to Todd, who was repeatedly kicking the door... each kick more violent than the other.

"So what? You're gonna just stand there and let'em kick the damn door?"

"You know me better than that, Sky." – The tall blonde sporting the crew acknowledge- "I don't do the babysitting thing."

"Un fucking believable!" – Sky cried out, then snatched open the door – "Last time T-Man, stop kicking the door!" Before Todd could respond, Sky slammed the door on him. "Take these clowns over to the spot," – Sky ordered – "Put Franky in the blue room and wait for me there, oh yeah, no phones!"

Agent Sky was starting to get that old feeling back, the one where he could feel Nije slipping away. If he had let the intruder go into the house unannounced, there is no telling if his mole would have made it out alive. But the question he asked himself was, "What if?" what if he just let it play out? What if, by him showing his face too soon, he might have blown three-plus years of his life chasing a man only to see his overreacting impulse cause him to lose in the eleventh hour? This was the closet he'd come to nailing Nije's ass to the cross, but at the same time, this would also be his last time in a long time if ever he got another chance of this magnitude... the hourglass was officially turned over, and Agent Sky was now face-to-face with the falling sand. From that point on, he knew he was on borrowed time. Sky had to think quickly, putting his trust in the hands of an ex-junky turned D-boy. It wasn't good enough; he needed more assurance that all three men would be more than willing to help his cause. Strapped with a few push-buttons, Sky headed back to the station.

"We've been in this room over two hours now!" – Hope acknowledged.

"You know I saw them jump on Franky."- Todd said – "I tried to stop..."

"Where is Franky?"

"I've been in here with yo crying ass, how should I know?" – Todd let out a laugh.

"Not right now, Todd, not right now!"

"But that is a good question... where is that nigga? I hope he alright."

"I hope he ain't telling."

"Telling! Telling what?"

"Todd, man, I don't trust that old head. He too much for self! He even tried to get me to go behind your back and make things live again! I'm telling you something ain't right with your uncle."

"My uncle?"

"Yeah, nigga... yo uncle! Trust when I tell you he's not cut from the same cloth like me and you."

"Where is all this coming from?"

"Just hear me out, family," – Hope slid up on Todd – "I don't think that these are regular cops, and nothing they're doing is standard... why me and you together but not Franky? Homeboy on the phone... jump up and run to the back, then them people come, and they talking bout everything but what's in their face! I'm telling you something ain't right! They got there too fast! Too fast!"

Everything Hope was saying was making sense – All but Franky making Hope go behind his back and start slanging again; Todd knew Hope loved money and understood how hard it would be for him to walk away from the street life and all the fame that came with it... money, hoes, clothes...etc. But that didn't change the fact that Hope was his main man and that no matter what, he would always have Todd's back – but at the same time, Todd didn't want to overreact; moving out of impulse was a mistake he'd seen many before him make, a mistake a great deal of them couldn't bounce back from. The one thing that stuck in Todd's head was the statement Hope made about the cops not being regular... that statement alone let Todd know that two things would have to happen in order for them to have a fighting chance. The first thing was to find out which branch of law he was dealing with and what they wanted from them. Secondly, he had to make sure whatever they had on them – if they had anything‐ was not legit but limited.

"You think they feds?" – Todd asked.

"Ain't no telling who these crackers is!" – Hope shot back – "All I know is we knee deep right now, babyboy."

"Once we find out who we dealing with, we'll know where to go from there?"

"I need to know where that uncle of yours is at and who he talking to?"

"You'll get your answers soon enough." – Todd replied.

"You said that to say what?"

"All I meant by that was all this is about to come to a head, and when it do, I just want for us to be on the same page... just want for us to be ready for whatever."

"You need to tell your uncle that next time you see his goof talking ass," – Hope responded – "You know how I get down... nigga you ain't just meet me!"

"Man, chill out." – Todd gave'em some dap. "I'm just saying!" – Hope mumbled.

"I know homeboy" ‐ Todd gave'em some dap – "but listen, you know they about to split us up?"

"Good cop, bad cop." – Hope suggested.

"Not on this one." – Todd chimed in – "I think we're dealing with a different beast on this one. I might be wrong, but I think it's going to be me against you and you against Franky or whoever else is tied into this here."

"Me against you? You think that's how they are going to play it?"

"Like I said, I might be wrong... I just got that feeling."

"Well, these crackers need to show their face so we can get this show on the road, ya feel me?"

While Todd and Hope were sharing a few more conspiracy theories, Sky was in the elevator heading up to the seventh floor to go and see Franky. But before he went, he stopped by to plant a seed into the heads of Todd and Hope.

CHAPTER 28

For some reason, Jamie felt like Lewis, Rumerez, Peet, Howard, Sneed, and Todd Patrick were all a part of some big scheme. So many questions with no one to answer them. She thought she might have had at least a foot in the door, but Mrs. Jams never showed up to their meeting; that left her with just one more rabbit to pull out her hat.

"Hey, Kevin... please tell me you found something?"

"You might want to sit down for this one."

"That bad?" Jamie asked.

"I'll let you be the judge of that," Kevin answered.

"So, what is it?"

"Let's see... well, for starts, the mayor just got arrested for having sex with a minor."

"Yeah, I just saw that on the news, but why is that important to me?"

"It's important to you because he mentioned Peet's name."

"Peets name. What Peet has to do with that?"

"He's claiming Lewis and Peet helped him get girls."

"Not my Peet," Jamie said without thought.

"Jamie, he has proof," Kevin said.

"Proof!", "What proof!"

"According to him, he paid Peet hush money on three occasions."

"Are you sure it's my Peet?"

"Yes."

"And Lewis?"

"Lewis, along with Rumerez and..."

"That's Rosco.", Jamie chimed in.

"Oh, okay, so you know about Rumerez and Macki?"

"Carlos Macki?"

"According to the mayor, he was assisting Macki in bringing down Lewis and Rumerez."

"Son of a bitch!" Jamie snarled into the phone.

"Excuse me?"

"Can you get that in black and white for me?"

"Yeah, but it'll be unofficial."

"That's fine. Let me call you back."

Things were starting to make sense, Jamie thought as she started to place all the pieces together. But there was that million-dollar question she needed answered: WHERE WAS CURLY AND WHAT WAS HIS NEXT MOVE? Seventy-two hours; that was all the time her captain gave her to bring Curly and whoever else to Justice – with fourteen hours gone, she had less than sixty hours to get her man. It was now or never.

"Leslie? Yeah, this is Jamie from Homicide – I need a favor off the record."

"Talk to me."

"Want to know if I can swing by with a dozen or so prints for you to match for me?"

"Why would that be off the record?"

"The person you're matching it to is one of ours," Jamie explained.

"Another witch hunt!"

Jamie could hear the disappointment in his voice. "It's not like that," Jamie pleaded.

"I don't know, Jamie. I almost lost my job the last time you asked."

"He killed Peet Leslie. That son of a bitch killed Peet!"

"What do you mean he killed Peet? The kid on the bike killed Peet."

"No! Curly killed Peet just like he killed Rosco. The kid was just following orders."

"Who is Rosco?"

"The Rumerez case."

"You talking about the garage you got shot?"

"Yeah, Rosco was shot in his office by Det.Macki. I need you to run his print with all the prints in that room."

"Jamie."

"You're the only one who can help me.", Jamie stressed.

"Jamie."

"Will you help me?"

"Fine! Fine, okay."

"Thank you, Leslie... thank you."

"Can you be here within the next hour?" Leslie asked.

"I'm on my way!"

CHAPTER 29

Elevator music was always strange to Agent Sky. Being in the bureau and riding a lot of elevators meant listening to a lot of elevator music, and for Sky, it was fourteen years of unwanted aggravation. What was the purpose of putting music in an elevator? Why would someone make music just to be played in an elevator? What type of person likes this type of music? Sky would always think those thoughts [to himself] the second he stepped into an elevator, and just as bad as he hated stepping into one, he felt even worse stepping out at that particular moment... just as the doors parted, Agent Sky saw Todd, Hope, and Franky being escorted towards him by a slender white male with red curly hair.

"Where the hell you think you're going." Agent Sky demanded.

"Cracka, we out'a here."

"My ass," Agent Sky shot back.

"Agent Sky?" Curly extended his hand. "I'm special Agent Macki."

"I give a rat's ass who you are.", Agent Sky said while refusing to shake Curly's hand. "These are my prisoners, you little prick! You don't just come into a man's house go in his icebox!"

"I guess inmate was too big of a word for the whiteboy," Todd heckled.

"Agent Sky, I have direct orders from up top to leave this building with these three gentlemen," He handed Agent Sky a folded piece of paper bearing the Federal Bureau imprint. "It's all in there. If you have any questions" – He handed him a card – "call that number and ask for a Jack Braves."

"You have your orders."

"Screw your orders," Agent Sky barked as he reached out to grab Franky.

Special Agent Macki pulled the side of his coat back with one hand, exposing his sidearm while extending the other out towards Agent Sky. "Is this really what you want to do?" He asked with a hostile sneer.

"This isn't over, asshole!" Agent Sky suggested.

"I'm afraid it is." Special Agent Macki responded, and just as Hope, Franky, and Todd came in as Agent Sky's ace in the hole, they were leaving, taking not only his last chance to catch Nije but also his last trump card. As all four men climbed into the elevator, Franky and Sky met eyes for what seemed to be the last time. No words were exchanged between the two, but Franky was able to flash a smirk and give a head nod, which was clearly taken by Agent Sky as some sort of victory taunt.

"I'll be back," Agent Sky mouthed in silence as he watched the elevator doors shut close.

* * * * * *

"You wanted proof," Jamie tossed a blue folder on the desk of her captain, "Here's your proof," she announced proudly. The captain picked up the folder, read the contents, and then tossed the folder back onto the desk.

"It's not enough."

"What do you mean?" Jamie asked, shocked at what she just heard. "His prints were on the victims' gun, for Christ's sake."

"Not enough," he stated once more.

"What about his prints on the desk handle? That son of bitch planted that gun on him!"

"I believe you. I'm just saying I need more than the fingerprint of acop on the gun of a wanted killer."

"He killed Peet, Rumerez, and that kid on the bike to cover his tracks!"

"That's why I gave you seventy-two hours to bring me solid proof that I can show my supervisors."

"Now what?" Jamie asked, flopping onto the couch in defeat.

"Now is when you pull yourself together and do what you gotta do to get what you want." He walked over and sat next to Jamie, "This just as important for me as you. I have a lot to lose if this blow up in my face. My ass on the line as well. In our line of work, it's like suicide when you accuse another officer of killing another cop without solid proof."

In Jamie's heart, she knew the captain was right, "I understand," Jamie acknowledged.

"That doesn't mean I want you to lay down. Just be smart. That's all, the captain replied."

"So, what exactly do you need to put that S.O.B. in prison?"

"The first thing I need is for you to bring whatever you find to me, and me only. As far as Mack is concerned, see if you can get'em on tape saying why he killed Rosco, Peet, or the kid. A tape confession would be just needed to put him away for a long, long..."

"What did you just say?" Jamie asked. Her face showed her confusion.

"What? About having it on tape?"

"No. Right before that."

"Get your head in the game, Lightbourn. How you plan on catching Macki if you can't pay attention to simple instructions!"

"I'm sorry, I just thought I heard... never mind."

The captain looked to his watch and then to Jamie, "Is there somewhere you need to be?"

Bewildered, Jamie pondered on the question before realizing what her captain was insinuating. A little embarrassed, she bounced to her feet and headed towards the door.

"Lightbourn?" the captain barked, stopping Jamie just as she pulled open the door.

"Yes, sir," Jamie asked.

"Remember, whatever you find, bring straight to me."

"Will do, sir," Jamie responded, closing the door behind her. The captain was right, Jamie thought as she walked down the corridor to the elevator. She had to make sure that whatever evidence she had against Curly was proof; she understood the margin for error was slim to none and that time was not on her side. She just wished the captain would have given her a little more time. Maybe he only gave her seventy-two hours because he felt she could do it in such a short time? Or maybe he didn't believe in her but still gave her the benefit of the doubt? For Jamie, it really didn't matter why. She wrestled with her concerns for half a second before pushing them out of her head. She had to. She had a killer to catch, and she had to stay focused; no ifs, ands, or buts about it. As Jamie walked out of the elevator into the car garage, her mind rushed to find a way to get Curly to confess or find someone who'd testify against him. For some reason, the sound of the car engine turning over placed Jamie's mind back in time... flashes of her being shot by Rosco's men rushed her memory bank. Visions of Curly and Peet up in each other's faces transpired right before her very eyes; she could literally hear Curly call out the name "Rosco," and then it hit her! Her captain was called Rumerez by Rosco as well. How did he know him by that name? Did he know Rosco? Was the captain holding back information... nothing made sense. Too many holes to be filled. Catch Curly... Catch Curly, and all the pieces to the puzzle will come together, Jamie reminded herself. Just as she put the car into drive, her phone rang.

"Lightbourn"

"Hey Jamie, not sure if it will help, but the three guys from the Lewis case was arrested by the feds yesterday."

"Where are they now?" Jamie asked.

"They're still downtown at the federal building, last I heard," Kevin answered.

"Thanks, Kev," Jamie said.

"You're welcome, so are you going down there?"

"Yeah, gotta start somewhere."

"When you have time, I got what you asked for."

"Good. I'll be to see you soon. Thanks again, Kev."

"No problem. Anytime."

Being a federal agent would have been a dream come true for Detective Lightbourn. The feds only targeted the best of the best the criminal world had to offer; only on that level could a difference be made – Jamie knew that better than anyone, and for a long time, she craved the chance to make her mark as a federal agent. After being denied numerous times, Jamie thought it would be best too if she kept her talents along with her desires in Orlando; being in homicide could not compare to being a federal agent, but it was no chop liver either... not to Jamie, but yet and still she always wondered what it would be like or if she truly had what it took to be one? She tried not to think too much about it when she drove the corridors, which was much harder than she had expected, but she was on a mission. She took two deep breaths, refocused her thoughts and walked up to the secretary sitting behind an oversized desk.

"Hi, how are you doing? My name is Jamie Lightbourn", she showed her badge, "I'm with the Orange County Police Department. Who do I talk to about interviewing two people you have here in custody?"

"Do you have an appointment?"

"No. Not really.", Jamie responded.

"May I see your badge?"

"Yeah, sure." Jamie handed over her badge.

The secretary wrote her badge number down, typed it into his computer, then handed it back. "Give me one sec."

"Okay," Jamie nodded in agreeance. She flashed a smile as she tried to eavesdrop on his phone conversation.

"Someone will be right down to see you," he acknowledged right before he replaced the backdown.

"Perfect," Jamie replied.

Feeling overcrowded, the secretary asked Jamie to take a seat on one of the couches across the room. A little embarrassed, Jamie did as she was told without questioning why. Ten minutes later, she was approached by an agent.

"Detective?"

Jamie looked up, then came to her feet. To her surprise, they stood eye to eye. Awkwardly, she extended her hand to him, but he refused to shake hands. "Yes. How are you doing?"

"Who are you looking for?" he asked bitterly.

"I'm sorry, but are you in charge.... maybe I need to talk to..."

"Don't apologize," He insisted.

"Come again?" Jamie asked.

"I'm just a little upset right now. That's all. But how can I help you?"

"I was told that a Todd Patrick and Howard..."

"Sneed."

"Yeah. Howard Sneed and Todd Patrick were arrested by you guys, and I really need to talk to them." Jamie explained.

"I'm sorry, Agent Ski," he extended his hand toward Jamie. "How do you know them?"

"You with narcotics?"

"No. Homicide."

"How could three drug dealers be of help to a murder?" Ski asked.

"The case centered around a dirty cop who was dealing drugs," Jamie explained.

"Was! Is he dead? Did they kill him?"

"No. but I believe they can help me on something else."

"Yeah"

"Who was killed, if you don't mind me asking?"

"My partner," Jamie acknowledged, fighting to hide her emotions.

"Sorry to hear that."

"Do you think it's possible for me to talk with them?" Jamie asked.

"I'm afraid you're too late. Appears your three amigos are very popular right now."

"I don't follow."

"Some redhead prick with freckles just came and snatched them right out my hands."

"Was he with homicide?"

"Locals don't have that authority, detective." He handed Jamie the card he was given.

"So, what, they just walked out?"

Agent Ski flopped onto the couch, placed his hands over his face and rested the back of his head against the wall. "Yeap!" his words muddled from behind his fingers.

"Where did they go?"

"If you have any complaints, call the number on the card." Agent Ski said mockingly.

Jamie studied the F.B.I. card for a few seconds, then handed it back to Agent Ski. "There's no name on it?"

"Only the ones who want you call back have them."

"Did you arrest them, Agent Ski?"

"With my own two hands," He stared blankly into the palms of his hands.

"Do you mind me asking for what?"

"I don't mind you asking, but I hope you don't mind me not telling you?"

"Of course," Jamie said disappointedly.

Seeing the thwarted look on Jamie's face made Agent Skie realize Jamie was feeling the same defeat he was feeling and decided to help. "What exactly are you trying to do?"

"About what?"

"About this case you're working on?" Ski asked.

"Are you offering to help me?"

"I think so... what can I do?"

Jamie pondered on his inquest a few seconds before answering, "I need to run a background check on a dirty cop."

"You gotta name?"

"Macki. Carlos Macki."

"Special Agent Macki?" Agent Ski asked.

"Curly. Special Agent? I don't think so," Jamie let out a light laugh.

"Well, the guy who took the guys you're looking for is Carlos Macki... Special Agent. Carlos Macki."

"Curly..."

"I don't know, this Curly character you're speaking of, but if Curly's last name is Macki and his first name is Carlos… we're talking about the same guy."

"But Curly works homicide."

"Still want to do a background check?"

"Right now?" Jamie asked.

"Follow me." Agent Ski led Jamie to his office on the sixth floor. While on the elevator, she filled him in as much as she could. After explaining how everything was off the record until she had solid evidence and how her captain had her on a timetable, Ski assured Jamie that whatever they found would stay between the two of them. Instead of logging onto the office computer, Agent Ski pulled out his personal laptop.

"Give me just two minutes," Agent Ski asked as he made a call on his cellphone.

"Want me to step out?" Jamie asked.

Agent Ski motioned for her to have a seat. "It's me… I'm going on in three minutes. Okay. Okay. Yeah." Agent Ski placed the phone on the table, waited three minutes, and then logged onto his laptop.

"Can you look up anybody on that?" Jamie inquired.

"Anyone but the president and a few execs," Ski acknowledged as he surfed the laptop.

"What will it be able to tell us?"

"Everything you want to know," Ski turned around the laptop, showing a picture of Curly.

"He looks so young," Jamie spoke without thinking.

"There's no way he was in homicide," Agent Ski commented.

"Is this accurate?" Jamie asked as he read through a slew of accomplishments and accolades.

"You're in over your head, detective." Agent Ski closed his laptop.

"What're you doing? I was reading that."

"And now you're finished. I thought I could help you."

"Are you serious?" Jamie asked bitterly.

"Listen. This isn't good cop, bad cop detective… walk away," he advised her.

"You ever had a partner killed Agent Ski?"

"I can't tell you I feel your pain, detective. But this guy can be bad news for you. Literally."

"I can't, and I won't!"

"I'm sorry about your friend…"

"Peet was more than a friend. I told you. He was my partner."

"Again, I'm sorry for your loss, but the guy you're chasing doesn't exist."

"Only one who's going to be sorry will be Curly when I nail his ass to the wall."

"Just walk away."

"Can I at least see the rest of the file?"

"Your funeral detective.", Agent Ski professed before opening back up his laptop.

"Thank you." Jamie snuggled up to the small screen and filled her brain with as much information as she could. The more she read, the more she realized that Agent Ski wasn't pulling her leg and that her life would be in grave danger if she pursued any further, but Curly killed Peet, and it didn't matter if Peet was on the take or not. Peet was her partner. Right or Wrong. Curly. Special Agent Macki, whoever he was going to pay for what he did – she was going to make sure of that. After taking a few more notes, Jamie thanked Agent Ski once more, then left. Shortly after Jamie left, Agent Ski picked up his cell phone and dialed out.

"Yeah, it's me again... I need a favor. I'm about to send you something – tell me what you think?"

CHAPTER 30

When Candy was a little girl, she loved to eavesdrop on the conversations her grandmother would have with her friends – the rule of thumb back then was for the children to be seen and not heard, but Candy always felt the child was never seen or heard, she was never allowed to partake in any of the discussions her grandmother or any adult had. Always a thinker, Candy had to find creative ways to get to her ear in listening positions, and when she did, she would hear some of the funniest, scariest and sometimes saddest stories. It was during those times she would hear about the emotions a woman would go through while carrying a child. Good and Bad. Today was one of those days when the bad emotions were getting the best of her. Today was the third time she and Todd were supposed to go and see the doctor together, and this was the third time she'd gone alone... within one minute, Candy felt angry, frustrated, and unappreciated with Todd because of Todd. Never the victim, Candy dried her eyes, fixed her face, then walked into the clinic.

"Hello, I have a three o'clock appointment with Doctor O'Ney," Candy tried her best to flash a smile.

"If you would have a seat, she'd be with you shortly."

Candy mustered up another smile and then took a seat next to a couple with the cutest little girl – From the bump in the woman's stomach, they were expecting another. Rather, he was the husband or just the baby's father, Candy felt somewhat jealous of how open-eyed he was. How attentive he was towards her and the little girl. The way he rubbed her stomach made Candy want her stomach rubbed. She really wanted to be there with her. After hearing her name being called, Candy went to the back to see Doctor O'Ney.

"Miss James"

"Hey, Doctor O'Ney." Candy walked over and gave the doctor a hug.

"I take it your friend didn't make it?"

"I still want to know what the sex of the baby is," Candy said matter faculty.

"Are you fighting because that's not healthy for the baby, you know?"

"If he misses another appointment, we will!" Candy mumbled as she stood on the digital scale.

"I'm sorry, sweetie, but what did you say?"

"Nothing. Is this scale, right?" Candy gestured.

The doctor looked down at the scale, jotted down in her file, then placed her hand on Candy's stomach.

"Sure is. But I would like for you to eat a little more – at five months, I would like for you to gain fifteen pounds."

"I'm already getting fat, and you want me to get even fatter?"

"First rule of motherhood... no more you. Always us."

"But I've gained. How much have I gained?"

"Thirteen pounds on the head." Doctor O'Ney giggled.

"Only if it's the best you can do, but if you can do better – do better."

"Yes, ma'am."

"Now, come and lay down so we can see what you're about to introduce to the world."

"I can't believe I'm having a baby." Candy laid on her back and placed both hands on her stomach.

"I remember the first time I was pregnant."

"Doctor O'Ney, you have children?"

"Well, don't look so surprised, Ms. Lady. I was quite the catch back in my day," she let out a light laugh.

"Are you married?" Candy asked.

"Yes, I am." She acknowledged proudly.

Candy removed her hands as the doctor squirted the clear gel on her stomach, "Do you keep that in the freezer?"

"Everybody asks that," the doctor mumbled while moving a small device around Candy's belly. "There we go."

"Can you see my baby? Can you see the baby?" Candy's voice went from nervous to excited.

"Well, what do you know!"

"I know Todd really wants a girl, but honestly, I want myself a little man."

"God knows best, sweetie... God knows best."

"It's a boy? Am I having a boy?"

"Look for yourself, sweetheart."

When Candy looked over to the screen, she felt her heart skip and breath shorten. This was the first time she'd seen arms moving, legs kicking, or the heart beating; She was officially a mommy. Being pregnant brought a lot of concern for Candy, but the movement she saw on the screen and the amount of joy she felt was beyond words.

Doctor O'Ney took a pen and placed it to the right of the screen. "This is your baby boy," she pointed the pen to the left side, pausing for a few seconds, "And... and this would be your little... little girl."

"Twins?"

"Yes, ma'am," the doctor professed.

"Twins. I'm really having twins.", Candy expressed with tears of joy.

"Congratulations, sweetie, congratulations. I told you God knows best."

* * * * * *

Todd, Hope, and Franky were taken to an undisclosed building somewhere in Sanford. As they sat blindfolded in small metal chains, the smell of mildew pipes and old water paint filled the room. Unable to move, all three sat in silence as the sound of dripping water bounced off the walls. Todd was the first to have his blindfold removed; he recognized the agent at first sight but was reluctant about saying it. After a few moments of silence, the agent spoke.

"Gentleman. I have an offer you can't refuse!"

"Man, take these damn cuffs off... my damn wrist hurt", Hope demanded.

"In due time, Mr. Sneed, but first, we talk business," Curly explained.

"Well then, talk!" Todd ordered.

"Mr. Patrick, this is not your show anymore, this you need to understand. You also need to understand that from this point on out, you will do what I say when I say it and how I say it?"

"Man, say what you gotta say," Todd requested.

"Fine. The three of you are going to work for me."

"Work for you?"

"Yes. Work for me."

"If that's what you talk about, saying a nigga can't refuse... cracker, you dun bumped you head. I'm not working for you. Silly ass cracker!" Hope explained matter factly.

Curly walked over to Hope and placed his hands on Hope's thighs, leaning in so close that their noses almost touched.

"Are you sure you don't want to take that statement back?" Curly whispered.

"Cracker fuck you!" Hope answered.

Curly exposed a small smirk, then nodded his head in agreeance with Hope's comment. Within a blink of an eye, Curly slapped Hope so hard he knocked him to the floor, splitting his lip in the process. "Is that your final answer?" Curly asked, his pistol aimed between the center of Hope's eyes.

"We'll do it!" Todd yelled.

"Glad to hear you're on board, Mr. Patrick, but I was talking to Mr. Sneed." Curly suggested.

"Hope tell the man you'll do it," Todd said.

Curly bent down and shoved the barrel of the gun into Hope's nose, "Yeah, Hope, tell me you'll do it," Curly commanded as he forced Hope's head back with the tip of the gun.

"Hope! Tell him you'll do it, my nigga! Man, tell the man!"

"I'll do it," Hope confessed through tears while tasting his blood.

"Never test me again, Mr. Sneed, or I will kill you," Curly said calmly.

"You wanna talk business... what we gotta do?" Todd asked, bringing Curly's focus back to him.

"Sell my dope!" Curly announced as he uncuffed Todd, then Franky.

"How much dope? And what's our cut?" Todd asked.

Curly tossed Todd the handcuff key, "Would you mind picking up your friend? Two hundred bricks a month... do that, and I won't lock your ass up for 30 years."

"If you did your homework, you would know we don't have the clientele to move that in one month."

"Well, Mr. Patrick, I don't think you were trying hard enough?" Curly responded.

"I go smart, not hard. Always!"

"Go home to Miss. James Mr. Patrick. I'll call you in the next three days to tell you where to pick up the dope. Like I said, this is an offer you can't refuse." Curly gestured to himself, then pointed towards a door behind all three in the far-left hand corner of the building. Todd led Hope and Franky through the narrow door, where they were once again blindfolded and put back into the truck. Forty minutes later, they were dropped off half a mile from Candy's house. They had to walk home.

* * * * * *

"Are you serious... twins?"

"Yeap. A boy and a girl", Candy patted the top of her stomach.

"Todd must be ecstatic?" Stephanie asked.

"Why not? Wasn't he there for the sonogram?" Stephanie questioned.

"I haven't seen or spoke to Todd in two days."

"Well, have you tried calling?"

"Like a thousand times already."

"Didn't you say he was a street person – think something might have happened?" Stephanie asked.

"Like he went to jail or something?" Candy suggested.

"Yeah."

"I doubt it, if that was the case, he would have hit me up by now."

"Well then, don't trip. He'll be home sometime today, and you can tell him you're having twins."

"Don't trip?" Candy repeated with a big smile, "That's what's up." She started laughing.

"What! What? Why are you laughing? I said it correctly... didn't I?" Stephanie asked.

"Yes, Stephanie. You said it right."

"What are you still laughing at then?"

"Trust me. I'm laughing with you, baby girl. Not at you," Candy implied.

"Have you thought of any names?" Stephanie asked.

"Not yet, but I will."

"Wow! I can't believe you're having twins." Stephanie leaned over and gave Candy a hug.

"I'm scared, Stephanie," Candy whispered during their hug.

"Scared of what sweetheart? You're going to be a great mother." Stephanie pointed out.

"Everything. Little things. Big things."

"Like what, sweetheart?"

"Will my babies have all ten fingers and toes? How can I be everything for them, and how can I make sure nothing will happen to them? Will Todd... Todd might not even be here to see them being born or grow into young adults; I don't know, I guess I'm just..."

Stephanie chimed in, "Being a mother?"

"I'm just having a lot of uncertainty right now, that's all," Candy implied.

"What great mother wouldn't?" Stephanie asked.

"Were you scared when you first got pregnant?" Candy asked.

"Honey, I was shaking like Don Notts," – Stephanie started laughing, "but I was seventeen and immature, unlike you, who is more focused than I was at the age you are now and more established as an adult than I was. Being scared just shows that you are putting that baby first... as should be."

"Thank you." Candy leaned over and gave Stephanie a hug.

"Anytime, sweetie... anytime."

Candy went into the kitchen to fix the two of them some of her famous tea. Waiting for the water to come to a boil, she thought about all Stephanie had said to her; some things she knew in her heart but needed to hear, while other things she just needed to know. After the first girls' night Candy hosted at her house, Stephanie was the one Candy felt the closest to; the two became best friends. Candy was pleased that she had another woman to share things with, while Stephanie was just as happy to have a friend mature enough to trade thoughts and share dreams with. Each one shared her life story with the other. Stephanie told stories of her overly aggressive alcoholic mother beating her as a child. Candy talked about her drug addict mother and not knowing her father until she was almost grown, but it wasn't until Candy told her about being raped by Rosco and his goons that Candy realized how special Stephanie was to her.

Lost in thought, Candy's daydream was short lived as the whistling from the teapot brought her back to reality. Little did she know her perfect day with her BFF was about to come to an end. Forever ready to go from bad to worse, Candy was right on point when Todd, Hope, and Franky came into the house hooting and hollering about some white boy who think he's tough.

Walking back to the living room, Candy heard her uncle saying something about being pistol whipped.

"You know that White boy gonna cross us!" Franky expressed.

"Man, fuck that cracker!" Hope shouted.

"Both of y'all need to relax," Todd shouted.

"Nigga, you the one yelling!" Hope shouted back.

"Ain't nobody yelling my nigga, I'm just saying chill out," Todd explained.

"What happened to your face!" Candy pushed herself between Todd and Franky walked up to Hope.

"Nothing," Todd responded.

"What happened to his face?" Candy asked again, never taking her eyes off of Hope's face.

"Pussy ass cracker hit me with a gun!" Hope answered.

"I'll be right back." Candy went to the bathroom and came back with a washcloth. "Franky, get me some ice."

"Candy. I'm about to go. Call me later." Stephanie suggested.

"That's my friend.", Candy said harshly.

"Man, right now ain't the time for that hoe to be over here!"

"Boy you done lost your mind." "Don't call her that!" Candy said with anger.

"Who you talking to?" Todd walked up to Candy.

"Todd. She's pregnant," Stephanie cried out as she stood between the two of them. "She's pregnant."

"What's ya name, white girl?" Hope asked.

"My name is Stephanie!"

"Let me walk you to your car," Hope suggested.

"Are you okay, sweetie?" She asked Candy.

"Yeah. I'm good."

Stephanie looked at Hope and then back to Todd. "Okay. I'll call you tonight."

Hope walked Stephanie out of the house and to the car, then came back in. "What you plan on doing with that whiteboy?"

"Don't know yet," Todd answered.

"What whiteboy? Is that who hit you?" Candy pointed to Hope.

"Didn't the whiteboy say he'll be calling a day after tomorrow?" Franky asked.

"So, we got until tomorrow to come up with something" Hope responded.

"None of this makes sense. First, homicide all over us for some cop being killed, then they back off. Now the feds grab us... we don't even know if they still gonna charge us for the body? But now some dude take us from him talking about two hundred bricks a month."

"What body?" Candy asked with panic.

All three looked to Candy and then one another. "Candy, go fix me a drink, please," Todd said more as an order than a question. Reluctant to do so, feeling she was being ignored, she did it anyway.

"So, what you think, FBI?" Franky asked.

"Can't really say who he is, besides, too many agencies to be sitting here guessing on that." Todd voiced firmly.

"For now, at least until I can come up with an exit plan."

"What about old girl?" Hope questioned.

"Who? Candy! What about her?"

"What about Candy?" Candy asked as she came back carrying a few drinks.

"Nothing!" Todd said sharply, simultaneously giving Hope a threatening eyes.

"Nothing?" she looked to Hope and Franky for some insight before turning back to Todd, "Let's try this again."

"You tell her everything else! Yell her what's up!" Hope blurted out.

"What that be bout?"

"I'm just saying my nigga", Hope shot back.

"All she need to worry about is that baby," Todd gestured to Candy's stomach.

"We all need to be worried because right now, we don't know who's who or what's what?" Franky said.

"Man... fuck all that! I'm tired of trying to figure this shit out! Come Friday, we'll know how the white boy likes his who's and what's – I'm trying to blow one! Nigga twist one up," Hope looked to Todd.

"I'll blow one later. I need to wrap with Candy right quick." Hope busted down a blunt for him and Franky to smoke, and Todd and Candy walked to the backroom.

"So, what you think they going to do about the body," Franky asked skeptically.

"So, this how you gonna play it?"

"Play what?" Franky asked with a guarded tone.

"How long the whiteboy been on us?"

"I don't even know if he's DEA, FBI, ATF... hell I'm supposed to know that!"

"Who told you that cracker was coming through the window?" Hope asked.

"I don't play the indirect games, youngster... say what you gotta say!"

"Sound good, but you still haven't answered my question?"

"Don't play with me!" Franky voiced with aggression.

"So what? You didn't think we were smart enough to peep game? You a rat, my nigga!"

"Something told me wasn't right that day in the car you mentioned the connect was Haitian."

"Man, I don't know what the hell you talking about?"

"What you getting out'a this shit?"

Hope slammed his fist into the palm of his hand. "That's why the police went to see Todd at the hospital. That's how that lady cop was all over us, and that's how you knew the whiteboy was coming through the window – yo rat ass been working with them, people." Hope lunged from his seat and dove into Franky, taking the two of them to the floor where he wildly swang his arms, plunging his fist numerous times into Franky's face. Hope was full of anger; he swung his arms as fast and as hard as he could. Hope blamed Franky for everything; Candy being raped, Todd being shot. The three of them were charged with murder. Him getting beat up by that whiteboy. Everything.

"Get the fuck off of me!" Franky screamed as he kicked Hope donkey-style into the coffee table, breaking it into pieces like a cat. Hope bounced to his feet and squared off with the old man. Before either could throw a punch, Todd and Candy came storming into the living room.

"Who broke my table?" Candy cried.

"Man, what the hell y'all doing?" Todd questioned.

"Yo uncle a big ass rat... he broke yo table!" Hope pointed to Franky.

"This girl's couch flipped over, her table broke, and her flowerpots knocked down." – Todd gestured to all three items – "Fuck y'all fighting for?" Todd asked.

"I told you. Ratboy the reason why we all fucked up! Everything. From you being shot, us going to jail the other night... even Rosco fat ass raping yo Georgia peach, nigga!"

"Raped?" Todd looked over to Candy.

"Yeah! And it's all because of him," Hope pointed to Franky.

Hope's words literally took the air from Candy's lungs, causing her knees to buckle and forcing her to grab the first thing closest to her – which just so happened to be Todd. Candy couldn't believe what Hope just did. What was more shocking was that he even knew what happened to her. Stephanie warned her not to keep that secret from Todd – told her he had a right to know, but Candy was too afraid to tell him, too ashamed to let anyone else know how she was taken advantage of. In her heart, she knew Todd loved her, but she also knew that Todd would look at her differently. Treat her differently. Act differently, and for Candy, that would be worse than being raped. Emotionally, Todd was built to handle anything, but mentally, he was unprepared for the devasting news hope so inconsiderately placed in his life.

Todd sat Candy down then took a few steps back. "Is the baby mine?"

"Babies," Candy mumbled.

"I'm having... we're having twins."

"How do you know they mine?"

Candy looked over to Franky and Hope. "I need for the two of you to leave," Candy stated harshly.

"Yeah. Y'all need to bounce," Todd concurred.

Candy gathered her thoughts and then spoke from her heart, "I was never going to tell you I was raped."

"Tell me something I don't know."

"You asked how I know the babies are yours? I'm five months pregnant. Those bastards raped me four months ago. That's how I know."

"You should've told me. I had the right to know."

"You would have left me if I'd told you." Candy confessed.

"I wouldn't have left you." Todd acknowledged.

"Then don't leave me now!"

"I have to go, we'll talk later."

"Where are you going?" Candy asked as Todd headed out the front door.

"Get this whiteboy off my neck," Todd replied as he closed the door behind him. Candy knew she had to do something to keep her family together. She had to find a way to help Todd get whoever it was off his neck; once he was free from the streets, the four of them would be able to live the life she so badly wanted. Feeling she had nothing to lose, Candy pulled a small card from her purse and dialed the number printed at the bottom. After the third ring, a voice came on the other end.

"Lightbourn?"

"You said you would help Todd if I called," Candy's voice appeared desperate and blocked.

"I'm sorry, but who am I speaking to."

"Candy James. I mean Casondra. Casondra James."

"I can't get your boyfriend out of jail, Miss. James."

"Todd isn't in jail, detective. That's why I'm calling you…"

"You've seen him? Is Sneed with him?" Jamie chimed in.

"You already know what's going on?" Candy asked.

"All I know is that the feds have them or had them in custody," Jamie answered.

"Who is forcing them to sell dope? And who beat up Sneed?" Jamie asked.

"I think they said he worked with FBI and ATF and CIA?" Jamie said without sureness.

"Where are you, Miss. James!" Jamie asked with urgency.

"At the house. Why?" Candy said, picking up on Jamie and pressing one of his voice.

"Who's there with you?"

"No one. They all left."

"I'm on my way!"

"No! I'll come to you." Candy retorted. They both agreed on the place and time and met up later that evening where Candy told Jamie everything.

CHAPTER 31

"Bonjour monsieur"
"Everything is everything come Friday."
"Excellent. I've been looking forward to this."
"So have I... talk to you in a few weeks."
"Will do, my friend," the old man said as he pushed the end button on his cell phone.
"Sorry I just popped up to your crib, but this is important," Todd explained.
"How can I help you?" the old man asked.
"You can't. I'm just here to tell you in person that I'm walking away."
"Yeah, Hope already told me that," Nije answered.
"Hope? When did Hope tell you this?"
"About three, four months ago... you'd just been shot, I think?"
"And not today?"
"No. Last time I spoke with Hope was about two weeks ago. To be honest, I thought you were him, coming to bring me some money, actually."
"I never told Hope to come and talk to you."
"Well, he did, and when I didn't hear from you, I figured it to be true."
"It is now," Todd stated firmly.
"Why now? If it's about the prices, Hope and I have worked out new numbers that will be beneficial for both sides."
"I'm not tripping on the prices. I get my money; just have to work through some thangs, and I don't want you caught up in my bullshit, that's all."
"What, you in the middle of some turf war ignorance!" Nije inquired.
"I wish it was just some cats tripping... man, I'm just gone tell you what the lick read: Feds bammed me and my dawgs yesterday, but some other agency snatched us from them."
"What do you mean snatched from them?" Nije chimed in.
"Make a long story short. I believe they want to use me to get someone else?"
"And you feel it might be me?" Nije asked.
"Maybe. Maybe not. All I know is you and me straight. You always kept it G with me, and I'm a real nigga, so you know how that goes", Todd said proudly.
"So, what makes you think they want you to set someone up?"
"You know when you get that feeling that something is more than what it seems? Something about this redhead fuckboy is telling me I'm caught up in something way bigger than me!"
"Redhead? Who is redhead?" Nije inquired.
"I'm just calling him redhead because he got red hair... some agent putting the press game on me and my people's." "I see. So, what's your next move?"

"Don't know yet. He should be hitting me up by Friday... take it from there. I just wanted to let you know what's what," Todd responded. Nije and Todd exchanged a few more words before Nije walked Todd to the front door. Later that night, after supper, Nije retired to his quarters to have himself a nightcap. The conversation he and Todd shared was pulling on his spirit something heavy. It appeared Curly was after him after all – that would explain why Hope came to him behind Todd's back. Nije was starting to feel like the political pitch was a ploy, smoke and mirrors. What if he was the cat's paw of a bigger scheme? Or maybe the ends to a means? Nije spent all that night rationalizing over every conspiracy theory with two shots of bourbon until he finally passed out. He woke up the next day with a hangover, dry mouth, and paranoia. He made up his mind that if he was going down, he was going down swinging.

* * * * * *

"I didn't think you would show up," Jamie said offhandedly.

"Can you help us?" Candy asked.

"I believe so?" Jamie answered.

"That's not good enough." Candy shot back as she turned to walk away.

Jamie grabbed her arm and turned her back around. "I can help you! Tell me what you know."

"Promise me no one will know what I'm about to tell you."

"Okay... promise", Jamie agreed.

"That cop who was killed – Todd, Hope or my uncle didn't do it."

"Which one?"

"The one you asked about the first time we met," Candy explained.

"You mean Detective Lewis."

"Him and Rosco was trying to set up Hope with that car full of dope, but Todd ended up behind the wheel when Hope went to jail."

"Go on."

"Rosco kidnapped me; that's how Todd got shot... trying to rescue me."

"Go on."

"The newspaper said that Rosco killed detective Lewis... you guess killed Rosco, and I'm thinking we can go on and live our lives now, but some redhead super-agent is trying to have Todd sell their dope for them," Candy said tearfully.

"Redhead?"

"Todd has been doing business with some old man named Nije..."

"The redheaded man, have you seen him for yourself?" Jamie chimed in. "No. but listen, these drug lords... I don't want anything to happen to Todd just because some drug lord thinks Todd is trying to cross him!"

"Who does he work for?"

"Who, Todd? Todd doesn't work for anybody." Candy declared.

"Not Todd. The Agent."

"One of those big agencies FBI, DEA, CIA..."

"And how do you know all this?" Jamie asked.

"Todd told me earlier today."

"Who else knows about this?" Jamie asked.

"Just me, Todd, my uncle, and Hope."

"How much dope we talking about?"

"Todd told me they want him to sell two hundred keys a month. They told them if they don't do that, Todd will be charged with the death of some white man who tried to break in my house!"

"Someone was killed at your house. When did this happen?" Jamie demanded.

"Day-before-yesterday, but Todd didn't do it!" Candy pleaded.

"Was he there?"

"Yeah."

"Then it doesn't matter!" Jamie insisted.

"Todd can't move all that dope in one month. That's why I called you. That's why I need your help!"

"He's going to have to do something until I can get everything put into place.", Jamie suggested.

"It might be too late... Todd might be changed with murder before you have things in place."

"I don't know."

"You're going to have find out and tell me", Jamie requested.

"Okay," Candy answered.

"Also, I'm going to need for you to plant a bug on Todd," Jamie asked with a note of skepticism.

"You talking about a wire?" Candy asked in disbelief.

"Hear me out before you go AWAL! You told me Todd is being forced to do that... A wire will give me solid proof of just that. Do you want that drug lord to kill Todd or that agent to put him in prison for murder? Think about your baby! You have the power to make all this go in your favor. It's your life, your family, your choice."

Everything Jamie said Candy could feel in her heart was true, but in her head, it said trouble. Candy thought about everything she and Todd had been through and didn't want the twins to be exposed to any of that. Jamie was right. Candy did have the power to offer the twins a better life. A drama-free life where both parents would be in their lives, she felt she had no choice but to go all the way. It was now or never.

"Okay, detective, tell me what I got to do."

"When you know for a fact that everything is in motion, you call me! We'll start from there. Until then, go back home and be there for your family." – Jamie placed her hand on Candy's stomach – "And remember, you're doing the right thing. Trust me." Jamie reached over and gave Candy a hug, then walked back to her car. Contemplative about her next move, Jamie decided to go against her first mind and call Agent Ski instead of her captain concerning the new information she was holding. Her heart told her the Federal Agent would be of more help than some local cop, even if he was a captain. She was right. Agent Ski seemed very uninterested in her new findings and wanted her to come to his office ASAP – something about old man Nije had him all worked up.

CHAPTER 32

Friday 3:45 A.M.

"Hello?"

"Meet me at the warehouse off of Mercy Drive and Pine Hills Road."

"Now?" Todd asked tiredly.

"No. Not now. Right now!"

"We'll be there in half an hour," Todd announced.

"Just you, Mr. Patrick."

"I thought we..."

"Just you", he repeated.

"I'm on my way."

"Mr. Patrick, wear a plain white tee and blue jeans." He instructed.

"Okay. Fine.", Todd responded before hitting the end button on his cellphone.

"Where you going?" Candy asked lethargically as she watched Todd get dressed.

"That was the Agent... want me to meet him over on Mercy."

"Drive?" Candy asked with surprise.

"Yeah. Over at the warehouse", Todd answered while going into the bathroom.

"Do Hope and Franky know you're going over there?"

Todd stuck his head out of the bathroom. "I'm going solo... they'll be aight."

"Maybe you should take at least one of them with you, just in case!"

Todd came out of the bathroom and sat on the bed to put his shoes on. "Told me to come by myself," Todd explained, hoping to ease Candy's mind.

"When will you be back?"

"You going soft on me, now?"

"I just asked when you coming back", Candy responded defensively.

"Man, long as we've been together, you ain't never ask a nigga when I'm coming back from handling business. What's up with that?"

"You really have to ask me that?"

Todd looked at his watch, "I gotta go. I told the man I was on my way. We'll talk later." Todd leaned over and gave Candy a kiss before leaving the house. Thirty minutes later, he was pulling into the parking lot of the warehouse.

* * * * * *

"Has she come to you with anything we might take as a treat?" Curly asked with a hint of suspicion.

"Thanks to you, her nose is wide open now!"

"What does that mean?" Curly asked.

"It means your prints were on Rosco's pistol and on his desk handle."

"So what! That's nothing."

"So, the plan was for you to make it appear like your life was in danger, not leave your prints all over the place. If you would have followed orders right the first time, we could've been retired by now and Lewis wouldn't be dead."

"Lewis is dead because Lewis was being Lewis, and let's not forget who signed off every time large amounts of drugs were taken from the evidence room. Captain!"

"You just make sure you stick to the plan, and I'll handle Lightbourn." "You do that," Curly responded.

"Don't forget we need to meet up within the next couple of days."

"Gotta go, Mr. Patrick is here," Curly announced as he rudely hung up the phone in mid-sentence.

When Todd walked up to Agent Macki, he could see the pure evil in his eyes; for Todd. He felt like he had sold his soul to Satan. "Let's do this," Todd said with dismissal.

"Follow me," Curly commanded as he tossed Todd a car key. As Todd walked through the oversized parking lot, he wondered if all the people he'd seen were there for the same exact reason he was, and if they weren't, did he look out of place, a new face and all. What seemed odd to him was the fact that everybody – including the agent was wearing blue jeans and white tee shirts.

"We gotta go somewhere else to pick up the dope?" Todd asked as the two of them climbed into the empty van.

"Just drive... you acting like the police with that dumb ass question," Curly insisted.

"Where we going?" Todd asked, embarrassed by Curly's last comment. "Just drive," Curly repeated. He instructed Todd to get on I-4 and head west. Todd did as he was told – Fifty minutes later, they were on Interstate 4.

"How long you plan on forcing us to do your dirty work?" Todd asked.

"When it's over, I'll let you know," Curly stated facetiously.

"So, are you at least going to tell me how this little operation is going to work?" Todd asked.

"If you stop asking so many damn questions, I'll tell you what you need to know! Like, for once, I changed the amount of kilos you and your crew will have access to."

"You mean how much dope we'll move for you in a month," Todd responded.

"Something like that. But also, how you will deliver the money once you make it – just remember being short on money isn't an option, neither is being late, my friend," Curly stated.

"How much more you talking?"

"Instead of two hundred a month... you'll be doing three."

"You know that's some bullshit!" Todd shot back.

"No. What's some bullshit is you locked up for life and that pretty little thang of yours out here by herself in the free world with people like me."

"What about price?" Todd asked.

"Oh yeah, about that... instead of fifteen. Sixteen."

"Three hundred at sixteen a pop... that's what, four point eight?"

"You get to keep one-hundred fifty for living expenses," Curly proclaimed off-handedly.

"A piece?" Todd asked.

"Of course not. I'm not in the business to make drug dealers rich. Besides, I didn't want to give you that much, but I told you so."

"So, you're not the boss?" Todd asked with a small smirk.

"I'm the boss of your ass! Better not forget that.", Curly answered.

"Which exit to get off of?" Todd asked with a bit of an attitude.

"I'll let you know before you get there. Now, about the money? Once you sell everything, you'll call me, and I let you know where to pick back up in the van. You'll place the money into the hidden components, lock the doors, and push the alarm button on the key. A week later, you'll go back to the warehouse. Sametime as this morning, wearing the exact same clothes."

"So, the dope is already in the van?"

"Yeah. And it will be every time I call you, so when you get that call, b-line your ass straight over there and pick up the van – it'll always be the fourth can from the end of the third row."

"But where do I take the van once I put the money in it?"

"What time is that?"

"They close about eight o'clock at night.", Curly explained.

"So, how do I get into the hidden compartments?"

"Real simple. To open the bottom floor, all you have to do is hold down the off button on the radio while turning the volume knob all the way to the left. To open the ruff up, you have to turn off the engine. Place the gear shaft in drive two and push down on the gas pedal."

"So, this can will hold up to three hundred bricks?" Todd asked with wonder and approval.

"Three hundred on the head," Curly answered.

"So that's it?"

"One more thing... make sure all the bulls are twenty's and up. If possible, nothing but hundreds and fifties." Curly and Todd went over a few more details before Todd dropped Curly off in Tampa. Halfway back to Orlando, he called Hope to meet him at the house, where he later explained what was told to him by Curly. The amount of money involved made it clear to Todd that whoever was pulling the strings wasn't going to let him, Hope on Franky, just walk away. Todd knew first hand that when the stakes are that high, someone will have to die in order for someone to live.

CHAPTER 33

This was only Jamie's second time stepping foot into the Federal building downtown, but the feeling it gave Jamie was beyond words. Walking into that building early that morning made Jamie feel like she was a part of the team, a part of America's most privileged fraternity that worked day in and day out to rid the mother of all the free worlds from any and everything detrimental. After Jamie received her visitor pass, she jumped on the elevator to meet Agent Ski at his office. The moment Jamie stepped foot into the Federal building brought a noticeable cockiness about her; Her confidence was growing so much it was becoming borderline arrogant. She took that vibe with her straight into Agent Ski's office, where it was amusingly picked up on.

"Someone's feeling good.", Ski chuckled as Jamie strutted into the office.

"No crime in feeling on top of the world, Agent Ski," Jamie proclaimed with a hint of sassiness.

"No crime at all, detective. So, tell me, what does your informant know about Nije Culpa?"

"Well, she's not an informant… just decided to share some info to help get someone out of trouble."

"So, what did she say about Nije?"

"Nije, huh? Agent Skie, do you have a personal interest in this Nije character? If so, do I need to be worried that I may become a means to an end?"

"I have no more personal interest in this than you do, detective.", Ski suggested.

"I just don't want to be caught up in someone else's bedeviled witch hunt.", Jamie insisted.

"Look, detective, you and I have our own reasons for doing what we do, and we have different ways of getting it done. How about we do this together? Get our man. Call it a day? You want the cop killer. I want the drug dealer, simple as that!"

With less than twenty-eight hours left to bring her captain heard proof, Jamie was in no position to be barking out demands of any sort, if Curly was to be brought to justice, Jamie knew Agent Ski was her best chance and accomplishing such a feat. "Okay. We do it together", Jamie conceded.

"I didn't think you would let apples and oranges stop you from getting your man… come over here, I want to show you something." Ski flipped open his laptop and angled it towards Jamie.

"Is this what I was looking at yesterday?" Jamie asked.

"Yes and no.", Ski answered.

"So, what am I looking at?"

"See for yourself," Ski responded.

Jamie took the next twenty minutes reading an extensive profile put together on Agent Macki. All the questions she'd had were finally answered, but now, she was realizing just how hard it was going to be to bring him to justice. His rankings super exceeded her pay level – she was starting to doubt if Agent Ski would be able to help her. Maybe he already knew that he couldn't when he kicked her out of his office the first time? Maybe he just needed Jamie to catch the Nije Culpa character? Jamie walked numerous homicide cases, and whether the motive was clear or not, Jamie had a hard time reasoning why someone would casually take a life - in a way, that was what made her such a good homicide detective; infuriated, she would stop at nothing to catch such a stony-hearted person – but after reading what she read she understood why Rosco killed Lewis. Why Curly killed Rosco, and why Peet was gunned down like a dog. They all had to die in order for the mission to be met. Now, her mission was to end theirs.

"Where did you get this?" Jamie asked, somewhat fascinated.

"We're about to get into some really muddy waters... you know that, right?"

"How many times have you read this?"

"Three. Maybe four times."

"So, who do we go to first?" Jamie inquired.

"We do this alone, detective... can't bring anyone else in at this point."

"So, what do we do?"

"Good old-fashioned police work.", Ski implied.

"Have to be fast, whatever we do! My captain only gave me seventy-two hours to wrap this thing up."

"What would make him do that?"

"Been reckless a few times early in my career... didn't want this to blow up in either of our faces, I guess? My captain is one of those people strictly by the books."

"Fine. Go to him, tell him what you got, see what he says, and we'll go from there – but don't tell him about me... I have my own ass to watch out for."

"You do that, and I'll continue to work my mojo on this side." After Jamie left, Ski decided to go out and rattle a few cages. Ski knew the only way to put a kink in the armor was to cause dissent in the ranks. United stood, but if Ski had his way, divided, they were going to fall. The first cage he deemed to rattle first was agent Carlos Macki, from there, he would go to Nije himself. Old-fashioned police work, he thought as he walked out of the office. Old fashioned police work.

* * * * * *

"I'm guessing the first shipment went through?"

"Yeah. He got a call early this morning."

"So where is he now?"

"Not sure... might be with the rest of the crew."

"Where did he have to go and pick it up?"

"Some warehouse on Mercy... I mean off of Mercy."

181

"You still want help?"

"Would I be calling if I didn't!"

"Fair enough. Clear your schedule for today, I have a meeting in about five minutes. I should be finished by lunch; you can come to my office and…"

"… I'm not coming to your office!"

"Why not?"

"I'm not coming there. Period!"

"I'm. Not. Coming. To your office. Period!" Candy repeated sincerely.

Jamie knocked on the door, waited a few seconds, and then walked in. Awaiting her entrance was her captain. He spoke, but Jamie threw up a finger, requesting silence. "You're going to have to figure out if you really want to help Todd or not… call me around twelve o'clock if you serious." Jamie shoved the cell phone into her purse and took a seat on the office couch.

"That sounded serious?" The captain replied.

"Did you know Curly was once CIA?" Jamie asked.

"And he's a part of this big drug scheme with some drug lord named Nije Culpa… according to my sources, there's also people above both our pay-level involved as well," Jamie suggested.

"Jamie!" the captain retorted, trying his best to appear surprised.

"Captain, I'm serious. That's why I'm here. I have solid proof!"

"You have proof Curly is involved with some drug lord and that there are people above the CIA who might be involved as well?" "Not above it, just within the ranks."

"Well, hand it over."

"I don't have it", Jamie responded.

"Did you leave it at the house or in the car?"

"My partner has it."

"What partner? I never assigned you a partner."

"Not like that. He's the one helping me. He's fed.", Jamie announced proudly.

"You went to the feds and didn't ask first?" the captain snarled. "Relax, captain, I didn't go the feds… his case and mine are tied in."

"You don't have a case! I told you to bring me evidence to see if you have one!"

"And I got it."

"No! You don't have it because I don't have it in my hand. He slapped his hands together."

"What if I told you I could have Curly and the drug lord by the end of this month?"

"I don't have time for this bullshit, Lightbourn." The captain barked.

"I have someone on the inside," Jamie stated.

"Who? Or are you not at liberty to share that info either?" The captain seethed.

"Come on, captain. What good cope dimes out their mold?"

"The only thing I'm getting is that you came here to tell me you can't tell me what you know. Who you're working with or who this mold is."

"End of the month, that's all I'm asking?"

"You bring me something before I go home, and we have a deal."

Jamie looked at her watch. "Deal. I just have to go and tie up a few loose ends, and I'll be back with something worth the wait."

"Fine. I guess I'll be here doing real police work until you come back."

"Thanks, captain."

"Yeah, yeah, yeah. Now get out my office." He mumbled as Jamie darted out the door. While Jamie was waiting on Candy to call, Ski was on his way to have lunch with the last person on Earth he could have imagined doing such a thing with, but on the other side of town, Todd, Hope, and Franky were tucked in some fancy hotel going over their strategy for selling all the kilos of cocaine they were being forced to distribute. For Todd, it was simple, sell the dope until he could find a way out, but for Hope, he found it more difficult to comprehend Todd's plan because of a multiplicity of interrelated elements, mainly Franky. Hope didn't trust him and had no problem letting it be known – the other was him, along with his best friend, being forced to make millions for some white boy who was going to bury their assets the minute he didn't need them anymore. Franky had a less painful and less disruptive set of fixed ideas; his only problem was turning Hope's distrust for him into a more focal point against or towards the Haitian Nije. With so much going on inside their circle as well as outside their circle, Todd knew he would have to stay extra sharp if all three had any chance of walking away with only a few bumps and bruises.

"You know that cracker gave me a hundred more bricks to move." Todd explained.

"Figures," Hope shot back.

"A hundred a piece," Franky chimed in.

"Nigga you act like we getting paid for this shit! Nigga we ain't getting paid for this shit."

"What else the white boy stressing?" Franky asked.

"Nothing really... oh yeah, he did say that when we drop the money off to put into large bills so it will fit into the van. You know. Fifty's. Hundreds. Shit like that."

"Man, this white boy trippin! He putting an extra mill and half on us, and we ain't started yet." Todd could see the frustration resting on Hope's face like dried concrete. He hated to be the one to add on to his homeboy's grief, but he knew it was for the better to get everything out in the open. "He's also adding an extra stack on each brick," Todd said disappointedly.

"I know you know where this is going?" Hope looked to Todd with pleading eyes.

"Yeah, I thought about that coming back from Tampa?" Todd confessed.

"Thought about what?" Franky's request fell on deaf ears.

"So, you know, right!" Hope asked with a new calmness.

"Know what?" Franky asked.

"I'm hoping it won't come to that," Todd expressed remorsefully.

"What the hell are you talking about?" Franky asked with a blank look on his face.

"None of your muthafuckin business nigga!" Hope retorted.

"Hope, chill out… we were just feeding thoughts and ideas, that's all.", Todd answered.

"Where the dope?" Franky asked.

"In the parking lot," Todd informed them.

"You don't think that's being a little too relaxed, young blood."

"We straight… that dope will never be found in a hundred years."

"You said you were in Tampa, hell you doing Tampa?" Hope asked.

"That's where he had me drop'em off," Todd answered.

"Man, this shit crazy.", Hope mumbled as he lit up a blunt.

"Before we leave, I want to explain something. We only have a month to jump everything, so y'all gotta be on the grind on some real heavy grind shit. I know we in a rock and a hard place, but I think I can pull us out this shit… we gotta stay focused, though! Divided, we fall, my nigga. Our plans haven't changed. We still got the stock market thang going on; The old head for that jumping, so we making money, so don't trip on that. Y'all wit me or what?" Todd asked sternly.

"I'm always with you," Hope shot back.

"I'm wit it," Franky proclaimed.

"Then let's do this!" Todd exclaimed. For the next hour, all three shared various scenarios on how to make the best out of a bad situation. As usual, Hope supplied a fresh batch of what he would always call – that sticky icky – to help them with the thought process. Coming home from prison, Todd had imagined his life going in a different direction, he'd studied so many different ways to live a productive drama free life. If he would have been asked the day of his release what he was going out to do, he would have told you he was going to become an architect and later on own a few grocery stores… Now, as he sat in the hotel room submerged in thick marijuana smoke, listening to Hope and Franky draw up different conclusions as to how things might turn out. He realized his past and his future had come full circle. The harder he pulled on the blunt, the lower Hope and Franky's voices became. Finally, he could no longer hear them speaking; He could only see their lips moving as his own thoughts started to speak to him directly. Guiding him. Ten minutes later, he snapped out of his daze and shared his vision with Hope and Frank. I'm not sure if his plan would work; they both agreed anyway. They meet back up to split up the dope as planned, and as discussed, they all make it their personal mission to stay focused until Todd can pull off his master plan or at least that was the plan.

* * * * * *

"I don't know, sweetie, this sounds dangerous.", Stephanie confessed.

"I have to do something, or my children might not have a father to grow up with."

"But what if something happens to the mother?"

"What do you mean?" Candy asked.

"From what you've told me, these people Todd is involved with are scary, to say the least."

"I won't be involved with them directly. The detective just wants me to switch hones with Todd and tell her when things might change up", Candy explained.

"Something could go wrong... they always go wrong with those type of people, Candy!"

"Todd needs my help! The babies need my help!"

"No! What those bundle of joys need is to first be born, then to have both parents alive when they do come unto this Earth – that's what they need!" Stephanie stated firmly.

"Please don't fight me on this. I really need your support because I'm feeling alone on this and I'm scared... I'm scared for me, my babies, Todd..." Candy began crying.

Stephanie reached over and gave Candy a big hug. "Stop crying, sweetie, I'm here. I'm here. I won't fight you on this... hope that boy appreciates what he was with you?"

"He loves me, Stephanie. He really, really loves me," Candy mumbled.

"He better," Stephanie whispered as she began to laugh and cry at the same time.

"Thank you for letting me meet the detective over here."

"About that... I should've myself in the ass for agreeing to this! I don't know why I can't tell you girls no."

"Yes, mother dearest," Candy replied with a slight giggle.

"You're so silly, you know that," Stephanie said right before she went to answer the door. Ready to get things up and running, detective Lightbourn came fully prepared. With her, she brought the same model phone Candy told her Todd uses. Along with a few wire bugs, she'd plan to place throughout Candy's house and into Todd's car. Stephanie directed her towards the living room before excusing herself to the kitchen. When Jamie walked into the living room, the first thing she noticed was Candy drying her eyes.

"I hope nothing's wrong with the baby?" Jamie announced as she walked in.

"The baby's fine, we were just having a girl's moment before you came."

"So I brought the phone and had the number you gave me put on it as well," Jamie pulled several small devices out of her purse.

"What are those?" Candy asked.

"I plan on putting these in the house and in your car."

"Why would you want to do that?"

"These are listening devices. I'll be able to hear what you can't." Jamie implied.

"Not going to happen. I told you I'm not wearing any wire, and I'm damn sure not putting any bugs in my house! Besides, Todd doesn't move like that. He's not longing the streets to our home."

"Under the circumstances, I don't think you can say what Todd will or won't do."

"I'm not doing it! I'll switch phones but nothing else."

"Mrs. James, this will help Todd in more ways than one."

"I'm not helping you, detective; I'm helping my family."

"Mrs. James, if you just..."

"I wasn't sure what would go good with orange tea, so I just made P- Jay's. I hope you like them; I toasted the bread to give them a little kick.", Stephanie chimed in, cutting Jamie off.

"P-Jay's are fine," Candy said approvingly.

Stephanie grabbed a sandwich and then sat next to Candy. "Sugar's in the bowl if you want, detective." she flashed a smile.

"I'm okay, miss?"

"Heart. Stephanie Heart," she answered.

Candy could see the need for privacy growing on the detective's face "You can speak in front of her, detective. I told her everything. She's my friend, and I trust her." Candy reached over and grabbed Stephanie's hand. "I see, well, here's the deal, you need to switch out the phone so we'll know who's all involved on the law enforcement side. From there, we'll get arrest warrants because you're reluctant to wack a wire or put the bugs in place, it could take more time on our part to wrap this thing up, now if you hear or know anything you need to call me whether you think it's small or not..."

"Will she be safe?" Stephanie asked sternly.

"Very safe.", Jamie responded.

"What else do I have to do? Detective?"

"That's about it for now, Mrs. James."

"Well, if we're done, I need to get back home. Todd might be there."

"If you change your mind about the wire or anything else, let me know."

"I won't", Candy said matter factly.

"Mrs. James, make sure you switch out phones today. When you do, call me so we can start our end."

"It was nice meeting you, detective," Stephanie announced as she walked Jamie to her car. When she came back into the house, she and Candy ate P-Jay's and drank tea. She never brought back up the situation about Todd, and Neither did Candy. They both enjoyed the lunch as well as each other's company. An hour later, Candy went home to do what she thought she'd never do... help the detective who was trying to lock Todd up for murder.

CHAPTER 34

When Franky left Hope and Todd, he went to go and see one of his main buyers. He explained to him that from now on, he would have kilos of cocaine for sixteen thousand a piece and that the coke was ninety six percent pure. After the buyer agreed to purchase twenty kilos a month, Franky explained when and where for him to pick the dope up and how the money was to be paid in large bills. That day, Franky went to see four other buyers he knew who were buying twenty kilos or more a month; they all agreed except for one, he already had a connection who was giving them him a thousand less per kilo. Franky tried to persuade the young man a few more times, explaining to him the pureness of the coke, but he was unsuccessful. The young man declined, and Franky went about his business. Franky needed one more person to buy twenty kilos a month in order to move his share of the three hundred. Franky had one more person in mind; the potential buyer hustled on the part of the town that was heavily patrolled by the cops, so Franky went home to put up his pistol, to his surprise, Agent Ski was sitting in his living room.

"We need to talk.", Ski insisted as Franky walked into the living room.

"No! We don't need to do anything. You need to get out my house." Franky demanded.

"You have no idea what you've got yourself involved in."

"What I've got myself involved in?", Franky repeated sarcastically.

"You know what I mean."

"As much as I like having a white boy with his foot on my neck, I'll pass on the threesome if you don't mind," Franky seethed.

"Whatever you're involved in, he's going to cross you... you do know that?"

"So, what you planned on doing about the body... was just going to let I go free, huh?"

"I can help you, all of you. Walk away, scoot free." "Just like you let me walk out that hospital, right?"

"What exactly are you involved in?"

"Who says I'm involved in anything," Franky responded.

"This thing, whatever it is, is going to end badly for you and your crew."

"As I said, my neck isn't big enough for two feet, detective. I mean Agent Ski."

"So, I guess you're ready to die?"

"Nice try, white boy." Franky gave off a light chuckle.

"I'm serious! You and your crew are a means to an end. Everyone he deals with either dies or comes up missing. The day you ended up with that dead cop' drugs tied you into something you weren't ready for. It goes back further than that, but that's where you and your crew got on the bus, and whether you know it or not, that bus is on its way straight off a cliff." Agent Ski's eyes matched the intensity in his voice.

"Are you finished!" Franky asked coldly.

"Do you still have my number?"

"Are you finished!" Franky repeated through cliched teeth.

Agent Ski pulled a card from his pocket and tossed it on the table. "Now would be the best time to choose the least of two evils, my friend... gamble carefully. Dead broke a bitch."

"So is life! Now get out my house.", Franky ordered.

"Just remember our deal, Mr. Big Timer... you owe me, Nije.", Ski said threateningly. "Whatever," Franky mumbled as Agent Ski walked out of the house and climbed into his unmarked. Franky knew half of what Ski was saying was true, but the other half, he felt Ski was just a running game. It was apparent Agent Ski had no clue to what was going on and was fishing for clues; what bothered Franky was how confident the agent was about him being in grave danger. It made Franky feel as if he was holding back on something. The initial plan was to help the DEA arrest the Haitians, but now he was thinking along the lines of staying alive and walking away with as much money as possible. Franky decided a long time ago that it would be every man for himself. His plan was to follow suit until he saw the perfect cynic route, then disappear a rich man. But what he didn't know was that Hope had seen Agent Ski coming out of his house and had a plan of his own to put an end to whatever plan he had in place.

* * * * * *

In the back of the captain's mind, he knew what Jamie was capable of when it came down to solving cases; a pitbull in a skirt who was tenacious and perseverant, Jamie had a way of always getting her man. The captain knew that better than anyone. He practically groomed her himself when she first came to the prescient they were assigned to. The death of Detective Lewis almost made the big three relocate their operation, which would have meant the loss of an opportunity to go to Washington plus tens of thousands of tax-free dollars. The captain chose the money and promotion over the life of his fellow subordinate.

"What do you want?" Curly asked without interest.

"We have a little situation you need to fix."

"Or do you mean you want me to clean your mess up!"

"It's Lightbourn... she's way too close."

"So, you want her removed. Is that it?"

"I spoke with the others, and we have the green light," the captain declared.

"Well, captain, it's time you get your hands dirty, she'll never see it coming." Curly laughed.

"I thought you would've jumped at the opportunity to..."

"To what? Do your dirty work. No, my friend, this one is all yours." Curly suggested.

Seeing how reluctant Curly was, the captain accepted, "Fine! I'll do it."

"Good. With that bitch out the way, it should be smooth sailing."

"I just have to figure out a way to make it seem like an accident," the captain professed.

"It's not that hard, you know... put two in her head and put the blame on some street punk," Curly implied.

"You didn't want to do it, so let me figure out how to do this. Okay."

"You just make sure you do it! We have no room for soft hearts my friend."

"I said I'll do it!"

"Call me tomorrow when you finish, there's something we need to talk about."

"About what?" the captain asked.

"Just call me tomorrow.", Curly acknowledged before he hung up. The captain thought of many ways to kill Jamie, but only one stood out as being efficient and realistic.

The time had come, and he was all in.

CHAPTER 35

"Didn't I tell you that fool was working with the police!"

"Man stop yelling in my ear and calm yo ass down.", Todd commanded. "The police leaving this nucca right now." Hope continued to scream into the phone.

"Man, quit yelling! And who are you talking about?" Todd asked calmly. "Franky ratass! The DEA dude that kicked the door in was at his house. Hanging out for about twenty minutes... I'm sitting here watching this shit, I'm telling you, his ratass is playing both sides! This clown gonna get us killed with this bullshit! I'm telling ya.", Hope voiced with ill will.

"He's at Franky's house right now?"

"He pulling out the driveway right now!"

"Don't move. I'm on my way over there, if anyone else shows up, hit me up ASAP. Don't go in the house. Wait until I get there."

"We should have been dealt with this here!" Hope said disappointingly.

"Just wait in the car, and we'll deal with this together."

"Well, tighten up, nucca. I'm ready to deal with this ratass fuckboy!" Hope hung up the phone and tossed it over into the passenger seat. He was furious. Hope pulled half a blunt from the ashtray and lit it up as the intoxicant smoke filled his lungs and chest. Hope's anger blustered out. For every pull he took on the blunt and every lung full of smoke he swallowed, Hope had more and more of a reason to run up into Franky's house and give him an old fashion ass whipping. He looked at his watch, ten minutes had passed, and Todd was nowhere in sight. He decided to give his homeboy ten more minutes. Two minutes later, he checked his gun over, tucked it in his waistline, and then exited the car after taking the last pull on the blunt. With blood in his eyes, Hope had one thing on his mind, and that was to make Franky suffer for being the ratass fuckboy he was. "Ready or not," Hope mumbled just as he turned the handle to the front door.

* * * * * *

After leaving Candy's friend's house, Jamie wasn't sure how far Candy would be willing to go to protect Todd and the babies. Placing those bugs in the house would have been a major accomplishment for her and Agent Ski, and even though Candy gently denied access to her domicile, she still agreed to switch out phones; that was a victory within itself and something she would have to build on positively if she were to have any chance at bringing Curly or Curly and his silent partners to justice, and just when she thought to call Agent Ski and her phone rang.

"Detective Lightbourn."

"So, how did the meeting go?"

"He told me show'em something in black and white by the end of the day, and I got the green light," Jamie explained.

"What else he said?"

"That's pretty much it in a nutshell."

"Can you trust'em with what we got?" Ski asked skeptically.

"He's my captain. Remember."

"Don't fall asleep on me, detective. This is serious business. I'll ask you again. Can we trust him?"

"Yes." Jamie hesitated.

Agent Ski picked up on her dubiousness but only made note of it. "Okay, so what would you like to show'em?"

"Do you have the document he gave you when he took over custody of Sneed and Patrick?"

"Yeah. Matter of fact I have it in the car with me." "Good, bring it down to the station."

"Why don't you come down to the building and get it... have a few more leads to pin-up.", Ski responded.

"Fine. I'll be there in twenty minutes."

"I'll see you soon, detective." Agent Ski hung up the phone and B-lined to the federal building. Agent Ski was good at dotting his I's and crossing his T's, so when Jamie was shilly-shally about whether her captain could be trusted, he hurried to the office to do a background check on the captain. "No stone unturned," Ski said aloud as he jumped on the east-west expressway.

* * * * * *

"I knew yo ass was a rat!" Hope voiced coldly as he entered the living room.

"Man, I don't have no time for the bullshit, Hope!" Franky suggested.

"But your ratass have time for the police?"

"Man, get out my house, stupid ass nucca!" Franky implied angrily.

"So, what you and the whiteboy talking about... you some shit!"

"What the hell you talking about? What whiteboy?" Franky stuffed a card in his pocket.

"This shit ends right here, right now!" Franky said viciously.

"If you talking about the DEA cop, it ain't even like that."

Hope pulled out his gun and pointed it at Franky. "You better start talking, old man."

"So, what, you gonna kill me?"

"Yo ass better start talking, or it is what it is.", Hope advised with cold eyes. Franky brought his hands up to his chest submissively. "You wanna talk? Put the gun down, and let's talk." Franky took a seat on the couch.

With only a small table separating the two, Hope took a seat directly in front of Franky, placing the gun in his lap. "Talk!" Hope commanded.

"I didn't have to tell that whiteboy a goddamn thang! He been on our trail for God knows how long."

"I just wanna know why you ratted us out... Nucca, we was feeding you!"

"Ain't nobody rat you out! He don't even want us stupid ass nucca! He wants the Haitian. Not us." Franky explained.

"And you had no problem agreeing to that dumb ass shit!" Hope asked furiously.

"It was either him or us... you wanna do twenty years in prison?" "You some shit! I told my dawg you were some shit... you still haven't told me what all you told that whiteboy. All this time, I think Todd trippen thinking the Feds was on us, and here you are right up under a Nucca nose working with the Feds!"

"Right now, you're looking at the tree and not the forest."

"Naw! I'm looking at yo ratass, nucca!"

"It's bigger than you think, youngblood... right now, all we can do is make this shit work for us the best way we can. You wanna be loyal to a person you don't know, and I'm looking out for you. Not me. Us!"

"Naw. See, that's where you get the game fucked up! Nucca, I'm true to this shit! It's rules with this bitch, and you broke the first one – don't rat on yo people!" Franky leaned to the edge of the couch. "The game only has one rule, youngblood, and that's to always be mindful that the game has no rules. It never has and never will... it's a dog-eat-dog world. You get in. You get out."

Hope picked up the gun and aimed it towards Franky. "Maybe that's how you roll, but I don't get down like that. I live by the G-code. Always have. Always will. Just like I said, this shit ends right here, right now!" Hope announced with spite. "Killing me won't make none of this go away. You kill me, and you're only adding to your problems... Hope listen to me! Fuck that Haitian! You think he gives a shit about us? You always see in the newspaper how one of them big drug lords turned state on the people they were selling that shit to! I have a plan that will guarantee us our freedom as well as enough money to relocate and start over.", Franky acknowledged.

Hope stood up and pointed the gun down at Franky. "Not my style. I've never been cool with being a rat", Hope responded, and just when he was about to pull the trigga, Franky hurdled over the table towards Hope. Able to get off three shots before losing the gun and falling to his back, Hope was able to shoot a hanging mirror and the stereo; only one bullet managed to hit Franky, which turned out to be a flesh wound to his upper ear. Franticly, the two wrestled on the floor for possession of the pistol. Like animals, they kicked, punched, and scratched as each one took turns grabbing and then losing the gun. Franky was the last to have the gun knocked from his hand before they began a more traditional first-to-cuffs. Hope was younger and stronger, so he hit much harder than Franky, but Franky was much wiser and far more advanced in fistfights, which proved to be much more of an advantage for him as he began to manhandle Hope in the living room. With precise punches, Franky delivered damaging blows to Hope's ribcage, stomach, and throat. When Hope fell to the ground, Franky made his move for the gun, but Hope's youth allowed for a quick recovery as he was right on Franky's heels. Running full speed, Franky tried to bend over and pick up the gun, but his momentum carried over, causing him to lose his balance and fall down. Hope made one last attempt as he dove in the air towards Franky just as he was turning over - gun in hand – and without warning, Franky squeezed off two rounds, hitting Hope once in the neck and the other in the head. Hope's body instinctively slumped over Franky. Horrified, Franky pushed Hope's body to the side and crawled to the corner of the wall. He couldn't believe what he just did.

* * * * * *

When Jamie walked into the office, Ski was typing feverishly on his laptop, so much so he didn't hear Jamie knock on the door or notice her standing in front of him – it wasn't until the scent of her perfume disrupted his train of thought that Ski finally came up from the air.

"Is that perfume you have on?" Ski asked, almost in disbelief.

Not sure if she should feel embarrassed or insulted, Jamie ignored the question altogether, "What had you all worked up when I walked in?"

Ski handed Jamie the documents she requested. "This should light a fire in your captain to get'em on board," Ski insisted.

Jamie took the two-page documentation, looked over it, and then shoved it in her purse. "You never said what had you going when I came in. You run across something inestimable?" Jamie asked quizzically.

"Not really. Just trying to finish up some paperwork." Ski answered untruthfully. He was doing a profile on her captain and thought it would be best if she didn't know for the time being.

"I know how that is. I hate paperwork... do you think we can bust this thing wide open and take down the ones pulling strings?" Jamie's tone came off iffy.

"That's why you became a detective... to solve these types of cases, right?"

"To be honest with you, I've never been a part of something this magnitude."

"All cases are the same detective because at the end of the day, you either solve the case and catch your man or woman or you don't, and the perpetrator gets away; the only thing that differentiates one from the other is your detective."

"What does that mean?" Jamie questioned comically.

With a straight face, Agent Ski answered, "It means if you think you can't solve a particular case, then you won't."

That was the second time Jamie put her foot in her mouth being around Agent Ski. She made a note not to talk too much around him – she figured that would at the least help her save face. Agent Ski carried himself just as Jamie imagined a federal agent would: that was the last thought Jamie had as she climbed into her car and headed back to the station to show her captain the proof he asked for. Thinking about what Agent Ski said about solving cases made Jamie realize that she had what it took to be a federal agent after all. If going hard on every case put you in that category, Jamie knew she was right at home, and she'd made her mind up to prove just that.

CHAPTER 36

When Todd pulled up behind Hope, he turned off his car and jumped into Hope's car, but Hope wasn't in it. "I told his ass to stay in the car," Todd said aloud, disappointingly, as he slammed the door shut. With everything going on between Candy and the babies and him and his being forced to get money for someone other than them, he was becoming more and more agitated with Hope and Franky's catfights. Todd knew he had to put an end to all things negative in order for all three of them to make it scoot-free – with that in mind, Todd sped up his steps to the house... "I Hope these clowns ain't in here fighting again.", he mumbled just before walking in. The living room was a total disaster; broken glass everywhere, tables smashed, and sofas flipped over – but what garnered all his attention were the bullet holes in the wall and what happened to be one in the stereo. Cautiously, Todd pulled out his pistol, scanned as much of the house as he could without moving, and then called out for Hope and Franky, but neither one answered. Todd yelled out a second time for his comrades, but again, no answer. He took a few steps forward, and that's when his heart dropped. Sticking out from behind the couch was an Air Nike, which Todd knew belonged to Hope – instinctively, he ran over to see what he'd already known in his heart, lying in a pool of blood was his best friend. Unable to control his emotions, Todd began to yell and scream for Hooe to get up, but Hope was nonresponsive. It wasn't until he turned Hope over that he saw the bullet wound to the head and neck. Frantically, he pulled out his phone and dialed nine, one, one.

"Nine, one, one – What is your emergency?"

"Somebody shot my dawg, He need help!" Todd yelled hysterically.

"Where was your dog shot, sir?"

"Okay, sir, where is your friend shot at?" the operator asked calmly.

"Looks like the head and neck... please send someone over here, my nigga ain't breathing... please don't die, Hope... please don't die."

"Sir, are you on a cellphone?"

"Lady, please send somebody," Todd placed.

"I don't know the number to the house," Todd repeated with panic.

"Can you go outside and look at the front of the house?"

"Hold on!" Todd ran out the door.

"Sir, Sir. Sir, are you still?"

"Ten-fifty-seven!" Todd screamed.

"Help is on the way, sir, we're tracking your phone as we speak," the operator confirmed proudly.

"Please hurry... what the fuuu!"

"Sir? Sir? Who's shooting at you… sir!" the operator signaled to dispatch that rounds were being fired at the residence the EMT was headed to and to proceed with caution. She tried her best to get Todd back on the phone; shots continued to blast through the phone, giving little Hope that the person on the other end of the phone would return.

"I didn't want to shoot'em, but he made me!" Franky screamed as he left off two shots at Todd.

"What the hell are you doing?" Todd asked panickily as he stared at his pistol lying on the side of Hope.

"He was gonna kill me!"

"So, what now? You gonna kill me?" Todd asked, ducking behind the large couch.

"I'm no fool, Todd… he was your best friend. I know you wanna kill me for hurting him."

"The cops are on their way, Franky."

Franky, as well as Todd, could hear the sirens approaching, he let off three more shots in Todd's direction and fled to the back of the house, where he was able to leave the scene without notice. As the sirens became louder and the gunshots ceased, Todd made it his business to follow suit. Quickly, he ran out the front door, jumped in his car and fled from the screen, but not before retrieving his pistol and cellphone. With his best friend dead and the team decimated, all Todd's hopes of freedom lay motionless in Franky's living room.

* * * * * *

A few more minutes and Jamie would have missed not only the captain but also her last shot at moving forward on the biggest case of her life.

"I was starting to think you wasn't coming."

Jamie handed the captain the three-page document. "Read this," Jamie suggested firmly.

"Where did you get this?" He asked, peeping up at her and then back to papers.

"The person I'm working with is real resourceful," Jamie answered.

The captain flipped to the next page. "He better be! This is high-ranking stuff."

"So, what do ya think? I have your blessing or not?"

The captain turned to the last page, read it over, and then tucked the documents into his back pocket. "Are you sure you don't want to let the big boys handle this?"

"You're not going back on your word, are you?" the panic in her voice was showing.

"Relax, detective, I'm not going back on my word, but I will be honest with you when I tell you I have a bad feeling about this." He pulled the papers out of his pocket, "This is telling me that this is a very serious, very sensitive situation we're dealing with. It's like picking up stick with one side that says good, and the other says bad… once you pick from either side, you have to take the other as well," the captain explained.

"I can do this, captain, and you know it!" Jamie professed.

"How do you know you can solve this?"

"Have I not always got my man, captain? Am I not the best at getting their man."

"I don't know, Jamie... I have a bad feeling." The captain expressed uneasiness.

"You won't be sorry. I promise. Captain, I can do this.", Jamie stressed firmly. After taking a few seconds, he finally agreed, "Okay, Lightbourn, but I swear if I think this needs to go to the FBI, I won't hesitate to pull the triga."

"Okay. Well, I'll call you tomorrow to let you know how I plan on attacking this thing; that way, you'll be brought up to speed on everything... oh, I need those papers back."

"No can-do detective. Have to keep them just in case I have to bring in reinforcements. Just like you had to bring me proof." – he gestured to the folded papers – "I'll need to do the same thing. But don't worry, they're safe with me."

"Fine. Just make sure you don't lose them", Jamie requested as she walked out the door. After Jamie left, the captain was more certain than ever that Jamie had to die, but after Jamie showed him the documents, he realized Jamie had tied herself to someone with a lot of pull and that he would have to find out whom that person was before he killed her; Only a person well connected could have gotten a hole to those papers, and the captain was well aware of that. He immediately called up Curly to give him the bad news.

* * * * * *

The images of Hope laying on the floor, bleeding from the head and neck, became a permanent fixation in Todd's memory, his adrenaline began to evaporate, tears started to fill his eyes as his anger turned to sorrow, and while his body turned numb, his mind struggled to come to grips that his best friend was really gone. Too much was going on in Todd's head. He was feeling out of control and unstable. He pulled over on the side of the road, put the car in park, and broke down crying. What he was feeling was unbearable, and for the next ten minutes, he pulled, punched, and banged his head on the steering wheel. It wasn't until the continuous ringing of the cell phone that pulled him from his fit of rage that he stopped. Taking a few minutes to regain his composure, he finally picked up the phone and pushed send.

"Who is it!". Todd asked angrily.

"Is that any way to speak to your future wife?" Candy asked jokingly.

"What do you want!"

Candy took the phone from her ear, looked at it, and then brought it back to her ear. "Hello?" She asked if she dialed the wrong number.

"I'm here. What's up?" Todd responded nonchalantly. "Hello? Todd, is that you?" Candy asked with unease.

"I said I'm here... what's up?"

"You sound like something's wrong... bey, you scaring me."

The image of Hope lying on the floor rehashed in Todd's head, and instantly, he thought Candy and the babies might be in danger. "Where are you?" he asked in hysteria, sending red flags straight to Candy.

"Okay, now you're really starting to scare me... what the hell is going on!"

"Where are you?" He repeated.

"At the house. Why?" Candy asked concerningly.

"Lock all the doors and windows... don't go out the house. Don't answer the door. Don't do anything until I get there!" Todd said.

"Where's Franky and Hope?" Candy questioned.

"Don't open the door for no one! No one, Candy! I mean it!" Todd barked.

Candy never questioned Todd about his intentions or her well-being, so when he began barking orders, she listened more to what he was saying and not so much to the manner in which it was being delivered. "Okay. I'm doing it now. Just hurry up and come home... okay."

"I'll be there in twenty minutes," Todd answered, then hung up. Candy and the twins were all he had left, and there was no way he was going to let anything happen to them. Franky had already killed Hope and tried to kill him as well, who's to say he wouldn't try to harm Candy – even if she was his niece? Todd wasn't about to take any chances. He couldn't take any chances.

CHAPTER 37

Nothing short of a miracle was all the EMTs could think of as they rushed to place Hope in the ambulance. With a faint pulse and barely breathing, somehow, some way, Hope managed to hang on to life until help arrived. Once they reached the hospital, Hope was taken directly into surgery. The bullet wound to the neck caused major damage to his esophagus, but the doctor's main concern was with his head trauma; the shot he took to the head was close enough to be considered point-blank. Due to such an injury, Hope developed swelling in the brain. For hours, a team of doctors worked with due diligence to give Hope a fighting chance at having an opportunity to have a shot at living a normal life and successful recovery, and after six and a half hours of operative astuteness, the unwanted pressure on the brain was alleviated. But, like many before him, Hope wasn't out the words yet. Head injuries of any kind warrant concern, and in Hope's case, a grave concern as with any serious head injury. After the surgery, the doctors figured Hope would have a seventy percent chance of walking out of the hospital fully recovered but that he would also have a real fight on his hands. Two hours after surgery, Hope fell short in the first round of that fight as he slipped into a coma. With nothing else they could do, the doctors had Hope placed on a breathing machine and everything else in God's hands.

* * * * * *

"Seems like our little point of focus has went out and got some wind up under her wings."

"We don't have time for this bullshit!" Curly stated harshly.

"I'm going to hold off for now until these smoke and mirrors clear up."

"Any idea who it might be?"

"Whoever it is was important enough to grab a copy of the documents you used to attain custody of our three little friends." The captain suggested.

"Is she still coming to you with whatever she finds?" Curly asked.

"How you think I got the documents?"

"So you have them?"

"Yeah. She tried getting them back... I have them for safekeeping."

"What else she's talking about?"

"For starters. I believe her silent partner might become a thorn in our side if we don't find out who he... or she or they is."

"You need to come to Tampa ASAP!" Curly demanded.

"I was thinking you would say that. I'm already on I-4 as we speak; should be in Tampa in about thirty minutes."

"They say the more you teach them, the dumber you get."

"Don't worry. School is almost over for little student of the game.", the captain assured Curly in a calm but cold manner. After his discussion with Curly, the captain decided to call the big three and bring them up to speed about Jamie and the potential threat of her silent partner. What he was told was about to change everything. He didn't like it, but he understood why, and he respected it. The only thing left was to explain to Curly what was said and why.

* * * * * *

Before Todd reached the house, he'd calmed down a great deal. To his surprise, Franky hadn't been over there or at least it didn't look like it. Normally, he would have called Candy just as he was coming up to the house, but nothing was normal anymore. Todd realized that nothing was normal from the day he was released from prison, with that and so many other things in mind. Todd checked the grounds of the house with extreme caution before he went into the house, where he was met at the door by Candy, who was also on heavy alert status due to Todd's erratic behavior on the phone. Immediately, she took notice of his tear-stained face and somber eyes; without a word, she grabbed his hand and walked him to their bedroom. There, she pulled him close to her as they both lay in the bed. For the next ten minutes, Todd cried the last tears he was holding inside from the death of his best friend. He'd come to grips with the fact that no matter what happened next, Hope wasn't coming back and that he needed to move on with his life.

"None of this is making sense. Why would Franky do such a thing?" Candy asked befuddling.

"Hope seen the agent coming from his house... guess Hope was right," Todd mumbled.

"But I thought the Agent was making you sell all his dope," Candy responded.

"Not that cracker. The one who kicked the door in. The one holding the body over our heads."

"When you explained what was what, I assumed you were speaking of the same agent?"

"Naw, it's two of them, and because of one of them, my dawg dead," Todd seethed.

"Are you sure Franky killed Hope?" Candy questioned, desperation immersed in her voice.

"Just as sure as I am, he tried to do me as well," Todd retorted.

"Maybe he's acting out? He might be back on drugs and don't know how to control it?" Candy knew she was reaching the moment she opened her mouth, "Maybe..."

"I know that's your uncle and all, but he killed Hope, and the nucca tried to kill me as well. It is what it is." Todd chimed in on Candy's thesis about her uncle's maliciousness. Candy loved her uncle more than anything, but her loyalty was to her family, and Todd, along with the twins, was her family. So much had changed for Candy from the time she crossed the Georgia Florida line, but what didn't change, what would never change, was her love for Todd or what she would do to protect him. He recognized from that point on out it would be her and him against the world, and she was up for the challenge.

"So, what do you have in mind? What's our next move?" Candy asked fittingly.

"First, I need to put you up somewhere safe. That way, I can move the way I need to move, knowing you and the baby's straight." Todd placed his hands over Candy's stomach.

"But I want to help... don't want my kids growing up fatherless."

"You wanna help? You really want to help? Do what I tell you to do."

Candy trusted Todd with her life, and because of that, she gave in, "Okay, I'll do whatever you tell me to do." Candy stated passively.

"Good. Go and grab some clothes so we can bounce."

"How much clothes do we need?"

"Now us. You... about a week," Todd explained.

"Where am I going?"

"I'll explain in the car, but I need you to tighten up, bey," Todd responded. About to respond to Todd's decorous tone, Candy decided it would be better suited if she used that opportunity to switch phones while gathering up a few outfits before hitting the road; for all she knew, she might not get to see Todd for days at a time. After packing her bag, she snatched Todd's cellphone off the bed and tossed it in her bag of feminine hygiene. It wasn't until they were long gone from the house that Todd remembered he'd left his phone on the bed.

"Here," Candy pulled out a phone from her purse.

"Good looking. I was just about to bust a 'U' and go back and get my shit." The relief in his voice was all the confirmation Candy needed.

"No problem, bey... no problem."

"Still wanna know where we going?"

"Sure do!" Candy responded matter factly.

"Touch your nose." Todd started laughing.

"Whatever!" Candy shot back.

"Don't worry, you'll love it." Todd flashed a smile as he turned on the radio. A new joint from Jill Scott came on. Candy loved Jill Scott.

"When did you have time to go out and buy the new CD?"

"Come out yesterday... thought of you. Went out and coped it."

Candy leaned over and gave him a kiss. "That was sweet of you," Candy said girlishly.

"When all this is over, we out'a here," Todd stated firmly.

"I know," Candy acknowledged as she leaned her seat back. The two of them didn't speak another word the whole ride; the only voice to be heard was that of Jill, which wasn't such a bad thing to be listening to.

CHAPTER 38

Being a Federal Agent required having a few set skills, skills that would allow the agent to go above and beyond when it came to catching some of the more sophisticated criminals the world had to offer. Agent Ski not only possessed those skills, but he owed the most important one of them all – Instincts. Instincts he'd grown to trust and obey, and those same instincts advised him to put a tail on the captain. As usual, his instincts were right. Because of his intuitiveness, he was able to spy on the captain and special Agent Macki Sub-Rose Rendez-Vous. Armed with a high-powered lens camera, Ski took pictures as Macki and the captain engaged in what appeared to be an intense conversation.

"It's over!" The captain waved the three-page documents irefully, then shoved them into Curly's chest.

"What's over? What are you talking about?" Curly looked over the paper then pushed it into his pocket.

"They're pulling the plug... too risky. Try next year, that's all," the captain explained.

"Well, I haven't heard anything, so it's business as usual for me," Curly informed him.

"You think I drove way to Tampa just to see your little pretty face? I came to tell you face to face it's over. I was sent to tie up the loose ends."

"What does that mean? Tie up loose ends?" Curly asked angrily.

"I'm just upset as you are, but before things get too out of control and we end up exposing our hand, it's best we just walk away for now." The captain suggested.

"Out of control! Out of control! You fucking kidding me! You fuck up, and somehow, you've convinced them to what – pull the plug! This is your fault. Not mine."

"Like I said, I'm here to collect the money, collect the dope, and report back."

"What money? I just gave them the dope this morning, you moron!"

"Well, call them, tell 'em to bring it back, arrest their ass for murder, and we start off fresh next year." The captain implied firmly.

"No!"

"This isn't up for debate, Macki, and I'm not asking either."

"I don't have until next year, and if you know like I do, neither do you."

"So what! You're the ultimate tough guy now? You're gonna bite the hand that feeds ya?" The captain questioned with contempt.

"You just don't get it! There will be no next year, and whatever you did to get them to pull the plug flushed any enhance, you had to move up right down the toilet."

"If it was meant to happen, so be it."

"Don't give me that bull crap philosophy! You had your reasons for coming aboard, and if the reward wasn't greater than the risk, you would not have jumped the fence... I'm not willing to walk away from my dreams. Not like this."

"I don't have a problem with that little scenario... like I said, risk and reward."

"So, what you want me to tell them?" He asked disappointingly. "Tell'em I've got everything worked out and not to worry," Curly answered calmly.

"You sure you wanna do this?" The captain questioned.

"Yeah, I'm sure. Don't worry about Lightbourn, after tonight, she won't be a problem."

"Your call. Your life." The captain mumbled as he walked back to his car. When the captain pulled off, Curly remained seated on the park bench. Agent Ski decided to remain with him to see who else would show up – no one did, and Curly left twenty minutes later. Although Ski couldn't hear what the captain and Curly were discussing, Curly's animated hand gestures and facial expressions, along with the captain's cool demeanor, told Ski that something had gone wrong. Terribly wrong. This would be the best time for him and Jamie to attack hard while they were vulnerable. There was definitely tension between the two, which more than likely meant bad news for Jamie, being she had some sort of connection to them both. It was time to move now, and Ski planned to do so while the iron was still hot.

* * * * * *

With Candy back in Atlanta, Todd knew he would be able to handle his current situation accordingly. His first order of business was to get back a hundred bricks he'd given to Franky the day before all was shot to hell. The second and maybe the most important thing he had to do was to keep both agents out of the loop; with Hope dead and Franky on AWAL status, Todd figured his only option was to collect the dope, max it out to the highest dollar then move somewhere he and his family would never be in harm's way again in their lives. He thought about living on one of those small Bahamian islands but figured they were too close to Florida. After five hours of thinking on the highway, he narrowed his choices to either Canada or Europe. Now, all he had to do was handle his business. But Todd wasn't the only one planning for the future, Candy was making a move or two of her own. As soon as Candy figured Todd to be back on the highway headed back to Florida, she called Detective Lightbourn to inform her that the phones were switched out; that was all Jamie needed to hear. Ten minutes later, she had a team of three listening in on everything Todd and Special Agent Macki had to say. That was the big break she prayed for and got.

"Agent Ski!"

"Yeah, it's me... we're in."

"She switched the phones."

"We've made a few recordings already. Nothing significant, but were in."

"At the federal building – on the third floor."

"Well, stay on the line. I have a feeling Mr. Patrick's phone is about to take on a life of its own.", Ski expressed openly.

"You know something I don't?"

"Nothing solid, just a hunch," Ski answered.

"You coming in to offer another ear?"

"Yeah, I'm on my way now," Ski answered.

"I guess I'll see you in a little bit," Jamie responded.

"Hey, Lightbourn."

"What's up?"

"I think I might have a clue to go off of. Call your captain and tell'em to let you hold the documents for a few hours... we're going to need the originals to do what's needed to be done," Ski stated justifiably.

"What exactly are we looking for?"

"Can you get the papers or not!" Ski demanded without answering to her question.

"Yeah. I'll call right now." Jamie retorted, feeling uneasy about Agent Ski's barking tactics.

"I need them before" – Ski looked to his watch – "before, two o'clock detective."

"Didn't I say I'll get them!" Jamie barked back. Unscathed by Jamie's mimicry, Agent Ski explained his motives [in part], answered a few more questions, and then hung up. Jamie did as she was advised to do; she remained online, and good advice it was. Curly wasted no time calling Todd the second, he and the captain parted ways.

"I want this on tape for evidence... I think this it?" Jamie ordered confidently while Jamie was gaily listening to Todd and Curly – Curly wouldn't be so cheerful, although his words were every bit colorful:

"I'm afraid the plans have changed," Curly spoke matter factly.

"Changed? Changed how?"

"You and the others no longer have a month to deliver..."

"So, what is it?"

"More like three weeks," Curly imposed obtrusively.

"Are you crazy! You want me to move three hundred bricks in three weeks!"

"Here's your deal, Mr. Patrick... you do that, and I let you and the others walk. Clean as a whistle."

Todd was starting to feel like a caged animal. His brain began to work in overdrive as he tried to map out an exit plan while simultaneously trying to read between the lines of what Agent Macki was insinuating. Was the whole thing some sort of ruse? A ploy. Todd was beginning to feel more and more like a cat's paw: Could the agent be setting him up for some grand scheme to boost his career? And if so, was he planning on killing Todd or, even worse, Candy and the babies to cover all leads tracing back to him and whomever else? Todd thought about all those things before he responded to the agent's audacious requisition. "Seems like I don't have much of a choice," Todd fretted.

Curly began to chuckle. "No such thang, Mr. Patrick, there is always a choice to be made... the consequence for making that choice is what you wouldn't have a say in!" Curly informed Todd.

"I'll have the money for the first two hundred in two weeks, but you have to give me another week and a half to get you the rest of the money."

"I hope you're not planning on doing something stupid, Mr. Patrick," Curly forewarns Todd.

"You want all your money or not?" Todd implied bitterly.

"Careful, Mr. Patrick," Curly cautioned.

"Listen. Ol'boy went out'a town with the dope, soon as he's back, I'll bring yo thirsty ass the beard."

"I told you to be local, you lil dumbshit! We can't protect you outside the box! Jesus Christ. You and the other two shitheads are unbelievable."

"Whatever. Like I said, I'll have the money."

"You better!" Curly snarled before hanging up the phone. He couldn't believe the balls of Todd talking to him like that; he thought about teaching Todd a little lesson in mannerisms after he got the money. But Curly wasn't the only one looking to teach a lesson. After eavesdropping on Curly and Todd's conversation, Jamie had all the proof she needed to put Curly away for a long, long time. But Jamie wanted Curly to go to jail for more than just dealing drugs. She wanted Curly to suffer the shame of killing a cop, she wanted Curly to die in prison from old age, and she wanted to teach Curly that crooked cops never last in her world, and now she had the proof to school him.

CHAPTER 39

The first observation Agent Ski made when he walked into the compacted communications room was the look of victory on Jamie's face. Solving a case always brought a certain feeling of attainment, but when that same case involved elements on a more significant level, the gratification for solving that case could never be described in words; It could only be felt and cherished. Ski remembered that feeling, and seeing that look on Jamie's face made him feel like a proud big brother. After seeing her so giddy, he was more determined to help.

"Did we get in it?" Ski asked anxiously.

"We sure did!" Jamie announced simultaneously with one of the technicians.

The technician looked at Jamie, smiled, and then said to Ski, "Yeah, we got in... just waiting for him to pick up the phone."

"Waiting for who to pick up the phone? All we have to do is go and arrest Curly when he meets up with Patrick to collect the money for the drugs." Jamie acknowledged with certainty but yet feeling somewhat confused.

"I need to talk with the detective, so if anything comes up from the second tap, call me immediately," Ski ordered as he gestured to Jamie to come with him. As the two rode in the elevator, Jamie had an uncanny feeling that whatever Agent Ski wanted to talk to her about wasn't good. As soon as Jamie took a seat in his office, Agent Ski came clean.

"I believe your captain and Agent Macki are somehow involved?" Ski informed Jamie.

"That's not possible!" Jamie responded, feeling a little insulted.

"Hear me out, detective," Ski advised with firmness.

"I'm listening," Jamie replied.

"When you and I talked earlier, I was with the captain when he and Macki were engaged in a heated discussion... about what I don't know, but my gut is telling me that the two of them have a hand in this thing."

"How were you with the captain but couldn't hear what they were saying?"

"I wasn't with him, with him. I was tailing him where they met up in some park in Tampa," Ski explained.

"They could have been talking about anything," Jamie said with uncertainty.

"Did you call and ask for the papers back?"

"That's what I was about to do before you drug me up to your office!"

Agent Ski walked over to Jamie and pulled her phone out of her purse. "Call him. Call him and tell'em you're coming over to make copies of the paper." Ski demanded reluctantly. Jamie grabbed the phone and called her captain. He picked up on the first ring and said, "Yeah, it's me. I need to drop and make a copy of the papers."

"What papers?"

"The ones I'm going to use to put Curly away for a long time," Jamie answered.

The captain searched his coat pocket for the papers only to realize that he'd given them to Curly. "Uugghhh, call me back, Lightbourn. Somethings come up," the captain explained, then hung up. He immediately called Curly to get the papers back. Meanwhile, Jamie stood dumbfounded as Agent Ski looked at her with an "I told you" face.

"Let me guess, he blew you off?"

"I'm not understanding this," Jamie confessed.

"Don't worry. It happens to the best of us," Ski confirmed slyly.

"This whole time, he's been playing me," Jamie's anger started to show.

"In this business, you better learn how not to take things too personally."

"Like the way you didn't take it personally when Curly lifted Sneed and Patrick right out'a your hands!" Jamie suggested sarcastically.

"It's only advice, detective, you can take it or leave it." Ski responded, a little embarrassed.

"You're right. So, what do we do now?" Jamie asked.

With his game face on tight, Ski looked Jamie square in the eyes, "We're going to do what we do best. Catch bad guys and lock'em up for a long time."

"Any suggestions?" Jamie asked, her tone semi-defeated.

"I have a plan!" Ski implied with a devilish grain. For the next twenty minutes, Agent Ski went over the best scenario he felt would allow himself and Jamie the opportunity to arrest her captain as well as Curly: Jamie made it clear that she wanted Curly and the captain to be down for the death of Peet, but that she would accept if not for the murder of her partner, then at least the rest of their lives for something else. She could sense that a showdown was inevitable and was mentally preparing herself – if need be – to either take down or take out her long-time friend, boss. Mentor.

* * * * * *

Two weeks had passed since Todd held his best friend's slumped body in his arms, and no matter what he did or how hard he tried, he couldn't get the image of Hope's head and neck bleeding the way it did. The more he thought about Hope lying on that floor like some crazed dog shot down, the more upset he became with himself. Hope didn't deserve to die like that, and he didn't deserve to be lying up in some hospital morgue rocking a toe tag. All Todd could think of was what type of friend he was not to give his best friend due right and send him out the right way with a proper burial. He decided to check all the hospitals for Hope's body so he could say goodbye to his homeboy the right way. The respectful way. After collecting all of the money he had floating through the streets, Todd went to the house to begin his search for Hope's body. Being that O.R.M.C. was the biggest hospital in Orange County, he figured he'd start there first. But after hours and hours of calling four hospitals, he would come up empty. Hope's body was nowhere to be found, and to make matters worse, there wasn't anyone fitting Hope's description that was brought into the morgue that day or that month. Flustered, Todd decided to smoke a blunt, regroup, and come up with a plan "B." Halfway through the second blunt, Todd figured out what might have happened to Hope's body – the only logical answer affordable at the time: Franky had to have doubled back and grabbed the body before the cops showed up so he wouldn't be implicated in Hope's murder, being the body would've been found in his house. Most likely, he either dumped the body into some lake or buried it somewhere remote. Todd figured he would kill two birds with one stone and find Franky, but first, he called Agent Macki to let him know he had most of the money to deliver him.

"I need to see you."

"Right on time. But I must admit that I didn't think your type practice in punctuality." Curly's words came off coldish.

"Whatever! Man, where you talking about meeting at?"

"Come to the Hilton Hotel in Altamont... room one-fourteen."

"What time?"

"Be there before three o'clock."

"Check this out, though. I don't got all the money, but I got most of it."

"Why not!" Curly demanded.

"We ain't going through all that. You'll have all your money, and when you do, you can leave me and mine alone."

"Just get my money up and lose the tougher than leather attitude, which reminds me, do you remember how to use the van?"

"I can't till this shit over!" Todd mumbled.

"So, I take that as a yes?"

"Yeah. I know how to work the van," Todd answered regretfully.

"How much are you bringing, anyways?"

"Seven-fifty," Todd answered.

"That's it? Seven-fifty all you bringing! You don't need the van for seven fifty. You can put that in a shoe box and bring it to me!" Curly snapped. "I told you that shit wasn't going to be like that. Three hundred in three weeks – man, I ain't cut like that." Todd tried justifying his shortcomings, "I have a call coming in, we'll talk later." Curly hung up with Todd, then switched over to his other line – "What do you want!"

"I just got off the phone with Lightbourn, and I believe she's about to make a move on ya. Also, the big three are sending someone to bring you in. I told them what you said, and they didn't like it."

"He's bringing me the money at three o'clock," Curly professed.

"It's out of my hands, Curly. Risk and reward, remember?" The captain admonished Curly.

"You think you're safe, you're stupid," Curly cautioned the captain.

"They want the money in dope back so they can set up in another state."

"Did you hear what I said? He's bringing me the money."

"Don't make this any harder for yourself. You're ready to fight a losing battle, my friend."

"Friend? Friends don't throw friends into traffic - and you call yourself a Marine? No man left behind, or have you forgotten." Curly questions scornfully.

"I've never broke honor. Never!" The captain chide.

"I never accused you of breaking honor. I'm asking you to be to me what I am to you? What will I always be to you? Right or Wrong. A brother."

"What are you asking me?"

"You know what I'm asking you," Curly replied.

Wrong is wrong, and right is right, but all marines lived their life one way, and that way was the marine way; reluctant to do what was breaded in him, the captain followed his heart and not his head. "Let me see what I can do. I can't promise you anything, just let me see what I can do."

"Huw-raw," Curly called out boastfully.

"Huw-raw," the captain shot back halfheartedly before hanging up.

* * * * * *

Agent Ski and Jamie sat on the third floor of the federal building in the cramped technician room, patiently waiting for either Curly or the captain to make another phone call - but neither one of them did.

"This doesn't make any sense!" Jamie blurted out in frustration.

"You can't confuse greed with stupidity, detective."

"I don't follow?" Jamie admitted.

"My guess is that they use different lines to talk to one another... I thought that's why you wanted a tap on Mr. Patrick's phone?" Ski avow.

"Big boys, huh?" Jamie said rhetorically.

"As long as we have Mr. Patrick online, we're good."

"No. That's still good. Just gotta Hope he slips and calls the captain on that phone so we can get a better read on everything, that's all." Curly stated apprehensively.

"Maybe it's me, but I'm getting the feeling like this is pulling away from us."

"Nothing is slipping, and no one is pulling from us. This is just the quiet before the storm. All you have to do is stay ready! Believe me, when everything comes to a standstill, your ass better be ready for the bumrush."

The certainty in Agent Ski's voice brought comfort to Jamie as she took heed to the season veteran caveat advice. Jamie also realized that the federal agent arena hosted a variety of cat and mouse games she wasn't accustomed to. The elite thinkers of the criminal minded played vicious games

- games Jamie knew she had to learn and learn quickly if she were to have any chance of surviving in the underworld. With that understanding clearer than ever, Jamie simply nodded her head in agreeance and passively said, "Okay." Jamie was about to ask the agent a question, but his phone went off, he threw up a finger, cutting her sentence short to answer the phone. To his surprise, Franky was on the other end; in a quivering voice, he confessed to killing Hope and begged for the Agent's help. In exchange for the agents' help, Franky agreed to tell Agent Ski all he knew about Curly, Todd and the three hundred bricks. Agent Ski calmly told Franky to stay put and that he

was on his way to come and get him. Three minutes later, Agent Ski and Jamie were in the car headed to the west side.

CHAPTER 40

When Agent Ski and Jamie pulled behind the abandoned schoolhouse, skepticism entered their head coincidentally. Ski looked over to Jamie and automatically knew what she was thinking; rather than giving her a pep talk, he simply produced half a grin and then motioned with his head for her to follow as he exited the car. Jamie, a few steps behind Ski, began to fall further back as her Jimmy Choos continued to stick into the tall grass of the baseball field. She called out for him to slow down, but he never did; instead of yelling, she picked up her pace, and just when she was gaining ground, she broke a heel. Out of frustration, she hobbled to the corner of the cafeteria and fell to one knee. "They're ruined," Jamie thought as she wiggled the broken stem back and forth. She couldn't believe she'd broken her heel, and as soon as she felt the cold piece of steel pressed against the back of her head, she couldn't believe how she had just gotten caught slipping.

"Please don't shoot!" Jamie begged.

"What is this, a setup?" Franky asked in dismay.

"Please. Don't shoot me?" Jamie repeated fearfully.

"What the hell are you doing here... where's Ski?"

"Put the gun down, Franky!" Ski ordered calmly – his gun aimed at Franky's head.

"Why is she here? Why did you bring her?"

"I told you I was gonna help you, right? Well, she's gonna help me help you, but first, you gotta put your gun down, Franky... gotta put the gun down."

"You're gonna help me?"

Agent Ski looked to Jamie, then to Franky. "Yeah, I'm gonna help ya."

Franky removed the gun from Jamie's head and backed up. "I don't know what to do... I didn't mean to kill'em, it just happened."

Jamie got off the ground and took a few steps towards Ski. "You sure he's dead."

"Yeah, he's dead. I shot'em twice, once in the head," Franky confirmed.

"You said it happened at your house, but you never said what it was all about."

"You. It was all over you!"

"Me, how was it about me?"

"He seen you leaving or coming to the house – it happened right after you left."

"Who else was there?" Jamie chimed in.

"Todd came after I shot'em. He tried to kill."

"Why are they trying to kill you?" Jamie asked.

"Because I agreed to give up the Haitian when your partner here forced my hand, but come to find out, he doesn't have that much pull, and now the other agent is forcing us to sell three hundred bricks for them, almost for free."

"You're referring to Curly... I mean, Agent Macki?" Jamie asked.

"Yeah, the one who pulled us away from him." He gestured to Agent Ski.

"Who else is involved besides Agent Macki?" Ski inquired.

"I didn't see anybody else. All I know is that the white boy got his foot on my neck."

"You willing to testify?" Jamie blurted out.

Franky looked Ski square in the eyes and answered Jamie's question, "I want the whole nine if I do; I'm no fool, I know these big boys we playing with."

"Agreed." Ski extended Franky his hand.

"One more thang," Franky went and grabbed a black duffel bag. "Here", he tossed the overly-sized bag next to Jamie.

"What is that?" Jamie asked.

"That's your evidence and my show of good faith.", Franky announced. Jamie opened the bag where on the inside were countless square blocks duck taped in various colors; she cracked open one, and the smell of pure cocaine drove up her nose – the smell was so strong she lost her balance.

"That stuff smells like pure cocaine," Jamie admitted as she bounced to her feet.

"Top of the line, detective... top of the line," Franky concerned.

"Who are you calling?" Jamie asked.

"Need to get an interference on the warrant they might have on him."

"Think they'll have one this soon? It's not twenty-four yet." Jamie responded.

"Just making sure, that's all. We also need a place for him to crash until all this is over.", Ski recommended.

Jamie watched Ski spit out four to five one worders before stuffing the cell phone back into his pocket. "So what did they say?" she asked curiously.

Ski glanced over to Franky and then back to Jamie. "Said he'll get back to me."

"What does that mean? He'll get back to you?" Franky questioned.

"It means he'll get back to me, but in the meantime, I'm going to house you until further notice." Ski answered sharply.

"So, where we going?" Franky asked.

Ski lifted the duffle bag up and patted Franky on the shoulder, "It's a surprise.", Ski acknowledged. Franky hated surprises, but with all that was going on, he welcomed it with open arms. Ski threw the bag into the trunk, and they all loaded into the car and headed to the unknown destination.

* * * * * *

When Curly opened the door, Todd could see signs of irritation resting on the agent's face. He was fifteen minutes late, and Curly hated when people were late. Without saying a word, Todd squeezed by the agent and then went and tossed the money onto the bed.

"That's seven-fifty," Todd confirmed.

"I thought I told you to be here by three o'clock? Not three-fifteen."

"Relax. I had to charge my battery up before I came," Todd explained.

"I don't believe this! Are you telling me you called me from another phone?"

"You trippen! Ain't you the police? I know you ain't trippen bout no phone."

"You can't be that stupid!" Curly screamed.

"You gonna count the money or what?" Todd asked sharply.

Curly looked at Todd with daggering eyes, "Don't ever call me from another phone."

"What difference does it make? You, the police! You straight!" Todd retorted.

While Curly thumped through the ten-thousand-dollar stacks, he thought about killing Todd right where he stood. He couldn't believe Todd's naivete – for someone to be a big-time dealer, he figured Todd to be very stupid, to say the least. But Curly's greed suede Todd's life, or for the time being, halfway through counting the money, Curly heard a knock on the door. Instinctively, he grabbed his firearm and rushed to the door; once there, he turned to Todd and placed a finger to his lips – commanding silence.

"Come back later, I'm in the shower," Curly disguised his voice as a woman.

"Man, you trippen!" Todd mumbled as more knocks bounced off the door.

Curly turned back around in an animated manner and demanded Todd's silence – even though his infraction was a more whisper. Todd followed suit; more knocks came.

"Come back later," Curly once again disguised his voice.

"Open the door, RuPaul," a voice familiar to Curly's ear responded. Curly turned back around and stared at Todd like a deer in headlights – he panicked. For Todd, this was uncharted waters, he'd never seen the super-agent cop so indecisive; watching him panic was as easily welcomed as it was denied. Not sure what the crooked agent was involved in, Todd pulled out his pistol just to be on the safe side. He had no intentions of helping Agent Macki, he just wanted to make sure he didn't catch any bullets not meant for him. Curly finally snapped out of his mini trance and snatched open the door – afforded, to his disappointment, stood his long-time comrade, the captain, who didn't seem too pleased to be standing in the doorway of some hotel room staring at some stranger in the room holding a gun.

* * * * * *

"Are you sure it's them?" Ski asked strongly.

"What's up?" Jamie asked with much interest.

"And you say they're at the Hilton in Altamont?"

"Who's in Altamont?" Jamie asked.

"Okay, yeah, yeah, okay.", Ski voiced sternly before hanging up and turning to Jamie. "What's the fastest way to the Hilton hotel in Altamont."

"We need to jump on I-4... who's at the Hilton?"

"I'll give you two guesses," Ski said slyly.

"Macki!" Jamie shot back.

Ski looked Jamie in the eyes, "I hear he has company."

"The captain?" Jamie asked with surprise.

"No! But Mr. Patrick's there. That was the third floor informing me they just heard Macki and Patrick set up an appointment to meet up at the hotel at three o'clock."

Jamie looked at her watch, "But it's three-fifteen." Jamie acknowledged.

"That's why I emphasized fast.", Ski responded.

"Are we going to arrest them once we get there?"

"We'll let them decide that.", Ski responded as he jumped on the highway. Fifteen minutes later, they were pulling into the Hilton hotel parking lot – Ski parked all the way in the back. Both checked over their pistols. Jamie put hers in her purse while Ski tucked his in his pants line. They waited a few minutes, then entered the hotel through the pool entrance.

"What room they in?" Jamie asked as her eyes jumped from room door to door.

"One-fourteen," Ski whispered.

Jamie looked to the next room door, "Should be up there," she whispered back.

"Don't stop at the door, just see if you hear anything."

"If we hear something, then what?" Jamie expressed concern, but Agent Ski didn't respond. When they passed by the room, both could hear voiced coming from behind the door.

"Didn't I tell you never to bring a gun when you come to see me!" Curly's tone was both threatening and fearful as he walked over and snatched Todd's gun from him.

"Relax, Macki," the captain said calmly.

"He was just leaving," Curly stuttered, unaware the captain knew where he was staying.

"Yeah, I was just leaving," Todd agreed with quickness.

"How about you stay... the three of us need to talk," the captain suggested firmly.

"About what?" Todd questioned.

"Yeah, he doesn't need to stay... besides, he needs to leave so he can go and do that thang I was telling you about.", Curly implied timidly, but the captain was in no mood for negotiating on debating, and because Curly desperately needed his help he submissively sat down; gesturing to the couch for Todd to follow suit. Reluctant, Todd did as ordered and sat directly across from the captain, who was still standing by the door.

"I believe I've found you away, Curly?" the captain flashed half a smile.

"I had a feeling you would come through for me, so everything is back to normal?"

"Let's hear it!" Curly asked satisfyingly.

The captain pointed to Todd. "You brought all the money?"

"Did they agree? What's the new plan? Move forward, how?" Curly babbled.

"Curly. Relax. Now, did he bring all the money?"

The tone of the captain's voice led Todd to believe things were about to get a bit harried, so much so his eyes advertently ran all over the room looking for a safe exit. Whatever troubles Agent Macki was a part of, Todd wanted nothing to do with them.

"Look. Whatever you two got going on ain't got shit to do with me! I brought the money, it's in that bag on the side of the bed."

"Not all of it, but he should have the rest tomorrow," Curly chimed in.

"Exactly how much did you bring?" the captain seemed to be caught off guard.

"Seven-fifty," Curly answered.

"Seven hundred and fifty thousand dollars from three hundred kilos!"

"It would have been more, but one of them took a hundred with him out of town."

"And you fell for that? The oldest trick in the book, and you fell for it!"

Curly looked to Todd for confirmation, "It's no trick! He knows better than to try me like that... two dead bodies equals capital murder, which means the death penalty."

"The rest of the money will be here tomorrow," Todd tried to sound convincing.

"Is that what they want... they get the money, we back in business?"

"Something like that," the captain responded.

"Well, why you ain't just say so. Patrick, grab the money," Curly ordered.

A million thoughts ran through Todd's head as he got up to go get the bag. Something about the agent's partner wasn't sitting right with him; something was wrong, and every time he got that feeling, something bad always happened – and just as his hand gripped the handle of the bag, his phone started ringing. He let go of the bag and answered the phone. It was Candy.

"Candy, let me call you back?" Todd asked, panickingly.

"The babies are kicking like crazy!" Candy announced joylessly.

"Baby. Let me call you back," Todd stressed with more panic.

"Did you hear what I said? The babies are..."

"Okay, that's sweet, baby girl. I'll talk to you when I get to the house." Todd cut Candy off in mid-sentence.

"Babygirl! Who are you talking to... bey, are you in trouble?" Candy finally picked up on Todd's vibe.

"That's my girl," Todd mumbled.

"Who is that on the phone? Hang up the phone!" The captain ordered.

"Let me call you back," Todd said painfully.

"Todd, who was that man? Bey..."

The captain pulled out his pistol and pointed it towards Todd. "I said, put the phone down. Now!" the captain walked over and snatched the phone from Todd.

"Todd? Todd? If you can hear me, don't hang the phone up, leave the phone on... police will be able to help you, she said she would protect you; your phone is being recorded by the police..." Candy confessed. But instead of Todd's ear on the end of the phone, it was the Captain; what he heard brought him to a boiling point instantly. He became so angry Todd could see the white of his knuckles as he squeezed the cell phone out of disgust. It became apparent to Todd that his life might be in danger when the captain broke the phone in half.

"He's been playing with you all this time!" the captain yelled at Curly while still holding the gun on Todd.

"What are you talking about?" Curly asked skeptically.

"Some girl on the phone was saying he's working with the cops – his phone is tapped, you idiot," the captain explained vehemently as he pointed the gun towards Curly.

"What the hell are you doing?" Curly asked in dismay.

"You should have listened!" The captain informed Curly.

"Listen to what? What the hell is going on?" Curly became frantic.

"You took a chance... now we're all exposed," – the captain looked to Todd – "you put me in harm's way, Curly. You're a liability now," – he looked back to Curly – "Time to move on," the captain insisted.

Curly put his hands up as if to shield himself from any harm. "What!"

"Lightbourn, do you have a visual?"

"Not that good. But Curly and the captain are both in the room."

"Are you sure? Communications said Curly and Patrick were the ones meeting at the room."

"Patrick's there. But the captains there too," Jamie whispered.

"Where are you positioned, detective?"

"Behind some bushes by the sliding glass."

"Can you see anything now?"

When Candy looked up, the captain was the only one in clear sight, not wanting her cover blown, she quickly ducked back into the bushes, but not before seeing the captain pointing his gun. "Something's wrong," Jamie announced.

"What do you see?"

"Call for backup... he's pointing a gun at Patrick or Curly."

"Goodbye, Curly.", the captain mumbled before letting off six shots into Curly's chest. He quickly aimed the gun at Todd let off three shots, but Todd dived behind the bed – barely escaping the hot lead. Just as the captain was about to walk over and shoot Todd, the sliding glass door shattered, and Detective Lightbourn came crashing in. The captain shot two rounds towards the person, crashing through the glass door, then fled through the front door. Once in the hallway, he let off three more rounds. Through all the commotion, Todd was able to slip out the back door; just as he was climbing into his car, he could see a slew of remarks flooding the hotel parking lot. It wasn't until a few moments after he remained ducked behind the mob tent that he realized he dropped his pistol. Meanwhile, Ski was ducking bullets being thrown his way by the captain as he came charging down the hallway. Rather than chase the captain, Agent Ski ran into the room to assist Jamie. When he entered the room, Jamie was getting off the floor.

"Where's Patrick?"

Jamie looked around the room "I don't know... he's gone."

Ski walked over to Curly and placed two fingers on his neck, just below his jaw. "You said you seen the captain shoot'em?"

"Only thing I seen was the captain pointing his gun... couldn't see at who."

"Why did you just charge in the room like that?"

"I heard shots... just reacted, I guess," Jamie confessed as she walked over to the side of the bed, where she would find Todd's gun along with the money.

"Did the captain get away?"

"I'm afraid so," Ski acknowledged as he placed latex gloves on his hands.

"You keep latex gloves in your back pocket?"

"Yeah. Don't everybody," Ski responded. Skeptically opening the bag. Not sure who the money belonged to it was obvious it was enough to kill for.

"That's a lot of money," Jamie blurted out.

When Ski looked up, the room started to fill with DEA agents. "Any sign of either of the suspects?" Ski questioned the tall blonde, rocking a crew cut.

"We have one detained in the parking lot, but the other two..."

"Who's in the parking lot?" Jamie asked immediately.

The tall blonde looked to the floor where Curly lay dead. "I guess only one is on the run." He pulled out a small hand device and showed a picture of Todd.

"They got Patrick," he informed Jamie, who was already walking out the door at the same time the EMT was coming in. Agent Ski gave his men their orders and high-stepped behind Jamie. Handcuffed in the back seat of an SUV was Todd; Jamie walked up and snatched the door open.

"You've been a busy boy, Mr. Patrick... a busy boy indeed."

CHAPTER 41

Killing Curly turned out to be a bittersweet moment for the captain, but he knew Curly had to die. His sole purpose for following Curly to the hotel was to take him out. The big three deemed it fit that Curly be removed from the situation after the captain informed them that Curly had lost half the shipment and that he was bringing unwanted exposure to the whole operation.

The big three ensured the captain another opportunity to be promoted if Curly was killed. For the captain, killing Curly was simply a means to an end, but not being able to recoup the seven hundred fifty thousand dollars left a bad taste in his mouth. Whoever that was who jumped through the glass door coasted him big time, and if he was ever to find out who it was, he had seven hundred fifty thousand reasons to knock their dick in the dirt. With Curly dead, everything went back to normal. The captain figured things would be pushed back six months to a year, but after that, everything would be back in full swing; the only thing left to do was kill Todd Patrick. The only person who could place him in the room and finger him as the killer of Detective Macki. He would soon get his wish. Jamie called the captain, telling him he had Todd Patrick in her custody along with the murder weapon and seven- hundred fifty thousand dollars; she explained that due to the unusual circumstances involving the case, she would need his help hiding Mr. Patrick until his trial date. The captain agreed to help, he asked Jamie if he could call her back, and when she said yes, he hung up and called the big three. The big three were more than happy to hear that Mr. Patrick would soon be dead and that all loose ends would be cut. The captain called Jamie back and told her about an old aircraft hanger on the outskirts of Oviedo that would be perfect for hiding Mr. Patrick. He noted it had a built-in living quarters to accommodate long stays. Jamie got the address and told him she would call him in a few days after Mr. Patrick settled in, but the truth of the matter was that Jamie lied, what was thought to be Todd turned out to be a guest at the hotel – and to make matters worse the only resemblance he and Todd shared was they both were black. Lucky for Jamie, the captain didn't know that, but the bad part is that she has a trap but no bait.

"How long will it take for you to have that place mic'd up?" Jamie handed Ski the address to the hideaway spot.

"An hour. Tops."

"Cameras?"

"Yeah, the whole nine... you know where Patrick is?"

"Not right off the bat. No! You know where he at?" Jamie tried not to sound too desperate.

"No. But I'm pretty sure I can get him to come to us." Ski returned.

"Good luck on that one." Jamie looked at Ski with a skeptical eye.

"No, seriously."

"Let's hear it?"

"Sneed isn't dead. He's in a coma."

"How do you know this? But Franky said…"

"Franky said what Franky believed to be true. That's all.", Ski insisted.

"Ms. James!" Jamie mumbled as she snatched her phone out of the purse and pushed speed dial seven. Four rings later, Candy's voice was on the other line. Jamie looked over to Agent Ski and gave him a wink of the eye – once again, he'd saved the day. Jamie's phone call was short and simple. Without mentioning a word to Todd, Jamie notified Candy that Hope was alive and that he was in a coma. She informed her that he was being looked after at the Orlando Regional Medical Center and for her to contact the hospital as the next of kin. Unable to hide her emotions, Candy thanked Jamie and agreed to take her advice; she hung up the phone and whipped away her tears. "As soon as your daddy gets here, we're going to have the biggest surprise for him… yes, we are." Candy chanted to her stomach in joy. Two hours later, Todd crossed the Florida-Georgia line. When he arrived in Atlanta, it was a little after midnight, and to his surprise, Candy was wide awake.

"He's not dead!" Candy shouted just as Todd was walking in the door.

"Who's not dead?" Todd asked insignificantly, obviously tired from driving. Candy walked over, gave Todd a hug and kiss, then handed him a small slip of paper. "Hope. Hope's alive, baby, he's not dead. Your best friend's alive." Todd stared at the paper, then looked up to Candy. "What are you talking bout." Candy pointed back to the paper. "You didn't even read it… read the paper." As he was told, Todd read the slip, "A coma? This says he's in a coma?"

"Baby, he's alive, and we're going to see him tomorrow."

"Where did you get this?" Todd waved the paper in Candy's face.

"Baby, he's alive, what does it matter?"

"The… I got a call from the hospital."

"When? And why would they…"

"I don't know. I got a call asking if I know a Howard Sneed."

"When. When did they…"

"Why are you asking me all these questions? We should be on the road going back to Florida to see our friend – your best friend!" Candy implied.

"When did they call?" Todd reiterated angrily.

"Last night… they called last night," Candy mumbled submissively.

"We're not going anywhere, and you ain't leaving G.A.," Todd commanded.

"That boy in the hospital with no one by his side!"

"You heard what I said!"

"So, what, you just going to leave him there?"

"I'm tired. I'm going to sleep. We'll talk in the morning." Todd walked into the back room and went to sleep, and just like that, it was over. At least, that's what Todd was thinking right before his head hit the pillow. Candy, on the other hand, was beating the drums to a different beat. Furious, she wrote Todd a letter explaining that she was, in fact, going to see Hope and that, with or without his permission, she was doing it all on his behalf. She packed a small bag, placed the letter on the side of the bed and left.

* * * * * *

"So, when do you plan on telling Franky that Sneed's alive?"

"I don't... still need him to think he's a murderer."

"If you say so, puppet master," Jamie said facetiously.

"He came to me thinking he killed him... right now. He needs me."

"And you think that Patrick is gonna come to the hospital?"

"You tell me," Agent Ski responded rhetorically.

"I arranged for Franky to be transported to the aircraft hangar."

"Why would you do that?"

"Thought it might buy us some time," Jamie explained.

"It could also blow up in our face!"

"Bad idea?"

"It's not a bad idea, I'm just thinking out loud."

"But you think it might blow up in our faces?"

"When you've been in this game long as I have, you believe in all possibilities; I just don't like when all my eggs are in one basket. That's all."

"Do you think I could make it as a DEA?"

Ski looked to Jamie with a puzzled stare, "Sure. I guess. Why not."

"I was just asking," Jamie acknowledged.

"Yeah, you'd make it on this side of field."

"I was only asking, you know," she tried not to sound too serious.

"It's not that hard detective. You catch the bad guys, and you lock them up for a long time... you do it every day. We just get to do it with all the cameras rolling and the lights flashing – that's all."

"Well, when you put it that way." "What other way is there to put it?"

"All this time. All this time, the captain has been playing me!"

"I had a feeling once I found out the two of them served together. On thing I know about the military is that it creates strong bonds between people of all walks of life," Ski said proudly.

"That was very sincere?"

"Navy seal. Eight years, I just know what they breed. That's all."

"Excuse me if I don't want that type of bond... death doesn't look that good on me."

Ski gave off a chuckle, "I guess not."

"Navy seal, huh? Impressive... Oh, I plan on calling the captain by Wednesday, even if Patrick doesn't show up."

"Why not let him call you? More evidence," Ski suggested.

"Just don't want this thing to get away from me!"

"From us... and it won't!" Ski stated firmly.

After a few moments of pondering over Agent Ski's request, Jamie gave in, "Okay. We do it your way."

"You sure?"

"Yeah, I'm good."

"Call and cancel Franky's transfer. Anything hary jump off can't afford him being there."

"What else?"

Ski looked over to Jamie and flashed a smile, "Nothing. Everything else is perfect... all we have to do now is wait for the curtain call."

CHAPTER 42

Todd couldn't believe that Candy would defy him after he told her to stay away from Hope, but to wake up to a note justifying her insolence really got his blood boiling. Without as much as brushing his teeth or washing his face, Todd stormed out of the house, got back in his car and rushed back to Florida. More upset with himself rather than Candy for not explaining his reasons for demanding she stay away from Hope. Todd prayed he would reach Florida in time before Candy ended up doing something that might get both of them and the babies killed. Candy, on the other hand, had further thoughts of being killed; her focus was fixed on seeing Hope, which at the moment was becoming more and more like a mission impossible. Frustrated, Candy reached out to the one person she felt could help. Thiry minutes later, detective Lightbourn and Agent Ski were at the hospital. Five minutes after their arrival, Candy was being escorted into Hope's room. The sight of Todd's best friend being hooked up to the various machines and a tube coming out of his mouth brought instant tears to Candy's eyes. She pulled up a chair beside him, sat down and placed her hand in his.

"Can he hear me?" Candy turned around and asked the nurse.

"I like to think that they do," the nurse confided with Candy before leaving the room to give her privacy. Not sure what to say or not to say, Candy took the next half hour and spoke from the heart. At first, she felt awkward speaking to Hope, knowing he couldn't talk back, but the more she opened up, the easier it became, and before she knew it, she was telling Hope all her business – She told him about the twins and how she wanted them to be raised. She talked about all the trouble Todd was in and how she wished he wasn't in a coma so he could help Todd square everything away. She told him that she was sorry for what Franky did to him and that she would never forgive him for that. She talked about her involvement with the detective and how she has regrets for betraying Todd the way she did; she even shared her thoughts on why she thinks Todd forbade her from coming to see him, and while Candy sat in the room pouring her heart out to Hope, Agent Ski and detective Lightbourn were out in the hallway trying to figure a few things out.

"What do you think they're talking about?"

"Not much," Jamie walked over to the water fountain.

"That's right. Dumb question. He's in a coma," Ski responded to Jamie's offhand remark.

"My question is, where's the boyfriend."

"He's coming, trust me!"

"Why you said it like that?"

"Who wouldn't chase after her... she's gorgeous."

"Chasing her? Where did that come from?" Jamie tried hiding her envy of Candy.

"Figure of speech," Ski answered.

"Okay, figure of speech," Jamie retorted.

"All I'm saying is that a woman as physically attractive" – he gestured to Jamie – "such as yourself would have men coming out the woodworks." Agent Ski replied. Even at seven months pregnancy, there was no denying that Candy's physical attributes were ranked in the upper echelon of finest; Jamie would've been the first bare witness to Candy's overwhelming allurement, and from the instant lust filled eyes of Agent Ski, she wisely diverted the conversation back to the matter at hand.

"Do you think she knows her uncle was the one who tried to kill him?"

"From what you've told me about her, I think she knows more than we're giving her credit for," Ski voiced with firmness.

"Can you have her followed twenty-four?"

"Yeah. That's a good idea because he's not coming here, but I'm willing to bet he'll show up wherever she's laying her pretty little head."

"More than likely, she's going back to her place," Jamie suggested.

"Not if she thinks we're looking for him she won't," Agent Ski informed Jamie, who happened to be standing in front of Hope's door and just as Agent Ski began to explain his supposal and emotionally drained, Candy was heading out. After saying a short prayer, she promised Hope she would come back the next day. She kissed him on the forehead and walked to the door; it wasn't until she reached for her keys that she overheard Agent Ski and Detective Lightbourn talking about Todd on the other side of the door when she decided to eavesdrop.

"I can understand what would make you think like that, but I've given her no reason not to trust me. She believes I'm here to help him, not arrest him."

"Who you think she's most loyal to."

"Between the boyfriend and uncle."

"I mean, if you had to guess?"

"They say blood's thicker than water," Jamie answered.

"Yeah. I've heard that before."

"What does her loyalty has to do with anything?"

"Just trying to figure out who I'm dealing with, that's all."

"Speaking of her uncle, I need to call and make sure the airplane hangar will be cleared out."

"Does everything in Florida have an Indian name to it?" Ski chuckled.

"Spanish or Native American, you choose... welcome to Florida," Jamie announced.

"So, just what do you plan to do with the boyfriend."

"Whatever happens to him will be his own doing. They make their own bed when it comes to me; My question is, what you got planned for the uncle and how you plan on using him once Mr. Patrick show up?"

"The right thing."

"And what might that be?" Jamie asked curiously.

"Straight to prison."

"Fed or state?"

Agent Ski gave Jamie a facetious glare, "There's nothing like the B.O.P."

"And the drugs he gave you to show you good faith?"

"Icing on the cake." Ski flashed a big smile.

"I think we should have a team ready to trail her the second she leaves the hospital," Jamie insisted.

"I'm on it," Ski announced before hitting speed dial. Jamie was about to say something when Candy came through the door with a full head of steam, so much so she bumped straight into Jamie. Shocked by what she had just overheard, Candy wanted nothing more than to get as far away from Detective Lightbourn as possible and nothing to tell Todd all she'd just heard – including the whereabouts of her uncle.

"I'm sorry!" Candy said in frustration.

"That's quite all right, Ms. James," Jamie said.

"I'm gonna take this down the hall," Ski mumbled as he walked off.

"That's fine." – Jamie waved him off, then focused back at Candy – "So, did they say how long he'll be in the little situation?"

"I don't think little is the right adjective to describe his... situation."

"I didn't mean it like that, Ms. James."

"Of course, you didn't," Candy replied somewhat bitterly.

"Okay," Jamie mumbled, "you do know I'm here to help you? That's why I called you in the first place... to help you. I figured you'd want to know that your fried wasn't dead."

Candy ran both hands through the sides of her hair. "I'm sorry. You're right, you have only tried to help me and the babies. I'm just dealing with a lot of feelings right now, and being pregnant isn't helping." Candy sighed, then chuckled.

Jamie flashed the palms of her hand towards Candy. "That's understandable."

"I've never seen him look so vulnerable."

"You mean Sneed?"

"That could have been Todd."

"This is what I've been trying to tell you all those months ago," Jamie warned.

"Where is Todd?" Candy demanded.

"I was hoping you could tell us that."

"Who is us, and who was that white man with you just now?"

"That's my partner."

"But I thought your partner was killed in a drive-by?"

"If you're talking about Peet. The one who came with me to the hospital when your boyfriend was shot... yes, he was killed. This is my new partner Ag... detective Ski."

"Well, I haven't heard from Todd since I switched his phone."

"Do you have any way of contacting him?"

"Is something wrong?"

"We believe the person who shot your friend might be coming after him."

"But you said you would protect us."

"I can only do so much, Ms. James. You're gonna have to help me help you."

Candy thought about the detective's last comment and took it as a slap in the face after hearing earlier her conversation with her so-called new partner, and figured she'd heard enough. "The last thing I want is to have to see Todd lying in a bed like that."

"None of us want that," Jamie said sympathetically.

"If I hear anything or he calls me, I will call you, but right now, I need to go home and lie down. I feel... I feel sick."

"Can I help you with anything?"

"I'm fine. I'll call you when Todd calls me.", Candy mumbled. Never in a million years did Candy think her actions – intentional or not – would cause Todd at any point grief or harm, but after hearing the two detectives' animus, she did just what she thought she'd never do. Cause Todd's pain. Barely out the front entrance, Candy pulled out her phone and called Todd but quickly hung up. Todd's phone was being tabbed – no things to her = and what she wanted to say wasn't for the world to hear, especially not Detective Lightbourn... "Fool me once, shame on you. Fool me twice, shame on me!" Candy thought as she climbed into her truck and drove home. Home. The one place she knew Todd would show up, especially after the note she left and how she snuck out like a thief in the night. For now, all she could do was wait and pray and hope that God would put her cry for help on the top of his to-do list.

CHAPTER 43

A thousand and one thoughts raced through Todd's head while he sat motionless in the dark, waiting for Candy to show up. He figured a few warrants had been issued for his arrest, so he decided to play it safe and not be in bird's eye view, but Candy was making that mission almost impossible with her impulsive behavior and reckless demeanor. Always a cool camper, Candy was starting to show signs of being rash and foolhardy – something that began to scare Todd half to death. Something he planned to get to the bottom of the second Candy showed up. And only after an hour's wait she came knocking.

"About time!" Todd declared before waving Candy into the room.

"I know you're angry with me, but I had to go see him."

"What in the hell has gotten into you lately? You need to let me know what's going on with you. Like right now!" Todd demanded.

"Could you at least turn on the lights?"

Todd walked over and hit the switch on the wall. "Okay. Now talk."

"Baby, you need to go see him. He looks so helpless."

"We been strong for too long; For the bullshit, and you've been acting real funny. So, what the fuck going on!"

"Did you hear what I said about Hope?" Candy stated empathetically.

"Candy, don't play with me... either you tell me what's going on or else."

"Meaning what? Or else what?"

"Oh, it's like that."

"Life what you make it, and right now, you either make us or break us."

"You would leave me like that?" Candy questioned, her words stuck in her throat as her eyes began to slowly tear up.

"You need to be real straight up with me right now, baby girl."

Todd meant too much to Candy for her to lose him, so much so that she took the few moments of silence that stood between them to imagine a life without him. And for all the obvious reasons as well as the ones not so obvious – she couldn't. There, standing in front of her, was the man of her dreams and the father of her unborn children. The man she wanted to spend the rest of her life with. The man she would give her life for or take the life of another for, but, in a not so perfect world, that same man who stood just two feet away from her was the same man she skillfully betrayed. As her mouth began to dry, Candy could hear her heart pounding inside her chest; the reality of what all she'd done had come full circle and the dilemma she faced the moment she agreed to help Detective Lightbourn became her white elephant in the room.

"Cat gotcha tongue?" Todd quip

"You once told me that we didn't need a ring or piece of paper. You still feel that way or not?"

"What the hell do that..."

"Do you still feel that way?" Candy chimed in.

"You gotta talk to me, Candy. With everything that's going on, I gotta know we still one hundred." Todd walked over and placed her hands into his.

Candy started crying, "I didn't want to lose you. Our children need their father."

"Lose me how?"

"The detective said that dirty cop you were selling the dope for was going to kill you."

"The detective?" Todd dropped her hands and took a few steps back.

Candy took a step towards Todd, but he took one backwards. "She said they would kill you!"

"She? She? She? Naw! Not the white girl. Man, you let the white girl play you like that? Man, this shit here crazy!"

"I didn't know what else to do! I thought you were going to die!" Candy screamed.

"Who the fuck you yelling at!" Todd asked aggressively.

"I didn't mean to yell, but I'm trying to explain..."

"Damn right you gonna explain. You gonna sit yo'ass right there and explain everything, and I do mean everything," Todd commanded.

"Please don't leave me," Candy pleaded woefully.

"Nobody's leaving anybody," Todd confessed, and with that said, Candy felt comfortable enough to open up. Candy did her best to paint the perfect picture so Todd could see why she did what she did, she also informed him of what she heard the two detectives discussing while at the hospital, making sure not to leave out the part of her uncle's whereabouts. Trying to manage all his emotions as well as put everything into perspective, Todd knew he was in dire need of an exit plan. But an exit plan with no money was like being a fish out of water, and unfortunately, he'd given a chunk of the money to the Agent, who just so happened to get killed right after he gave it to him. Luckily for Todd, he knew where Franky was, which meant he either had all the dope or all or most of the cash – either way, Todd needed one or the other. After reassuring Candy he wouldn't leave her, he talked her into going back to Georgia. He told her he would send for her when the time was right, but for now, he needed to do one more thing. They both stayed the night at the hotel, made love and by morning, Todd was gone.

* * * * * *

"So, you really think that little trick of yours is gonna work?"

"Just as sure I think the sun is going to rise and set tomorrow."

"And if it don't?"

"Oh, it's going to work," Jamie said arrogantly.

"What makes you think she was even listening to us?"

"Did you see the look on her face? She heard us and couldn't wait to tell it."

"But that doesn't mean he'll go to the hospital."

"If his profile is accurate, he'll show up."

"What about your captain."

"As far as what?"

"You still got'em on ice?"

"Barely! That's why I had to set that little stage play."

"Think he's playing you?"

"Who knows!"

Agent Ski was about to deliver one of his sly remarks when his phone rang. He answered it, then threw up a finger at Jamie, asking for silence. "Yeah. Umhmm, okay. I'll be down in a minute." – He looked to Jamie – "You want anything to drink? Gotta run downstairs a minute."

"Yeah, bring me back a pop."

"I'll be right back," Ski informed Jamie as he darted out the door, leaving Jamie to herself as she secretly prayed for Todd to show his face so she could finally and unofficially close and solve her case. But while Jamie was praying that Todd show his face, Todd was praying that his new face would bring him a safe passage.

"Maaaay, I, heeelpp, you?" the young clerk as in shock.

"Yes. I was told my nephew Howard Sneed was a patient here?" Todd delivered in his best Whoopie Goldberg impersonation, but the young clerk – in total disbelief – just stared at Todd in shock. He couldn't believe how ugly she or he looked or how badly his, her or its makeup was applied, and because of his incredulity – he was unable to respond, making Todd not only nervous but agitated. "Are you going to tell me if my nephew is here or not?" Todd demanded.

"Did you say Sneed?" He asked indifferently, his attention focused more on the imperfect blending of Todd's makeup rather than the question being asked.

"Yes, sir. Sneed, S-N-E-E..." Todd repeated once more like Whoopi Goldberg.

"Yes... Howard Sneed. He's here."

"What room?"

"New policy." He reached out his hand to Todd. "I need some identification."

"I.D.! For what? Just to see my nephew?" Todd's voice faded in and out, – male/female.

"Not my rules, sir! I mean, madam, besides, you never know what type of freak you might run into?" the young clerk gave Todd a bogus smile.

As Todd patted himself down, he could clearly see the young clerk was fully aware of his antics. "I think I might have lost my identification somewhere."

"Well, when you find it..."

"Oh! Here it is." Todd pulled out Candy's school I.D. and gave it to him.

Even more, after seeing a picture of Candy and then looking up to Todd, the clerk, had to take a double look. "Misss. Jamesss?" He asked awkwardly.

"That picture was taken before the accident," Todd responded scornfully.

"But this ID says you're 5'2, and you..."

"Give me my damn I.D.! You making fun of me?" Todd snatched back the I.D. card.

"No. No!" the clerk blurted out.

"I know you think I'm ugly."

"I didn't say that" – the clerk looked around – "you know I didn't say that!"

"I know I'm fucked up! I know I'm ugly, but you can't just..."

"I don't think you're ugly... A little fucked up, yes, I mean maybe! But could you stop yelling at me? People are starting to look at us." The clerk begged.

"Where is my nephew? Where is Pokey? I wanna see Pokey!"

"Okay. Okay! He's in room thirteen fourteen, geesh! Jesus Christ!"

"Thank you.", Todd mumbled, rushing off as quickly as he could in high heels. Not knowing what to expect, he tried not to expect anything, but when he entered Hope's room, he instantly knew he wasn't mentally or emotionally ready to see Hope.

* * * * * *

"Hello?"

"What's up, capt? I got your message to call you ASAP. Something wrong?"

"You can say that. It's Jamie. Again. She's doing what she does best."

"Rambo or T.J. Hooker?"

"How about James Bond on this one."

"Let me guess... a cloak and dagger stunt."

"Close. Apparently, the star witness in some big case she is working on has mysteriously disappeared out of protective custody, and once again, I have to save her butt yet again..."

"How long ago was this? Because I just spoke to Jamie two days ago."

"Did she happen to tell you about her little mission being impossible?"

"From what I gathered, the guy you're talking about was still in protective custody. Matter of fact, we're the ones who had him moved."

"You had him moved from the Airplane Hangar."

"Yeah, but if I would've known she was..."

"We both know how Jamie can get at times. The thing is trial is set, and because of the complexity of the case, it's been moved down to Palm Beach. I just wanted to get a jumpstart and have him moved before nightfall. I have a team ready for transport, but I need him brought back to the Hangar or else

Jamie's ass is in a sling."

"I can call her and..."

"She'll only fight you on it. You know she always thinks her way is better. Besides, my reason for calling is to bring little to no attention to all this, and I'm glad I did, now that I know you had a part in this..."

229

"I'm not getting screwed, so relax. But I do need the witness to be brought back ASAP... I don't think this type of insubordinate behavior would be conducive for anyone in our line of work," the captain warned.

"I agree. I can't believe I let her get me caught up in some more of her bullshit! Give me an hour, and he'll be back at the Hangar."

"I don't want you to beat yourself up over this. Jamie's a good cop, she just sees things a little different, that's all," the captain suggested.

"Well, like I said, give me an hour, and everything will be back the way it was."

"After all this is over, I'm going to have a serious talk with her! This bullshit has to stop! And I can't keep saving her ass, putting mines in harm's way!"

"I'll call you when it's done."

"You make sure you do that.", the captain insisted, hanging up the phone. He had a feeling Jamie was stringing him along, but now that he was a step ahead of her, he would be able to finish what he started and move on with his life. "Sometimes you're just too damn smart for your own good." The captain chuckled as he looked at his watch and began counting down the minutes to victory.

* * * * * *

"I didn't know if you were one of those healthy freaks, so I brought you a piece of fruit, a donut, and some sun chips."

"What is all that for?" Jamie asked, somewhat confused.

"Do you even eat? Because I've yet to see you eat."

Jamie walked over and grabbed the fruit. "A banana? Are you serious? A banana?"

"What?"

"A banana? You wanna see me eat a banana?"

"What! What? It's fruit," Ski chuckled as he handed Jamie her pop.

"Men! At least you got the right pop, and no, thank you on the banana. But I will have the sun chips."

"That's what happen when you don't eat. You get defensive," Ski chuckled.

"Just give me the damn chips," Jamie managed not to smile but still gave up a smirk.

"Your boy might be a no show," Ski mumbled.

"You know they're best friends."

"Who? Sneed and Patrick?"

"Yeah, and to some people, that means something."

"And you're betting on their loyalty," his tone expressed his agreeability.

"Some people are just built that way," she smiled, winked, then popped a chip in her mouth.

"We'll see?" Ski responded.

"Gotta stay positive. Here, put some joy in your life," Jamie offered him some chips. Just as Ski reached for the bag, his phone rang. "Agent Ski?" Yeah. Are you sure? Did she show any I.D.? What are you talking about? What operation?" –

Ski motioned for Jamie to grab her phone – "How long ago was this? Cassandra James?" – Ski signaled for Jamie to call Candy – "Hold on for a minute."

"You want me to call Ms. James?" Jamie asked.

"See where she at?"

"Who's that on the phone."

"Just call her. I'll explain later," Ski insisted.

Jamie did as was told, and seconds later, Candy was on the phone. "Miss. James?" Jamie looked to Ski for directions.

"Sorry for the hold... is she still there?" Ski asked insidiously.

"I was just checking in to see how Mr. Sneed was doing." Jamie was right on point with Agent Ski.

"How long has she been there?" Ski asked.

"Oh, I just figured you'd be going to see him today... if you like, I could meet you down there just to give you a little company? No, I understand" – she looked to Ski – "but if you change your mind. No. Okay. Bye, Miss. James."

"Listen to me... call security and have them guard that room. Tell them not to let her leave the hospital... that's fine. That's also fine... I'm on my way." Ski hung up the phone and gave Jamie that look of relief.

"It's Patrick, isn't it?" Jamie asked.

"Whoever it is, it's not Miss. James." Ski retorted.

"I'll drive," Jamie shouted as they both darted out the door. This was it. This was the last piece to the puzzle Jamie needed to trap off her captain and finally bring some closure to all her madness. This was it. The light at the end of a very long tunnel.

CHAPTER 44

Todd never grew up a religious person – and the only time he could remember going to a church was for a funereal; he'd never read the bible – and up until he walked in and saw his best friend draped in various tubes and colorful wires, he wasn't even sure he believed there was a god; but that was then, and he was now. Now. Now, he found himself practically begging for some higher power to change Hope's condition, fix what needed to be fixed, and allow his best friend to walk out of that hospital. Awkwardly, Todd walked over to Hope's bed, removed his wig and kicked off his high heels. "If you ever tell anyone you seen me like this, I'll deny it." Todd tittered while pulling up a chair. Surprisingly, Todd found it to be quite easy for him to talk to Hope. He even joked aloud that by Hope having a tube in his throat, he wouldn't be able to argue with him if he said something he didn't agree with. The only thing discomfiting was when Todd found himself having three ongoing conversations – one with Hope, himself, and his newfound higher power. Todd's sole purpose for going to the hospital was just to show his face and pay respects to his homeboy. But those intentions quickly converted into something else – something more therapeutic and soul soothing. Just like Candy, Todd found himself having the same dilemma Candy faced as he pieced together his version of a heart to heart. Feeling time was against him, Todd tried his best to cram in everything he had to say, which was exactly what Agent Ski and Jamie were attempting to do. But instead of cramming words, they were trying to cram milage. Feeling the pressures of limited time, Agent Ski and Jamie traveled at speeds well over the speed limit in hopes of getting there before Todd, who they expected to be, left Hope's room. But despite their egocentric effort, their person of interest was gone. The only signs that indicated Mr. Sneed had a visitor were that of a blonde wig and high-heeled shoes. Infuriated, Jamie stormed out of the room to the clerk's desk. Incompetence was something Jamie absolutely hated, and the young man sitting behind the desk was about to find that out firsthand.

"You had a direct order to call us if anyone came to visit room fourteen fifteen," Jamie said just as she first slammed into the countertop.

"Whore, don't come in here yelling at me, talking bout no damn direct order shit."

"Whore!" Jamie repeated, then swung the palm of her hand towards his face in full force, only to have Agent Ski catch her wrist mid swing.

"Stupid is a stupid does." Ski insisted while firmly holding onto Jamie's wrist. Jamie tried pushing forward, but Ski was too strong. "Fine! I said I'm okay, so let me go!" Jamie demanded.

Reluctantly, Ski gave in and let her go, "Now's not the time, detective."

"I apologize for taking a swing at you," Jamie said off-handedly.

"Apology accepted," the clerk responded.

"How long did he..."

"You mean she... poor thang was super ugly, but that's not reason..."

"That she was a he," Jamie stated matter-factly.

"No, it was a she. She just looked like that after the operation."

Jamie looked at Agent Ski, "This isn't working."

"Sir, could you just please tell us when that person left the room?" Ski asked as calmly as he could.

"They never left the room," the clerk stated.

"Are you sure?" Jamie asked.

"Of course, I'm sure!" the clerk rolled his eyes at Jamie.

Ski walked to Hope's room and returned with the wig and high heels. "Did he have this on when you gave him the room number?" Ski asked disappointingly. With a look of shock, the clerk placed his hands over his mouth, "He tricked me."

"Imagine that," Jamie sarcastically mumbled. Contemplating her next move, Jamie had her thought process cut into by her phone ringing. Frustrated, he pulled the phone from her purse and hit send.

"What's up, Kev?"

"What's up is you dragging me into your bullshit again! But this time, I am not going with you!"

"What the hell are you talking about?"

"I'm talking about these personal missions you impulsively go on, taking the innocent with you regardless of the consequences," Kevin said acrimoniously.

"You need to calm down and tell me what's going on."

"What's going on is that you asked me to transport a witness for you, when, in fact, that witness wasn't in your custody."

"Of course, he's in my custody... where's this coming from?"

"Just so you know, I had him taken back to the original spot."

"You what!" Jamie screamed.

"Maybe you take your job as a joke. But I don't."

"Kevin, why the hell would you do that?"

"What you need to do is thank your captain for saving your ass again."

"The captain? When did you speak to the captain?" Jamie asked with grave concern.

"You really need to think about your future, Jamie, or you won't have one!"

"I need to know when you last spoke to the captain, Kevin?"

"Why you always..."

"Damn it, Kevin, when did you last talk to him?" Jamie commanded.

"Five minutes ago," Kevin answered.

"Kevin! Listen to me. The captain is corrupt. I need you and your men to meet me at the Hangar."

"Have you been listening to me? You're on your own."

"He helped kill Peet, Kevin!" Jamie stressed angrily.

"That's not gonna work this time, Jamie. I'm sorry, but I'm out."

Infuriated, Jamie hung up the phone and turned to Ski. "Let's go! Franky was taken back to the Hangar, and the captain his on his way over there!"

* * * * * *

All that was told to Franky was that he was being brought back to the Hangar by direct orders and not to get too comfortable because he would be moved again within the next hour or so. Franky politely nodded, flashed a less than genuine smile, and then requested something to eat – twenty minutes later, he was brought a turkey sandwich, chips, and a pop. Halfway through his meal, Franky realized the shortage of officers assigned to watch over him; He remembered at least six to eight more cops being present during his first stint at the hideaway. Unfazed, he finished his meal and decided to catch a quick nap before he was to go on his mysterious trip. But just as fate would have it, right when he was about to fall asleep, he got an unexpected visitor, not to mention a hard slap to the face. The initial blow to the face created a burning feeling from Franky's left eye down to his jaw line – and every in between. Bushwhacked, Franky tried calling for help but was instantly gagged by the barrel of Todd's gun as it was forcefully shoved into his mouth – breaking a few teeth in the process.

"You try that again, and I'll kill ya!" Todd whispered.

"Please, young blood! Don't kill me! Please!" Franky uttered in a low, inarticulate voice.

"Did you show any mercy!" Todd asked coldly.

"Please, man... please don't. The boy was trying to kill me!" Franky tried to plead his case, but his words repeatedly fumbled over the barrel of the gun, and to make things worse, Franky finally noticed the silencer attached to the gun – knowing the meaning behind having a silencer caused Franky to piss on himself, simultaneously releasing what little breakfast he'd had that morning.

"Can't hold your mud ol'head?" Todd drove his fist into Franky's fag, "Where them slab's at Nicca?" Todd whispered, pushing the tip of the gun well into Franky's throat – so much so Franky threw up his lunch.

"The agent took the dope from me!" Franky's words were barely audible.

"Oh yeah? So, if there's no dope, your services no longer needed." Todd announced as he stood over Franky and aimed the gun at his head. Franky closed his eyes and asked God to save him – his prayers were answered. Within seconds of pulling the trigger, Todd was hit over the head with a blunt object, knocking him out cold. Because his eyes were closed the whole time, Franky didn't realize what was going on until Todd fell on top of him.

"He was gonna kill me!" Franky sputtered, pushing Todd off of him.

"Well, lucky for you, I got here in time." the captain helped Franky to his feet.

"Where the hell were you?" Franked pointed to a few cops standing behind the captain. "Now you wanna play cop!" Franky watched as Todd was cuffed and placed on the couch.

"What type of police work is this?" The captain asked with harshness.

"But that's what we were trying to tell you... no one informed us the witness was brought back," the young officer insisted.

"So, how the hell he got by you?" The captain pointed at Todd.

"He must've snuck in while we were loading up the vans."

"Can I get some type of medical help?" Franky implored.

"Cuff him." – he gestured to Franky. "And put both of them in my car."

"Sir, have you heard from Detective Lightbourn."

"Do I look like a babysitter to you?" The captain snapped.

"I was only asking because..."

"You sure you wanna go there with me?" The captain warned.

"I'll put them in the car," the other officer chimed in nervously.

When Todd finally gained consciousness, he awoke to a massive headache and cold handcuffs. Slumped in the back seat of the captain's car, he painfully lifted himself up. With his vision partially intact, Todd was still able to make out Franky, but he had no such luck with the driver. The driver was talking in riddles, and Todd's baring headache wasn't helping. He tried focusing on his words, but all he could come up with was something about being born in the light and two birds carrying a stone. Unwilling to continue to deal with his headache, Todd slumped back into the corner of the car door and closed his eyes. He remembered hearing Franky saying something but couldn't make out what it was, so he decided to deal with it once his head stopped hurting.

CHAPTER 45

"Are you sure about this shortcut?" Ski questioned.

"Trust me... I used to date this cab driver who loved to watch planes go up. Anyways, she would bring me out here all the time."

"But why this way?"

"We'll be able to sneak up on the captain and whoever else," Jamie stated.

"The cop on the phone, ah friend?"

"Not sure anymore. He's the reason Franky was brought back."

"But you said the captain..."

"I know what I said!" Jamie cut into his sentence.

"Left or right?" Ski asked.

"Damn it! You missed it, turn back around," Jamie demanded as she looked at her watch. Time was starting to turn against them, and Jamie was feeling the pressure. As ordered, Ski made a hard left onto a one-lane dirt road. Halfway down the road, Ski noticed a dark blue unmarked coming head on at breakneck speed, and without warning, two live rounds came crashing into their windshield.

"Son-of-a-bitch!" Ski screamed as he angled off, avoiding more shots and a possible head-on collision.

"That's him!"

"What would make you think that!" Ski retorted as he turned back over the engine and began the chase.

"Stay with him!"

"Relax! I got this.", Ski demanded as he pushed down on the accelerator while Agent Ski was showcasing his driving skills, Jamie decided to call in for help. "This is Detective Lightbourn of homicide! I have two-sixty-two in progress requesting backup; the suspect is headed westbound in a dark blue Crown Victoria... I repeat, dark blue Vicky with the big brother tag – four, zero, seven, Casey, Peaches, Tommy..."

* * * * * *

The sound of Jamie's voice came blasting through the speakers of the captain's car. He could hear her calling in for backup and warning their fellow comrades that he'd taken shots at her and some federal agent and that he should be considered armed and dangerous, as the dispatcher called for all cars available to assist Detective Lightbourn and for air support, the captain was beginning to feel his walls caving in. But he wasn't the only one. The moment Franky was shoved into the backseat, he knew nothing good was going to come out of him taking that ride, but he did think that he would have a little time to put something together – but after hearing the dispatcher call for troops, labeling the driver of the car armed and dangerous, Franky knew his time to do something was now. And right now, it was just what Jamie was feeling. Thanks to Agent Ski's stirring wheel tricks, the pair were able to catch up with the captain, but after nearly fifteen minutes of putting the peddle to the metal, the captain made an erupt stop at a green light with Jamie and Ski only two car links behind; and what appeared to be a knee jerk reaction, Jamie attempted to jump out the car to go and arrest him.

"Are you crazy!" Ski yelled as he pulled Jamie back into the car.

"What are you doing!" Jamie seethed, trying to break free of Ski's grip.

"Get your ass back in the car, detective!" Ski yanked Jamie back in "Too many people. It's too dangerous."

"But he's right there," Jamie pleaded as the angry motorist started blowing their horns.

"What the hell is he doing?"

Jamie reluctantly closed the door. "What the hell are we doing?" Jamie questioned.

"What the hell are you doing?" Ski mumbled softly.

"This is bullshit!" Jamie blurted, then reopened the door. Just as she was climbing out of the car, the captain gave her three good reasons to get back in as three bullets came crashing down on them. Two into the windshield and one through the passenger window, one that was inches away from her face. The captain was playing a serious cat and mouse game, and as soon as the light turned red, he dashed into traffic, barely making it across.

"God damn it!" Jamie screamed out in frustration.

"He does that again, and I swear I'm gonna kill him!" Ski acknowledged.

Jamie reached over and started blowing the horn. "Turn on the right so they can get out our way before we lose him."

"I'm already on it." Ski answered, then hit the switch and began back chasing the captain.

"Where the hell is the air support?" Jamie questioned.

"Call in! See where they are." Ski darkened as he blindly raced down the intersection. Luckily for Jamie, the police helicopter had spotted the captain's car and was tracking his every move; the dispatcher called into all pursuing cars to give the whereabouts of the wanted suspect, but because the captain also had a radio, he was able to listen in on how they planned on apprehending him – and for that, Jamie was unlucky. Franky and Todd, on the other hand, were neither lucky nor unlucky; they were more or less stuck between a rock and a hard place. But if Franky had any say in the matter, that was all about to change. Just as the captain was eagerly listening for anything that would help escape, so was Franky. After hearing the police helicopter had read on the car, they were in Franky and decided it was now or never. In the back of his mind, he thought the crazy white boy might use him and Todd as leverage for his freedom but, in the end, would kill them as well as himself if things didn't go as planned. Franky knew whiteboys didn't fair too well in prison – especially dirty cops – and most of them rather kill themselves than go to prison, even for one day. Franky would never kill himself, but his mind was set on do or die, and he was all in. Now, all he had to do was get Todd to help overtake the white boy.

"I know your head hearting youngster, but you gotta get yo ass up," Franky whispered to Todd before giving him a sharp nug. But all Todd did was moan, then mumble. Franky knew his time was running short, so he gave Todd another sharp nug but with a lot more thrust behind it. "If you don't help me take out this cracker, he's gonna kill both our asses."

"Stop screaming in my ear," Todd muttered.

"Ain't nobody screaming. You trippen. Can you bring your arms from behind your back?"

"I think so," Todd answered, it was evident he was still in great pain from the blow to the head as he attempted to bring his legs through his arms just minutes after Franky did it. But unlike Franky, instead of swift, precise movement, his was awkward and clumsy, which proved to be costly as it drew the attention of the captain. At that moment, Franky thought it was his gun and grabbed the steering wheel. Todd Tried his best to assist Franky but was repeatedly slammed around the backseat as the car frequently bounced off of pedestrians, parked cars, light polls and other moving vehicles while Frank and the captain fought for control of the steering wheel. Each one tagging to the left or the right.

"Todd, help me!"

"Let go... of the steering wheel.", the captain yelled, then drove his feet deep into Franky's face, causing him to fall onto the floor. Instinctively, Todd plunged to the front of the car, landing directly on the captain's neck, crushing his chest into the dashboard. As the captain tried desperately to hold himself up, the weight of Todd's body took him, along with Todd plummeting down to the floor. Unconsciously, Todd latched on to the steering wheel, yanking it down with him, and without warning, the car flung in the air, flipped three times, came down on its roof, and flipped over two more times, tossing Todd out in the process before landing on its side, and sliding up on a tree.

* * * * * *

"The captain just crashed out."

"I heard them," Ski replied.

"Make that right at the light. Dispatch said the crash happened on fifty."

"Lucky for us, air patrol stayed with him because he damn sure lost us." The vibration from the engine, charged up by all the horsepower, sent an elective volt into Jamie's already tense body as Ski drove the unmarked as hard as he could in order to reach the crash site. For Jamie, this was the last I to be dotted and her last to be crossed, and in less than five minutes, she understood her world – no matter the outcome – was going to be different from that point on out. The ma she was rushing to arrest was not only her captain of ten years but someone she considered a friend and confidence. Not allowing herself to think of the captain in that manner, Jamie pushed aside all emotions and conformed to beast mode. At the other end of the tailspin was the captain. Momentarily knocked out from the crash, the captain was quickly awakened by the sound of a helicopter hovering over him, blended in by police sirens in the distance. Pretzeled between two legs, the captain struggled to free himself. Realizing his arm was broken, he used his legs to break free as well as push himself out of the car. With the sun beaming in his face and blood dripping in his eyes, the captain found it quite difficult to hold his balance standing on the side of the door. He looked down and saw half of Franky's body was being crushed by the car and realized the legs he was entangled in belonged to him. To make matters worse, he and Jamie met eyes just as he was lifting back up his head.

Shocked by both the crushed corpse and Jamie's face, the captain lost his balance and fell.

"I can't believe that son-of-a-bitch survived that crash," Ski admitted.

"Oh my god! Is that Franky pinned under that car?"

"Call it in," Ski ordered as he slung around the car to shield them from any gunfire.

"I don't think he's alive," Jamie admitted.

"Just call it in, detective." Ski reached for his vest before cautiously climbing out of the driver's seat. Wisely, Jamie followed suit.

"He's hurt," Jamie said.

"The way that car looks, he should be more than just hurt."

"Before he jumped down, I didn't see any gun."

"Trust me, he has one."

Jamie got on her radio and called the helicopter. "Okay, guys, I need your eyes."

"Suspect isn't moving," the pilot said.

"Do you have a clear shot?" Jamie asked.

"Negative. Suspect is being shielded by the tree," the pilot confirmed.

"Hold your position!" Jamie ordered just as more and more reinforcements arrived.

As Jamie was running over to instruct the others what she needed done, she noticed a familiar face. She saw a friend.

"Figured you might need a hand."

"Thank you."

Kevin always had a soft spot for Jamie, and thank yous were never needed. "What's the plan."

"Right now, we're putting up a perimeter. Visual is bleak, so we gotta find a way to get in there."

"What about the hostages?"

"He's dead."

"He's dead? What about the other one?" Kevin asked.

"We wasn't aware... wait! Who said there were two of them?"

"We went back to the Hangar looking for you, but you never showed up. The two cops told us the captain left with two people; one a witness, the other suspect."

"Damn it, Todd!" Jamie expressed scornfully.

"Who the hell is Todd?" Kevin asked, confused.

"A pain in my ass!"

"What now?" One of Kevin's men blurted out.

"Now we do what cops do best. We go in and get our man," Ski announced walking up.

"Patrick's in the car," Jamie said to Ski.

"You sure?"

"Yeah, Kev just informed me."

Ski handed Jamie a bullhorn. "Everyone's in position. Your move."

Jamie grabbed the bullhorn, checked her surroundings, then walked back to the car.

"There's nowhere to go. It's over, captain. Just give up," Jamie instructed.

"Fuck you! Fuck all of you!" The captain yelled.

"Let the hostage go, and I give you my word you won't be harmed."

"Don't you think it's a little late for that?" The captain asked sarcastically.

"He could be hurt. Let us come and get him."

"You promise not to hurt me?" The captain asked apprehensively.

"I give you my word," Jamie said matter factly.

"Okay. Come and get'em."

Jamie looked over to Ski and then to Kevin, "I'm gonna need you to toss your gone out."

"Where's the trust detective?" The captain asked in disbelief.

"I'm trusting you'll do the right thing, captain. Just like you taught me."

The captain tossed his pistol from behind the car. "I guess you were listening after all. Come on and get him." He voiced calmly. With a stained look, Jamie gestured to two blue coats to go in and bring back Todd – who she figured was still in the officers. Immediately, a team of shooters returned fire until both men were brought back safe, but without Todd.

"What the hell was that!" Jamie screamed through the bullhorn.

"You tried me, Jamie... you really tried me."

"Damn it, captain! You gave me your word," Jamie pleaded.

"We both know how this is going to end, detective," the captain suggested meekly.

"You have the power to end this peacefully," Jamie said stoically as she began directing officers to gain more ground for a possible kill shot.

"He's not going to be taken alive, detective," Ski insisted.

"What about Patrick?" she asked.

"Team three. Can you see inside the vertical?"

"Affirmative.", the unknown voice came blaring through Agent Ski's radio.

"I need a read on the second passenger in the car."

"Negative sir. There's only one body in the vehicle, or should I say half a body."

Ski looked at Jamie and said, "Are you sure?"

"Affirmative. One body, sir."

"Your call, detective... for whatever reason, Patrick's not in that car."

Jamie held the radio firmly up to her mouth, her grip so tight the whites of her knuckles were showing. "Listen up! We're going in hard and fast. I want him alive, and I want him to pay dearly. On my call, it's a green light."

"You're going in?" Kevin questioned while observing Jamie putting on her vest.

"Didn't you just hear me say we going in hard and fast?"

"I just thought..."

"Kevin, right? You might wanna put your vest on... look like we're about to dance." Ski gave Kevin a pat on the chest and then walked over to Jamie.

"This is your last chance, captain. You have thirty seconds to decide how this is going to play out?" Jamie announced. But no longer than ten seconds after her announcement, the captain came hobbling from behind the battered vehicle with a gun to his head.

"Life is what you make it, detective," the captain yelled out in defeat.

"Sir! You didn't have to do this... just put the gun down." Jamie pleaded.

"Everybody, stand down!" Ski ordered, then fell back into the crowd.

"Put your guns down!" Jamie screamed.

"You're only as good as your last one... today you were better than me, Jamie."

"You don't have to do this."

"Team four, do you have a clean shot?"

"Negative."

"Team five, do you have a clear shot?"

"Yeah, I got his ass."

"Sometimes your shit do stank." The captain mumbled before squeezing the trigger. A single bullet came crashing through his shoulder – knocking him down instantly. In one breath, all five teams, along with Ski, Jamie, and Kevin, converged on to captain. A member of team three got there first to kick away the captain's firearm. He was handcuffed within seconds.

"Killing you would've given you an undeserved victory," Jamie vented.

"He's gonna need a medic to treat that bullet wound, detective," Ski indicated.

"Read'em his rights and get'em out my sight," Jamie commanded. It was finally over, and Jamie couldn't help but feel a great sigh of relief and sorrow removed from both her heart and her shoulders. Many people had died over the few months, and seeing Franky's body being placed inside a back bag made Jamie realize that even though a person may choose his or her own path. They will never be able to choose the outcome or consequences. Proudly, Jamie removed her vest and threw it in the backseat of her car. She ordered a sweep of the area to look for Todd's body, then climbed in the car with Ski.

"Why such a big smile?" Ski asked curiously.

"You ever wondered if your shit stank?"

"No! I know my shit stank. How bout I buy you dinner?" Ski asked as they both laughed.

"Sounds good to me," Jamie retorted as they drove off.

CHAPTER 46

TWO MONTHS LATER

"Hey, you?"

"What they do?" Hope responded.

"Why is it every time I come to see you there's fresh flowers in here?"

Hope looked over to the pink roses then to Candy. "Pink roses, huh?"

"They're cute," Candy gave a slight giggle.

"Let you tell it," Hope shot back with a smile.

"So, who is she?"

"Detective Lightbourn," Hope answered.

"She still looking for Todd?"

"She never asked for him directly, but yeah, I believe so," Hope answered.

"Did she tell you about the car crash?"

"Yeah."

"About Franky?"

"Yeah."

"You believe Todd was in the car when it flipped over?" Jamie asked mournfully.

"I don't know what to believe... she said they have on tape him being forced into that cop's car." Hope hated talking about Todd with Candy. He hated the fact that he would have to entertain the thought that his best friend just might be dead, but what was hurting was the numb look Candy would have on her face whenever her due date would come up. He knew he was going to be there for her and the babies, but at the same time, he understood his presence would never be equal to Todd's.

"So, when you get to come here?" Candy tried putting on her happy face.

"Doctor said in about two weeks." Hope confirmed with a kool-aid smile.

"You know the babies will be here around that time," Jamie softly patted on her stomach while blowing kisses at the twins.

"Do you have everything for the babies?"

"Everything but their father!"

"Stay positive," Hope reminded Candy.

"I don't want to raise the twins by myself... a child needs both."

Hope chimed in, "I don't know much about kids, but I do know I gotcha."

Candy wiped away her tears. "I'm sorry. I didn't come up here to spoil your day. I just miss Todd and..."

"I feel ya. Things understood, don't need explaining."

"What's wrong?" Candy noticed Hope was grimacing.

"I'm just ready for my body to be back all the way."

"I thought you were going through physical therapy?"

"I am! Hell, that old lady be working my ass something decent." Hope laughed.

Candy started laughing, "Boy, yo butt is sooo silly… working you."

"You should see her. Bending this. Twisting that. Working my ass!" While Hope was giving his best impersonation of the female therapist, he didn't notice Candy clutching her stomach as she fell to her knees; it wasn't until she turned over the lunch tray that he figured something was wrong. Sill confined to the bed, Hope yelled out to Candy, but she never answered. The hospital bed sat up high and was blocking Hope from seeing what was happening to Candy. He tried not to panic but failed horribly. That's when he heard Candy yell out like a wounded animal. Although he managed to push the distress button, the sounds of Candy's cries echo so violently through the hospital a team of nurses came pouring into Hope's room way before the panic signal reached the nurse station. This was the most pain Candy had ever felt in her life. Her water had broken, and the twins were coming – with or without her permission.

"Doc! Doc! What's wrong with her… what's happening to Candy?"

"Miss! Miss, what is your name?" the nurse asked.

"My water broke! I can feel the babies coming!" Candy screamed out in anguish.

"Somebody help her!" Hope yelled out in panic.

"Go get the doctor," the lead nurse advised one of the nurses as another ran to get a wheelchair. Quickly, Candy was placed in the chair and ushered to the west wing of the hospital; one of the nurses stayed in the to get as much information from Hope about Candy. As big as Candy's stomach was, it was inevitable that she would give birth. But, for Hope, the moment her water broke, the unavoidable became more of an ambush than an anticipation. As unsure as Candy was about Todd's whereabouts, Hope wished there was more he could do for his best friend's baby mother – he at least wanted to be in the room with her when the twins came into the world. He figured a familiar face would help her situation as opposed to her being in a room with no family, surrounded by a bunch of strangers. As the bad thoughts began to overpower him, his frustration was unleashed, and he slung his TV remote against the wall.

"Them people gone make you pay for that shit." Todd insisted while sneaking through the window. At first sight, Hope wasn't sure if he was spazzing out or if Todd was actually standing in front of him.

"Why would you let that girl think yo ass was dead?" Hope snapped.

"How long you been out the coma?"

"Fuck all that! That gurl think yo monkey ass is somewhere dead!"

"When the last time she came up here to see you?"

"You know as well as I do that girl is fucked up cause you…"

"Let me explain," Todd asked with pleading eyes.

"That girl come up here damn near every day, crying and shit," Hope snapped.

"You gonna let me explain?"

"Talk!"

"First. Please tell me you still got them bricks."

"Man, this ain't bout no dope my nicca! This about that girl and them twins."

"Hear me out."

"Hear what? You ain't said shit."

"If I could stay, I would, and you know I would, my nicca. But right now I gotta get ghost – out'a sight, out'a mind. Ya, feel me?"

"So what, you gonna leave Candy and the twins?" Hope asked scornfully.

"That's why I came to holla at you."

"You came for the dope!"

"You gonna hear me out or what?" Todd insisted.

"Yeah. Cause you need to make me understand this shit."

"Franky's dead. The redhead whiteboy dead – some other cop killed him…"

"I know bout Franky punk-ass," Hope admitted.

"If you know that, then you know I have a warrant out for murder."

"Murder! What murder!"

"That's why I gotta get ghost. And that's why you gotta hold it down for me until I can get this shit squared away. And that's why you can't tell Candy I came to see you… what the hell is that smell?"

"Candy," Hope answered.

"What type of smell is that?"

"No. That's Candy. She's having the babies, what you smelling is her water. Her water broke when she was in here about twenty minutes ago."

"She having the twins?"

"Yeah. Like right now. As we speak," Hope responded.

"Man, this shit is crazy," Todd mumbled as he clasped his fist into his hand.

"Do like Denzel did in John Q," Hope suggested.

Todd looked at Hope with disappointed eyes. "John Q went to prison for that bullshit."

"I'm just saying," Hope shot back.

"I gotta go," Todd said despondently.

"You have to see the twins before you leave, or it'll kill you while you're away."

"I can't win from losing!" Todd vented.

"I'll do my part while you're gone, but you got to see the babies before you go. Candy don't need to know. You can see the twins at the rooms they put all the newborns in."

"You right. I'll do that, then go get that dope… you never said where you put it? Where you stashed it at?"

"I don't know. Candy put that shit up – don't look at me like that! I didn't ask her to do that. She just did."

"Where she put it at?"

"I said I don't know."

"Never mind the dope. Listen. I'm leaving the country tonight. I'm leaving everything to you and Candy…"

"How you gonna leave the country with no money?" Hope chimed in.

"I'm good. All my arrangements are taken care of. I just can't be late getting to my pick-up spot," Todd answered.

"So how long you'll be gone?", Hope asked just as Todd was about to answer. A nurse knocked on the door and came in at the same time; the hand in the cookie jar looked on both Hope's and Todd's faces and raised a red flag in the nurse's head, but she was relevant to show it.

"I'm sorry. I was unaware you had a visitor. If you like, I could come back later to take you to your physical therapy appointment?"

"I thought that wasn't until tomorrow?"

The nurse gave a quick look over, then focused back on Hope. "That is correct, but you were rescheduled for this afternoon."

"Go ahead and get your body right… I'll see you soon," Todd implied.

"You sure you don't want to stick around… enjoy a little bit of life with me?"

"I was leaving anyway," Todd answered. He walked over to Hope, whispered something in his ear, gave him some dap, and then walked out of the room. Hope wasn't sure if he would ever see Todd again, but he was certain that he would keep his word and take care of his best friend's family until he came back, whenever he came back. As the nurse placed Hope into a wheelchair and began pushing him down the hall, Hope closed his eyes and said a prayer. He asked God to watch over Todd and see him safe. He asked that Candy be given extra strength to hold up until Todd made it back, and he also asked God not to lay a burden on them they wouldn't be able to bear. After his quick prayer, Hope went into his therapy session with a light heart and an easy spirit, believing his prayer would soon be answered.

For Candy, things were just the opposite. The pain in her heart matched the pain she felt every time she was having a contraction; unsure about her future or the future of her children was taking a toll on her. Why was God doing this to her? She wondered. Was Todd dead? In her heart of hearts, she knew Todd had to be dead… death would be the only thing that could keep Todd away. He had to be dead.

"Okay! She's crowning, people," the doctor announced, enthused.

"I can't take this pain!" Candy screamed.

"You're doing fine, Miss. James. Now, give me another good push."

Candy clapped down on the bed rails and pushed as hard as she could. "It hurts!"

"Just one more push, Miss. James. The baby is almost out." The doctor encouraged.

"I can't push anymore."

"Just one more push. You can do it."

Candy began to cry. "Todd, where are you? I need you. Baby I really need…"

"First baby's out." The doctor said proudly, quickly cutting the umbilical cord and handing off the newborn to the nurse. "One down. One to go," he reminded Candy just as a wave of contractions drove through her body.

"I feel the baby coming," Candy bellowed.

"Come on, Miss. James... push. Push hard!" Candy pushed and pushed until she passed out, but not before delivering her second child. When she awoke, she was in a different bed in a different room. To her surprise, someone took the liberty to clean her up. But nothing could have prepared her when she saw Hope holding the twins. At that moment, she forgot about all her worries. The twins were finally there.

"You ready?"

"Yeah. I'm ready."

"Don't worry, I've got everything in place over once you reach the island. My people will take good care of you."

"You know I became a father today?"

"Is that right!"

"Yeah, man, I'm a daddy," Todd stated proudly as he climbed onto the boat.

"Congratulations!" Nije walked over and shook his hand.

"So what now?"

"Do as I have instructed you, and all this will be behind you very soon my friend."

"I hope so?"

"Trust me. You'll soon have back your life, but for now, just stay focused." Nije informed Todd with encouragement. As Todd began to drift into the ocean, he thought about everything he was leaving. Everything that was being taken away from him. He thought about Candy. The twins. Hope. He understood what he had to do in order to get everything back.

"In due time, Candy girl... in due time." Those were the last thoughts Todd had before he went to sleep.

About The Author

Distinguished Author, Accomplished Entrepreneur, and Visionary Business Owner, B.E Harmon is the driving force behind the success of Harmon Media Group LLC and West Brown LLC's innovative ATM solutions. Born in the vibrant community of Eatonville, Florida, in November 1975, B.E Harmon brings a wealth of experience and passion to both the literary and business worlds.

As an Author, B.E Harmon weaves compelling narratives that captivate readers, providing them with thought-provoking and unforgettable experiences. Simultaneously, B.E Harmon is the architect of Harmon Media Group LLC, a trailblazing enterprise dedicated to pushing the boundaries of creativity and communication.

In the realm of business, B.E Harmon leads West Brown LLC, where cutting-edge ATM machines are crafted to redefine convenience and accessibility. With a commitment to excellence, B.E Harmon has not only created a mark in the literary landscape but has also carved a niche in the business world.

Family holds a special place in B.E Harmon's heart. As a devoted spouse and proud parent of two children and four grandchildren, B.E Harmon finds inspiration in the warmth of personal connections.

Step into the world of B.E Harmon, where literary prowess meets entrepreneurial acumen, creating a unique blend of creativity and business innovation.